THE CANNERY ROW MURDERS

A JOHN GRANVILLE & EMILY TURNER HISTORICAL MYSTERY

SHARON ROWSE

THREE CEDARS PRESS

THE CANNERY ROW MURDERS

A John Granville & Emily Turner Historical Mystery

By Sharon Rowse

Published by Three Cedars Press
www.threecedarspress.com

ISBN: 978-1-988037-257

1

TUESDAY, AUGUST 7, 1900

It was a hot day, even for August, and the faint breeze carried the the salty smell of the ocean from the beach a few blocks away. John Lansdowne Granville strolled down Hastings Street, noting the rush of businessmen hurrying from some appointment or other—all formally dark-suited and hatted in defiance of the heat.

He was no better, Granville thought with a grin as he glanced down at his own well-cut suit. Good thing he didn't wear the thick beards so popular now—he could just imagine how unbearable that would be in this heat. Though he'd begun to consider a mustache.

Crossing the street, he waved off the driver's good-natured cursing as he narrowly avoided being clipped by a furniture-delivery wagon. He laughed aloud at the incongruous sight of an oak china cabinet, finely carved, swaying in time with the clop of the job horse's hooves.

Between two mansions looking out over the harbor, Granville found his destination. The Vancouver Club was an ivy-clad, two-story brick building, with a gabled roof and a heavy stone arch over the doorway. Pushing open the heavy walnut doors, he swiped at the sweat beading on his forehead and gladly handed his hat to the attendant.

The interior was blessedly cool. Clad in dark wood paneling, it felt similar to London's best clubs. Which was undoubtedly the intent of the members, many of whom were English themselves, and still spent time there on their frequent trips 'home'.

Two years digging for gold in the frozen ground of the Klondike had given Granville a different perspective on such clubs—and while he still felt at home in these environs, he found them a little stifling. The formality of the Vancouver Club felt odd to him here—in this newly built city carved out of the wilderness—in a way it never did in London, with its long-depleted forests and centuries of existence.

Still, it was an excellent place to do business. Its members represented most of the businesses in the city—and most of the money. If the Terminal City Club was a place for the up-and-coming businessmen, the Vancouver Club was home to those already well-established.

Granville took the stairs to the first floor, his feet sinking into the thick pile carpet. Turning left, he entered the wine room, which served as the bar. He paused in the doorway, scanning the sparsely-filled room.

"Granville. There you are," Angus Turner said, walking up to him and holding out a welcoming hand. His future father-in-law looked like he belonged here, with his full beard, expensively tailored dark suit, and satisfied expression. "Come along, there's someone I want you to meet."

Following the portly figure across the room, Granville wondered what Turner was up to. They had agreed to meet here for a drink to celebrate Granville's acceptance as a member of the club, since his future father-in-law had sponsored him. Apparently Turner had another motive.

His suspicions were confirmed when Turner marched over to a tall, thin man with a full beard and a commanding presence. He'd been sitting in one of the leather club chairs near the window, but stood as they approached.

"Alex, this is my daughter's fiancé, John Granville. John, Alexander Ross-Murray."

Inclining his head in acknowledgement, Ross-Murray held out a hand, one equal to another. "Pleasure," he said, a faint burr of his Scotland in his voice.

Granville shook hands. Ross-Murray? The family was a good one, from the Scottish borderlands, he thought. And he'd heard of Alexander Ross-Murray.

He was one of the city's most influential businessmen, and a stalwart member of Vancouver's upper class. He was also an acknowledged leader in the canning industry, having founded the British & Canadian Packing Company some years before.

So why would a canneries magnate want to meet with him? Granville knew very little about the industry. But like Ross-Murray, he was the son of a good British family—his late father had been the 5th Baron Granville. And to his amusement, Granville had found Vancouver's businessmen—including his prospective father-in-law—to be surprisingly class-conscious, for all the city's declared independence from the colonial mentality. Did the same hold true for Ross-Murray?

"I've been hearing good things about your firm's investigative work," Ross-Murray said. "And Turner here tells me you're trustworthy."

Good to know, Granville thought with an inward grin. He inclined his head in acknowledgement. And waited for the man to come to the point.

"Please, have a seat," Ross-Murray said, gesturing to the empty leather-covered club chairs clustered around a heavy coffee table. "Can I offer you a drink? Whiskey?"

Granville nodded, and Ross-Murray motioned to the uniformed attendant, holding up three fingers. Turner beamed at both of them as they sat down and the whiskey was served on a silver tray.

Ross-Murray raised his glass to them. "What do you know about the local canneries?" he asked.

"Other than the recent fisheries strike?" Granville said. "Not a great deal."

Ross-Murray nodded. The answer didn't seem to concern him. "What you need to know is that salmon canning is now British Columbia's major industry. The output from our canneries grew one hundred and sixty percent last year alone."

Those were impressive figures. Granville wondered if they were sustainable. He'd learned about salmon's four year cycle from the Indians in the north, whose lives had depended on the size of each year's salmon run. As did Ross-Murray's fortune.

"Go on."

"In a very real sense, the success of the province—and this city—depends on the success of the fishing season. We have already lost most of July to the fishermen's strike—no salmon were caught, and none canned. And the salmon will run for only another two, two and a half months, at most. We must make up our losses in the time we have left."

He looked hard at Granville. "Nothing can be allowed to prevent that."

Interesting. Ross-Murray clearly spoke for his fellow cannery owners as well as himself. And he was undoubtedly right about the impact on the economy if the canneries did poorly. And the impact on the fishermen and the cannery workers as well, though Ross-Murray hadn't mentioned them. They too must need to make as much money as they could in what was left of the short fishing season.

"I see. And why come to me?" Granville asked.

"I have a job that needs doing," Ross-Murray said. He paused a moment, watching Granville's expression. "It's a sensitive issue, one that will have to be very carefully handled. Otherwise, we're likely to be facing another strike, and as I said, neither the city nor the province can afford that."

"Go on."

"I'm speaking on behalf of the B.C. Salmon Packers' Association," Ross-Murray said. "We'd like to hire your firm to handle this job for us."

The association represented all of the canneries in British Columbia. But what kind of situation could require this kind of build-up?

"I'm flattered," Granville said smoothly. "What is the job?"

"They've found a body at the Gulf of Georgia Cannery in Steveston. Or rather, they've found the bones."

EVEN ON THE mining fields of the Klondike, Granville had heard stories about Steveston's infamous Cannery Row. But still. Finding a human skeleton? At a cannery?

How was that even possible?

Granville raised his glass—of heavy crystal, he noted absently—as he considered Ross-Murray's matter-of-fact offer. The rich taste of good single malt whiskey coated his mouth. Around him the low buzz of quiet conversation mixed with the clink of glasses as drinks were served. Sunlight poured in from clerestory windows, in direct contrast to the dark subject of their conversation, while slow-turning ceiling fans kept the room cool.

"Whose bones?" Granville asked.

"One of the workers, most likely."

"Then it's a recent death?"

"So it would seem." Ross-Murray waved an impatient hand. "But this soon after the strike settlement? We can't afford to have rumors of this unfortunate fellow's death reigniting the tensions that are still simmering from the strike."

The government had called in the army on the striking cannery workers—specifically the Duke of Connaught's 6th Regiment. Probably urged on by the cannery owners. Granville wasn't surprised that there were still bad feelings between the parties.

"What are you most concerned about?" he asked, forcing a neutral tone.

"There are rumbles of another strike," Ross-Murray said. "Or worse."

The official reason for the government's intervention had been to prevent further threats against Japanese fishermen, who had settled with the canneries and gone back to work. The real story was unclear, but the newly formed Fishermen's Union had cried foul. Granville remembered reading about it—during what proved to be the last week of the strike—and wondering how the fishermen had felt, facing an armed regiment.

No wonder the cannery owners were worried.

"What steps have you taken so far?" Granville asked.

"We've kept things quiet while we looked for the right person to handle the situation for us," Ross-Murray said.

"Then you haven't brought in the police?"

"No. This needs to be dealt with quietly," Ross-Murray was saying.

"You know we'll have to bring them in, if we take the job." Granville wasn't compromising on this one.

Ross-Murray's face was impossible to read, until he broke into a smile. "A man of honor, then, are you? Good. That's what we need." He leaned forward. "And what will it take for you to accept this job?"

'To start, I'll need more information," Granville said. "Who was found, where, and when."

"The dead man—or rather his bones—was found early yesterday morning. In a lye bath at the Gulf of Georgia Cannery. We have no idea who he was."

In a lye bath? He grimaced at the thought of what lye could do to a body. "Could it have been an accidental death?"

Ross-Murray shook his head. "I'm afraid not."

Which meant they were looking at a murder. And one with no body—and presumably no witnesses. Just bones.

This would be a difficult case. And different from anything his investigative agency had yet attempted. Granville and Scott Investigations had been in business less than a year, but they were slowly becoming known for their ability to take on complex cases—and solve them. He wasn't ready to risk that reputation on a hopeless case.

On the other hand, it would be a challenge. And he'd never been able to resist a challenge, even one with long odds.

"And who knows about this discovery?" Granville asked.

"The only ones who know so far are the shift foreman, the cannery manager, myself and several of my fellow cannery owners, and now you," Ross-Murray said. "None of us will talk about it. We can't afford to have word getting out."

"None of the workers know?"

"Just one. A Chinese fellow who maintained the lye bath. He's been let go, and the Chinese contractor will make sure he doesn't talk."

"The Chinese contractor?"

"All the canneries hire them," Ross-Murray said. "The 'China Boss' is responsible for providing all the Chinese workers a cannery will need for the season. He's responsible for them—makes sure they show up, feeds them, takes care of any complaints. And since they're Chinese themselves, the contractors know the language, the customs. It's a good system."

It sounded like a convenient one, at least for the cannery owners. And maybe for the workers, too, since most of them wouldn't speak English. "And what are your expectations on this case?"

"That you will find out who was killed, by whom, and why. I trust that you will do so in a discreet manner."

He raised his whiskey glass, glanced at Granville over the top of it. "And I sincerely hope that your finding will be that this man's death had nothing to do with the strike, or with tensions between the Japanese and the white workers," he said, and drained the glass.

"And if the death proves to be related to the strike?" Granville said. "What do you expect of my firm then?"

"Then it will be up to you how you choose to handle it. Which is why I needed to hire an honorable man."

That decided him. He hoped Ross-Murray meant what he was saying, because once he took on a case, he followed it through. "Then we accept the job."

"Good."

"I'll need to see the cannery where the bones were found."

"Yes, of course. Someone will be in touch later today." Ross-Murray stood and shook hands. "I'm glad you've decided to take this on. You're one of us."

Beside him, Turner had nodded. In approval?

Granville couldn't decide how he felt about Ross-Murray's statement. Was he was flattered to be treated as a peer by this very successful businessman, or appalled?

What did "one of us" mean in a murder investigation?

2

WEDNESDAY, AUGUST 8, 1900

The Gulf of Georgia Cannery was built on a pier suspended over the deep waters of the Fraser River on long poles—poles the size of tree trunks, sunk deep into the mud. Seeing the thick encrustation of barnacles and seaweed on those poles, smelling the creosote that sealed them—it seemed as if they'd stand forever. Granville had spent enough of his childhood in and around water, though, to know that the river wouldn't allow anything to last forever.

Inside the sprawling wooden building, he was met by the foreman, and quickly taken to the canning room. Even from the doorway, the heat of the canning room was overwhelming, the noise beyond belief. But it was the smell Granville couldn't ignore. The steamy air stunk of fish guts, machine oil and sweat.

Steeling himself, he walked into the huge room. He could see both of the working canning lines, running the length of the building. Two strings of men and women—standing for twelve, fifteen hours a day in that noise and that heat—whose labor resulted in the cans of sockeye salmon that had ended up on his breakfast table when he was still in London.

There was something frantic in the air here. In the clattering of the machines. The hissing of steam. The quick motions of the cannery workers as they slung the fish along the line.

They'd lost all of July to the fishermen's strike, so none of them —not the owners, not the fishermen, not the cannery workers themselves—could afford to lose any more time. Or money. The salmon run was too short as it was.

The foreman waved him forward—Bob Dirks, another Brit, and London-born by his accent. Assigned as his guide, Dirks had proven eager to please a guest of Alexander Ross-Murray himself. Dirks walked Granville the length of the building, past the hectic pace of the workers on the line, until they reached the far end, where huge wooden doors stood open to the river, letting in a gust of air, cool from the river. It was a welcome relief.

Against the near wall stood large wooden bins on wheels. The floor inside the doors was mounded with thick-bodied salmon, which two Chinese men were slinging into those bins in an endless rhythm, fish after fish.

As they got closer, Granville could see through the big doors to the fishing boats on the river below. Two men were unloading sockeye salmon from the boats. Hundreds of them. Fifteen, twenty pounds apiece. Sides gleaming silver in the sun.

Two more men shoveled the salmon into bins, loaded them on a trolley. Another winched the trolley up a ramp into the cannery, where its contents were dumped onto mounds of salmon already there.

Granville had never seen so many fish in his life.

The foreman pointed at the bins full of fish, shouted something —his words lost in the din—then guided him towards the next station.

Two rows of long narrow wooden benches, mirroring each other, each with two of the wooden bins behind it—one full of salmon, one half-empty.

More than two dozen Chinese and Japanese men, knives flying, were butchering the fish. Slicing off heads, tails and fins, slitting the bellies, gutting them.

Each knife moving so fast it almost sang. Whssst.

The butchered fish tossed into the half-empty bins. Heads and entrails pushed off the bench. A new fish reached for. Whssst.

"These men are the butchers, they do four, five fish a minute," Dirks yelled in his ear. "They have to be fast, or it slows down the whole line. 'S why they're paid so much, nearly a quarter as much as me."

Granville was mesmerized by the flashing knives, the quick, precise movements. And repelled by the smell, the blood staining their aprons, the table, the floor, until it fell through the cracks in the cannery floor to the river below.

Dirks was tugging his elbow, moving him along. Following the route the salmon took, they stopped at a double row of waist high benches fitted with cutting boards and rubber hoses gushing water.

Rows of women—mostly native Indian, some with babies on their backs—were cleaning and washing the butchered salmon. Busy knives flying. Bits of entrails pushed into a trough below their cutting boards. Water splashing everywhere.

"Sliming station," the foreman yelled. "Cleans the fish."

Granville noted the water lying in pools at the women's feet. He could feel the breeze coming in from the open doors, and sneaking through chinks in the cannery walls. It helped with the heat and the smell, but these women must be freezing—standing here hour after hour with wet hands and feet.

Faces calm, the women's hands flashed as they moved the fish along, talking to each other as fast as they worked. He wondered how they managed to hear anything through the din all around them.

Dirks was pulling him along again, as they followed the cleaned salmon to the next station. "Gang knives," he said. "Fast, but deadly."

Protectively garbed Chinese men were feeding whole salmon into the whirring blades, which cut the fish into thick steaks. Granville instinctively clenched his fists—it was obvious how little it would take to lose fingers or a whole hand to the machine.

But the foreman was already moving on, pointing out the machines that packed the one pound cans of salmon. Granville watched in fascination as the clattering, whirring machine moved the tins forward at dizzying speed.

"Half-pound cans are filled manually. Costs more, but we can charge more," Dirks yelled gleefully. "The cans are all made before the season. Stored in the can loft. Kids drop them down this chute to us." and he pointed to the metal chute coming down from the wood ceiling above them.

Children? Here? He'd have to ask to see the loft as well, Granville thought. He could only imagine the heat building up in there.

"Crimping machine, then soldering machine over here for the lids," Dirks said.

Granville watched as can after can rolled out of the soldering machine, and quick hands stacked them one row deep in large baskets made of strips of wrought iron. He tried to imagine trying to keep up this pace all day long. Couldn't.

"These men punch a hole in each lid to let out the steam." Dirks nodded at them. "Then they run them through the steam bath."

The foreman patted the side of a machine. "Got this one two years ago. Saves us at least four workers a shift." He didn't seem to care if the men working the steam bath heard him.

"The cooled cans get resealed by hand," Dirks waved at the tables of workers, bent over the trays of cans with soldering irons, carefully re-sealing the hole. "Then it's off to the cooking line."

The smell of cooking salmon was everywhere. It smelled anything but appetizing mixed in with the stench from the rest of the plant.

Granville tried not to smell it. Fresh caught and cooked salmon had become a favorite of his since he'd moved to Vancouver. He'd hate to have his enjoyment of it permanently spoiled by this experience.

"Soon's they're cooked, it's into the lye bath to clean 'em off," the cannery foreman said, waving in the direction of a large steel bin.

Granville glanced at Dirks's indifferent face, wondering if he knew about the bones found here. Surely he must. Did he care so little, then?

Granville looked back at the lye bath. This was what he'd come to see. About three feet by four feet across, it stood nearly four feet high. He could smell the caustic odor of the lye, cutting through the overall stench of the place. And he was tall enough to see easily into the thing.

The heavy tub was three quarters full of a clear liquid with the distinctive sharp burning odor of lye. He could see that it easily held several crates full of cans. More than big enough to hold a body. And there was no lid on the thing.

How could people work like this?

And why had a man died here?

3

The man who might be able to give him some answers had an office in a wing on the town side of the cannery. Andrew Boyd was the manager of the Gulf of Georgia Cannery, responsible for the running of the cannery, and every man, and woman, in it. Presumably that extended to the bones they'd found in the lye vat.

Boyd's office was at the end of a long hallway. The whole section was closed off from the cannery line by several walls and two sets of doors. The smell and the noise were much less here, but it was still present. As he rapped on the closed door, Granville wondered how long it had taken Boyd to adjust to the working conditions.

"Come in."

The cannery manager was a short, rotund fellow, who looked like he ate far more beef pot pie than he did the fish he canned. He came forward with an outstretched hand. "I'm Andrew Boyd. Very pleased to meet you. Alexander Ross-Murray called himself to advise us you'd be here today. I hope your tour was satisfactory?"

"John Granville," he said, shaking hands. "And yes, very satisfactory, if a little overwhelming."

He glanced around him. Boyd's office looked like a typical business office, with a heavy oak desk and bookcase, and a water cooler sitting beneath the window that looked out on Cannery Row. A jumble of papers on the desk completed the impression. It was as far from the noise and stink of the cannery line as it was possible to get while still remaining in the same building.

Boyd smiled. "Please, have a seat," he said, waving at a group of comfortable leather club chairs grouped around a small mahogany table. "Graham Owens, one of our owners, will be joining us for this meeting. I'll just let him know you're here."

Granville pulled out a chair and sprawled comfortably in it, listening to Boyd's call. Boyd's tone was obsequious, and his fingers tapped nervously on his desk. After a moment he hung up, and joined Granville at the table.

"He'll be just a moment. He had business in the village this morning. Can I get you a coffee?"

"No thank you," Granville said politely. His nose still hadn't adjusted to the stink of the building. He didn't want to add coffee to that, in case he could never drink the stuff again. And he was fond of his coffee.

"Very well," Boyd said. "You said you had questions. Perhaps we can start with those while we wait."

"Perfect," Granville said. "I'm interested in the lye bath. That's a fairly large tub."

"Yes, it is. It has to be. Once they're cooked, the sealed cans are loaded into crates that are placed in the lye bath. That's why the crates are made of wrought iron—lye won't corrode iron."

"And the lye is to clean the cans? Of what?"

"Extra bits of fish, blood, even scales—whatever may have ended up on the outside of the can. It's a messy process, canning—you may have noticed."

"I did indeed," Granville said with a wry grin. "How do you stand the smell, day after day?"

Boyd looked surprised. "I don't even notice it any more."

"How long did that take?"

"I can't even tell you—one day I simply didn't notice. Now, you had another question?"

He did. "Isn't it dangerous to have the lye baths so large?"

Boyd frowned at the question, as if it had never occurred to him. Or maybe he was just annoyed. "No, it isn't dangerous. And we do have safety regulations, you know."

He was annoyed.

Granville found that interesting. Usually men who got angry when questioned were either very arrogant, which Boyd lacked the self-confidence to be. Or they had something to hide.

Granville wondered just what Boyd might be hiding.

And which safety regulations they were ignoring.

"The sides are too high for someone to accidentally fall in," Boyd was explaining. "And the smell keeps them at a distance in any case. It's built that way to accommodate more crates. For efficiency, you know. We can't afford anything to slow down the canning line."

"Has anyone ever fallen in?"

"Certainly not."

Boyd was growing increasingly defensive. Why?

"What about the fellows who load the tins into the lye bath? Could one of them slip and fall in?" Granville asked.

"No. Of course not. Oh, they get the occasional lye burn on their hands or arms, but nothing serious."

An occupational hazard, Granville thought. Just like the missing fingers on some of the workers operating the gang knives. Surely the line could have been built more safely? "And how long are the cans left in the lye?"

"Three or four minutes," was the answer.

"And how many people work the lye bath?" Granville asked.

"Four. Two on each side. That way there are always several crates of cans being cleaned at any given moment. Which is an asset on the line, because otherwise it could create a bottleneck and back up all the stations," Boyd said with some pride.

"Do the workers take breaks?" Granville asked. "And are they replaced?"

"Of course they take breaks. Every eight hours, there is a thirty minute break for dinner."

He couldn't imagine how they maintained the pace he'd seen earlier for that long, with no break for eight hours, and in all that heat and noise. He doubted he'd have survived three hours of it. And he considered himself in good shape.

No wonder the workers he'd seen were all fined down to muscle and sinew. "And does someone else take on the work when they're on their break?"

"Oh yes, someone from elsewhere on the line."

"Has there ever been an accident?"

"No, no. Nothing serious, anyway. Nothing where the line had to be shut down," Boyd said.

Before Granville could ask his next question, they were interrupted.

"No, don't bother announcing me," boomed a voice from outside the door.

The door was flung inward, and Graham Owens strode into Boyd's office with a broad grin and energy to burn, shown in by Boyd's beaming secretary. Granville had heard the part-owner of the Gulf of Georgia Cannery had worked in canneries for most of his adult life, loved everything about them. It showed.

Sharp gray eyes took in the two of them seated at the table. "You started without me?" Owens asked. He did not look pleased.

"No, no," Boyd said, rising to his feet. "We've been waiting for you. Mr. Granville here simply had some questions about the line after seeing it earlier."

Owens frowned. Before he could say anything, Boyd waved a hand towards Granville, blinking nervously as he did so. "Graham Owens, this is John Granville."

Owens gave the cannery manager a hard look, then strode over to where Granville sat and held out a hand.

Granville stood to shake hands. "Pleased to meet you."

"Likewise. So, what did you want to know about the line?" Owens said as he pulled out the chair between Granville and Boyd.

As they all sat, Granville noted that while Owens pushed his own chair back, stretched out long legs comfortably, Boyd had edged his chair a little further from his boss's. The cannery manager gave Granville a worried glance, before focusing his attention on Owens.

Granville felt sorry for the fellow, but he wasn't going to sweeten it for him. Their reactions could be a critical piece in unraveling this ugly death.

"Mostly specifics about the lye bath, and how it's run," he said calmly.

"Oh? And did you get all your questions answered?" Owens asked, darting a glance at Boyd that Granville couldn't read.

"Not yet. Can you tell me how often the lye bath is cleaned? And how it's done?"

"It isn't cleaned that often," Boyd said, after a worried look at his boss. "Maybe once a fortnight. Doesn't really need it more often, you see. The lye dissolves everything, leaves a dark red sludge behind. And not much of that."

"Everything except bones," Granville said.

Boyd flushed. "Well, it dissolves salmon bones," he explained. "So we clean it when it gets too dirty. We empty it. Scrub out the tub. Then refill it."

"Where do you empty it?" Granville asked, though he suspected he knew.

"Into the river. The water dilutes the lye until it's harmless."

Which was probably true. And olives were lye-cured. But he'd suddenly lost the desire to try those crabs under the pier, the ones which reportedly grew so large from feasting on salmon scraps.

"And was the lye bath cleaned out over the weekend? Is that how the bones were discovered?" Granville asked.

"No, surprisingly, it wasn't," Owens said. "The Chinese worker whose job it is to maintain the lye vat arrived early, as he does on a Monday. Which was lucky for us, in a way, because most of the line weren't in yet. He saw the bones lying on the bottom, because the lye mixture was still mostly clear. He did manage to go and tell the foreman before he fell apart, so we've been able to contain the news of the discovery."

"Lucky indeed," Boyd agreed.

They called anything lucky about finding a skeleton in the lye vat? Granville looked from one to the other, but refrained from comment. "How did you retrieve the bones without anyone learning about it?"

"Fished them out with a metal skimmer," Boyd said, looking pleased with their ingenuity.

"You didn't drain the vat?"

"There was no need," Owens said. "The tub had been emptied the week before, so there was very little sludge. We were easily able to fish everything out. Do you want to see?"

"Of course," Granville said immediately. He wasn't looking forward to it, though. Bodies he'd dealt with before, but not skeletons. For some reason the skeletons seemed worse.

Owens nodded. "Boyd, get the bones," Owens said.

Boyd nodded and scurried off.

Owens smiled at Granville. "I find the things unsettling, myself, so I'm glad our association has hired you to deal with the matter. The last thing we need is more labor unrest."

"Yes, I can imagine," Granville said.

"Once Boyd retrieves them, you might as well take the bones with you," Owens said.

"Actually, I'd like your permission to send them to the coroner in New Westminster, Dr. Findler. I understand he makes something of a study of bones."

"As long as it's kept strictly confidential," Owens said. "We can't have word of this getting out."

"Of course not," Granville said. "The matter will be handled in the strictest of confidence, you have my word on that. Though the number of people who know will have to expand somewhat—I'll need to involve the Steveston police, as I'm sure Ross-Murray informed you. They will be the ones to ship the bones to the coroner."

"Very well," Owens said. "With you directing the investigation, I have no problem with handing the bones off to the police when they request them."

"Thank you," Granville said.

The door opened and Boyd came back, carrying a medium sized cardboard box in his arms. Whatever Granville had expected them to have done with the skeleton they'd found, this wasn't it.

THE CANNERY MANAGER half-dropped the cardboard box of bones on the table in front of Granville and Owens, and let out a relieved breath. He pulled out a handkerchief and mopped at his flushed face.

Granville couldn't decide if the box was too heavy for Boyd, or if the cannery manager was bothered by its contents.

The box itself was perhaps two and a half feet long by two feet wide by one and a half feet deep. It was made of ordinary brown cardboard. And it held what had once been a man.

Granville found it hard to believe that a human being could be reduced to this little.

Boyd pulled open the flaps—it hadn't even been sealed—and exposed the contents.

"This is all you found in the lye vat?" Granville asked. "You're sure no small bits were left behind in the—sludge, you called it?"

"Oh yes. I'm very certain," Boyd said. "The Chinaman was very careful. Once he got over his nervous fit after finding the bones, that is."

"Yes, he would be careful," Owens added unexpectedly, surprising Granville. "A person's bones, especially an ancestor's bones, are very important to the Chinese. Important enough that their association has hired several bone collectors, who travel through the province recovering the bones of the Chinamen who died while building the Canadian Pacific Railway."

His fiancée, Emily Turner, had told him something similar, Granville recalled, while they were working on the lost mine case. Her parents' Chinese houseboy, Bertie Wong, had a cousin who was a bone collector. Bertie had arranged for the fellow—en route to the Fraser River goldfields—to deliver a message from Emily to Granville.

Granville had thought the notion of bone collecting—returning the remains of those who had died overseas to their homeland for a proper burial—commendable, if a little macabre, then. He found it even more commendable today, looking at what had once been a man.

Now it was only a collection of bones stuffed haphazardly in a cardboard box.

His firm had been hired to solve this man's murder, which inevitably meant learning who he was. But looking at the contents of the cardboard box, Granville suddenly had a much stronger reason to do so.

He was determined to see that these bones got a proper burial. And to ensure that the dead man's name and cause of death were known to his loved ones.

He looked more closely at the jumble of bones in the box. The skull was easy to pick out, and a couple of long, heavy bones that must be thigh bones. He couldn't begin to identify the rest.

It was a very good thing Owens had agreed to release the skeleton to the coroner.

The bones themselves were clean and very white. Every surface was pitted. Probably from the caustic action of the lye. They also looked fragile, as if a blow would shatter them. He'd have to ask the coroner if that was the effect of the lye, or whether the victim had been in poor health.

But tucked into one corner of the box, Granville saw the glint of metal. He reached out, then paused, looking at Owens. "May I?" he asked.

The latter nodded.

Granville reached in, and carefully removed a round metal disk. It was the size and weight of a coin, with a rectangular hole cut into the middle of it. "Where was this found?" he asked.

"In the lye vat. At the bottom, mixed in with the bones and the sludge from the body," Boyd said.

Granville examined it. It was shiny after its immersion in lye, and heavy for its size. Possibly iron. The edges of the disk were worn in places, and both sides were smooth to the touch.

There were symbols on one side, blurred with wear. The other side was worn completely smooth, and it was impossible to tell if there had ever been a design on it. Granville looked more closely at the symbols. He didn't recognize them, though they resembled Chinese characters, possibly stylized or simplified, surrounded by circles.

He ran his thumb over the front of the disk, feeling the raised design. The feel of it was pleasing, but it told him nothing more. However, the shape and markings on the disk looked remarkably similar to the ancient Buddhist tokens that had figured so largely in the missing heir case they'd undertaken a few months before.

Which might suggest their victim was Chinese. Or at least Buddhist.

"Do either of you recognize this?" he asked the two cannery executives, passing the piece to Owens.

Owens examined it carefully, rubbing his thumb over it as Granville had done. He shook his head, and passed it to Boyd.

The cannery manager turned the piece of metal over several times. "No," he said, and passed it back to Granville.

"What about the symbols?" Granville asked.

Boyd glanced at Owens. "I don't know," Boyd said.

Owens held out a hand, and Granville dropped the disk into it.

The cannery owner held the disk closer to his eyes, angling it towards the sunlight streaming through the window, turning it this way and that. "Could be Chinese," he said after a moment. "Or Japanese."

"The symbols could be either Chinese or Japanese?" Granville hadn't known that.

"Yes. Easily."

"But you don't recognize them?"

"I'm afraid not."

Granville turned the disk over in his fingers. "I'd like to take this with me, if I may," he said. "I'll see if I can identify it."

Boyd started to protest, but Owens nodded. "Of course," he said.

Looking from the bones to the two men, Granville asked his most important question. "Have any of your workers been reported as missing since Monday?" he asked.

"You mean the Chinese workers?" Boyd asked. "Or the Japanese?

"Any men, of any race, that normally work here," Granville said. "And haven't been here since last Sunday. Don't forget, we are not just looking to identify the victim. We are also looking for his killer."

Boyd and Owens exchanged glances.

"Not to my knowledge," the owner said.

Owens had chosen his words very carefully. Granville found that interesting.

He smiled at Owens, glanced over at Boyd. Then back. "You're certain no-one is missing from your crew?"

"Yes. I just told you…" Owens began. Then he too glanced at Boyd.

"Have any of your workers not shown up since Saturday?" Granville asked Boyd directly. "Perhaps someone you might not have mentioned to Owens here."

"No, that is, no, I don't think so," Boyd said, stammering a little. "Both lines are running full out, as you saw."

"But I understand from Ross-Murray that many of your men are contracted. If the former owner of these bones was Chinese or Japanese, would you know if he was missing?"

"You mean if the China Boss or the Japan Boss had someone ready to take his place at the start of the shift?" Boyd said.

"Yes, exactly," Granville said.

"No. We wouldn't," Owens said unexpectedly.

Boyd frowned. "I'm sure the foreman would have noticed," he said.

Having met the man, Granville doubted it. "If the replacement worker knew the work, and didn't slow the line, are you sure Dirks would have noticed?" he asked.

"Maybe not," Boyd said. "We pay a lot of attention to the speed of the line."

And not so much to the workers, obviously, Granville thought. "How many people are working on the cannery lines here on a given day?"

"Nearly three hundred," Boyd said.

Picturing the two cannery lines in his mind, that number didn't surprise Granville. Still, it was quite a few people to keep track of. Would Dirks know them all by face, if not by name? Somehow he doubted that, too.

Just how expendable was an individual worker? "So it's possible the deceased could have been one of your workers?"

"Yes, it is," Owens said. "Poor fellow."

"Of course it's possible. But I doubt it was one of our workers," Boyd said. "The contractors would have said something."

Boyd scratched at his elbow, as if it suddenly itched. "But if he was one of ours, he was still alive when his shift finished on Saturday," he said.

"What makes you say that?"

"Well, the body would have been visible in the lye bath. So it wasn't there," Boyd said.

"This man must have come from somewhere," Granville said. "It's possible he was killed on Sunday. But it's too early in the investigation to ignore any possibility. If this was one of your workers, is there nowhere in the cannery a body could have been hidden during the work day?"

Boyd and Owens exchanged glances. "I don't see how…" Boyd began.

"There are several places where it might have been possible," Owens said, interrupting him. "This is a big place, and the lighting isn't the best, as you'll have noticed. I can't imagine how it would have been done—but yes, in all the confusion, it might have been possible to hide a body here."

"He could as easily have been one of the fishermen," Boyd said. "Quite a few of them bring their catch in late. And there are sometimes feuds over the fishing grounds."

Probably true enough. And worth following up. But Granville needed to know as much about the deceased as the coroner could tell him before he could even begin to figure out what was going on here.

Or ask these two any more questions.

"Thank you for your time," he said as he rose. "You can expect to hear from the police chief—likely tomorrow—regarding the arrangements for shipping these bones to the coroner."

"Yes, of course," Owens said.

Boyd's gaze slipped to Owens, then slid away. The cannery manager looked more nervous than ever.

Did Boyd know something about the bones he wasn't telling them?

4

The journey by stagecoach back to Vancouver had been long, crowded and hot. And Granville hadn't been able to get Boyd's nervous expression out of his mind. As he climbed the creaking stairs to his office on the third floor, Granville was still trying to puzzle out what the fellow might be hiding. And why.

Was the cannery manager involved in the murder? Or perhaps covering for someone?

He ran a hand through his hair, surprised to find it still damp. He'd expected it to have dried by now, but the muggy heat had defeated that plan. Still, it had been worth the detour to his cramped apartment for a shower.

Today was a scorcher—as his assistant, Trent Davis, was wont to say—and the heat had seemed to worsen the smell that had clung to him ever since he'd left the cannery. The expressions of the other riders on the stagecoach back from Steveston had confirmed that he smelled just as badly as he'd thought he did. All the passengers had looked unhappy when he got on.

Once they reached Vancouver, he'd walked from the livery stable back to his apartment, rather than take the trolley and endure that reaction again.

At least now he was clean and cooled off. Which wouldn't last. Not in this heat.

The hall door on the third floor stuck, as usual, and the hallway carpet looked tired. He opened their office door and glanced around the office.

Papered in soft cream with a faint blue stripe, the mahogany desk and upholstered chairs spoke of prosperity. The second, smaller desk of dark-stained oak had clearly been added later, making the space feel crowded and less welcoming. Through a door on the left, another small desk of dark-stained oak was visible, surrounded by shelving. It had once been a storage room, and it made a poor office.

Both of the oak desks were empty. Their clerk, Laura Kent, sat at the mahogany desk. She seemed to be the only one in the office.

She glanced up as he entered, giving him that very professional smile of hers, with just a hint of warmth around the edges.

"Afternoon, Miss Kent," he said, pausing in front of her desk. "Is Scott in?"

She nodded. "Yes. But Trent is working on the Barton case and your fiancée is at the realtor's."

The Barton case was a new one they'd taken on—a fairly straight-forward surveillance. He and his partner, Sam Scott, had decided it was the perfect chance for Trent to work solo. He just hoped the lad wasn't getting too bored.

He grinned at the thought. Surveillances were often tedious, and Trent had proved rather too fond of taking risky chances. A little boredom might be good for him.

He wondered how Emily's meeting with their realtor was going. She'd been invaluable in real estate matters for months now. Though he was glad he wasn't in the fellow's shoes. Miss Emily Turner was proving herself a fierce negotiator.

It was thanks to her they wouldn't be renting this office much longer, Granville thought as he opened the door to the inner office he and Scott shared. Soon their firm, Granville and Scott Investigations, would own the entire office building. They'd made an offer in June to the building's current, less than effective, owners.

And the deal would close at the end of the month.

It didn't seem quite real. No doubt the renovations that Emily was planning for them would bring it home, he thought with a grin. They were likely to live with disruption for months, judging by the last set of plans he'd seen.

SCOTT's massive frame dwarfed the desk chair he'd had specially built. His dark brows were pinched together over whatever file he was reading, but he looked up when Granville closed the door.

"Granville. I expected you back an hour ago."

"I had to shower first," Granville said, removing his jacket and rolling up his shirtsleeves before sitting down on his side of the double-size partner's desk that he and Scott shared.

He glanced around their cramped office. In addition to their heavy oak desk, there were four chairs lined up along the wall, two on each side of the door. This room also served as the office meeting room, and it was proving woefully inadequate. Overhead, a fan squeaked away, moving very little of the air.

A renovation—any renovation—would be welcome.

Owning the building would give them an opportunity for a much needed expansion. And bring in rent money that could offset —hopefully unnecessarily—slow periods in their business. Or slow-to-pay clients. Another business hazard he'd been reluctantly learning about.

"So what did you think of Steveston's Cannery Row?" Scott was asking. "It remind you of Dupont Street?"

"Dupont Street?"

Scott grinned at him. "You know—opium dens? Bars? Brothels?"

"Yes, I know Steveston's reputation. But aside from a few bar signs near the stage depot, all I noticed today was canneries." Lots of canneries. And sky. But he didn't share the latter thought. "We'll have to check out the rest of it tomorrow."

"So how did it go with the canneries?"

"It was very informative. And worse than you can imagine."

"What happened?"

"Have you ever seen a cannery in operation?"

"No."

"Suffice it to say I needed that shower to make me fit company again. The reek of the place is beyond anything I've encountered before."

"Worse than a miner's cabin at the end of a Klondike winter?"

"Far worse. But you'll find out."

"I look forward to it." Scott said with a grin. He leaned forward. "But what did you learn?"

"Very little, yet. The cannery lines are running, with full crews, as long as there are fish to can. Which often means twelve to fifteen hours a day. Afterwards, most of the workers—including the cannery foreman—go home, while a small crew washes the entire cannery down with steam hoses."

He glanced at Scott's expression, grinned. "It's not as bad as you're envisioning. The cannery is built out over the river, so everything washes through the cracks and down into the river below. Fish heads, fish blood, fish guts, everything. Apparently the crabs in that section of the river are unusually large, and make very tasty eating."

Scott made a face. "Okay. So what happens when the place is clean?"

"The cleaning crew lock up and go home. There's a night watchman, whom I haven't met yet."

"So when did the dead guy get killed?"

Granville sat back and stretched out his legs under the desk. "Presumably after the cleaning crew had left on Saturday. Which still leaves all of Sunday with the cannery virtually empty. And with nothing but bones to examine, the coroner will be able to tell us very little about when the poor fellow died."

"Tough case."

"It gets worse. Since the cannery was hosed down again on Monday night, and again on Tuesday, any traces of the killing will be gone. If the poor fellow was even killed there."

"It seems likely though, doesn't it?"

"Perhaps. It can be hard to dispose of a body, though, and the lye bath might have provided an easy solution for someone," Granville said. "Especially if they didn't want the dead man identified. Soaking in lye for a few hours takes care of that."

Scott grimaced. "Yeah, but the river's right there. Toss him in, a body'll be out at sea in no time."

"Currents can be unpredictable. Perhaps the killer couldn't afford to have his victim wash up on a beach somewhere. And a lye bath does a thorough job, from what I saw."

"Maybe. Just bones you said?"

"Yes. Very clean bones, with some of the edges eaten away. And a bit of metal." Granville pulled the small disk out of his shirt pocket, and passed it to Scott. "This was found in the bottom of the lye vat, with the bones."

Scott made a face as he accepted it, then turned it over in his fingers. "Looks like the ones Weston was looking for. The Buddhist coins. You think these are the same?"

"They are clearly newer. And this one might be a coin, rather than a religious token."

"Yeah. Could it be Chinese?"

"Yes. Or possibly Japanese, apparently. We'll need to find someone who can translate the symbols for us. Especially since at the moment it is our only clue to the identity of the victim."

Turning it over several times, Scott rubbed his index finger over both surfaces before handing it back to Granville. "Anyone recognize it?"

"Neither the cannery owner nor the manager admitted recognizing it."

"Or so they claim?" Scott said with a grin. "You trust them?"

"Too early to tell. Owens seems honorable enough, but I suspect

Boyd is hiding something. He looked nervous when he heard we were sending the skeleton to the coroner's office in New Westminster."

"You think he's involved?" Scott asked.

"He may be. Though he doesn't strike me as having the stomach for it. Or the nerves."

"Sometimes the weak ones are the nastiest," Scott said. "If you give them any kind of power."

Granville thought about Boyd's interactions with Owens. As the cannery manager, Boyd had a fair bit of power. But only when Owens wasn't around. That had to chafe.

"You might have something there," he said. "And I'll find out what Boyd is hiding."

Scott grinned. "Yeah, you never liked the ones who attack from behind," he said. "If Boyd is involved, any idea why?"

"Why he'd be involved in a murder? No. Not yet," Granville said. "We'll need to gather more information first. At the moment, the only man I know that Boyd and the owner would probably be glad to see vanish is the fisheries union organizer, Frank Rogers. And he's still very much alive."

"He the guy behind the recent strike?" Scott asked.

"One of them. And he's popular with the fishermen."

"Might be worth talking to, then."

"Might be," Granville said. "But it depends on how this case unfolds. And what the coroner has to say about the bones.

"Anyone from the cannery been reported missing yet?"

"No-one."

"And everyone was accounted for on all the shifts?"

Granville nodded. "Yes. Or so they say. That's why they called us in. Not only do they not have a killer, they can't even identify their victim."

"Nor can we," Scott said practically. "So what do we do next?"

"We identify him, of course. What else?" Granville said.

"But all we have are bones," Scott said. "Where do we even start?"

5

THURSDAY, AUGUST 9, 1900

They started with the Steveston police.

The following morning found Granville and Scott descending from the stagecoach on Moncton Street in Steveston, having rattled their way over planked roads and the most cobbled-together looking bridge Granville had ever seen. Both of them paused to get their bearings.

Granville was caught, as he had been the last time he'd come here, by how very present the sky was. It was the first thing he noticed—an endless expanse overhead—that bowl of burning blue the poets talked about.

It certainly fit today, when the August heat had burned off any clouds. He'd had the same feeling when he'd worked for a short time on the prairies. It was the flatness of the land, and the lack of trees.

But he hadn't expected to find it here, not so close to Vancouver, where the circling mountains were the first thing you noticed. Unless it was raining, of course, when grey clouds and fog became your world. Just like London, in fact. Maybe that was why he felt so at home in this climate.

He glanced at Scott who was scanning that part of the village they could see from where they stood. "So where's the red light district?" Scott asked.

"You're looking at it," Granville said, pointing along Bayview Street. And taking a closer look himself.

On one side of the street, facing the water, livery stables and feed lots mixed with dilapidated shacks as well as numerous pubs, bars and saloons. He could also see a number of pastel painted two-story houses—probably bordellos. All the buildings were plainly built and wood-framed, their exteriors badly weathered by the sea air. Even the bright trim on the bordellos had a tired look. None of it was particularly memorable.

So this was Cannery Row.

No wonder he hadn't paid much attention to it yesterday.

Across the street, cannery after cannery sprawled down to the river. He could see at least seven from where he stood, which meant there was another five he couldn't see. All the canneries faced the river—which must be quite a sight from the water—and their enormous back lots were covered by a motley collection of roughly-built huts, bunkhouses, native-style longhouses and lean-tos, where the cannery workers lived, ate and found their entertainment. Well, most of it.

Between the canneries they caught glimpses of the slow, muddy river, full of fishing boats. A whole long string of fishing boats was being pulled out to sea by a tug, hitched together like some over-sized child's plaything. It was an extraordinary thing to see.

The air was hot and heavy, nearly still in the heat. There was a sly breeze blowing off the water, but it provided no relief as the stench of the canneries settled over them. He thought he detected a hint of opium's distinctive burnt odor, but it vanished again, and he couldn't see any signs of the opium dens he'd expected to find.

"This is Steveston's infamous Cannery Row?" Scott said. "This?"

"I'm afraid so."

"Huh."

"Probably we should see it at night. Might be a good place to ask questions."

"Yeah." Scott inhaled as if testing the smell. Grimaced. "Mining I understand. Criminals, gangs even. But canning? I don't know enough about it to even ask good questions."

Nor did he.

"So we'll learn," Granville said with a shrug. "As investigators, it's to our advantage not to know everything. It means we'll notice things others miss or take for granted."

"Huh. So where do we start this learning of yours?"

"You mean of ours, don't you?" Granville said with a grin.

Scott clapped him on the back on place of an answer. It felt more like a wallop.

It was a good thing Scott was on his side, Granville thought, not for the first time, walking towards Third Avenue and the police station. His friend was a formidable foe, and just as useful an ally. Even if he didn't much care for new situations.

They stopped in front of the small, white-painted building with the word "Police" painted in blue over the door, glanced at each other. It wasn't very big, and it looked like a good storm would knock the place over.

As Granville reached for the tarnished brass doorknob, he wondered what he'd find inside. He'd read the sensationalized press coverage when the village's Police Chief had been murdered in February, ambushed by a trio of Chinese thieves. The remaining squad now had an acting chief, Bert Gates, but the murder of their senior officer had to be demoralizing. How would they react to the news of another murder here, and a bizarre one at that?

He stepped inside, to find four desks facing the door, two of them occupied by men in blue uniforms with silver buttons in need of polishing. A fan turned lazily overhead. "Acting Chief Gates?" he asked.

The younger of the two men gestured to a closed door at the rear of the building. "Back there," he said.

Mentally shaking his head at the lack of discipline, Granville headed towards Gates' office. Behind him he could hear Scott's heavy tread. Granville gave a quick rap on the closed door, waited for the acknowledgement. Then opened the door.

"Chief Gates," he said as he walked into the fellow's office, which was orderly and neat.

Gates, who had thinning brown hair and worried eyes, placed his fountain pen back in its stand and pulled a sheet of blank paper over his notes. "Yes?" he said.

"I'm John Granville. This is my partner, Sam Scott. We're with…"

"Granville and Scott Investigations, in Vancouver," Gates said, standing up to shake hands. "Yes, I've heard of you. What brings you out this way?"

Well that was a surprise. Granville hadn't expected Gates to have known who they were—not when they'd been in business less than a year. He was pleased, though. It would make things easier.

And it meant their firm was beginning to gain the kind of reputation he'd hoped for. Even without an affiliation with the Pinkerton's Agency.

Which sparked a twinge of anxiety. The meeting he'd arranged with the Pinkerton's Investigations Agency—to explore the possibility of their firm affiliating with that storied agency—was approaching fast. And he still didn't know which direction would be best for their firm. Or how Scott really felt about it.

He shoved the thought away. They had a job to do here. And they might be treading on sensitive toes. "We've been hired by the Salmon Packers' Association to look into a body found at one of the local canneries," he said.

"I've heard nothing of this," the Acting Chief said, his shoulders tensing under the stiff uniform.

"No. The association preferred to keep the matter private, for fear of starting a riot."

"Or another strike?" Gates said wryly. "Given the violence of the last one, I'm not surprised. But why are you here?"

"They gave us latitude to involve you if we chose. And it is our firm's policy," and Granville's look included Scott, "to involve the police as early as possible."

Which policy they interpreted rather liberally, depending on how corrupt a local police force proved to be. So far, he liked what he'd seen of Acting Chief Gates. The fellow might not be the best leader, judging by the apathy he'd seen in the outer office, but he cared.

"You know this village, these people," Scott said. "We don't."

"True. Though sometimes I wonder," Gates said with a smile that didn't reach his eyes. "This is a village of transients for most of the fishing season. More than six thousand of them, pouring into a village that is at most four thousand people in winter. It's not an easy place to police. But sit down, both of you."

No wonder Cannery Row stories abounded, Granville thought as he sat. With that many transients every summer—far from home, without roots here—it was amazing there was any semblance of law at all.

When all three were seated, Gates leaned forward, his gaze intent on Granville. "Now, who was murdered. And how?"

Granville crossed one leg over the other, appreciating the way the fine wool draped. It was good to be buying quality clothing again—the rough clothes of the gold miner had been something of a shock.

"We don't know who was murdered," Granville said. "Which is part of the problem. A skeleton was found in the lye bath at the Gulf of Georgia Cannery on Monday morning. They have no idea who he was, and as of yesterday, no-one has been reported missing."

Gates frowned. "The lye bath?"

"It's where they clean the cans of salmon before labeling them," Granville said. "Lye will dissolve nearly anything."

Gates winced. "I suppose we're lucky this hasn't happened before."

The Acting Chief tapped his fingers on the desk. Stopped as

soon as he noticed them watching. "So, we have no idea who their victim was. And I suppose after the lye bath, there's no indication of how he was killed?"

"Nope. Nor where he was killed," Scott said, bracing huge hands on his knees. "If he was killed at sea, he could've been hidden under a cargo of fish easy enough. Then been brought in to the cannery dock."

Clearly Scott had been thinking about the case overnight, Granville thought. And Scott was right. This case grew more complex the more they thought about it, dammit.

Gates was nodding. "But if the victim was brought in by boat would mean there are two killers—one man can't handle those boats."

"Or an accomplice," Scott put in.

"Risky," Gates said. "If they knew about the lye bath, though, it might have seemed safer than risking a body drifting on the incoming tide to somewhere it might be found. Though if they were far enough out to sea, they could have anchored the body with something, made sure it was never seen again."

"If they had something in the boat that was heavy enough," Scott said. "Maybe they didn't."

"Maybe not, at that. Though it might have been challenging getting a body into the cannery without anyone noticing," the chief said.

"He could have been killed in the cannery even more easily," Granville said.

Gates looked from Scott to Granville. "It seems this case offers little in the way of clues. Where did you plan to start?"

"First, can you tell us anything about the Gulf of Georgia owners, manager or foreman?" Granville said.

"There isn't much to tell, I'm afraid. We've had no dealings with any of the owners. Graham Owens is the only one of them who lives in Steveston, and he's had no run-ins with the law. Nor has Andrew Boyd, the cannery manager," Gates said.

"Bob Dirks, the foreman, is another matter. He's been pulled in after a few saloon brawls. Has a vicious temper when he's been drinking, that one. Nothing out of the ordinary, though."

Dirks would bear a closer investigation, Granville thought. "Any problems with the cannery itself?"

"Other than the recent strike? No. Nothing there either, I'm afraid," Gates said with an awkward shrug of thin shoulders.

"The bones will need to be examined by the coroner in New Westminster," Granville said. "And I've heard that the fellow also makes a private study of bones. He might be able to tell us something useful."

"That would be Dr. Findler," Gates said. "Good man."

"Could you arrange for Findler to see the bones?"

"Yes, I'd be happy to do that," Gates said. "If the cannery is willing to release the bones?"

"They are. On the condition that either Scott or I be present to hear the coroner's report."

"Along with one of my men," Gates said.

"Agreed," Granville said. "The manager at the Gulf of Georgia Cannery has the bones, and is expecting your call."

"Then I'll set it up. You can expect to hear from the coroner's office in a day or two."

"Thank you. And would you be willing to have your people work with us?" Granville asked. "You have the local knowledge that we lack."

"I have limited resources as it is, and a varied and difficult community." Gates picked up his pen, walked it over his fingers and back again, the movement mesmerizing in its smoothness. "But Constable Ingram, the man responsible for the cannery area, is dedicated and enthusiastic. He might well make the time to be involved in this case. At the least, he can give you a bit of background on the canneries, and who the players are."

Even that would help, Granville thought, though he hoped the constable would be intrigued enough to do more. "When might we speak with him?"

"He'll be back in the office after lunch. You can talk to him then," Gates said. "Mind you don't make it sound more exciting than it is. The lad's young, yet."

Grinning at the thought, Granville promised.

6

It was nearly one when Granville and Scott returned to the police station. They'd spent half an hour walking the fourteen blocks that made up the village of Steveston, trying to get a feel for the community. The village had been laid out on a grid system, with was focused towards the river.

As they sauntered along Chatham Street from First to Seventh Avenue, Granville had noted the mix of people—everyone from fishermen to farmers to bankers. Most of the village's businesses— from seed shops to ship's chandleries, and even the plainly-built wooden Opera House—seemed to be on Second and Third Avenues, running between Chatham and Moncton.

They strolled back along Cannery Row. Seen close-up, the red light district along the Steveston riverfront seemed like a blend of the rough bars near the Vancouver docks and the brothels and opium dens of Dupont Street in Vancouver's Chinatown—brought together here every summer by those who fished or worked for the canneries.

Cannery Row was their escape from hard physical labor and punishing hours. And the violence and debauchery common to such places was likely to make his job harder.

They'd eaten a properly greasy fish and chips lunch in one such bar, washed down with a half-decent ale. Clearly a hangout for working men, the place was rough—with plank walls and a dirt floor—and rowdy. They hadn't picked up much in the way of gossip, but the mood had been boisterous—workers letting off steam—not tense or uneasy. Which suggested a lack of rumors about the discovery of the bones.

Constable Ingram was waiting for them by the door of the police station, and Chief Gates had been right—he was eager to help.

On the short side, Ingram was wiry and intense, with a shock of sandy brown hair he kept pushing back, and sharp blue eyes that missed nothing.

"Billy Ingram," he said with a broad smile and an outstretched hand. "I'm a local. We came here when I was ten. From Finland. My uncle's a fisherman, so I know something of the fishing industry."

"Pleased to meet you," Granville said, and introduced himself and Scott. They all shook hands.

At Ingram's instigation, they moved along the porch so they were standing away from the windows, but still in the shade. Granville stood at a slight angle to Ingram, so he could watch both the constable's face and the street behind him. Scott leaned against a pillar, arms crossed.

"The Chief filled me in," Ingram told them. "And I'm really glad you chose to involve us. So how can I help?"

"We need to understand how the cannery industry fits into this village, where the tensions are," Granville said. "Starting with the repercussions from the strike last month. And it sounds like you might be the man to help us with that."

Ingram's smile died. "I hope so. And those are the right questions. It isn't just about the unions, you know. It gets personal. Too many people depend on the money coming from the salmon run every summer in order to live."

Granville nodded. "That's what I thought. And are you hearing rumors?"

"No, I'm not," Ingram said with a slight frown. "All I've run across is relief that the strike is over, and without more violence. There's still outrage that the militia was called in against our men. But that's to be expected."

Granville wondered if Ingram's words reflected an underlying racial tension in Steveston. "How are the Japanese seen here?" he asked Ingram.

The constable shrugged. "You know there are two fishermen's unions?" he asked instead of answering.

"Yes."

"Well, the Fishermen's Union would rather see the Fishermen's Association—which is Japanese—disappear. Along with all their members," Ingram said. "They feel the same about the Chinese. Most of our citizens—Canadians, Americans and Europeans alike —feel that Orientals are taking away good jobs from men who need them."

Which explained why the cannery owners were so concerned that the skeleton they'd found might be Japanese, Granville thought. It could stir up the resentment left from the strike into a confrontation that would affect their bottom line. "So that tension is always there?"

"Yes. But it doesn't seem to have flared up, or be any worse than usual," Ingram said.

Interesting. "What do you know of the Gulf of Georgia Cannery?" Granville asked.

"The Monster Cannery?" Ingram said.

Granville smiled at the name. He hadn't heard it before, and it struck him as particularly appropriate for this monstrosity of a case.

"And why is it called that?" Scott asked.

"Because it's the biggest," Ingram said. "They run two canning lines, with the option of a third they could set up next year, when the sockeye run will be even bigger."

At Scott's blank look, Ingram explained. "The salmon return

here to the Fraser River to spawn and die. Their offspring journey to the sea, then four years later, they too return to spawn and die. This happens every year, but one year in four, the run is much, much bigger."

"How come?" Scott asked.

Ingram shrugged. "No-one knows why. But the bigger runs are predictable. And those monster runs have saved many a failing cannery. If they can take advantage of them, that is."

"Take advantage how?" Scott asked.

"On a fourth year run," Ingram said, "the fish are so numerous, the canning lines can run all day, every day. They call it an embarrassment of fish, hereabouts."

"Isn't that how they're running now?" Granville asked.

"Trust me, next year will make this one look like nothing. This year, everyone's working until every last fish is canned, because they were all shut down in July by the strike. They're doing everything they can to fill shipping quotas and make up for that loss," Ingram said.

"But it's different with a big run. Those years, there are so many fish, that even those like the Monster Cannery, who can put on extra lines, end up overwhelmed and unable to buy all the fish the fishermen catch."

"What happens to the fish that aren't bought?" Granville asked.

"They're just dumped into the river outside the cannery," Ingram said with a frown.

Granville had learned about the salmon runs from the Kispiox Indians up north, but Ingram's explanation told him a lot about the culture here. The Kispiox looked on the salmon runs as a bounty nature provided to them, one that should be reverenced and properly honored. And never wasted.

"Those who can't run efficiently throw back far more fish," Ingram was saying. "And their costs are too high. Often they don't make it."

"Why not?" Scott asked.

"They have to hire more workers—if they can find them—which raises their costs," Ingram said. "Canneries trying to expand to meet the demand only one year in four have it tough. They end up running with too few workers in some areas and too many in others, depending on which workers were available. Or they hire people without the skills they need."

The young constable grimaced. "They can't run efficiently. So they lose more money. And the banks foreclose, or the investors pull their support."

It sounded all too familiar, Granville thought. Anything that impacted the ability of the canneries to turn the salmon run into canned salmon could put a cannery under. Like the strike.

Or the bones in the lye bath?

The strike had impacted all of them. If the bones had the potential to do the same—no wonder the Salmon Packers' Association had hired him to deal with those bones.

"There've been no troubles that are specific to the Gulf of Georgia Cannery, then?" he asked Ingram.

"Not that I've heard."

"Any rumors about their manager?"

"Andrew Boyd? Nothing one way or the other. The fishermen don't respect him much, though," Ingram said after a moment.

"And why is that?"

"He lets Dirks—that's his foreman—get away with too much."

"Such as?" Scott said.

Ingram glanced from Scott to Granville, grimaced. "He doesn't like his work. And he takes it out on those around him. Sets impossible standards, then penalizes those that don't meet them. And since everyone from the fishermen to the cannery workers are paid on a per piece basis, his tactics can cost people their living."

That explained the looks Dirks had received when he'd toured the cannery with him, Granville thought. "Does Boyd know?"

Ingram shrugged. "He chooses not to know. It would be pretty obvious if he ever went out on the cannery floor."

"He doesn't?"

"Not if he can help it, from what I've heard."

Interesting. "Before we looking into the murder itself, we need to get our own sense of where the tension lies," Granville said.

"Where did you want to start?" Ingram asked.

"Show us your village," Granville said.

BY FIVE, Granville was more than ready to leave Steveston. If only to get away from the smell of the canneries that pervaded every corner. After a full day of touring the village and its environs, he'd had quite enough, and he could tell Scott felt the same.

Their first impression of a sleepy little farming village transformed into a place where anything goes by the annual run of salmon had been confirmed. But they'd seen little of the kind of tension that they'd expected. The kind that leads to murder.

Constable Ingram had proved a good—and indefatigable—guide, determined to show them every nook and cranny of a village he evidently loved. Right down to the opium dens.

Hidden in rickety shacks on the back lots of the canneries, the opium dens were built snug to the back of the bunkhouses for the Chinese workers. Directly across Moncton Street from the bars and the brothels of Cannery Row.

No wonder he and Scott hadn't seen them.

It still seemed odd to Granville to find the respectable shopping district of the village only a half-block away from the red light district. And it said a great deal about the importance of the canneries to the village that the red light district was so large. When he said as much to Ingram, the constable just shook his head.

"Cannery Row," he said, sweeping his arm to encompass all of Bayview Street. "It's here because the canneries are here. And Steveston wouldn't exist without the canneries. Everyone here knows that. They may resent it, but they know it."

And he turned to lead them back up Fourth Avenue.

Everywhere Ingram took them, people were busy. Every store, every restaurant was buzzing. People were buying and selling, running errands. No-one was lingering to talk. Block after block was the same.

Granville had seen the same thing that morning, but it was only now—seeing it through the young constable's eyes—that he was gaining enough understanding of the place to make sense of it.

He turned to Ingram, stopping him with a hand on his shoulder. "The lingering effects of last month's strike—it's more than the tension amongst the races, isn't it?"

Ingram frowned. "What do you mean?"

Behind the young policeman, Scott was looking from Granville to the busy street around them, nodding. He'd seen it too.

"Everyone lost money," Granville said. "And I understand that the salmon run only lasts another few months. Perhaps a week or two into November, if they're very lucky."

"Yup, that's right. But I don't get what you're asking?"

"While the salmon run lasts, practically everyone in Steveston has a chance to make money, a chance that won't come their way again until next year's salmon run."

"That's right. So?"

"So who would risk disrupting that opportunity to make money by killing someone at one of the canneries?"

"Oh," Ingram's face went blank, but evidently his brain was working furiously, for he immediately nodded.

"No-one would," the constable said. "No-one thinking, anyway. They'd wait until they'd made all the money they could from the run first."

"You've got it, Scott said. "This attack is personal. Someone either was in a rage and attacked..."

"Or leaving that particular man alive for even one more day was too big a risk for someone," Granville finished for him.

Ingram was looking from one to the other and back. His eyes

were bright. "So then it's all about finding out who it was that was killed, right?"

It had always been about finding out who the dead man was. But unfortunately, there were no reports of a missing man. Nor was there talk of one. Not even whispers. Not anywhere they'd been.

But someone, somewhere, knew who he was.

All they had to do was find him.

ON THEIR WAY back from Steveston, Granville had the stage driver drop them two blocks from Garrity's Steak house. After the day they'd had, they both deserved a decent steak. And after spending all day breathing in the reek of the canneries, it needed to be somewhere that didn't serve fish.

Garrity's was hot from the ovens, and crowded, filled with conversation and low laughter. It should have felt confining in this heat, but Granville reveled in it. His back against the comfortably smoothed planks of the wooden booth, he looked around him at the cheerful crowd.

It was as far from a murder investigation as anything he could imagine.

And the food. The air was full of the rich, meaty smell of a perfectly charred steak. A waiter walked by holding two platters loaded with food. He could smell fried onions and crisp bacon.

His stomach growled, and Scott grinned at him. "Have some bread," he said as the waiter came up behind Granville.

The fellow put a small round loaf of sourdough, still hot from the oven, on the carving board in the middle of their table. Added a breadknife and a dish of bright yellow butter. Slid glasses of whiskey—double shots—in front of each of them.

"Now that's more like it," Scott said, reaching for the knife.

By the time the food arrived—huge plates brimming with perfectly grilled steak, fried onions and huge baked potatoes smothered in sour cream, butter and crisp strips of bacon, Granville was feeling mellow. He was still hungry, but no longer ravenous. The loaf of bread was gone, as was the whisky.

The server glanced at their empty glasses, and at Granville's nod, brought refills.

Granville tasted his, relishing the burn and the mellow flavor spreading over his tongue that followed. It might not be the best whiskey, but it served its purpose. He looked across at Scott, who was engrossed in demolishing his steak. His partner was a big man. He probably should've ordered two steaks to begin with.

"So what's your impression so far?" Granville asked.

Scott looked up, a big piece of steak impaled on his fork. "Of the case?"

Granville raised an eyebrow. "Of course."

His partner grinned at that. "Well, you could've been asking about the food."

Granville just waited.

Scott put his fork down. "It's an interesting place, Steveston. There's a lot under the surface. But it's a cannery town."

"Except for the farming."

"Yeah. But this one's all about the canneries. And we're outsiders. Trying to find a killer in a village where all the residents know each other—and could tend to band together.

Then there's the people here just for the fishing season—thousands of them. And none of them know each other. On top of that, we're dealing with three groups who won't be much interested in talkin' to us."

"The Japanese Fishermen's Association. The Chinese workers. And the Fishermen's Union," Granville said. "True. But Ingram is an insider, and more than willing to help us."

Scott rolled his eyes. "I'll say. He's trying so hard to help that he'll drown us in detail. We'll never get anywhere."

"Only if we do it his way. Which we won't." Granville paused, thinking over the day. "We do have a feel for the place now. And for Ingram. He's just green, needs some guidance. And he's excited about working with us. Which is good, because he knows the village, and they know him. They'll accept him where they won't accept us."

"Maybe." Scott picked up his fork, ate the piece of steak. "But I noticed you didn't show him the disk you found with the bones."

"It's too soon."

"Uh huh. Well, we're supposed to keep this investigation quiet, and I don't see us doing that and also finding out who died. And how. We'll need to ask questions."

"We will."

"Without antagonizing the cannery owners?"

"They trust us to use our discretion in how we solve this."

Scott snorted. "Right. Of course they do. Right up until the moment they don't like what we do."

"That's their problem. They hired us," Granville said.

"And they can fire us, too."

Just let them try it. "They could," Granville said. "But they've already paid us a very large retainer. Which is non-refundable."

"Uh huh." Scott drained his whiskey.

"And I'm beginning to doubt that the murder had anything to do with the cannery ownership."

"Because everyone here is so focused on the money?"

"Yes, that's part of it. But it feels personal, too."

"You mean the killer using the lye bath."

"Yes. He eliminated every trace of his enemy."

"Didn't do us any favors, either."

Granville laughed.

"Personal or not, we still need to get information from people who have no reason to trust us," Scott said.

"Maybe they'll trust Ingram."

"You really think so?"

Maybe not. "We'll find a way to solve this one, Scott. We always do."

"You feel the same way about Pinkerton's?" Scott asked.

Leaving Granville without an answer.

Just before the silence became uncomfortable Scott grinned, shook his head at him. "So where do we go from here?" he asked.

Scott knew him too well.

"We order another round," Granville said. "Clear that smell out of our heads. Then tomorrow we talk to the team."

7

FRIDAY, AUGUST 10, 1900

Emily Turner sat at the small desk she'd set up in the outer office of Granville and Scott Investigations, several sheafs of blueprints in front of her. Across from her, Laura Kent sat at the larger reception desk, her typewriter keys rattling in a lively rhythm. Other than the two of them, the office was empty. It wasn't even nine yet.

Despite the early hour, Emily's new seersucker suit was sticking to her back in the heat. And the overhead fan just blew in the dust and the smell of manure from the street below. She could hear the yells of the delivery men, and the clattering of the tram one street over.

August in the city. The *Daily World* said it was one of the hottest in a decade. And the weather showed no signs of breaking.

Glancing around to be sure none of the men were in yet, she pulled her long skirts away from her legs, hoping for some coolness. It didn't help. This was one of the downsides of working in an office that she hadn't anticipated.

Resignedly, she turned back to the stack of blueprints in front of her. She flipped one over, and the others threatened to cascade to the ground. Only a quick grab saved them.

Emily sighed. Her desk wasn't really big enough for looking at blueprints. Which was why she was doing this.

The firm needed more space. They'd grown out of what they had, and the layout of this office didn't allow for improvements. They either needed to move to a new office, or redesign this one.

And since the firm had just bought the building their office was in, they had options. She still couldn't quite believe that the deal had come together—or that Granville and Mr. Scott had taken the risk. At the end of the month, they would be landlords.

It was still several months before the house that Granville had also bought would close. It would be his home. And hers.

And she was alternately thrilled and terrified by the idea.

All of the excitement of convincing Granville that he could afford both investments, all the thrill of negotiating with the realtor—those had worn off. Now she was faced with the reality—an office building for which they would be responsible. A home where Granville wanted her to live. With him.

It was just cold feet, she told herself. They needed better office space. And the rents from the building would mean a steady cash flow. If nothing went wrong.

She did want to marry Granville, and soon. And she loved the house. Marrying him as soon as the house was ready and living in that house was a dream come true.

But she hadn't yet told her mother. And Mama was still busily planning an extravagant society wedding for them—to be held nearly two years from now. She'd told Granville that she'd tell her mother once the house was his. He'd grinned, but accepted it.

Emily dreaded the idea of a society wedding. And waiting two years for it. She wanted to marry Granville sooner. She did.

But first she had to tell her mother.

Annoyed with herself, Emily focused on the blueprints. Which were fascinating in their possibilities. The potential layouts for their new offices seemed endless, each better than the last.

Until she realized she'd already gone through the entire set and was looking at the first sheaf of drawings again. And those had become her new favorites.

She put the drawings down with a sigh, and looked over at her friend. Laura's fingers were flying over the keyboard, each key thunking onto the ribbon authoritatively, as she transcribed what looked like some of Mr. Scott's notes for the case file.

She'd recognize that looping scrawl anywhere.

"I don't know how you can read Mr. Scott's writing," Emily said. "Let alone type that fast."

Laura smiled without missing a keystroke. The keys flew faster. Finally, she looked up.

"Done," she said, resting her hands in her lap and looking up. "And you know you could type every bit as fast, if you wanted to."

She was just trying to be nice. "No, I can't," Emily said. "Really."

"You could," Laura said. "If you typed as often as you do other things."

Emily was about to protest when Laura held up a hand. "Like negotiating with realtors and choosing office plans," she finished with a wink.

Emily could feel herself flushing. Laura was right. Typing was a skill she was glad she'd learned. But she'd far rather do more interesting things—like investigating.

"Is Mr. Granville coming in today?" Laura asked.

"I think so," Emily said. "I know he intended to talk to all of us about the new case they've taken on. But I think it depends what happened in Steveston yesterday. Will Trent be in?"

Laura glanced at the clock on the wall. Emily's gaze followed. Both watched as the second hand swept past the twelve and the hour hand moved to the top with a soft clunk.

"Nine," Laura said. "He should have been here by now."

The sound of running footsteps in the hallway interrupted her, and then the hallway door burst open.

"I'm here, I'm here," Trent said, his words made jerky by his harsh breathing.

Trent was neatly dressed in a single-breasted navy suit with a plaid bow tie, but his reddish-brown hair stood half on-end, and he'd missed a streak of dirt by his eyebrow.

Laura had pursed her lips in the way that said she was trying not to laugh, and Trent was looking at the closed door to Granville and Scott's office with an aggrieved look on his face.

"I run all the way here, and they aren't even in yet?" he demanded. "How fair is that?"

"They might not even come in today," Emily said, just to watch his expression.

She wasn't disappointed.

Trent was biting his lip, and looked like he was going to explode. His face had gone red enough to hide his scattering of freckles, and he began to pace the floor.

He was copying Granville, Emily thought, stifling a most unprofessional inclination to giggle. Her fiancé also had a tendency to pace when he was annoyed. Trent was definitely picking up Granville's mannerisms. She wondered if either of them realized it.

"How is the Harvey case going?" Laura asked diplomatically.

It was the right thing to say.

Trent stopped pacing and turned to face her. "It's been very boring, but I think I'm finally getting somewhere," he said. "Last night, Mr. Harvey left the house after dinner, and didn't come back until after midnight."

"Where did he go?" Emily asked, riveted despite herself.

Trent flushed a little, and his gaze moved from Laura to her and back again. He cleared his throat uneasily. "Ummm... downtown. He went downtown."

Emily laughed, she couldn't help it. Trent's embarrassment, and his attempt to spare their feelings, was too funny. Even if he needed to learn to treat them as colleagues, she couldn't really fault him.

After all, most women of her acquaintance seemed to want to be coddled. It was really quite annoying.

"You mean he went to Dupont Street," she said, naming the most notorious red light district in town. "So he is cheating."

"Well, ummm, yes," Trent sputtered out. "At least, I think so. I tried to follow him, but they wouldn't let me in."

"So what did you do?" Laura asked.

Again, just the right words and tone to mollify Trent, Emily thought. Laura really was good at this.

And she was going to be a bigger asset to the office—and to the team Granville was building—than he had any idea of.

8

G ranville opened the door into the main office to be confronted by three sets of eyes, all staring at him.

Miss Kent and Emily were both seated behind their desks, while Trent stood in front of Miss Kent's desk, looking slightly embarrassed. Since he also looked like he'd been battling high winds—and there was no breeze this morning, to say nothing of the all-enveloping heat—there had to be a story there.

Granville wondered if he wanted to know what it was. Quickly decided he didn't. "Morning all," he said, and then to Scott, behind him. "It looks like they're expecting us."

Emily smiled at that. "We've been hoping you'd fill us in on the cannery case," she said. "Trent has been especially eager to hear about it."

Trent's ears turned red, and he glared at Emily, who looked demure. His fiancée had never been demure in her life. What was she up to?

Granville glanced at the pile of papers on her desk, recognizing some of them for blueprints. She'd been working on the building purchase again. No wonder she was teasing Trent.

As far as he was concerned, reviewing blueprints was the most boring task he could imagine. He couldn't seem to make the connection between how the space would look and the smudged blue lines on the blueprint. Though Emily seemed to enjoy it, for some odd reason. A fact for which he was truly thankful.

"Conference room?" he asked all of them with a grin.

Scott laughed as they all followed Granville into their cramped inner office. Emily sank into his office chair, Miss Kent into Scott's. He, Trent and Scott all pulled up chairs from along the wall.

"So?" Trent asked.

"So," Granville said. "We spent most of yesterday in Steveston, getting a feel for things there."

"The stagecoach journey is a treat," Scott put in. "Topped only by the smell of the canneries that hangs over the place."

Granville threw him a grin. "We have an unidentified corpse, or rather skeleton, and no suspects, in a small seaside village with an infamous reputation. The place takes over an hour to reach—on uneven roads, I might add—and stinks to high heaven. And it's full of groups of people who don't like each other."

"So far, the only thing we've found that might be helpful is this," and he drew the metal disk out of his pocket, placing it on the desk in front of them. "It was found with the bones of the victim."

Emily reached for the disk, weighing it in her hand. "It's something like the Chinese coin which turned out to be a Buddhist token, isn't it? Right down to the square hole in the center. Though that one was stone, and this one is metal. And this one doesn't feel nearly so old."

She turned it over, looking at it carefully, then passed it to Trent. "The markings are a little different, too, I think, but they have a similar feel."

"The owner of the Gulf of Georgia Cannery thought the symbols could be Chinese or Japanese. Which suggests our victim could have been either."

"If this disk is also Buddhist, perhaps it might be symbolic, and carried for luck," Emily said.

"It would be helpful to know what the symbols mean," Miss

Kent said, as she placed the disk back on the desk. "Someone must know."

"We'll need to look into that," Granville said. "Especially since at the moment this is our only clue to the identity of the victim."

"The Japanese Fishermen's Association is in Steveston," Scott said. "Maybe we could get someone there to talk to us about the disk. Without letting on about the victim, though."

"Might be a place to start." Granville glanced around the circle of faces. "Any other questions?"

"Just one," Emily said. "Can I come to Steveston with you tomorrow?"

"Me too," Trent said.

Scott chuckled. "The more the merrier," he said. "And the sooner we solve this one and get out of there, the better."

"There, you see," Emily said. "We can help."

Only if he could keep her away from the Cannery Row, Granville thought. Then realized his reaction had more to do with the strict society rules he'd grown up with than it did with who Emily was. And it was decidedly unfair to her, since she'd already braved the dark side of Vancouver's Chinatown to save his skin. She'd handle Steveston's version with aplomb.

He'd just have to make sure he was with her—for his own peace of mind.

"Did you miss the part about the infamous reputation?" he said to Scott with a grin. "And we're supposed to be inconspicuous. Remember? The cannery owners don't want word of this murder getting out until we've solved it."

Scott rolled his eyes.

"But didn't you spend yesterday there with the police?" Emily asked. "Or are they not willing to work with you?"

"That's not the problem," Scott muttered.

Granville winked at him. "Yes, we spent the day with Constable Ingram, who showed us around."

"And you don't think people will wonder what you're doing

there again?" Trent said. "Sorry," he muttered when Granville gave him a level look.

"What have you told everyone about why you were there?" Emily asked.

Scott looked at Granville expectantly, as did the rest of the team.

When Granville remained silent, Scott let out a crack of laughter. "He told them we were looking to invest in the village," Scott said. "Maybe even buy land there. Or a cannery."

"There, you see," Emily said. "I'm the person you need with you if you're buying land."

"I'm not buying land," Granville said, but he knew it was too late.

"And if you're investing in the canning industry, Scott and I can be your advance team," Trent said. "We can go in, ask questions, talk to people."

It was his own fault for coming up with the excuse, Granville thought. And they were making sense. The two of them—and especially Emily—would provide him and Scott with believable cover stories.

"I thought you had blueprints to look at?" he said to Emily, making one last effort to delay the inevitable. His desire to protect her from the dangerous side of the fishing village might not be rational, but it was real. "We do need bigger premises, after all."

She gave him a look. "I've looked at them. And you both,"—and her searing look included Scott—"need to look at the blueprints again, to see if they meet your requirements. Then the architects can sign off on them and the builders can get started. And I'll be free to join you in Steveston."

"To look at more real estate," Scott said with a broad grin.

"Or to solve a murder," Granville said, trying not to laugh at how neatly he'd been set up. "But you'll need to stay close to Scott or me while you're there."

Emily just smiled at him, and didn't say a word.

GRANVILLE HAD ARRANGED to meet Ross-Murray at his office. Which turned out to be a large corner office—very well appointed —looking out over Hastings Street and the ocean and mountains beyond. Yet for all its luxurious spaciousness, Granville found it oppressive.

Ross-Murray stood from behind his massive mahogany desk, and strode across the room to shake Granville's hand. "Good to see you, Granville, he said. "I hope you have news?"

"Yes, of a sort," Granville said. "The bones have been sent to the coroner in New Westminster for examination. And I've begun the investigation in Steveston. It's too soon to know much, but I wanted to update you now. I suspect our victim will turn out to have been either Chinese or Japanese."

"Japanese? That would not be good news." Ross-Murray frowned. "And why do you think that?"

Granville placed the token on the desk in front of him. "This was found with the bones."

"A coin?" Ross-Murray picked it up and turned it over in his hand.

"No. We believe it to be a Buddhist token, of either Chinese or Japanese origin, judging by the symbols. You'll notice the wear marks around the edges. Our first victim appears to have carried it with him."

Ross-Murray examined the token closely, turning it over in his fingers, and feeling the carvings. He was still frowning. "You'll need to determine its origin as quickly as possible then."

Granville nodded.

"Just keep in mind that we cannot afford to have another strike. You need to solve this, no matter what you have to do," Ross-Murray said, his gaze fierce.

For the first time, Granville wondered what would happen to his firm's reputation if this case turned into a nightmare. At the very least, it could impact their proposed deal with Pinkerton's, since several of the cannery owners were their clients. And at worst, it could irreparably damage their very new business.

Had he made the wrong choice in taking this case? And should they be backing out now?

No. Not while the victim remained nameless, and a killer went free.

"We intend to solve it," Granville said firmly, meeting that look.

Ross-Murray's frown smoothed out, and he smiled. "Good. I know a fellow who makes something of a hobby of collecting exotic coins and such," he said. "He's particularly interested in those of Oriental design. He might be able to help you with this. Shall I set up a meeting?"

"Yes, that would be most helpful. Thank you."

"Hold on." Ross-Murray picked up the telephone handset, gave the number, and waited for the operator to connect him. A brief conversation ensued, the upshot of which was that Granville had a meeting with one William Wardle, in his office, in an hour.

Granville thanked Ross-Murray for the information, and took his leave. As he strode along Hastings Street, his mind was made up. They would solve this thing. What the Salmon Packers' Association did from there was their problem.

WILLIAM WARDLE WAS A BANK MANAGER—WHICH perhaps explained his interest in old coins—and his office was the opposite of Ross-Murray's. It was on the first floor, with walls of solid, thick cut granite. Behind half-drawn blinds, his windows opened onto the wagons, carriages, businessmen and shoppers rushing along Pender Street.

Where Ross-Murray looked out on the railroads and the ships they served, the banker's view was one guaranteed to remind the fellow why he was here and whom he served.

Granville needed to make sure that his firm's planned renovations included that kind of focus. Many of their clients appreciated the fact that their current offices were at the end of a hall, giving them the option of discreetly taking the stairs, rather than the more obvious elevator to the crowded lobby. Though he suspected that Emily had already thought of the issue, and worked out a solution.

Wardle stood up with a smile and an outstretched hand. "Pleasure to meet you, Mr. Granville. Please have a seat. Ross-Murray says you have something of a puzzle for me?"

"Yes, I think I do," Granville said, drawing the disk from his pocket. "And I do appreciate your meeting with me on such short notice."

The bank manager waved it off. "You're doing me a favor—allowing me to indulge in my particular hobby-horse, and do a favor for one of our biggest clients at the same time."

Granville smiled at his honesty. "This coin, or perhaps token, was found in Steveston in the course of an investigation," he said, placing it on the heavy oak desk in front of the other man. "We're trying to learn what we can about it."

"Interesting indeed," Wardle said, peering at the coin. "May I?"

At Granville's nod he picked it up, running careful fingers over it, then turning it so that the carvings caught the light.

"This seems to be made of iron. Originally polished, I believe, and quite worn on the edges." All of Wardle's attention was fixed on the disk. "Not new, but not ancient either," he said as if to himself, turning the disk this way and that. His face was thoughtful, his eyes intent on the symbols.

After a moment he looked up. "Could it be Chinese? Or Japanese?"

"Yes."

Wardle nodded, and returned to his examination. "I think it might be Japanese," he said at last. "A token, not a coin. And most likely Buddhist. Either a religious piece, or a symbol for luck, or wealth. I can't tell you more without comparing it to some of my other things. Can you leave it with me?"

"I'm afraid not," Granville said. "I'll need it tomorrow. But I'll see if I can have a copy made that you could examine and then keep, if that would be satisfactory?"

"That would most satisfactory," Wardle said, beaming. "Just let me know when you'd like me to look at it."

"I will. And thank you again for your time."

"As I said, I'm happy to do it," Wardle said. "And if, as your firm becomes more successful, you are considering changing bankers I'd be happy to discuss the services we could offer you."

Granville had to smile. Wardle was a shrewd businessman, despite the genial, rather scattered impression he first created. "I'll keep that in mind," he said.

WHEN HE GOT BACK to his office, Granville immediately grabbed his partner's attention. They needed to discuss Ross-Murray's concerns about their handling of the case.

"It may be nothing," he said to Scott, who was going through papers on his side of the partner's desk they shared. "Still, you need to be aware that this could backfire on us. Badly."

Scott pushed his unsteady pile of documents to one side, gave Granville his full attention. "If we don't solve it, you mean?"

"No. If we do solve it, and our findings don't suit our employers. Or if they find them politically embarrassing, for whatever reason. Continuing to work on this case could be business suicide. We haven't been in business long enough to recover from a situation like that."

Scott just grinned. "This firm was your idea," he said. "It blows up, you'll just start something else. It's fine."

Granville shook his head. "You'd just start over?"

"Sure. Why not? Besides, you'll probably fix this one anyway. You always do."

Granville had to laugh. When it came to bullets flying, Scott had his back. In business, apparently, he was on his own.

Except for Emily. Who had an impressive head for business on her fine-boned shoulders. Perhaps there would an opportunity tomorrow to see what she thought about the situation with Ross-Murray.

He had a few questions for her, anyway. He took possession of their house at the end of next month. And she still hadn't agreed to move up the wedding date. He couldn't blame her. He wouldn't want to break that news to her mother either.

As long as that's all that was holding her back.

9

SATURDAY, AUGUST 11, 1900

Emily stepped down from the coach and looked around her. It had been a long and jarring journey by stagecoach. Granville hadn't been exaggerating the state of the roadways, and it felt good to be standing on solid ground. The first thing she noticed was the rank smell of spoiled fish mixed with the odor of cooking fish. Wrinkling her nose, she turned to Granville, who'd just stepped off the stage.

"I see what you mean by the smell," she said. It was like really strong blue cheese, searing the back of her sinuses.

She half-turned to look across the street, where she could see a number of sprawling buildings. Beyond them were hints of the wide river, and a very green bank beyond it. The air was still, and heavy. Above her, the sky was a rich blue, and it felt endless.

"Those are the canneries?" she asked, pointing to a series of long, low buildings that stretched along the river.

"Yes," Granville replied. "And to your right is Steveston's red light district. It isn't safe for you to walk there."

Emily looked down the street in fascination. The shopfronts didn't tell her much, but she could see several bar signs, and one for the Fishermen's Saloon. Mixed in were several very normal looking houses, painted in pastel colors that seemed incongruous in this setting. Hints of crimson detailing against fading white trim just made it worse.

She looked over her shoulder at Granville, pointed. "Those houses? Are they...?"

"That is exactly what they are," he said with a grin. "And we aren't going to discuss it. If you look across the street, however, you'll see that the Brunswick Cannery is to your far left, then the Lulu Island, the Steveston, and the Star Canneries. And off to your far right is the Gulf of Georgia Cannery."

Emily was still staring at those pastel houses. So that was what a brothel looked like. How very ordinary. And how horrified her mother would be if she knew.

Then, with a smile, she followed Granville's pointing hand, allowing herself to be distracted. She'd learned what she wanted to know, anyway. And she knew Granville would tell her more later, if she asked him.

Despite the rigid rules he'd been brought up to follow, Granville had never tried to hold her back. She thought it was his adventurous spirit showing through. And she was very grateful for it.

Turning her attention to the canneries, Emily memorized the names as he said them. Brunswick. Lulu Island. Steveston. Star. Gulf of Georgia.

"And all these buildings behind the canneries?" She lowered her voice. "The ones that look about to fall down?"

"Most of those are the bunkhouses for the workers, and built only for one season. They aren't expected to last beyond this year."

He put gentle hands on her shoulders, turning her slightly, so she faced the cannery he'd named Lulu Island Cannery. Emily liked the way his hands felt.

"See the longhouse there?"

Emily smiled. "It's just like the one at Kispiox. Are these Kispiox Indians, living here?"

"They might be," he said. "I learned yesterday that the canneries are hard pressed to find experienced workers since the canneries have expanded, and the Japanese, who once provided the skilled labor the canneries needed, now mostly work as fishermen. So Indian workers—from all over the province—and Chinese workers have filled that gap. A few of the Japanese fishermen have wives who work in the canneries, but most of their wives are still in Japan."

"You mean they left their families behind?" Emily asked. "But why?"

"Yes. They came here to earn the money to send home to their families. They plan to return home eventually."

"And home is in Japan?"

"Yes. Many of them came from the same province in Japan. They heard the fishing was good here—and there was no work for them at home."

"That's sad," Emily said. "That they have to leave their families for so long, just to support them. And to come all this way. They must not see them for months on end."

"It is more like years on end," Granville said. "The same is true for most of the Chinese workers."

"Yes, so Bertie has told me," Emily said. Granville had met her parents' Chinese houseboy a number of times, and Bertie had been helpful in several investigations. "Apparently there was a dreadful famine in his province, and there was no work and no money. They had no choice."

"So they came to Gold Mountain," Granville said, referring to the way the Chinese described North America. "Much as I left England to seek gold in the Klondike."

He winked at her. "It's a fool's game, chasing gold in other countries."

"But you're successful now," Emily said. "You have your firm."

"And a lovely fiancée," he said with a sideways look. "Even if she does argue with me."

Emily made a face at him. "I do not," she said, then bit her lip as she realized she'd just proved his point.

He grinned at her, then turned back to the canneries. "Constable Ingram told Scott and me that as many as one hundred and fifty Japanese fishermen bunk in that building," he said, pointing out a fairly small building. "And another one hundred and forty or so Chinese men in that one," and he pointed out a building which was even smaller than the first.

Emily frowned. "I can't imagine how uncomfortable that must be," she said.

"True. But they have work, and a roof over their heads, and food. And they will receive pay for their labor at the end of the contract."

He smiled at her. "It isn't an easy life, and it's certainly not what any of us would hope for. But it's better than the work I did in the Klondike."

"Which was just as hard, but in the end, for no pay," Emily said thoughtfully. "Was it worth it?"

"Lord, yes," Granville said. "It gave me a taste of independence and freedom that I'd never have found in England."

She rather doubted that, but chose not to tell him so. Granville would have been successful whatever he chose to do. He was handsome, charming, and very determined. He was also a natural leader.

Even if he didn't know it.

"But I think it was the harshness and beauty of the place," Granville was saying. "I wish you could see it. The land there—it gives no quarter. But it can take your breath with its beauty. And you have to struggle so hard just to survive—you come out with a new view of what's important, and a new appreciation for what you're capable of surviving."

Emily listened quietly. She'd never heard him so eloquent about his years in the Klondike. "Maybe one day we'll go there together," she said.

He looked swiftly over at her. "You really mean that?"

She nodded. "Yes. I'd love to see it. And in winter."

She grinned at him. "Though you might want to consider the hazards—no one else would even consider taking me there. And my mother would never forgive you."

He made a face and she laughed.

"Now show me the rest of the village," she said.

EMILY TUCKED her hand into Granville's arm as they turned away from the river and sauntered along what he told her was Second Avenue. This was a collection of modest buildings housing a variety of stores, and surprisingly, Steveston's Opera House. She wondered who performed there, and if they had ever had anyone famous. Glancing around her, it seemed unlikely.

Most of the buildings—including the Opera House—were plainly built one story buildings, some with flat roofs, some with peaked roofs. Several of the shops had false fronts, giving them a more imposing look. In the middle of the block was an unusual two story building which housed a number of shops on two levels, with the second level accessed by stairs up to a wrap-around balcony.

All of the buildings they passed had board siding, painted in deep colors—which seemed to her an odd contrast to the pastels of the brothels along the river—though bleached and weathered on the west side by the sea air.

They crossed Chatham Street—another main road—and he pointed out the police station, white-painted, with a wide front porch. Emily noted the heavy iron shutters that could be closed over the windows, and wondered how much trouble they saw here. She'd have to ask Granville later, when they were out of general earshot.

Looking farther down the street, she started to see one and two story homes clustered amongst very green acreage.

"These are mostly vegetable farms," Granville said. "They sell in Richmond, or ship their produce to New Westminster or Vancouver."

"And what are you supposed to be buying," she asked him. "A farm?"

"No," he said, drawing out the word.

"Not a cannery?"

"Wrong again. Though I have indicated interest in investing in one." Now he was grinning.

Emily thought about what they'd walked past. "The building on Second. The one with multiple stores."

He glanced at her. "Yes, that was one of the options. How did you know?"

"I'm starting to learn how you think," she said, keeping her face as neutral as she could manage.

"Oh, are you?" He placed her hand on his arm. "Then you can explain my real estate requirements to the local real estate agent."

"You aren't serious?" Emily said. He couldn't be planning on buying another building. They hadn't even closed on the first one yet.

Although their mortgage lender had mentioned that with the cash flow their new building would bring in, they would be happy to provide an additional loan. If her fiancé would be interested, of course.

Surely Granville wasn't serious?

"Just how do you expect to solve a murder by talking to a real estate agent?" she asked.

His grin widened.

10

Steveston Real Estate was easy to find. A small, white painted
building on First Avenue with a very large sign, it housed one
small man sitting behind a massive desk. The fellow—Randolf
Mayer, he said, standing to greet them—was at least four inches
shorter than Emily, making him five foot two or so. From his own
six-foot one, Granville felt as if he towered over him.

Mayer didn't seem bothered. He smiled broadly at both of them,
though there was a little extra warmth in his smile for Emily.

Granville didn't blame him. His fiancée was looking particularly
fine this morning in a light blue suit of fine cotton, with a fitted
bodice and a flaring skirt that just reached her ankles. With it she
wore a daring white straw hat—complete with an ornament of
bunched ribbon in the same light blue—perched forward over
one eye.

He'd noticed since their return from the Omenica that the suits
Emily wore for business—while still very professional—had
acquired an additional flare. He suspected Emily's friend Clara
Miles had taken her in hand, and helped her shop for the outfits.
Clara was notorious for her love of shopping, and she had an
impeccable eye.

He could only appreciate the result.

"And what can I do for you today," Mayer was asking. "Are you interested in property here in Steveston?"

"We might be," Granville said. "I do have an interest in the canning industry. However, at the moment I'm most interested in commercial properties. I will need to know more about the economy here, and especially the opportunities and challenges it offers."

Mayer's eyes brightened. "Please, have a seat," he said, waving them towards two chairs comfortably upholstered in a William Morris tapestry. "I'd be very pleased to tell you about our little village."

And for the next half-hour he did so, filling their ears with facts and figures, projections and his own observations. By the end of it, Granville had a clear picture of a resource based economy with a solid base and a great deal of room to expand.

The town of Steveston was built on fishing and farming. Its growth was held back by the lack of ready access to markets.

"If they build the railroad expansion that they've been talking about," Mayer said. "Then there will be no stopping this town. Being able to ship fresh produce from local farms and the entire output of the canneries directly to Vancouver would provide a huge impetus to our economy."

Emily had been listening attentively. "And that would drive the growth of shops to provide services to the farmers and the fishermen and the cannery workers, would it not?"

Mayer nodded. "It would indeed."

"Making commercial—especially retail—properties more valuable than they are today."

"Indeed, you have it exactly right. Several times more valuable, or I miss my guess."

Granville watched as Emily proceeded to dazzle their real estate agent with intelligent questions that showed her understanding of everything he'd been saying. They discussed the stability of retail properties, the current value of such enterprises, and the potential worth. She apparently impressed the fellow even further by seeking his opinion of which properties were currently the best deal, and which, in his opinion, would be the better deal when the railroad went through.

They concluded by choosing several properties that Mayer would undertake to show them that afternoon. One of which, he was amused to note, was the two-story building on Second which she'd already spotted.

That business finished, the two of them looked startled, as if suddenly aware of his presence. They'd been so caught up in their discussion that they'd forgotten him.

Emily flushed a little, and reached out a hand. Then withdrew it, as if she wasn't sure her gesture would be accepted. She really hadn't been valued in her family—her originality and intelligence seen as a handicap, rather than the gift it was.

Granville put his own hand lightly over hers, smiled at both of them.

Mayer looked a little shaken—probably he didn't often ignore a client—but relieved too. "You are in agreement with the properties your lady is interested in?" he asked.

"Very much so," Granville said. "I'm looking forward to seeing them as soon as possible. Perhaps tomorrow, if that is convenient? Though I do have several questions."

Mayer cleared his throat. "Yes?"

"The strike last month. If that had continued on for the duration of the sockeye run, what impact would that have had on retail operations?"

Mayer paled a little, but answered readily enough. "It would create a depression here. The canneries are important to the local economy. A good portion of our income for the year, in all businesses, flows from the canneries in one way or another. A year without the canneries running? It would cripple us."

The same would be true of the province as a whole, Granville thought. Based on what Ross-Murray had said about the canneries being the second largest employer in the province. He wondered what exactly the fellow expected him to accomplish with this investigation.

What if the skeleton proved to be that of a Japanese worker? Would the Salmon Packers' Association expect him to hide that fact?

Because he wouldn't do it.

"And are the retailers able to make up now for the sales they lost?" he asked.

"When money flows into the canneries, it flows into the village," Mayer said.

That made sense. "The cannery operations are cyclical, I understand," Granville said. "With one year in four being far more profitable because the salmon run is so much bigger."

The agent nodded. "Yes, that's true. Next year will be such a year, with the numbers of salmon returning to the Fraser River to spawn expected to be the biggest ever."

"How does that affect retail revenues? And what impact, if any, does it have on retail rents?"

"An excellent question, sir, if I may say so." Mayer looked at the sheaf of papers he'd brought out in the course of his explanations. He chose one page, handed it to Granville.

"As you can see here, retail revenues remain fairly constant, since the canneries' major expenditures are for tin cans and fish, and those are purchased directly from their suppliers. Only the purchase of fishing supplies for the cannery boats and food for their workers impacts our retail establishments directly," the real estate agent said.

He leaned forward a little, tapped a column on the page Granville held. "The canneries run every summer, and their requirements don't change that much in a boom year. They may hire more migrant workers for the cannery lines, but most canneries already run at capacity in non-boom years. Food costs don't increase much in a boom year. And a few more or less migrant workers don't impact us much - they spend very little money in the village. Very little indeed."

Probably because they had so little, Granville thought, looking at the column Mayer had indicated.

"Interesting," Granville said. "And this lack of impact the cannery workers have on the retail business. Does it extend to other businesses in the village?"

Mayer looked surprised at the question, but he answered readily enough. "For the most part, yes. With the exception of the establishments along the water that welcome the fishermen, of course. As you can imagine, a great deal of cash flows through those establishments."

He sent an apologetic look towards Emily. "But the cannery workers themselves? The Japanese—those who do not live here permanently, I mean—the Chinese, the Indian workers? We see very little of them. They may occasionally venture as far as Moncton street, but they work, eat and sleep on the cannery grounds. They have neither the time nor the inclination to come into the village."

All of fourteen blocks of it, Granville thought cynically. He couldn't imagine such a life.

Yes, he'd worked hard in the Klondike, gone hungry, been so cold he couldn't explain it, but the land itself was limitless. He walked miles every day. Nothing and no-one—beyond his own ambitions—had confined him.

Unlike most of the cannery workers. Who worked long, long hours in a punishingly noisy and unpleasant atmosphere, alternately roasting and freezing. Standing for long days. Falling into bed exhausted, only to get up and do it again.

Whose world was limited to the cannery and a crowded bunkhouse.

What kind of tensions did such a small life build up? And what happened when those tensions exploded?

Granville glanced at the numbers on the sheet Mayer had given him again. It did look as if retail revenues had been up every year for the last five. He was right, it was a good investment. For him. And for the canneries.

Just not for the cannery workers.

***

GRANVILLE WAS STILL THINKING about the working conditions in the canneries and the causes of murder when they left the real estate agent's office. With Emily lightly holding his arm, he stepped down to the street. And Constable Ingram walked up to them.

"Granville! It's a pleasure to see you again. And Miss...?"

Granville was forced to introduce Emily.

The young constable beamed at them both, and congratulated Granville on his engagement. Told him he was a lucky man, with a quaint little bow to Emily.

Ingram was exactly the same age as Emily, Granville realized. But she seemed far more mature. She had been growing up fast recently, he realized. Their trip north, and the way Emily had involved herself in his most recent case, not to mention the real estate negotiations she was handling—they'd changed her.

Her determination to keep learning, her sense of humor—they were still there. But she seemed more mature, somehow. More committed.

Her focus had shifted away from breaking out of the box her very traditional parents had tried to fit her into. Now her exuberant energy and enthusiasm were bent on helping him build their firm into one of the best in the city. It was an irony he could only appreciate.

Constable Ingram's formulaic words struck home in a way previous such words had not. He was a lucky man. A very lucky man.

Emily seemed to sense his regard, and looked up to give him a quick smile.

"I didn't know you were coming today," Constable Ingram was saying. "You didn't get in touch."

"No. We're waiting for the report from the coroner in New Westminster. Also, I wanted to make a few additional enquiries before taking up more of your time," Granville said diplomatically. "Do you wish to be present when the coroner makes his report?"

"Definitely," Ingram replied. "And I appreciate being included."

"Very well," Granville said. "I'll call the station to arrange it?"

"Yes, they'll know where I am," Ingram said. "And I'll be most happy to fit in with your schedule."

"You'll be hearing from me," Granville said. A thought struck him. "Would it also be possible to arrange to go talk to someone on one of the fishing boats?"

Ingram looked delighted. "Very possible indeed. I'm sure one of my uncles would be happy to answer any questions you might have."

"I'd appreciate it," Granville said.

"I'll arrange it, and leave word at the station," Ingram was saying. "Nice meeting you, Miss Turner."

And with a nod to Emily, he was off.

Granville watched him go, then turned back to Emily.

Who was laughing. "I see what you mean about Constable Ingram," she said. "He is very—enthusiastic, is he not?"

"He is indeed," Granville said, with an answering smile. "But he has the instincts of a good investigator, underneath it all. Now, shall we stroll by these properties Mayer suggested?"

"Of course," Emily said with a smile.

They looked at four properties before lunch. But it was the vision of the narrow life the cannery workers led that Granville carried away with him at the end of it. Was that where the roots of the lye bath murder lay?

11

That afternoon, Granville and Emily were back at Mayer's office, and ready to view the commercial buildings that they'd chosen as possible purchases. It made great cover for asking questions.

Mayer's office was even hotter than that morning, though all the doors and windows stood open to catch any hint of breeze blowing off the river. Unfortunately, it also brought in every bit of the reek from the canneries. The smell settled on Granville's skin, thick and dense, worse even than that morning.

Was it his imagination? Or was it some change in the canning process, or maybe the nature of the fish they'd caught?

Emily didn't seem to notice. She was engrossed in questioning the agent about every detail of the buildings they'd be seeing that day, asking several critical questions that Granville was glad she'd thought of. Because he hadn't. And they were important.

Or at least they would be important, if he was actually going to purchase property here. Which was unlikely. And they had a case to solve.

As soon as there was a break in the conversation, Granville gave

Mayer a nod, and the three of them set out on the tour Mayer had arranged.

The first building they saw was on Second Street, close to Chatham. Like many of the stores here, this one was wood sided, and shingled. Unlike the others, it was two stories tall, with a restaurant and a general store on the main floor, and a marine supply store and a dry good store on the second floor, accessible by a wide set of stairs from the front.

At their real estate agent's urging, Granville took the fellow's key and opened the door at the back, which was accessible from the alley. The back door opened onto a wide hallway.

"This is the back entrance to the shops," Mayer told them. "You'll notice there are two doors going into the restaurant. It's structured such that you could have a second shop in that space, if you ever needed to. Any builder could put up a wall for you in a jiffy, and it would increase your revenue."

"But doesn't the restaurant draw customers to the other stores?" Emily asked.

"Yes, it does," Mayer said, giving her a surprised look. "Which makes it worth the slight decrease in rents."

Granville was less interested in the revenue this building would generate, and more interested in talking to the various shop-owners. Especially in the general store on the main floor, and the marine supply store on the second floor. Those shop owners were the most likely to have heard any gossip that might be out there.

Scott wasn't the only one counting on gossip to help them catch a murderer.

Emily, however, was currently quizzing Mayer for details on income, and cash flow. The agent seemed to have the details at his fingertips, which was useful. And he seemed even more impressed with Emily than he'd been the previous day.

Granville knew Emily was interested in the real estate business, but he was beginning to suspect that she had a real genius for it. He still wasn't convinced that there was any logic in buying property in Steveston, though. If he was going to buy another investment property—and it was a big if— downtown Vancouver would seem a better choice. It was growing so fast, and expanding in so many directions, from the West End near downtown to the exclusive Shaughnessy on the south shore.

Even an apartment building in the East End, with rentals to workers from the mill or the docks, might be a better investment than this.

Mayer opened the door at the back of the general store and ushered them in. It was a long, narrow store, crowded with shelves from floor to ceiling, every shelf stuffed with bins overflowing with goods. Mayer introduced them to the owner, Ed Padgett, a genial man, as long and lean as any fisherman.

"Nice to meet you," Granville said. Then, on impulse, "You ever fish?"

Padgett smiled, wrung his hand. "Now, how'd you know? Yeah, I did some in my younger days. When the children came along, I came ashore. It's too dangerous a life for a family man."

He beamed at them. "And there are six of 'em, now," he added.

"Do you keep in touch with the industry?" Granville asked him.

"Sure. I have a brother, two cousins and a nephew—all fish-ermen now," Padgett said.

"This strike must have been hard on them?"

'It was hard on everyone. Especially not knowing when it would end. Then when they called in the armed regiment?" He shook his head. "Terrible thing, that. Terrible."

"It led to bad feelings?" Granville asked.

"Didn't mend matters, I'll tell you honestly. But people are too worried about getting the catch in and paid for to fuss about anything else."

"So no-one trying to get even, then?"

"Not that I've heard. Fisherfolk are pretty pragmatic. They have to be, living at the mercy of the sea and the weather. Once some-thing's done, it's done."

"What about those people working at the canneries?" Emily asked. "Are they also pragmatic?"

Padgett looked over at her. "It doesn't really apply. What those poor souls are is exhausted. Canneries have been running fifteen, sixteen hours a day, trying to keep up with the catch. And there'll be no throwing fish back this season, not after they missed all of July."

He shook his head. "Everyone needs to make the money to see them through the winter. And I mean everyone, from the owners to the fisherfolk, and on down."

He grimaced. "But those cannery workers? Standing on their feet the whole time, fish coming at them fast as you can breathe? I tell you, I don't envy them. Most don't, round here."

"Are people sympathetic?"

"Not the fellas who couldn't get jobs in the canneries. But they aren't trained, not like the Chinese and Indian workers are. And the cannery owners only hire trained workers. They've no time to waste on folk who don't know what they're doing anyway, but especially not this year."

This man was a gold mine of information. "Did you lose money here during the strike?" Granville asked.

"Not really. Folks still had to eat. And most of our business is from the restaurants and the farmers hereabouts. Not much from the canneries, strike or no."

Granville heard much the same story in the marine supply store.

If this was representative of the mood in the village, then it seemed unlikely that their murder case had anything to do with the strike. Ross-Murray and his fellow owners had little to worry about there.

But what was the connection to the cannery? Why had the body been left inside the cannery itself, rather than thrown out to sea, as Scott had suggested?

Did it mean the victim had worked there? That the killer worked there?

A man was still dead. And he wanted to know why.

1 2

Granville was still turning that question over in his mind when he walked into Mary's Diner. In company with Emily, Scott and Trent, he'd caught a late afternoon stage back to Vancouver, then walked the three blocks to Mary's, stopping at the office to collect Miss Kent along the way. They'd agreed that morning to meet here for dinner and compare notes.

Mary's was as crowded and noisy as ever. What it wasn't, despite the temperature outside, was broiling hot.

Granville eyed the lazily-turning big fans overhead. They seemed to do a better job than any in his office. And without all that racket, too. Perhaps their new premises could use something similar. He'd have to mention it to Emily, see what she thought.

Then he noticed that his fiancée's gaze had followed his. He caught her eye, and she smiled at him and nodded.

Apparently she was now a mind-reader.

The server came by to take their order, then Mary herself came over with a pot of coffee, which was unusual. In deference to the heat, her greying hair was twisted into a knot on top of her head, and the cheerful apron she wore was a light-weight cotton. She nodded to all of them, then winked at him, and filled his cup without asking.

Given the way Mary's dark eyes kept landing on Miss Kent, she was curious about the addition to their usual table. With a smile, Granville introduced them. "You'll be seeing Miss Kent again," he told her.

"Good," she said with a brisk nod. And left them to their discussion.

"Were there any urgent messages?" Granville asked Miss Kent.

She was sitting with her hands tucked demurely in front of her, everything about her attire neatly business-like. But her eyes were busily assessing and cataloguing her surroundings.

She'd probably never been in a diner before. He wondered what she made of it.

Miss Kent smiled at him. "Yes, one. The coroner's office in New Westminster called to confirm that he has begun the analysis of the bones from the cannery. You and Constable Ingram are to meet with him on Monday at ten."

"Good. And thank you," Granville said, well pleased.

They had so little to go on in this case. Perhaps the coroner would be able to provide some answers. Unfortunately, Ingram would also be there. He wasn't looking forward to another day of the young constable's exuberance.

"May I join you two?" Emily asked.

He should have seen that coming, and spoken to her separately ahead of time. He hated to turn Emily down, and especially hated that it had to be in front of everyone. But there was little choice. Dodging her request would be worse.

"I'm afraid that isn't possible," he said. "The coroner would be horrified by your presence. Vancouver and New Westminster are still very traditional cities, and the idea of a woman seeing an autopsy—even one where only bones were left—would be too much. I'm sorry."

Emily sighed and nodded.

It was hard to see her disappointment. But with Emily's new, more formal role in the firm's investigations? Accepting that was going to be difficult enough for the society she had to live in—and they'd pass that discomfort on to her. Adding the notion of a young lady witnessing the brutal reality an autopsy—and that included examining human remains in any form, even if they were just bones—would be too much.

Perhaps in a year or so things would be different—there were new ideas coming west all the time. Even the stodgily Victorian types who largely ran things here would eventually have to adapt.

"But when we next go to Steveston, I'll bring my camera," Emily said, setting her chin stubbornly. "That at least I can do."

"Good idea," he said. "Your photographs always capture elements that prove useful in the course of an investigation."

And her photography, at least, wouldn't raise any eyebrows. It was seen as a perfectly acceptable hobby for young ladies. Unless she somehow found a body to photograph. That would raise a few eyebrows, he thought with an inward amusement.

Trent broke the tension for all of them. "You'll never guess what Scott and I did," he said.

"Probably not," Granville said dryly. "Suppose you just tell us."

Trent quaffed down a good portion of his ginger ale, started to wipe his mouth on his sleeve, and glanced at Emily and Miss Kent. Changed his mind. "It's thirsty work!" he said.

Emily laughed, and Trent beamed at her.

"Well?" Granville asked him and Scott. "How did you make out?"

"Scott and I got jobs," Trent said with a wide grin.

Granville glanced at Scott, who nodded. "Where?" he asked.

"At the cannery. The Gulf of Georgia," Scott said. "I got thinking about it, and it makes sense to have us there. A man was killed, his body dumped there. Someone at that cannery has to know him, or know something about his death. Working there, we might have a chance to find out who."

Granville nodded. His partner was right. It did make sense. "The only problem might be getting them to talk to you," he said.

"I'm countin' on the rumors," Scott said with a flashing grin.

"But however did you manage to get jobs there so quickly?" Miss Kent asked.

"The salmon run is bigger than they thought, so they're short-handed," Trent said, and drank more of his soda.

Scott frowned at him, then smiled at Miss Kent. "We ran into the cannery manager in the village," he said. "Constable Ingram introduced us yesterday, so he knew me."

Then, to Granville, he said, "And you must have impressed him when you met with him on Wednesday, because as soon as I suggested it would be useful if I had a job there, he agreed."

He paused while huge platters were put in front of each of them. Emily and Trent had roast chicken, Miss Kent had the salmon, and Scott and Granville had steaks. None of them commented on Miss Kent's choice of meal, though Granville saw Emily turn hastily away.

Something about the smell of the cannery tended to put people off eating fish.

They were all hungry, so none of them spoke for a few minutes while they concentrated on their food.

Then Scott resumed his story. "He suggested that since they were short a line supervisor, and since those positions are filled by white men, I could sign on there. Undercover, as it were."

"So I asked if I could work there, too, and he said I'd be useful as an office boy," Trent said. "I'm not sure what that is. And we start tomorrow."

Granville saw Emily and Miss Kent exchange glances, then hide grins behind their napkins. He wondered what exactly an office boy would be required to do.

Trent, full of his new investigative role, didn't even notice.

"You and I can't be seen together. Not now I'm working there," Scott cautioned Granville. "So Trent and I will probably bunk out there. Gives us more chances to hear things."

"And keeps us out of that stagecoach," Trent said vehemently.

Obviously he hadn't much enjoyed their transport, Granville thought. He kept his amusement to himself, though. Trent was inclined to hurt feelings if he thought someone was laughing at him.

"We'll still need to meet," he told Scott. "And exchange information."

"There must be boats that go between the canneries and Vancouver," Emily said. "Can you not get a ride on one of those? It might be more in keeping with your work, as well as giving you the chance to talk to more people involved with the cannery.

She glanced between them. "That way you wouldn't run the risk of being seen traveling with us. And Trent could avoid the stagecoach." And she smiled at the lad.

Who blushed furiously, but smiled back.

"That'd work," Scott said, toasting her with his coffee cup. "Nice thinking."

Emily smiled. "I'm glad. And the sea air would help to clear the smell of the cannery out of your head, as well."

Scott grinned at her. "I'm guessing that after a day or two workin' there, we won't smell it anymore."

He was probably right at that, Granville thought.

"So how did you two make out?" Scott asked.

"Well, Granville found several properties to buy. They have the chance to make a great deal of money in a few years," Emily said, her tone nonchalant.

Scott stared at her, then at Granville. "You're really buying something?"

Probably not, but he couldn't resist pulling Scott's leg. Granville shrugged. "Emily is right, it seems too good an opportunity to miss. You want in?"

Scott choked on his coffee.

Emily leaned forward to pass him a napkin. "It might be a good investment for the business," she said. "If the numbers work out. You'll have extra money from the rents, you know. And money should always be put to work."

Granville stared at her. Surely she wasn't serious?

13

MONDAY, AUGUST 13, 1900

On Monday morning Emily donned her navy suit and white straw hat and set off early for the office. She narrowly avoided a long conversation with Mama about wedding planning—which was the last thing she wanted to talk about today. In fact, it was usually the last thing she wanted to talk about.

No matter how hard she tried—and to be honest, she hadn't tried that hard—Emily couldn't make herself care about the merits of a tulle veil compared to one of fine silk. Her friend Clara had been horrified when she'd tried to explain that to her. Clara cared very much about such things.

Was there something the matter with her? She hated Mama's vision of a big society wedding to be held two years from now, but she couldn't seem to think about the smaller wedding Granville had suggested having in a few months. And yet she loved being with him, working with him.

And the idea of living with him as man and wife made her face flush and her heart pound.

So why was she avoiding moving up the date of her wedding? It made no sense. Mama would be hurt and upset, of course, but that couldn't be helped. Could it?

Emily shook her head at herself, earning a frown from a thin, very tightly corseted old woman sitting opposite her on the tram. Smothering a grin, Emily pulled the bell for her stop.

Stepping down into the building heat, she wished she'd brought a fan. Even if she felt like a fool waving one, today even that little bit of cooling would have been welcome.

Reaching the office building, she climbed the stairs to the third floor more slowly than usual. The stairwell was already hot, and it would be baking by mid-day. Perhaps a second floor office really would be the right choice for their new location.

As she strode into the office, Laura looked up in surprise. "I thought you'd be with Mr. Granville today," she said.

"No, he has an appointment with the coroner this morning," Emily reminded her as she removed her hat, placing it on the empty coat rack. And he'd be gone most of tomorrow as well, since he needed to talk to the night watchman.

Leaving her stuck in the office, dealing with the architects. Though that was hardly fair, since it was what she'd asked for. But it still rankled. She'd rather be in Steveston, investigating.

"That's right," Laura was saying as she ran a finger down the day's calendar. "He'll be in New Westminster. I was thinking that was Wednesday."

"No, it's today. And apparently having me along would offend the coroner's delicate sensibilities. Or something," Emily said, seating herself at her desk and making a face that had her friend laughing.

"I didn't like to contradict Mr. Granville at dinner the other night, but I thought a coroner cut up dead bodies? How could he have sensibilities?" Laura said.

Now Emily was laughing, her funny bone tickled by the illogic of it all. "True. And since the poor man who died is just bones, I don't see why my being there should cause anyone problems. I could have taken pictures of the bones for them."

"But still, Emily. Human bones," Laura said with a shudder. "Doesn't that bother you?"

"Yes," Emily said. "It does. But I've told myself I can't think about it. Not if I'm to work with Granville and Mr. Scott."

"I'm glad I'm just the typewriter, then," Laura said. "I couldn't do it. I just couldn't."

"You're hardly just the typewriter," Emily said. "Look at everything you did on the Sinclair case."

"I did help, didn't I?" Laura said.

Emily nodded. "You did. You have a gift for seeing patterns—especially patterns in numbers—and I suspect you'll be called on again because of those abilities.

"You really think so?"

"Yes, I do." Emily glanced at the wall clock. "But I should be working on those blueprints. Did you make coffee?"

"It's too hot. But I can make some for you if you'd like?"

"I'll do it," Emily said, getting up. "It's better fresh anyway."

Ten minutes later they both had fresh cups of coffee steaming in front of them —Laura had been unable to resist when she smelled the rich fragrance.

Emily had spread out the blueprint of the office layout she liked the best, and was comparing it to her second favorite, then to the third. Each plan was based on a different location in the building that now belonged to the firm. The next step would be to evaluate the costs of each choice.

But first she compared each of the plans against similar designs which she'd rejected. It was important to be very sure she had the best choice for each location.

Was the space for the front office right? Had the offices for Granville and Scott, and the smaller ones for herself and Trent, been allocated enough space? Was it too much? And was the meeting room big enough to hold all of them, a consultant or two, and several clients? She thought it was.

Sitting back with a sigh, Emily rubbed her aching forehead. She'd been peering so hard at the slightly blurred lines and faint lettering that she felt like she'd tied her brain in a tight knot. But these were the final three.

All three plans even had an extra couple of rooms that could be used for offices for consultants like McAndrews. Or if the firm grew, they could become permanent offices.

She nodded, well-satisfied. Now she could think about the properties they'd seen the day before. Granville might not be serious about buying more real estate, but with the money this building would bring in every month, he could easily do so. And the Steveston properties seemed fairly valued, and likely to generate a nice income.

She opened the notes she'd taken, and got to work.

"Laura, could you put a call through for me to Mr. Marshall, please?" she asked an hour later.

The real estate agent would be surprised to hear from her today. And it might not be acceptable to discuss a property she'd looked at with one real estate agent with another. But she could ask.

And she did need to get everything sorted out so that Granville and Scott could make a final decision on the renovations for this building. Which meant she had to know all the of costs these plans would incur. Including the invisible ones, like the loss of rental income that would result from choosing a more expensive location than their current offices.

They needed more space, but not at the expense of the firm's prosperity.

<hr>

Mr. Marshall was a tall man, with sandy curls and an earnest look. His desk was awash with papers, but he stood up with an easy smile when his clerk announced her.

"Thank you for seeing me on such short notice," Emily said. She passed the plans she'd selected to the realtor. "We've selected three possible layouts for our new office, one for each of the currently available offices."

She watched his expressive face as he looked through them. It hadn't been easy to narrow it down to three possible designs.

One of their options had been to renovate their existing offices, which would have caused a great deal of disruption. Though with all of them except Miss Kent often out of the office with this cannery case, that might not be as bad an option as it sounded. And their clients did seem to appreciate the anonymity of their current location, with the stairs leading to the street just down the hall from their door.

There was another, larger office suite on the fourth floor which had just come vacant, but Granville was concerned about making his clients climb yet another flight of stairs.

The third option was on the second floor, and just few feet down the hall from the enclosed stairway to the street. This was her favorite—it was already better laid out than the others for their firm's purposes. And the closeness to the stairwell—not to mention fewer steps to climb—might prove an asset for those clients who would prefer not to be seen entering an investigator's office.

Emily grinned to herself at the thought.

She'd always enjoyed penny dreadful novels, which she had to sneak into the house to avoid her mother's censure. And to avoid having the books confiscated. The Pinkerton's P. I. yarns had been her favorites. A small fact that she hadn't admitted to Granville yet.

And now she was working as a P. I. herself, if not quite officially. And the firm was considering affiliating with Pinkerton's. Life really didn't get any better.

The real estate agent turned over the last diagram, then looked up at her. "What did you want to know?"

"Before the firm makes a decision," she said. "I'd like to know what effect choosing each location would have on the building's cash flow. That is, what would our total income from the building be in each case."

"That's a very interesting question," Mr. Marshall said. "But wouldn't you be better to look at which location will best suit the firm's needs?"

"Oh, we've done that," Emily said. "As you can see, each of these locations can be made to fit our needs quite well. And each has different advantages and drawbacks. So the only factor left to consider is the impact on overall revenue of each choice."

"I should have known you'd consider all factors," he said with a smile.

"But of course," Emily said with an answering smile. "So can you do it?"

"Absolutely. It will take us a few days, though. This isn't something we do often. Will that be all right?"

"Yes. We have an appointment with the architect early next week, so if it could be done by then, that would be wonderful."

"I'll make sure of it," Marshall said. "And may I say, it's been a pleasure working with you. Now, is there anything else I can do for you?"

Emily tried not to feel nervous. "Actually, there is. But I'm not sure if I should ask you or not. Whether it would be a—a conflict of interest, I mean."

Marshall smiled at her. "Why don't you ask, and I'll help you if I can."

Emily nodded. "During a recent investigation,"—she thought that sounded very discreet, and it had a nice ring to it—"Mr. Granville and I had occasion to view several commercial properties in Steveston. I know you aren't the agent for them, but I'd hoped to discuss the merits of such an investment with you. As additions to Mr. Granville's real estate holdings, I mean."

She finished all in a rush, and felt quite disappointed with herself. She'd thought she sounded quite like a proper detective, at least for a moment. And then she'd gone and ruined it.

Mr. Marshall didn't seem to notice. Instead he smiled at her again. "I'd be delighted to act as—what is the phrase?—a sounding board for you on such matters. If only because I'm impressed by your grasp of the real key to buying real estate."

"The real key?" Had she missed something?

He laughed. "Indeed. You seem to have already understood what most buyers take years to learn—if they ever do. It isn't buying and selling individual properties that will make an investor rich. It is the choice of many properties, and the way the holdings complement each other, that does so."

"Well, it just seemed to me that the excess cash flow from the office building could purchase a commercial building. And the rent from those…"

"Could purchase another office building. Or perhaps a warehouse or two, in locations likely to increase in value."

She hadn't thought quite that far ahead. "Yes, just so. So I suppose you've already answered my first question—my thinking makes sense."

"Indeed it does. And your next question?"

"Does purchasing a commercial building—one housing several shops and a restaurant—in a place like Steveston make sense? Or would it be better to buy a different kind of property? Or a similar one, but in Vancouver?"

He looked delighted. "Excellent questions, indeed. I don't suppose you'd like to work for me? You'd be a sensation. And make both of us a great deal of money, as well."

Was he serious? "Well, thank you, but I'm very happy where I am."

"And I suspect Mr. Granville would be most unhappy with the idea. And with me. So I'll simply tell you this—it is always good to diversify, both in kinds of properties, and in their location. As long as your commercial property is fairly valued, and its businesses don't depend more than thirty percent or so on purchases related to the canneries—which are too seasonal to be relied upon for more than that—I think it sounds an excellent purchase. There will always be time to buy more properties in Vancouver. And I hope that you'll consider me as your agent when that time comes."

Emily nodded, and smiled at him. He'd been very kind, to give her the information when he wouldn't make a penny from it. In fact, he'd just ensured that they'd buy from him again. She wondered if he knew it. And suspected he did.

Not that he showed it, by look or gesture. He courteously asked if there was anything more he could do for her, then showed her out when she said there wasn't.

Leaving her wondering what kind of purchase he might recommend for them next. And how Granville would feel about becoming a property magnate.

She suspected he wouldn't mind. Although he really didn't seem committed to buying that commercial property in Steveston yet.

She'd have to show him the numbers.

14

As Granville stepped off the tram in New Westminster, he glanced at the busy wharf around him. Several boats were loading, and the ferry for Victoria on Vancouver Island was just departing. The calls of the sailors, the clattering of wagons loading and unloading, the smells of creosote and muddy water—he felt a sudden shaft of longing for London. Though that busy harbor was far larger than this one.

It was a hot day, but there was a hint of breeze off the Fraser River, and the sight of green trees on the far side of the river was refreshing. He tipped his hat forward and straightened his single-breasted suit jacket in soft grey, pleased with the fit, and especially with the new, lighter, cooler weight of it.

The short walk to the coroner's office, along Columbia then took him past the city hall and through the heart of the downtown. A few blocks to the east he could see the concrete towers of the provincial penitentiary, and the green trees of the city park surrounding it.

The coroner's office was housed in a four-story brick building that held a variety the municipal departments. A sign directed him to the basement. Following a set of cement steps down, Granville took a breath, opened a door and entered into the dry, slightly acrid smell of the coroner's office. It was cool and though brightly lit, the large, white-painted room somehow seemed dim.

Dr. Findler greeted Granville cheerily, coming forward to shake his hand. "Mr. Granville, I presume? Your colleague has just arrived."

He motioned towards Constable Ingram, standing very straight in his uniform, on the other side of the room. The young constable looked a little pained, Granville thought, nodding a greeting to him. Or perhaps he was just nervous. Possibly Ingram hadn't been to the coroner's office before.

"You've provided me with a capital mystery, sir," the coroner was saying, waving at a steel-topped table where the pitted bones that had been found in the lye bath were laid out. "I must thank you. It isn't often I am faced with such a puzzle."

Dr. Findler obviously loved his work, Granville thought. Which was a good thing on this case. He needed all the help he could get. "What have you learned so far?" he asked.

"Well, to start with, the bones are definitely human."

Granville hadn't doubted that. Not given Ross-Murray's intensity. And he'd been sure from the moment he'd seen that skull grinning emptily up at him from a cardboard box.

"And we have one complete set of bones here," Dr. Findler was saying. "There's nothing here that shouldn't be, either."

Now that was something he hadn't considered—that there might be more than one victim. He was glad to hear that there was not.

"I believe the skeleton belonged to a male, probably in his late thirties or early forties," the coroner said.

Granville hadn't considered that their victim could be a woman either. And that was an oversight he'd have to be careful not to repeat. There were nearly as many women as men working on the canning line, after all. "Anything else?" he said.

"Your victim would most likely stand between five-five and five-seven, and he was sturdily built."

"Are you sure of these facts?" Granville asked the coroner.

Dr. Findler nodded, smoothing his tie. "Though you have to understand that this is not yet an exact science. There is a great deal more work needs to be done before this kind of information can be considered certain."

"I understand," Granville said. "And we'll treat the information as such. But how can you infer as much as you have?"

"I've made something of a personal study of bones," the coroner explained. "Do you know anything about them?"

Both Granville and Ingram shook their heads. Ingram looked rather pale, Granville noted.

Dr. Findler smiled at both of them. "Then this is your chance to learn," he said. "Determining that our victim was male was fairly straightforward."

He leaned towards the bones spread on the table, pointed to the skull. "We'll start with the skull. You'll note the slight ridge here, above the nose, the protuberance of the chin, and the heaviness of the bone here, where the neck muscles attached. All indications that this was a man."

He pointed lower on the table, where two bones lying next to each other reminded Granville of macabre butterfly wings. "And then there's the pelvic bones," Dr. Findler said. "You see the narrowness where the bones join? Definitely male."

"The bones of the pelvis can tell us quite a bit about age, also. Although in this case, because of the pitting of the bones caused by their immersion in lye, age is a bit harder to determine. I look at the fusion of the pelvic bones," he pointed to the edges where the two bones connected.

"The lye took care of the cartilage that would have been here, but the bones still tell their story. See here. The surface is pitted, which would normally suggest advanced age. But here at the joining, the rims of the bone," Findler's finger traced the area, "and the faint plateauing in the center suggest mid-forties. And despite the pitting, the shape is still regular. So, early-to-mid forties."

"How do you determine height?" Ingram asked.

"Mostly it's the length of the leg bones," the coroner said. "With a bit of guessing thrown in."

"What about his race?" Granville asked. "Is there any way to determine that?"

"No, unfortunately science hasn't progressed that far," Dr. Findler said.

That was unfortunate. But something in the coroner's expression as he said it caught Granville's attention. There was a fleeting hint of a smile, a brightening of his eyes. "You have an idea of his race, though, don't you?"

Dr. Findler smiled. "I see why the canneries hired you to investigate for them. That's a rather remarkable deduction on your part. Yes, I have a personal theory I've been experimenting with. It's fairly limited at the moment, and not guaranteed to be accurate."

"We're working with a set of pitted bones and looking for a murderer," Granville said. "We'll take any information you have, speculative or not."

Ingram nodded.

"Very well," the coroner said, picking up the skull and holding it cradled in his hands. "I've been studying teeth."

"Teeth?" Ingram said. "What can you learn from teeth?"

"A surprising amount, actually. But in this case, we look at the incisors, here," and he pointed them out. "These are shovel-shaped, rather than spatulate. Which tells me that the victim is in all probability an Oriental."

Chinese or Japanese, then. "How certain are you of that?" Granville asked.

"I've had occasion to examine quite a number of Oriental skulls over the years, and the shovel-shaped incisor has been consistent in every case. So I'm fairly certain, especially given where the bones were found."

"Why does the location matter?"

"The canneries hire a high number of Oriental workers."

"So he was Chinese or Japanese?" Ingram said. "You're sure?"

Granville rolled his eyes.

"Fairly sure," said Dr. Findler. "As I just said. However…"

"However you can't confirm that," Granville said. "Why not?"

"My research is at a fairly early stage," Dr. Findler said. "And I'd hate to mislead you on such a matter. And I have also seen the shovel-shaped incisor in the teeth of several Salish Indians I was able to examine. I haven't seen many, though. And there may well be other races who share the shovel-shaped incisor, whose skulls I haven't had access to," Dr. Findler continued. "So the only thing I can say is that he is likely Oriental."

He turned the skull in his hands, ran his thumb across the cheekbones. "Also, the cheekbones are lower than I would expect to see in an Indian. But that is also a theory, and a much less developed one than that of the teeth."

"So taking the teeth and cheekbones together, you'd suggest we would likely be wise to look for our victim in the Chinese or Japanese communities?" Granville said.

"Likely so," the coroner agreed. "No one factor is conclusive, you understand, but several factors taken together can often be relied on."

Granville nodded. He wasn't sure exactly what Alexander Ross-Murray had feared with the finding of the bones at the cannery, but he suspected that Dr. Findler's speculation as to the man's race would not be good news. Especially if he turned out to have been Japanese.

Ingram knew it too. He'd turned pale. He'd be aware of the impact the murder of a Japanese man in the cannery could have so soon after the strike.

"And there is the question of location," Dr. Findler continued. "The body was found at the cannery, after all. Since these bones belonged to a male, and since the Indian workers at the canneries are usually female, it is likely that these bones did not belong to an Indian man."

"But the Indian women bring their whole families with them when they come to work at the canneries," Ingram said. "And many of the Indian men fish for the canneries."

"So if the victim was killed outside the cannery, and then dumped there, we can't ignore the fact that our victim could be Indian as easily as Oriental," Granville said, with an approving nod at Ingram that had the young constable beaming.

"True," Dr. Findler agreed. "Depending on the reliability of cheekbone evidence. I can only speak to the probabilities, which is that your victim is Oriental."

They needed more. "What about time of death?" Granville asked. "Can you learn anything from the bones?"

Ingram gave him a startled look, but Dr. Findler smiled.

"Excellent question," the coroner said. "And no, I can't determine the time of death from the bones. But the state of the bones themselves tells us quite a bit. Chief Gates tells me that these bones were found in the lye bath at one of the canneries, yes?"

"That's right," Granville said. "They were found last Monday morning. The last shift worked was the Saturday night."

"And is the lye vat heated?"

"No. Why does that matter?"

"Heating the lye to boiling speeds up the process of decomposition. If it had been heated, the body would have spent only a few hours in the lye bath to reach this state of decomposition."

"So since the lye was cold...?"

"The body had been in there at least overnight."

"So our victim could have been killed there or brought in from somewhere else, but no later than the Sunday night," Granville said.

"It would seem likely," the coroner agreed.

"But how is that possible?" Ingram asked. "None of the canneries are ever left completely empty, especially when the salmon are running."

"That's our job to figure out," Granville said.

He turned back to the coroner. "Do the bones tell you anything about cause of death?" he asked.

"If they do, it isn't in any way I can read," Dr. Findler said. "There are no obvious injuries on what is left of the bones. Though it is possible that between the lye's dissolving action and the pitting any indications have been destroyed. If he was strangled, for instance, his hyoid would be cracked. But this body's hyoid was not recovered."

And the lye vat hadn't been emptied.

"Should I have them check the vat again for the hyoid?" Granville asked him. "If they missed it, it could still be in the sludge at the bottom." And wasn't that a cheerful thought.

Dr. Findler frowned. "No, I'm afraid that would be a waste of time. The hyoid bone is small, and rather thin—horse-shoe shaped, in fact—and not attached to any other bone. It would be the first of the bones to dissolve completely."

"I see," Granville said. "That is unfortunate. But I would appreciate your help with one other matter. This was also found with the body," he said, and reaching into his pocket, drew out the scratched bit of metal that had been found with the bones.

"Have you seen an item like this before?" Granville asked, handing the battered and pitted disk to the coroner.

Doctor Findler looked carefully at the piece. "Iron?" he said thoughtfully. "That would survive lye. May I?" And he waved towards a microscope that stood on a table under the window."

Granville nodded.

Dr. Findler spent some time peering through the microscope at the small disk, making various adjustments to the microscope as he did so.

"I'm afraid I can't help you," he said finally. I don't recognize this, nor the symbol on it. It looks as though there was also writing of some kind on the other side, but it's too worn to make out."

And he handed the coin-sized piece back to Granville.

"Writing?" Granville said, turning the disk over and staring at the seemingly blank reverse.

"You haven't seen it?"

Granville held it close to his eye, then ran a thumb over it. Nothing.

"You're welcome to look under the scope, if you like," Dr. Findler offered.

"Please."

Dr. Findler took the metal piece back, set up the microscope, then waved them towards it.

"Have a look," he said. "You turn this knob to focus it, and bring what you're looking at closer or farther away."

Granville looked through the barrel, fascinated to see the lines of scratches that immediately appeared on the metal. Adjusting the knob to change the focus, he found a setting where the scratches suddenly consolidated into something that was almost writing.

He looked for a long time, making minute adjustments until his eye began to feel the strain, but he couldn't get the almost-writing any clearer. Nor could he recognize it.

He stood back from the microscope, and beckoned Constable Ingram to take his place. The young officer did so eagerly.

"You saw it?" the coroner asked.

"Yes. But not clearly enough to make it out."

"Yes. It's badly degraded."

"Is there any way to make a copy of what's here?" Granville asked. "Like a rubbing? Or are the scratches too fine?"

Findler looked thoughtful. "It probably won't work for a normal rubbing, but there may be a way." He turned back to his long metal workbench, over which hung a custom-made cabinet filled with rows of little drawers and pigeonholes, and began opening and closing drawers.

By the time Constable Ingram had finished looking through the microscope, turning back to Granville with a frustrated look on his face, Doctor Findler had assembled a small stash of materials on his bench.

Granville took the battered piece of metal to him, then watched in fascination as Dr. Findler set to work.

First he tried a traditional rubbing, the kind the English were wont to make of tomb carvings, using a soft graphite pencil and a sheet of thin paper. He handed the result to Granville.

It showed a few of the scratches, but not enough to give the sense of almost-writing that he'd just seen. He passed it to Ingram.

Findler was now pressing the metal against an ink-pad, as if the metal was a stamp, then pressing it to a sheet of white paper. Again, the result was disappointing.

That didn't discourage the coroner. After cleaning the metal with some clear, astringent-smelling liquid, he softly tapped a black powder onto the metal, whisked it off with a small brush, then placed a rectangle of some kind of putty to the metal. When he pulled it off, he glanced at it, smiled, and passed it to Granville.

There on the surface of the putty were the lines of almost-writing, even clearer than he'd seen them through the microscope.

"But can you make a more permanent version?" Granville asked. "The putty will be hard to carry and show people.

"Of course," Findler said, already busy mixing a white powder with another clear liquid and pouring it into a shallow, rectangle made of rubber. A mold. "I'll make one for each side."

Then he rubbed the first, astringent-smelling liquid over the metal and tapped on more black powder. This time he waited a few seconds before brushing the powder off.

Then Findler tapped the white powder mixture, which had nearly set, and placed the metal piece on it, powder side down.

"Plaster of Paris," Findler said. "Should give us a good impression. But the trick is in the timing."

He pried the metal loose after a moment, cleaning the powder and bits of plaster off with yet another clear liquid. Which smelled worse than the first one. After another moment, he carefully released the solid plaster rectangle from its mold.

He smiled broadly, and passed the finished casting to Granville.

It was even clearer than the first.

And it told him nothing.

15

Low-slung and white-painted, with most of her lower deck open to the elements, the sternwheeler *Transfer* was much less elegant than those Granville had travelled on going up the Skeena River in the spring. She was built shallow enough to traverse the marshes along the edge of the Fraser, and made the daily run from New Westminster to Steveston and back.

Granville didn't mind the lack of amenities—it was exciting to travel so close to the water. And the *Transfer* provided a much less harrowing trip than the rapids of the Skeena had been, and one both faster and smoother than taking the stagecoach from Vancouver. Also, he'd grown fond of the sound of the sternwheeler churning the waters behind them, the water cascading up and over, the ripples spreading out in the shallows.

He noted several pairs of bald eagles swooping low over the river, and the splashes in the water that told of leaping salmon, fighting their way upriver. The eagles would dine well today.

Constable Ingram seemed oblivious to the sights of the journey, but then he'd lived in this place of natural abundance half his life. It was nothing new for him. The young officer was frowning slightly, and mostly silent. Which was uncharacteristic for what Granville had seen of him to date.

"So what did you think of the coroner's report?" Granville asked him.

"It was fascinating," Ingram said. "But I can't help thinking..."

"Yes?'

"How are we ever going to solve this?" the constable burst out. "I mean, the information about the bones and how much he could tell from them is fascinating and all. But it's so little. I mean, I'd hoped Dr. Findler could tell us something useful. We still know almost nothing about the poor man."

"We know a great deal more than we did," Granville said.

"More? What did we learn?"

"We know there was only one victim, a male. He stood five-five to five-seven, and he was sturdily built. And he was likely Chinese or Japanese."

"Or Indian. It isn't much," Ingram said.

"No, but it's more than we had," Granville said. "But if he wasn't white, or colored, it does narrow our investigation a bit. And the disk found with the bones also suggests he might have been Chinese or Japanese. Though we don't want to make too many assumptions at this stage."

"So where does that leave us?"

"You didn't recognize the inscription on the disk?"

"Me? No."

"Someone will," Granville said. "So we'll ask about that. And we know that who-ever it was, he had to have been tossed in the lye bath sometime on Sunday."

"Because by Monday morning there was nothing left but bones," Ingram said. "And the coroner said it would take overnight for a body to dissolve, since the lye wasn't heated."

So he'd been listening after all.

"That's right," Granville said. "So the killer had easy access to the cannery on a Sunday, when no-one would see him dispose of a body."

"I know it isn't usual, but you keep saying him. Could the killer not have been a woman?"

"Think about trying to lift a body into the vat that held the lye," Granville said.

Ingram frowned. "It'd be dead weight, wouldn't it? Hard to lift?"

"Perhaps. If the deceased was five-six or so, he would have been awkward to lift, and hard to carry. No woman could have managed it. It would take a strong man."

"Then the killer is unlikely to have been Chinese or Japanese, either, because they are mostly lightly built."

"Exactly. Though many of the Japanese and Chinese associated with the canneries do hard, heavy work. They will be much stronger than their build suggests."

"And what if there was more than one man?" Ingram said thoughtfully. "Moving him, I mean. Not necessarily killing him."

Granville smiled at his eager expression. "And that is a very good point. Well done."

Ingram flushed. "Except that it widens our pool of suspects again."

Granville nodded. "Yes. But if we're to find this killer, we have to keep our own assumptions out of it."

"So how do we find him?"

"We'll start by looking at the cannery workers, and work outward."

"Why?"

"Because the killer had access to the cannery."

Ingram nodded. "Yeah, that makes sense. Then what?'

"Then we are turn our attention to those who are not cannery workers."

"I see," Ingram said slowly. "But then what do we do?"

"We listen," Granville said. "We've talked about this before. Someone out there knows who our missing man is. We just have to give them the chance to tell us."

"Huh," Ingram said. "Yeah, I guess it's like when I question a suspect. You want to get him talking."

"Exactly."

"But since I've already arranged for you to talk with my uncle first thing tomorrow morning, before he goes out to fish," Ingram said. "We might as well ask a few questions, right?"

Granville just shook his head. He'd been charged with keeping this death quiet. That included the information he'd learned from the coroner.

Obviously he'd have to remind Ingram of the need for secrecy on the subject of the coroner's report. And find a way to make it stick.

"So what are you going to do next?" Ingram asked.

"That all depends. Is your Chief in today?"

"Gates?" Ingram asked. "Sorry, we're still struggling with Chief Mann's death. It doesn't seem quite right to call Gates "Chief". Not that he's not a good man, though."

"Of course not," Granville said.

"And yes, Gates is in. He's mostly always there."

"Then that's what I'll be doing next," Granville said. "Briefing your chief. And I'd like you to join me, if you're free?"

"Of course I am, and thanks for asking. I don't quite get what we're briefing him on though."

Granville just smiled. He would.

THE STEVESTON POLICE station was quiet when Granville and Ingram arrived. The only officer present greeted Ingram, and confirmed that Gates was in his office. Acting Chief Gates seemed surprised to see Granville, but stood up and wrung his hand.

"Granville. Nice to see you again. Ingram here proving helpful, I hope?"

"Very," Granville said. "But we've uncovered some information that I suspect could prove divisive, and I'd appreciate your wisdom on the matter."

"Certainly," Gates said. "Please, sit down."

As they did so, the chief clasped his hands together on the desk in front of him and leaned forward. "Now what have you learned that is so problematic?"

Gates would make a good administrator, Granville thought as he pulled the chair forward and sat. But he'd likely be replaced as Acting Chief as soon as they could find someone. He just didn't have the presence.

Which was a pity, because the man had good instincts for police work. And Granville suspected those instincts would go largely unused.

Well, not today.

"We've been to the coroner in New Westminster," he said.

"And was he able to help?"

"Indeed he was. He's made quite a study of skeletons. And he's told us that our skeleton belonged to a man in his early to mid forties, standing between five foot five and five foot seven tall, and sturdily built."

"An Oriental?" Acting Chief Gates asked.

"He says so," Ingram blurted out, then flushed, and looked apologetically at Granville.

"Dr. Findler's research suggests that the man is Oriental," Granville said. "But he can't verify that."

"So we still don't know the man's race?"

"No, I'm afraid not," Granville said.

"But he might have been Japanese?"

"Yes. Or Chinese."

"We can't have that information getting out now," Gates said. "I'd hate to see more rioting. And it wouldn't take much to set it off again."

Granville nodded. "That's the same conclusion I came to. With your agreement, I'd like to keep this information as private as possible. At least until we have some answers."

Gates nodded. "Makes sense. What information will you release?"

"Only that the victim was male. And that only to the few people who need to know. Otherwise speculation could create the explosive situation we're trying to avoid."

"That it would," Gates muttered. "That it would."

"What is the worst thing you fear could happen if the news got out?" Granville asked Gates.

"With no more information than you've given me?" the Chief said. "Another strike. We could deal with riots. We can't afford another strike."

"No, I rather thought not." Granville said. "I'll have to tell the Gulf of Georgia manager what we've learned, of course. And my contact with the Salmon Packers' Association. But I'd like to keep it quiet beyond them. Would you agree?"

"I would indeed. The longer we can keep this death under wraps, the better. And that especially applies to you, Ingram," he said, giving the young constable an admonishing look.

Granville hid his grin as poor Ingram blushed and shuffled his feet under his chair.

The constable meant well, and he had the makings of a good investigator—certainly his heart was in the right place—but that very enthusiasm could spell disaster for his investigation.

No-one could afford to have the coroner's findings spill too quickly.

"Was the coroner able to provide anything else?" Gates asked.

"No. Except that we only have one set of bones. And that the body must have been put in the lye bath no later than Sunday evening."

"That makes sense, I guess," Gates said. "Doesn't give you much to go on, though."

"No, I'm afraid it doesn't."

"How do you plan to proceed, then?"

"I'll want to verify whether there are any workers missing at the canning plant," Granville said. "I've been told there are not, but..."

"Good strategy," Gates said. "And from there?"

"Someone—somewhere—knows this man. And that he's missing," Granville said. "I'm going to keep asking questions until I find that someone."

He pulled out the metal disk the coroner had given him. "This was found with the bones. Do you recognize it?"

The Acting Chief reached for it, examined it closely. Passed it back. "It looks like some kind of coin, doesn't it? But I'm afraid not. Still, as you say, someone will recognize it."

"And I just hope it's someone who will share that knowledge with us," Granville said. "Not someone desperate to hide it."

Gates looked grave. "Yes. The murderer also knows who this victim is. And possibly what that token is."

"We may be looking for more than one killer," Granville said. "Ingram here suggested it and I think he may be right. Lifting a deadweight up and into the lye bath couldn't have been easy."

"Nice work, Ingram," Gates said. "You're quite right.

Ingram flushed again.

Granville hid another smile.

"So you're certain you're fine with my concealing most of the information on the victim for now?" he asked the Acting Chief, mostly to drive the point home to the young constable. "I've already asked Dr. Findler to keep it quiet, and he's agreed as long as you're fine with it."

Gates thought about it for a moment, and Granville liked him better for it.

Then he nodded. "Yes, I can see the value of what you're suggesting. We won't say anything, will we Ingram?"

"No, sir," Ingram said. He looked disappointed, but Granville suspected he'd keep his word.

"But do keep me informed, won't you?" Gates said. "I'd like to be forewarned if this thing is going to leak out. We'd probably have to call in reinforcements."

Granville rather suspected that if this case blew up, the Packers' Association would call in the militia again. And it wouldn't be pretty.

16

On the way into Boyd's office at the Gulf of Georgia
Cannery, Granville spotted Trent racing out of the clerk's
office, and flagged him down.

"C'n I help you?" Trent asked, fighting to hid a grin.

"I've a message I need delivered to one of your line supervisors.
Can you take it?" Granville asked.

"Yes sir," Trent said. "I'll get it to him right away."

Granville smiled, and handed him the note with Scott's name
on it. "Thanks."

"Welcome," Trent said, and shot off on his errand.

Wondering who had managed to teach the lad manners,
Granville turned down the hall towards Boyd's office, and rapped
firmly on his door.

When it opened, the cannery manager looked surprised to see
him, but smiled a welcome and swung the door wide.

"You're back," Boyd said. "Come in. Have you news?

Granville nodded, and followed Boyd to the round table they'd
used the previous week. "Yes. I spoke with the coroner this morning. According to Dr. Findler, the victim whose bones you found in
the lye bath was male. And the bones belonged to only one man."

Boyd paled. "I never thought of there being more than one."

Granville didn't think anyone had. "He also told us that the body must have been placed in the lye no later than Sunday evening."

"How could he know that?"

"From the condition of the bones. Something about the action of the lye."

Boyd swallowed hard. "I see. And that was all he could tell you?"

"That was everything he could confirm. And Dr. Findler seems to know his business," Granville said, choosing his words carefully to avoid mentioning the coroner's speculations about the man's race. Would Boyd notice?

Boyd just nodded. "Yes, Findler is known for it." He paused. "So you've still no idea who he was? The dead man, I mean."

"As I said, not yet."

"What about who killed him?"

The man really was a fool. Or he was trying to annoy Granville into quitting the case in disgust. The thought was more appealing than it should have been. "We have too little information at this moment to assume anything."

Boyd paled a little. Probably at the bite in his words. Granville hid a smile. The fellow had it coming. And it was time to put him on the defensive. "Has anyone who works here been reported missing since we last talked?"

"No," Boyd said. "I don't believe so." He pulled out a handkerchief and swiped at the sweat on his forehead.

"Are any of your workers simply away for some reason?" Granville asked.

"You mean the Chinese men?"

"Any men, of any race that normally work here," Granville said. "Who haven't been working since last Sunday. Don't forget, we're not just looking for the victim. We are also looking for his killer. And the only thing that the bones you found in the lye bath have told us so far is that the victim was definitely male."

"I supposed that's true," Boyd said.

"And I'd like to start by looking at the men who work in the cannery itself," Granville said. "So. Are there any of your men who might be away for some reason?"

"Not in the height of the season," was the reply. "But let me just check with my bookkeeper…"

"Before you do so, I need to ask you to keep everything I told you confidential until our investigation is completed."

"Of course. But I'll need to tell Owens," he said. "And possibly my foreman."

"Owens is fine. But not your foreman," Granville said. "If you can't make the promise in all honesty, then I'll have to give any news of our investigations directly to Owens."

That seemed to decide Boyd. "Very well. I'll honor your wishes."

He started to the door, then stopped and looked at Granville. "But I can't ask my book-keeper without telling him why, can I?"

"Probably not easily. But I could. Why don't I just talk with the fellow myself?"

Boyd looked startled at the request.

"Well, yes, I suppose that will be all right," he said slowly. "Ross-Murray vouched for you. Yes, that's fine."

"And I'll need to talk to your night watchman as well," Granville said.

Boyd's eyes shifted to the side, and he wiped his forehead again.

Was he about to lie? Granville had spent enough time at the poker table to immediately recognize the signs of a poor liar, and braced himself.

"The night watchman?" Boyd said. "Oh, but…"

"The victim's body was dumped into the lye vat between Saturday night and Sunday evening," Granville said. "Your night watchman may have seen something. You do want me to find the killer, do you not?"

"Of course, of course," Boyd said quickly. "Just let me know when you'd like to talk to him."

"Tonight, if possible." The sooner he talked to the fellow, the better.

But first, he'd see what the book-keeper had to say.

GRANVILLE MADE his way down the hall from Boyd's office to the far end, where the book-keeper for the Gulf of Georgia Cannery had his office. He rapped on the door.

When it opened, a small man with a wizened face and a twinkle in his dark eyes beamed up at Granville from his wheelchair. "I'm Leon. Grazzini. But call me Leon. Everyone does. Me, I been working here since Owens opened the place. Please, come in. Sit down."

Granville walked carefully into the tiny, crowded office. It was dark—with no window and only a desk lamp for illumination—and stuffy. There were papers piled precariously on every surface, looking as if one wrong motion would send them cascading across the floor. Probably destroying Leon's file system in the process.

He wondered if anyone else ever came in here.

Leon was sweeping a stack of papers off a wooden captain's chair tucked into one corner and swiping at it with a white handkerchief. Granville held his breath to avoid the choking cloud of dust that arose.

"Here, sit," the book-keeper said.

As Granville did so, the little man wheeled his chair back to the desk, then spun around until he faced Granville. He looked Granville up and down. "Boss says you have some questions you need answers to. And that I'm to keep our discussions confidential."

He waved a hand at the ledgers stacked on his small desk. "Me, I keep everything confidential. Maybe I have answers for you. Maybe not. But I'll try."

"I appreciate it," Granville said.

"Now, how can I help?" the book-keeper asked.

"I'm investigating absences among the cannery workers," Granville said. "Looking for patterns. I need information on any of the men who haven't been at work for any length of time, or for any reason, since the end of the strike."

Leon leaned forward in his chair. "I don't have that information on the Chinese workers," he said. "Or the Japanese. Only the China Boss and the Japan Boss would know."

"But your figures would show if the two bosses were paid less overall from one pay packet to the next?"

"Well, yes, of course. But I can't see how that would help you."

"It tells me which periods I need to discuss with the contractors."

Leon nodded. "*Capisco.* Okay, then. I'll see what I can find."

"Will it take long?" Granville asked.

"Not too long. Why? You want to wait?"

"If it wouldn't be an imposition?"

Leon laughed, a deep chuckle that fit oddly with his small size. "The imposition would be yours, sitting in this office. No air, no light. I'm used to it, but you wouldn't be."

Smiling in response, Granville found himself liking the man. "I'll handle it," he said.

Leon laughed again, and swiveling his chair around, he pulled out one journal after another. Muttering to himself, he began to flip pages, making quick notes on a note pad. After fifteen minutes of this, he swiveled around to grab a stack of files from where they'd been stacked haphazardly on a nearby bookcase.

Ignoring Granville, he turned back to his note-taking.

Twenty minutes later he swung back. "The Japan Boss pay packets are all the same. The China Boss too. Everyone else is working."

Granville's heart sank. Had he been so wrong?

He stood up, thanked the book-keeper and shook his hand. And left the cannery no further ahead than when he'd arrived.

GRANVILLE HAD CHOSEN to stay at the Sockeye Hotel, a sprawling, two-story building a block east of the Gulf of Georgia Cannery. It seemed fitting, plus it was close to the docks. He was to meet Ingram and his uncle there at four-thirty a.m.

His room on the second floor was surprisingly comfortable. The bed was well-sprung and the window, which actually opened, looked out onto Third Street. There was an oak desk and chair, and two deeply upholstered club chairs bracketing a small table.

He'd already arranged to have dinner for three sent up when he called for it. There was nothing to do but wait for Scott and Trent to show up. And think about the case.

He'd started by taking a sheet of the hotel's pristine stationery, and making a list of what they knew so far. And what they needed to know. The result was not helpful.

Now he was lying full length on the bed, arms behind his head, staring at the ceiling.

There was so little to go on.

He'd hoped the coroner would be more help. Though given the little the fellow had to work with— nothing but a few badly worn bones— it was surprising he'd been able to tell them anything at all.

The real blow had been the information the book-keeper had given him. Or rather, the lack of it. It looked like he'd been wrong. The victim hadn't worked at the cannery. Nor had the murderer.

Or else the murderer, or murderers, were brazen enough that they'd returned to work at the cannery on Monday as if nothing had happened.

Neither scenario helped his case at all.

Who was the murdered man? And how were they going to find him? He'd just decided a whiskey might help him think when there was a heavy rap on the door. Scott.

"About time you got here," he said, opening the door wide. His friend was wearing heavy boots and dark dungarees with some kind of rough cotton shirt, and brought with him the stink of the canneries. His eyes were tired, with dark circles under them. He didn't look like he'd slept.

Trent crowded in behind Scott. He didn't look much better than Scott did.

"It was early tonight," Trent said. "Yesterday they were canning until nearly ten and they kept me running errands. I didn't know I could be so tired."

"Are you hungry?" Granville asked, standing back so they could enter.

Scott nodded, and Trent put a hand to his stomach. "Starving," he said pitifully. Spoiling it with a wide grin.

"We can do something about that. Meanwhile, I'll pour us a drink."

He opened the window, then put in a call to room service. Retrieving the whiskey he'd bought earlier that day, and the glasses he'd borrowed from the bar, Granville poured shots for the three of them—a half shot for Trent—handed them around.

Trent looked surprised. "I get one too?"

"With the job you're doing? Yes," Granville said. "Just don't expect it every time."

Trent grinned at him, and drank off half of his glass.

Granville took that to be a bad sign, given that the lad's father was a drunkard. But he'd make that argument when he had to. He turned to Scott. "What have you learned so far?"

"Damned little," Scott said. "No-one's mentioned a missing worker. If anyone is missing a colleague, they haven't mentioned that, either. I talked to Dirks, and he's had no reports of anyone who hasn't shown up. Nor of any trouble."

"What do you think of him?" Granville asked.

"Who, Dirks? Not much. He's too careful to be polite and helpful with me, for one thing. Exactly the opposite with everyone else. Why?"

Granville nodded. "Just that I've heard similar rumors, and wondered if you'd seen it."

"Yeah, I have."

"Is it impacting the work?" Granville asked him.

"Not that I've seen. They all know they have to process as much salmon as they can while the season's still open."

"Everyone's just glad it's running so smoothly, from what I hear," Trent put in.

"Yeah. They all need the money. That strike hurt everyone," Scott said.

"So there are no rumors?" Granville asked, "No uneasiness in any of the crew?"

"Nope." Scott grimaced. "But people often don't know each other. This is transient work."

"Surely they'd notice that someone different was standing beside them as they work?" Granville said.

"They might. But no-one's talking, if they have. And Dirks does change the shifts up, even re-arranges the positions. Sometimes weekly. Usually on a Monday. Trying to get more efficiency out of people. And the body was found on a Monday, right?"

"Yes." Granville thought about that for a moment. "So if the victim was a cannery worker, whoever killed him knew about the shift changes, and knew how to minimize his risk of discovery."

"Yeah. So no-one knows this guy is even dead?"

"The killer knows." Granville said. "And the coroner says the bones are male, and likely Chinese or Japanese. Though there's a slight possibility he might be native Indian. We're keeping his race quiet for now. He was probably in his late thirties to early forties, and stood five foot six or so, with a sturdy build."

"All that from bones?" Scott said. "You learn anything else?"

"Very little. Unfortunately." Granville said. "And the book-keeper confirmed today that none of the workers are missing since Monday. This may be a case we can't solve."

"The Packers' Association mightn't mind," Trent said shrewdly. "Not if all they're worried about is setting off another strike. If no-one's talking about this guy being missing, then no-one's getting upset about it, either."

"The kid's right," Scott said. "Maybe we should just get paid and get out of there. No-one would know."

"Yes, but we'd know," Granville said. "No-one should be murdered and not avenged."

"That's all well and good," Scott said. "But we don't seem to be gettin' anywhere. How long are your principles going to keep us all working in that stink?"

His partner had a point.

"It's too soon to give up yet," Granville said. "I'm meeting with the night watchman at nine-thirty. Maybe he'll have seen something useful."

"And not reported it? Doubtful," Scott said.

Which was true enough. "You never know. He might not realize what he's seen. The only way to know is to ask. Besides, I've already stopped smelling it when I'm out there. Hasn't your nose adapted yet?"

Trent grinned at both of them. "Mine has. Scott's too. He's just pulling your leg."

Scott's grin said the lad was right. Granville just shook his head at the pair of them.

A knock sounded at the door. "This should be our dinner," he said. "Since we probably shouldn't be seen together. Steak okay?"

"Is there anything else?" Scott asked with a broad grin as Granville headed for the door.

17

Granville looked around him. An hour after sunset, and with the cannery deserted, it was evident how badly lit the building was. Deep pockets of shadow loomed everywhere. He could hear water dripping somewhere—likely the result of the cleaning crew.

The air was cooling rapidly with a slight breeze off the water, but he could feel the mugginess the steam left behind. Standing directly under a light bulb, he could see that the floor was clean, though water still pooled here and there.

The stench was gone. Or mostly. The smell of machine oil, entrails and cooking fish still lingered unpleasantly. It probably baked right into the rough planking of the walls all summer long.

So where was the night watchman?

Somewhere there was a slow, creaking sound. Probably just the dock, rising and falling with the motion of the tide. It was an eerie sound in the darkened and deserted cannery.

He heard a door open somewhere behind him. Then the lights went out.

The sudden blackness was a shock.

His eyes were useless—he couldn't see a thing.

Granville suddenly realized he should have asked Scott to join him. They still knew too little of this killer—and what he might have killed to protect.

Had the killer somehow learned that Granville was investigating this death? Found out he'd be here tonight?

Something rattled behind him, and Granville's hand fell to the knife on his hip.

He spun to face the sound.

To see the wavering light of a handheld lantern.

The night watchman. He let out the breath he'd been holding. To avoid any confusion—and being shot at—he called out.

"Someone there?" came a deep voice.

"I'm looking for the night watchman," Granville answered. "Are you him?"

The lantern light came forward, carrying a man in its brightness. He was in his late fifties, tall and fit, with the long, lean look of an outdoorsman. His face was weathered, with white showing in the furrows around his eyes and mouth.

"Howell. Albert Howell," he said, striding towards Granville and holding out a hand.

"John Granville."

"Sorry I didn't hear you come in. I was just finishing up my rounds outside," Howell said. "So what can I do for you?"

"You know why I'm here?"

"I hear they found a body Monday morning."

So who had told him? "They did," Granville said. "Though it's not common knowledge. Who told you?"

"Dirks. When he told me to expect you tonight."

Made sense. "You hear any rumors about how he died?"

"Not a thing."

"What about Sunday night? You see anything odd?"

"Nope. It was pretty quiet."

How was that possible? Even supposing the victim had been killed earlier, getting even a small body into that lye bath wouldn't have been easy. "Do you have a regular route at night?"

Howell nodded.

"Can you show me?"

"Sure can. I start here," He turned left and down along the hall to the offices. In the smaller space of the hall, the lantern seemed to burn brighter and clearer.

On their left was a large open area. Howell lifted his lantern, and Granville recognized the reception area, and several desks, including the one where Boyd's secretary sat. Granville noted a kettle sitting ready on a small stove, an earthenware teapot beside it. There was an open newspaper on the adjacent desk.

"You take your breaks here?" he asked as he followed the night watchman down to the far end of the hall, the lantern illuminating closed door after closed door.

"Sure. I walk my rounds every thirty minutes or so. Start here, through the canning plant, then outside and around the grounds."

"The same routine all night?"

"Except for my dinner break."

"When's that?"

"Around two. But I vary the time, so no-one can count on me being here at a particular time."

Which was smart, but it wouldn't be hard to watch Howell, and wait for him to be out of sight and hearing of the lye vat. It gave the killer time, if he was quick enough.

Especially if Howell's "every thirty minutes or so" was less than accurate.

Granville glanced at the open newspaper again. It would be very easy for the night watchman to lose track of time—to sit and read for an hour instead of half an hour—late at night, all alone in a quiet, deserted cannery.

"And on Sundays?"

"Same thing. I have the night watch then too. There's another fellow on during the day. Jones."

He'd have to talk to Jones, too.

Granville followed Howell back through the darkened building to the canning plant. The fellow was weaving his way down one side of the first cannery line, staying close to the far wall to avoid tripping over a projecting bit of machinery. He was moving at a fair clip, too. "You ever use the lights at night?"

Howell snorted. "Not likely. They figure it wastes money, when there's just me here."

The big building seemed huge in the dark, the machinery looming in the shadows. Their footsteps echoed hollowly, and the lapping of the waves was an eerie background in the emptiness. A cold draft from somewhere worked its way up his back, and the smell of the place was overlaid by the stench of rotting seaweed.

He coughed.

Howell grinned at him. "You get used to it after a while."

He didn't plan to be here that long.

They neared the big doors to the dock, closed now for the night. The air was fresher here, but colder. Howell turned up the middle of the huge room, walking between the two canning lines.

"When do those doors get locked?" Granville said.

"After the cleaning staff leave. It's the first thing I do when I start my shift at eight-thirty," Howell said.

"You ever check the lye vats?" Granville asked as they passed the washing stations.

"The lye vats? No. Why do you ask?"

They hadn't told him where the body had been found? That seemed foolish.

His question had apparently aroused Howell's curiosity. The night watchman moved towards the first lye vat, lifting his lamp higher. Holding his breath, he bent forward a little to look in.

Then stood back and sucked in a breath, making a face as he did so. "Phew. Even from here, that stuff stinks. But the stuff's clear, so it's easy to see all the way to the bottom. Nothing there."

With a grin, Howell turned towards the second vat. And froze. "This one's not clear," he said. "There's something in there."

GRANVILLE MOVED QUICKLY to Howell's side. Looked down.

The lye bath was cloudy, and bubbling. The liquid had a dark tinge in the lantern light. It was clear there was something in there. A large something.

Not again.

He turned to Howell. "I need a telephone."

The night watchman nodded. "In the offices."

After Granville had put a call through to a sleepy cannery manager, Howell turned to him.

"So that's where the first body was found?" he said. "In the lye bath?"

"Yes."

"And that's a second body we just found?"

"I'm afraid it might be."

Howell's jaw tightened. "So someone managed to dump a body in there when I was somewhere else and couldn't hear him?" He paused, frowned heavily. "But it could have been there when I got on shift. I didn't look."

Could it have been? "It's going to take Boyd and his men some time to get here," Granville said. Can we try something?"

"I guess."

Granville led them back into the cannery plant, and down the near wall to the doors that led to the dock at the far end. "Can I borrow your lantern?"

"I guess. But why?"

"Bear with me for a moment. You stay here. I'll be right back."

Holding Howell's lantern high, Granville retraced their steps along the aisle between the cannery lines, using the route Howell had been taking when they found the body in the lye bath.

He forced himself not to look directly at the lye baths, but let his gaze move slowly from side to side without focusing on anything in particular, as he'd seen Howell do earlier.

He worked his way the length of the aisle, then walked swiftly back to Howell.

Handing him the lantern, Granville waved towards the route

he'd just taken. "It's your turn. Just go back up the row as if this were any night. As if I hadn't been here tonight. Try not to think about the lye baths. Don't pay any particular attention to them."

Howell muttered something about elephants, but obeyed, moving up the aisle between the two canning lines with his lantern swinging from side to side.

He'd just passed the lye baths when he stopped dead, turning back to look at Granville, still standing at the end of the aisle where they'd started.

"You were right," Howell called, his voice echoing oddly. "I wasn't looking at the lye baths, but the difference between the two of them caught my eye. They caught the light differently."

It was exactly what he'd seen himself.

"I thought that might be the case," Granville said. "And you didn't notice it last time you came through here?"

"No," Howell said slowly. "I didn't."

"And when did you come through here last?"

"Just over half an hour ago. Say quarter to nine or so."

Nearly an hour ago by Granville's watch. So Howell's sense of time was imprecise. "So it was fully dark?"

"Yes."

"And was anything different from this time?"

"Nothing. Except I didn't notice any difference in the two vats."

"And two Sundays ago?"

"Nothing." Howell sighed heavily. "I didn't notice anything at all. What does that tell you?"

That last Sunday's victim had probably been in the lye bath a lot longer than half an hour before Howell had done his rounds that night.

It also told him that Howell himself could be the killer. Or perhaps his colleague Jones was one.

Granville didn't share either thought. "I don't know yet. What time did your shift start on Sunday?"

"Eight-thirty. Same as usual."

"So the cannery was empty after the cleaners left on the Saturday night?"

"Yeah. Except for me, and Jones during the day."

"And the cleaners finished up when?"

"Not sure. But the place was dry by the time I got here."

The cannery had to have been deserted for at least a couple of hours on the Saturday night, then. So maybe that body went into the lye early on the Saturday night, before Howell showed up. Earlier than the one tonight. Might that mean there would be no difference in how the lye caught the light?

But wouldn't Jones have seen something in the daylight on Sunday, then?

"Does that help?" Howell asked, his eyes on Granville's face.

"It might. It's too soon to be sure," Granville said.

He didn't particularly want to discuss the case with Howell. Not when he could be a suspect.

The sound of voices approaching the door provided a welcome distraction. "But I think we have company.

A HALF- HOUR LATER, all the lights in the cannery were on. There was a small crowd gathered around the lye bath.

Granville was standing off to one side, watching. Howell, the night watchman, was beside him. Boyd, the cannery manager, and Dirks, his foreman, were both in front of the lye bath. As was a nervous-looking Chinese man, whose job it was to clean out the lye vats. He was standing a foot from the vat, reaching in with what looked like a wrought iron net on the end of a long pole, also iron.

Whatever was in the lye—and Granville was uncomfortably certain it was another body—was too heavy to lift out with such a flimsy instrument.

The Chinaman had made several attempts, managing to lift something almost out of the lye, then having to leap back to avoid the caustic splash as whatever-it-was slipped back into the lye. He was looking increasingly unhappy. Finally he dropped his ineffective tool and turned to Dirks, waving his hands and saying something Granville couldn't catch.

He was surprised the fellow hadn't given up sooner.

Dirks clearly was not. Raising his voice and stepping forward menacingly, the foreman tried to force the Chinaman to return to work. Barely taller than the other man, Granville thought the cannery foreman looked like a bantam rooster, crowing over his flock. All one of him.

Who wasn't cooperating.

Granville stepped forward. "Whatever is in that lye bath, we need to get it out fast. Before the lye destroys any more of it. If this fellow can't do it by himself, we need more men here. Now!"

Boyd was nodding. "Yes, he's right." He turned to Dirks. "If this fellow has friends, get him to call them. If not, get the China Boss here. We need this done!"

Dirks glared at Granville, but turned to do his boss's bidding. "We need more men," he shouted at the poor Chinaman. "The kind who don't go talking about what they see. You get some. Now."

The slim man with the long plait down his back gave a slight bow. "I get them," he said clearly.

As he turned to go, he slid a glance at Granville, and inclined his head.

What was that all about? Granville wondered as he watched the quiet man vanish through the doors and out into the night. And who would he be bringing back?

His gaze moved to the others. Boyd and Dirks had shifted further away from the fumes of the lye vat—and its disturbing contents—and were talking quietly together. Judging by the way they stood, Boyd frowning and leaning forward, Dirks with his fists and jaw clenched, the cannery manager was unhappy with his foreman. And Dirks resented it.

Meanwhile Howell had removed himself even further from the scene of the murder.

Granville hadn't notice him moving, but the night watchman

now stood about ten feet from the doors through which the Chinaman had disappeared. His stance was so neutral that it was hard to tell if he was watching for the fellows return, or disassociating himself from the crime.

Granville looked back at the darkening liquid in the lye bath, and swallowed hard. Death was no stranger, but this dissolving of what was once a man being seemed—inhuman, somehow.

Returning a body to the earth in a ritual acknowledgement of man's fallibility, seemed fitting. Or maybe just familiar. But turning a man's body into pitted bones and a liquid that could end up dumped in the ocean? That felt ugly. De-humanizing.

It hadn't been enough to murder the man. This killer had felt the need to erase all trace of who his victim had been.

Granville turned his gaze away from the lye bath, quickly scanning the cannery. The place was huge. Even with all the lights on, and four of them here, it seemed shadowed and empty. He knew he could actually see from one end of the building to the other, but in this light, it seemed to disappear off into a shadowy distance that his eyes couldn't penetrate.

It also seemed far too quiet. Graveyard quiet.

The creaking of the wood, the occasional whistle of the wind through the cracks, the lapping of the waves beneath their feet— they were a lullaby compared to the racket of the cannery in full operation. As Granville breathed in the smell of canning mixed with a hint of salt air, his ears seemed to strain for sounds that weren't there.

It suddenly struck him just how quiet these two murders had been. The bodies were disposed of quickly and silently. There was no screaming. No sign of violence. No trace of blood.

Either these men had not been killed at the cannery, or they had been killed very quietly indeed.

But how? Strangulation? Poison? There should have been some evidence of a struggle in either death.

Unless the killer was much larger than his victims, and had overpowered him. Or—using Constable Ingram's theory—that there was more than one killer, so they'd been able to overpower and silence the victim very quickly.

He shook his head. This was a waste of time. He needed solid information, not guesses.

Mostly, he needed to know who the victims were.

Then he might be able to find their killer.

Or killers.

The outer door creaked, and Granville, suddenly alert, looked up to see the Chinaman had returned, bringing with him several of his countrymen. They all trooped over to the bubbling lye vat, and the first fellow spoke for some minutes, complete with gestures. Then the four of them argued for a short time in incomprehensible words, their tones rising and falling.

Eventually they fetched long wooden oars, and arranged themselves around the lye bath, one at each corner.

Granville wondered at their choice of implement. Wood was hardly impervious to lye. But as he watched them maneuver the long, sturdy pieces of wood, he realized his error.

The oars were long enough to keep them well back from any lye that might splash up at them. They obviously knew that the lye used in the vat was strong enough to cause serious burns on contact. They had to figure out a way to get an unwieldy body—if it was a body—out of the vat without allowing any of the liquid that would flow off of it to touch them. Or to splash onto them.

And the oars were strong enough—their blades heavy enough— to lift a body in one quick motion. While keeping any runoff far away from the four of them.

Which was evidently what they were planning to do.

Granville stepped back, well out of splashing range, and he noted Boyd and Dirks did the same. The four Chinese fellows moved a little closer to the vat. He admired their bravery.

Though Dirks hadn't exactly given them much of a choice.

The three new Chinamen looked at each other, then back at the first fellow, seemingly waiting for his signal. After a moment he gave a slight nod, calling out "*Yi!*"

Four oars dipped into the lye, four sets of arms flexed and shoulder muscles bunched as they dug in, maneuvering their paddles to get under the bulk of whatever was in the vat.

It took only seconds, though time seemed to have stretched. After a moment, each of them straightened, then set his shoulder to his oar handle. All three looked up at the first Chinaman.

Again he paused, gave that nod, and said "*Er!*" Quietly this time.

Four sets of arms dug in, pushed, lifted.

And a heavy mass of bloody cloth, flesh and bone was lifted up.

Then another quiet "*San*" and the dripping red mass was swung and out of the vat, and dumped on the wooden floor of the cannery. Without so much as a splash.

Granville looked away from the horrific image for a moment, but he could still see the corroded body. His determination to track down the killer who could do something like this intensified.

He just hoped that this recent victim had retained enough of his identity—after his relatively short immersion in the lye bath—to allow the coroner to provide him with an identity. And to give Granville some facts to go on.

Dr. Findler was an intelligent man, and committed to his work. If there were facts to be found, Granville was certain he'd find them.

It was late by the time Granville left the Monster Cannery. Cannery Row was very different at night. All the canneries were dark, and there were no streetlamps along Bayview. In the dim lights from the saloons and bars that lined the other side of the street, he could see dark figures moving up and down the street.

Here and there a dark figure sprawled motionless. Probably drunk and not dead, he realized, but their lack of movement sent a chill up his spine after the grisly discovery he'd made earlier.

It was almost cool at this time of night. The smell of the cannery was gone, but the air reeked of spilled beer and vomit and urine, overlaid by the smell of mud and river water brought by the faint breeze.

For a moment he caught the burnt smell of opium. The Chinese workers, taking their leisure. From the saloons he could hear tinny music, and men's voices, and howls of laughter.

He wandered into the first saloon he saw—the Palace, which it definitely wasn't—and ordered a whiskey. Not to talk, but to listen.

And to get what he'd seen tonight out of his mind.

18

TUESDAY, AUGUST 14, 1900

The following morning was painful. Granville was woken far too early by a call from the main desk, and blinked blearily at the time. Four-thirty a.m. And it had been nearly one when he'd got back to the Sockeye Hotel and downed several more whiskeys to erase the image of the corpse as it emerged from the lye bath.

Now the events of the previous night seemed unreal. The surreal atmosphere of the cannery at night, the finding of yet another body—he shook his head, as if to dislodge an unwanted memory.

Though he knew it would take more than that. He could still see the ugly image this morning.

Which had him regretting his early wake-up call all the more. Regretting ever arranging this chance to talk to Ingram's fisherman uncle, who needed to be on the water a half-hour before dawn. Meaning he had to be down at the docks by five if he wanted to talk to the man. After getting to bed at one.

But with two corpses, and a killer to find, he couldn't afford to miss an opportunity to learn more about the fishermen who worked for the Gulf of Georgia Cannery.

In any case, there was little he could do about the new corpse today. They'd temporarily commandeered a larger commercial refrigerator at the cannery for it overnight. Boyd would arrange with the Acting Police Chief for the body to be shipped to the coroner later today.

Granville just hoped Dr. Findler would begin his investigations quickly. He had a killer to stop.

A knock at the door brought a waiter with a small pot of fresh coffee and a plate of English muffins, bacon and two medium poached eggs. He downed a cup of coffee gratefully, then made short work of his breakfast. The food was hot and good. Though he was hungry enough to have eaten almost anything.

Once he'd finished, Granville set the tray aside and glanced at the clock. He had just enough time for a quick bath before heading down to the docks to meet Ingram and his uncle.

***

GRANVILLE STEPPED onto the plank sidewalk and turned down towards the river. It felt odd being out and about so early. The air was still cool, and a hint of breeze, salt-fresh, danced along the street.

He glanced up. With its low buildings all shadows, and its lack of trees, Steveston seemed all sky—and stars. He'd been too tired the night before to notice, but the sky overhead was filled with stars, some bright, some so faint they seemed a reflection. Someday he'd like to know enough to navigate by those stars.

He walked down Fourth Street towards the public wharf where he was to meet Ingram and his uncle. Cannery Row was dark. Nothing was open—it was too early.

Ingram, however, was already on the docks, pacing back and forth. Spotting Granville as he turned onto Moncton Street, the constable hurried towards him and beamed. "You made it!"

"I did."

Ingram looked at him closely. "You look tired. The hotel too noisy?"

"No. I worked late at the cannery—had a meeting with the night watchman last night. I wanted to see how he conducts his rounds. And hear what he had to say about his watch two Sundays ago."

"When they found the body? That makes sense," Ingram said. "But he didn't see anything that night, did he?"

"Apparently not. But I wanted to know how he could have missed it."

"Right. That's real detective work, isn't it? I wouldn't have thought to ask about it. How did it go?"

"Certainly not the way I'd expected it to," Granville said dryly. "We found another body last night."

"Another body? In the cannery?"

Granville nodded.

"Not—not in the lye bath again?"

"I'm afraid so."

"But—but that's horrible. We have two murders now? And it's the same killer?"

"Or killers, as you pointed out yesterday. It's too soon to say for sure, but it appears so."

"But—why are you here? We need to deal with this! We can't waste any time." The young constable looked frantically around him, as if searching for something out of place. But the street was deserted.

"I agree. But there is little we can actually do for the poor man today," Granville said. "At least until the coroner is ready to release his results. We might as well see if we can learn anything from your uncle. Especially if any of the Japanese fishermen are missing."

"I suppose so," Ingram said. "It just doesn't seem very urgent, somehow. Not when there's another murder just happened."

"Murder investigations tend not to be very exciting," Granville said. "Except perhaps at first. The rest of it is often mostly legwork. And we end up asking a lot of the wrong questions just to figure out what the right ones are."

"I suppose so," Ingram said. "What happens after we talk to my uncle?"

"I want to have another look at the cannery before the work starts. In the sunlight, this time."

"But they start at six-thirty."

"Exactly. And the sun's up at six."

"But the cannery is locked."

"I have a key."

Ingram frowned. "Don't some of the workers start earlier?"

"Not this morning, they don't," Granville said. "The cannery owners need these murders solved, and Boyd knows it. He's agreed we'll have the cannery to ourselves from six until six-thirty."

"So we need to be there by six. Both of us," Ingram said firmly, as if afraid he'd be left out. "I'm coming too."

"Of course you are. But we'll only have half an hour, so no questions until afterwards, all right? We'll go for a late breakfast."

Ingram nodded his agreement, then pointed. "There's my uncle."

INGRAM'S UNCLE JOE was a lean, grizzled man of medium height who looked to be in his mid-fifties. His arms were heavily muscled from hauling nets, and his face bore the signs of long days spent outdoors in the sun and the salt air. He stepped out of his boat and onto the dock with a nimbleness that belied his age, and came forward with his hand outstretched.

"Joe Ingram. But call me Uncle Joe, everyone does. You must be Granville. Good to meet ya."

They shook hands, and Constable Ingram got a hearty clap on the back from his uncle. "Billy here says you had a few questions for me. Something about investing in the canning business. Wanting to know more about how the fishing works here?"

Granville nodded, inwardly amused. There seemed no need to say more.

Uncle Joe pointed to the boat the crewman had snugged to a post. Granville estimated her to be about twenty-five feet long and nearly seven feet wide, with a fixed mast at the front and two sets of oar-locks.

"Lot of the boats here are like this one. Built her myself. She's round-bottomed, Columbia River-style. Good out there on the ocean. We built her up from the basic hull. Added the deck, and the cabin."

The boat was heavily planked and looked sturdy, despite floating low in the water. Granville looked for the name, and was surprised to see a combination of letters and numbers instead. The *G2977*.

"You didn't give her a name?" he asked.

Uncle Joe grinned at him. "It's a tradition around here, and a useful one. You'll see the same number painted above the door on people's homes. If a boat goes down, it makes for an easy way to find the right family and let them know."

Practical, maybe, but Granville found it a sad reminder of just how dangerous this business really was. He wondered just how many men died at sea every year, and made a mental note to ask Ingram later.

The *G2977* seemed small compared to any boat Granville had sailed on, especially if they planned to be out on the fishing grounds for days on end. "How many men does it take to sail her?"

"Usually two," he said. "But she'll hold four or five of us. And a lot of fish. The round bottom keeps her stable in the waves. And her mast's twenty-five feet high. Means we can follow the salmon pretty quick when we need to."

Granville was still thinking about the first part of his comment. If most of the fishing boats sailed with a crew of two, could both their victims be from one such boat? Perhaps the boat owner and his crew? But then why had the bodies been found at different times?

"How long do you stay out at sea?" he asked aloud.

"Depends how the fish are running," Uncle Joe said. "Usually from Sunday night to Saturday night. Sometimes we come back to Steveston to unload in between, like yesterday. Mostly we take the fish to the fish scows the canneries send out, and let the cannery's tender boat bring the fish back in."

"The fish scow?"

A brisk nod. "All the canneries have fish scows near the fishing ground—they weigh and credit your haul, then you get back to fishing and they take all the fish back to the cannery. Saves everyone's time."

"Do you contract with one cannery for the season?" Granville asked.

"Mostly. We sell to the Monster Cannery, unless they can't use more. Then we'll try the others. But we're lucky, we can do that. So can most of the Japanese fishermen. A lot can't."

"How so?"

"The canneries own a lot of the fishing licenses—and the boats, too—contract them out to a fisherman for the season with the understanding they'll fish only for them. If they aren't buying, too bad for you."

"And if you have your own license, you're paid more as well?" Granville said.

"Nah. That's part of what the strike was about—how much per fish. We settled at nineteen cents per fish." Uncle Joe shrugged. "You ask me, nobody won. But we get by."

From the little Ingram had told him about the Finnish community, who mostly lived in a collection of hand-built wooden shacks on what was locally known as Finn Slough, they did indeed get by. Barely. The community was largely self-sufficient, raising most of their own produce, using wood and coal oil for heat and light. He admired the independent spirit that had built a vibrant, self-sustaining community from literally nothing.

"It might be useful to meet some of the men who fish for the Gulf of Georgia Cannery. Would that be possible?"

"I can take you and Jimmy out to the fishing grounds today if you like. You'll meet 'em coming in."

Part of Granville was ready to leave immediately. But it was unlikely to get his case solved, unfortunately. "Thank you, but it won't be today, I'm afraid. But it's good to know it's possible."

"Sure thing. Just let Billy here know if you want to come out, and he'll set it up."

"Thank you. Have you heard anything about any of the fishermen going missing?"

"Nah, nothing like that. Weather has been easy lately, though. Last big storm was the previous Thursday."

Before the first victim was found, Granville thought. "So you'd have heard by now if a boat had gone down?"

"Maybe, maybe not. Should hear by the weekend, though. Most boats don't stay out longer than a week."

"But some do?"

"If their catch was bad, they might. Just drop their fish at the fish scow and go back to fishing."

"How quickly would it be noticed if a boat or a fisherman went missing?" Granville asked.

"Hard to say. Depends where they are fishing, and for how long. If visibility is bad and no other boats fish the same place, no-one might know if they went down. But if one of the fishermen on a boat went missing, the other would report it."

But not if both were missing. "Do the crew change often on a fishing boat?"

Uncle Joe shrugged. "Most crew sign on for the season. But things happen. One man leaves, another is hired. It happens."

"How well do you know the other fishermen?"

A broad grin. "If they're Fins, I know them well. Others, maybe a little."

It made sense, given what Granville had learned about the fishing community here. "So if I wanted to know if a particular fisherman was missing, I'd need to ask others in their community?"

"Yup."

Perhaps Ingram could suggest a name.

19

The interior of the cannery was still shadowy, despite the early morning sunlight peering in through the few windows and the cracks in the rough board walls. All the lights were on, but they barely reached into the shadows.

As Granville led the way down between the canning lines, he and Ingram both carried kerosene lanterns, held high. The lanterns provided a strong steady light, but the swinging of the lanterns meant the light wavered with their footsteps, chasing the shadows hither and yon as they walked. It was still an eerie place at this early hour.

Or perhaps he saw it so because they were seeking a killer.

"Where are we going?" Ingram asked, raising his lantern high and peering into the shadows, then looking nervously over his shoulder.

Apparently he wasn't the only one reacting to the atmosphere here. Reaching the lye bath where the body had been found, Granville pointed it out to Ingram.

The liquid within was mostly clear this morning, with nothing visible at the bottom. The Chinese workers had done a good job of clearing it out last night, especially given the poor light they had to work by.

"This is where the body was found?" Ingram asked, then held his breath as he moved to look into the depths of the bath. "I don't see anything."

"It was thoroughly cleared," Granville said. "Quiet, now."

Ingram subsided, frowning as he watched.

Granville gave him a half-smile, then concentrated on the job. He examined every inch of the floor around the lye bath, holding the lantern close. Looking for something, anything, that would indicate which direction the body had been carried from.

He saw nothing.

Which wasn't surprising, given the number of people who had walked back and forth in front of this vat last night, to say nothing of the four men who'd fished the body out of its corrosive grave.

In the slightly better light of the morning, however, he'd hoped to find signs of blood from the body. Small drops of blood would have sunk into the wood floor before the body was found, and thus been impervious to being trampled. But they hadn't been so lucky. He found nothing.

It was possible that the body hadn't bled. If the victim had been strangled, for instance—perhaps from behind, and thus killed without a fight. Then there would be no blood to find.

He widened his search, half crouching as he held the lantern out. He closely scanned one side of the canning aisle, first in one direction, then the other. Then he moved around to the other side, again scanning in both directions from the lye bath. Though this time he moved from the far end, near the entrance, and moved slowly down the aisle towards the doors leading to the dock.

Now he was looking for any sign that shouldn't be there after the cannery had been washed down.

And found it in a speck of mud lying in the aisle a few feet from the doors leading to the loading dock. None of last night's searchers had walked here.

Holding the lantern low, he scanned the area. Looking for something, anything, to help him find a killer.

Ingram began walking towards him, and Granville motioned the young constable back. He stared at the floor so long he began to feel he could see every grain in the wood. But it paid off.

He spotted a bit of grit, then another, both lying pale against the wood. A tiny smudge of mud. Then further over to one side, another smudge. Two people? Or one that took one path coming in, and another going out?

Or possibly just the marks that either the night watchman or he himself had made the previous evening.

He glanced up to see where Ingram was. The constable must have picked up on what he was doing, because he'd walked all the way around the other canning row to come out near the double doors, but on the far side, well back from where a murderer might have walked. He was holding his lantern high, which helped Granville see more clearly, but he was also scanning the area himself, his eyes moving slowly from section to section. Granville smiled, and returned to his own search.

He needed to find something that was clearly linked to the killer. Or killers.

Inch by inch he moved forward, moving carefully, scanning every bit of the floor. Then he saw it.

More of the bits of grit, lying in a little clump, as though they'd fallen out of the tread of someone's shoe. And back of that, a little line of grit, leading back to the door. And several smudges of mud, on the floor and in two widely separated spots on the door sill.

He looked down at what he'd found. He knew he hadn't stepped there, and he doubted Howell would have stepped on the door sill itself.

He looked from one smudge to the other. If there had been two of them, and if they'd been carrying a body…

It would have been awkward getting a body in through the doors. Yes, that would be about how far apart they'd have to walk.

Moving carefully over to the far set of smudges, he followed a faint path of grit and mud back towards the lye bath where the body had been found last night. He was able to find minute traces caught in the grain of the floor. The trail continued almost to the lye bath itself, where any trace must have been trampled into nothingness.

Two of them, then, bringing the body—dead or unconscious— in from the docks. From a boat? Carrying him between them down the aisle towards the lye bath. Dumping him in.

He wanted a record of the path they'd taken.

He glanced at his watch, then looked around for Ingram, who had moved to the other side of the canning line, and was staring down towards the floor with a slight frown between his brows. "Found something?" he asked.

"Maybe," Ingram said. "Come see what you think."

Moving carefully so as not to disturb the evidence he'd found, Granville made his way to the young man's side. "What is it?"

Ingram pointed halfway down the metal leg of the canning table just back of the lye bath. "There's something caught there," he said. "It looks like fabric."

Granville crouched down, held up his own lantern. Looked closely at a few scraps of what appeared to be pale thread caught up on a rough edge of the metal. "You're right. It is fabric."

"Someone in a hurry. Probably just a worker."

"They don't tend to hurry on the canning line," Granville said, his thoughts going back to his introduction to the cannery. "They work quickly, but at a steady pace, and they don't break that rhythm. Especially not so close to the lye bath, where a slip could result in serious burns from the lye. I saw enough lye burns on fingers to know that all of them understand the dangers."

"So our killer?"

Granville nodded, his thoughts on the theory he'd been formulating. "It's possible, anyway. So the killers carry their victim as far as the lye bath, down that aisle." He pointed. "But they know enough about lye that they don't want to risk being splashed when they dump the body in. They're probably not wearing protective clothing."

"Why not?"

"Too obvious if they're seen."

"Who would see them?"

"If they came in on a boat—other fishermen. If they came down the stairs from the village—anyone they passed."

"But if they had a body with them, it would be obvious."

"They managed to disguise it somehow. Or hide it. Perhaps the body was already hidden somewhere on the dock. We'll have to look for hiding places. But somehow they get the body here without being seen, carry it in. Then one of them moves quickly to this side, gets his trousers caught."

He glanced down. "There should be traces of grit or mud here."

"Yes, I see it," Ingram said, pointing to a bit of grit beside the table leg. "But why would he move over here?"

Granville moved to stand at one corner of the lye bath, squinted slightly to change his perspective. "If one man stood here, and the other on the same corner on the other side, they could lift the body by an arm and a leg. Then the man standing here walks towards the other corner, stretching the body over the lye bath."

Ingram nodded, seeing it now. "So then they lower it slowly, and avoid getting splashed."

He walked to the far end of the lye bath, put a flattened hand at the level of the top edge of the vat, moved his hand back against his chest, keeping it level the whole way. Looked at Granville. "They'd have to be tall, then. One of them, anyway."

Granville nodded. "The one standing where you are would need to be six feet or more, by my reckoning. And strong."

"You reckon he's the killer?"

"No, I suspect he's the muscle. The killer wouldn't rely on strength."

"I get that."

Granville glanced at his watch, then carefully gathered the bits of cloth that had caught on the table leg, and folded it into a sheet he tore from his notebook. He walked back to where they'd found the other evidence, scraped up some of the grit, and a bit of mud, folding each into a separate sheet of paper. Then he buttoned all three folded samples into his shirt pocket.

Ingram watched every move he made. Granville turned to him. "Can you help me map out the path of the debris our killers left?" he asked.

Ingram nodded. "Sure. But why?"

"We'll need a record of it before the crew gets in and tramples it," Granville said. "And we're almost out of time."

2 0

Granville and Ingram sat at a battered wooden table in a quiet corner of The Baithouse, a small restaurant down at the end of Number One Road that catered to fishermen. Overlooking the Fraser River, the place was spotlessly clean, and smelled of frying bacon. Sitting at one of the battered wooden tables that crowded the main room, they had the place to themselves.

"The food is good here," Ingram said. "And it's too late in the day for the fishermen, and too early for anyone from the canneries, so it's safe to talk."

He picked up a battered menu, glanced at it. "Plus the food is cheap and there's lots of it. And I'm hungry. I'll order for us?"

Granville nodded. Despite his early breakfast, he was hungry too. And that bacon smelled delicious. "And I could use a cup of coffee, too."

Ingram grinned, waved at the fellow behind the counter. "Two specials. And coffee, lots of it."

That got him a nod, and the fellow disappeared into the back. Ingram sat back, looking pleased. "Just wait till you taste it," he said.

Then he scowled at Granville. "But I don't get it. Why are we here, instead of out there inspecting the dock, seeing if we can find where they might've hid a body."

"Too many people around now," Granville said. "We're trying to keep our investigation quiet, remember? Especially now."

"Why now? We still don't know anything."

"Except that the bones we found could belong to a Japanese man. And that one of the men who dumped his body in the lye bath stands six feet or more."

Ingram's eyes widened. "Not Japanese," he whispered.

"Exactly. And likely not Chinese or Indian, either."

"You think he's white. And that he'd be taking his orders from another white man." Ingram was still whispering, despite the empty restaurant.

"Yes, I do. And if word gets out…"

"We could have a riot on our hands," Ingram said. "At best. But what about the other body? What if he's Japanese too?"

"I think we have to assume he is."

"Then you're right. We have to keep this quiet." Ingram stared at Granville, his expression tense. "But what about whoever got the body out of the lye bath last night? Won't they talk?"

The lad had the makings of a good investigator, Granville thought. "They're Chinese, and I've been assured that they won't. But we're going to have to work fast."

Ingram looked at him shrewdly. "You think they'll talk."

"What I think is that the more people who know about these deaths, the faster word will leak out. Someone will talk, eventually. Our job is to catch the killer before they do so."

"Yeah. But how do we investigate when we can't tell anyone about the murders?"

"Quietly," Granville said. "We need to talk to someone in the Japanese community. See if they've heard of anyone missing. But whoever we talk to, he'll have to be the right person, or this will escalate into the kind of mess the cannery owners are trying to avoid."

Ingram paled and nodded.

"Can you find out, quietly, who that person might be?"

"I'll do what I can," Ingram said. "It might take a while. It's probably someone in their Benevolent Association, but I want to be sure it's the right name. I don't want to make things worse here."

Ingram was learning.

"That's fine. Meanwhile, I need to talk to Boyd. Find out if there's a record of which boats unloaded fish that day," Granville said. "See who works on that dock, talk to them. Then we need to find out if those doors to the dock are locked at night. And whether it's feasible to enter from the land as well as from the water."

"I'll come with you."

"No," Granville said. "We need to avoid being seen together as much as possible. You're a police officer, and I'm officially just here looking at potential investments."

"Then why all the talks with Boyd?"

"I'm considering investing in the cannery, remember?" And he'd have to find out more about canneries as an investment. Or ask Emily to do so. He bit back a smile at the thought.

"Then perhaps you should come back with your fiancée. You'll be less obvious then," Ingram said.

Before Granville could answer, two steaming platters were dumped on the table in front of them. Each platter was piled high with food—eggs, bacon, flapjacks, some kind of mashed potatoes. Enough food for three men.

Granville drew in a deep breath. Everything smelled amazing. His stomach rumbled as he picked up his fork.

"Try the potatoes," Ingram said. "It's a hash made with smoked salmon, fried with sweet peppers and onions. It's really good."

Granville forked up a bite. Ingram was right, it was good. Very good. And the young constable was also right about bringing Emily with him. She had a good eye. And her presence would give him the excuse for another tour of the cannery property.

"I'll be heading back to Vancouver after breakfast," he told Ingram.

Right after he had another bath and checked out of the Sockeye. And talked to Boyd.

"And I'm planning to return tomorrow with my fiancée, ask a few questions. Can you follow up with your chief to be sure he's been asked to arrange the delivery of this latest body to the coroner? And see if you can quietly find out everything you can about the schedules for any suppliers to the Gulf of Georgia Cannery? Who delivers there and when?"

"I'll see what I can learn."

Granville nodded. "Good. Then after the coroner has delivered his findings on the latest body, we'll plan another night visit to the cannery."

GRANVILLE SAT in one of the uncomfortable wooden chairs which were all the Gulf of Georgia Cannery offered visitors. Boyd wasn't in yet, though it was five after nine. Apparently the cannery manager dealt with early mornings after a late night even less well than Granville did.

He was glad of the opportunity to observe the office routines. It seemed quiet this morning. One of the two office clerks had offered him coffee, which he'd declined, and was now typing busily on what looked like invoices. The other was making entries in a large ledger. Otherwise, the office was empty. He could hear the clatter of the canning lines through the doors.

Everything seemed as usual. Which suggested that Boyd had managed to keep the second murder quiet. Good.

There was no sign of Trent, which was unfortunate. He'd written a note for the lad to pass to Scott, filling him in on the murder, and what he'd learned this morning.

Granville glanced at the local newspapers lying on the low table in front of him, presumably to entertain visitors while they waited. He picked up a copy of the *Eburne News*, and glanced at the headlines. Nothing relevant.

But it was the edition he'd seen set out with the makings for the night watchman's coffee last night. Which led him to wonder how often Howell really made his rounds.

Just how long had the latest body been in the lye bath before they'd discovered it at ten? And what could it tell them about when the first man had died?

Boyd's noisy entry into the office distracted him from his thoughts. The cannery manager looked surprised and none too pleased to see him sitting there, but quickly hid his feelings behind a bland smile.

"Granville, how timely. I was hoping to talk with you today."

He was a poor liar. And a worse manager, from what Granville had heard so far. He wondered why Owens, who clearly knew the cannery business, and who struck him as a shrewd business man, had hired Boyd. And why he hadn't fired him by now. Boyd must have connections, somewhere.

"I'm sorry to arrive without an appointment," Granville said. "But I'm booked on the ten o'clock stage back to Vancouver, and I still have to collect my luggage from the hotel. So I don't have much time. I was hoping you could fit me in?"

"Yes, of course, of course," Boyd said. "Come with me."

Once seated in Boyd's well-appointed office, Granville watched the fellow hang up his coat, then try to make himself comfortable behind his desk. It was a losing proposition—clearly he was anything but easy at having to deal with Granville so soon.

"I have a few questions about the murder last night," Granville said.

"Oh, really? Already?" he said, his voice a little too high. "I mean, yes, of course. What can I tell you?"

"First, how is the cannery locked up? And who has responsibility for it?"

"Well, our policy is that everything is locked tight at the end of each day."

"And is that policy enforced?"

"Well, of course it is."

Granville nodded. "Then how would the murderer have got in last night?"

Boyd paled. "I assume they must have broken in."

There had been no sign of a break-in. "And who is responsible for ensuring that everything is locked up?"

"Dirks. He assigns that responsibility as he sees fit."

Dirks again. "I gather you have a Sunday watchman. I'll need to talk to him. Jones, is it?"

"Something like that. He's a recent hire. You'd have to talk to Dirks." Boyd grimaced slightly.

Dirks again. "I'll do that," Granville said. "Have you had any problem with theft here? Of tools, or equipment, I mean?"

"Theft?" Boyd said, his voice rising slightly. "Why would you ask about theft when you're looking for a murderer?"

Granville raised his eyebrows.

"No, nothing like that," Boyd said hurriedly.

"Thank you. I've talked to your book-keeper about whether you have any employees missing. And you don't."

Boyd looked pleased.

"So I need to widen the search. I'll need the lists of the suppliers you deal with," Granville said. "And a list of all the fishermen who work for you or sell to you."

"Oh, but..." Boyd began.

"In fact, I'll need lists of anyone who delivered fish to the dock outside the cannery yesterday," Granville continued, ignoring him. "And I'll need that list by Thursday."

"But that's the day after tomorrow. I—I don't think we can have it ready..."

"You have a murderer out there who has already killed twice. He's dumping the bodies at your cannery. And we can't keep it quiet much longer—word will get out. You have something more important than that?"

"Uh—no. No, of course not. I'll get you the lists."

"Thursday."

"Yes. Yes, of course. Thursday. Was there anything else?"

Granville smiled. "No, that's everything for now," he said, standing and holding out his hand. "It's been a pleasure."

As he walked back down the hall, he considered Boyd's less-than-firm handshake and befuddled look. The fellow was dangerous in his ineptitude.

The more he learned, the more he wondered why Owens had hired Boyd in the first place. And what could the owner feel he owed the cannery manager, to keep him on?

Granville checked his watch. He had just enough time left for a quick chat with Dirks.

Which he suspected the fellow wouldn't much enjoy.

As GRANVILLE WALKED through the cannery office, he ran into Trent, who was hurrying towards the corridor he'd just vacated. Trent grinned at him and stopped. "Didn't expect to see you this morning."

Glancing around to ensure they were out of earshot of the two clerks, who were focused on their work in any case, he pulled out the note he'd written.

"There's been another murder," he said in an undertone. "See that Scott gets this today, will you?"

Trent's eyes widened, but he just nodded, and set off in his original direction. The lad was learning.

Granville continued onto the cannery floor. With two lines in operation it was overwhelming. Heat, noise, smell. Too much, all of it.

He noted that the big doors were open at the far end of the building, letting in a hint of a breeze. Two Chinamen were shoveling in fish as fast as they could move, so at least one fishing boat was unloading down on the dock below.

He glanced around, looking for Dirks. It took a moment to spot him, caught in what looked like an argument with one of the butchers. The man's hands never stopped moving, even as Dirks was yelling at him. Further down the line, the already canned fish were being taken out of the boiler, dunked in the lye bath, then moved down the line for labeling and packing.

Just another day at the cannery.

Last night's murder might never have happened. Hadn't happened, as far as these workers knew.

Granville wondered what he might learn, if he were able to talk privately to each and every one of them.

He suspected he might have a solution pretty quickly—if he could get them to talk. But that opportunity would never happen. The politics were too volatile. And there was too much money at stake.

He'd have to find his answers the slow, hard way.

Granville turned his attention back to Dirks, who had apparently stopped yelling long enough to notice his presence, and was headed towards him. He didn't look much happier to see him than Boyd had. And he was even worse at concealing it.

"Why are you back?" Dirks asked as soon as he reached him, yelling over the noise of the canning lines.

"I have some further questions," Granville said. "Is there somewhere we can talk?"

Nodding to one of his line supervisors, presumably to take over, Dirks beckoned to him and headed for an office Granville hadn't noticed before. It was at the far end of the building, tucked away behind the packing plant, but with big windows looking out on the canning lines. Dirks flung himself down into a chair behind a battered desk piled high with paperwork, and gestured Granville to an equally battered but paperwork-free wooden chair in front of the desk.

"So?" Dirks said as Granville sat down facing him.

"I understand there's a new watchman working Sundays," he said. "Name of Jones?"

"That's right, Nick Jones. What of it?"

"When did he start working for you?"

"Soon as the strike ended."

Before the bones were found, then. "I'd like to talk to him."

Dirks hesitated, then nodded. "I'll set it up."

"Today if possible."

A smirk. "It isn't. He's a fisherman. Won't be back till Sunday. You can talk to him then, though."

"That's unfortunate," Granville said. "I'm looking into how the killer could have got into the cannery after hours. Boyd tells me everything is locked tight at the end of each day."

Dirks grinned. "If he says it, then it must be so."

"And yet we found a body in the lye bath."

"Maybe the body and the killer were already in the cannery."

He'd said it to annoy Granville, but it remained a possibility. For the first murder, anyhow. "That's entirely possible," Granville said. "But I can't figure out how he could have pulled it off. Can you?"

Dirks looked taken aback. "Well, we have all that equipment, for the third line that's not being used, off to the side. Light's not very good there. Easy enough to hide a body."

"What about the killer?"

Dirks thought about it. "Could be on the cleaning crew. Or, he could have hidden himself amongst that equipment. Come out and dumped the body after they left. Before the night watchman comes on, like."

"But how would the killer get out of the cannery?"

Dirks grinned. "Out those doors at the end, and down onto the docks."

"Yes, that makes sense. But I thought they were supposed to be locked at night?"

"Well, yeah. They are. But on these really hot nights, the doors are left wide open until the night watchman comes on. It's his job to close them and lock them up," Dirks said.

So the doors had been open until the night-watchman came on at eight-thirty.

"And sometimes I'll bet Howell doesn't lock them until late, like two or three in the morning, when everything's cooled off," Dirks added. "I mean, who's going to notice?"

Only the killer.

But the doors had been closed last night when Howell took him along on his rounds. And Howell said locking them was the first thing he did when he started his shift.

Was Dirks lying, trying to point Granville's investigation in another direction? Or had Howell changed his usual practices because he knew Granville would be coming?

Regardless, the killers had dumped another body in the lye bath. A body that had been brought in through those doors, which had definitely been locked by nine-thirty, when Granville first saw them. And Howell was prepared to swear it wasn't there at eight-thirty.

So when had the body been brought in?

He glanced at Dirks. If the man knew, he certainly wouldn't tell him.

"You ever get complaints about theft?" he said, to needle Dirks.

"Nah. Well, just small stuff. The usual. Nothing worth following up on."

Granville wondered how much Dirk's attitude was costing the cannery. It would be easy to steal small things, things the foreman clearly didn't care about, after hours. Which answered the question about who knew about the unlocked doors. Probably most of the workers.

Unless it was Dirks himself who was stealing from his employers.

He tucked that thought away for further consideration and pulled the disk that the coroner had copied for him out of his pocket, handed it across the desk to Dirks. "You recognize this?"

The foreman turned it over in his hands, scrutinizing both sides closely. Then shook his head. "Nope. Haven't ever seen this before."

"Or anything like it?"

"Nope," Dirks said. "This come from the dead man?"

"Yes. It was found with the bones."

"Funny that. Sorry, can't help you."

"I appreciate your time," Granville said dryly. "And your theory. I think you might have something there."

Dirks grinned. "O'course. I know how this place works."

But he seemed far less hostile as he ushered Granville out.

2 1

Emily re-read the numbers their real estate agent had provided on the various options for their office building one last time, and then stretched her arms to the ceiling. She'd been working on the renovation files all morning, until her back ached and her eyes burned.

But at least she was done. Finally. Maybe now she could get back to investigating. Meanwhile, she'd give anything for a glass of cool water.

It was hot in the office, and her white lawn shirtwaist was sticking to her back. She was just glad she'd removed her suit jacket and hung it over the back of her chair. After all, Granville, Trent and Mr. Scott were all in Steveston, and they had no appointments booked that day. There was only Laura to see her, and she wouldn't mind Emily's lack of professionalism.

Unless Emily gave in to her mad desire to do the same with her long, heavy skirts. She grinned at the thought.

"Laura, would you like a glass of water?"

"Yes, please," her friend said, her fingers still flying over the typewriter.

As Emily walked to the tiny sink, she considered the fan turning lazily overhead. It really didn't do a very good job of cooling the office.

She'd already asked that the architects put in the best fans available, but she'd have to ask whether more fans were possible. They'd be worth it in summer. And winter too, probably.

Emily ran the water until it was cold, then poured a glass and drank down a few mouthfuls. Much better.

She was tempted to pour the rest of it over her head just to cool off, but she refrained. Instead she refilled her glass and ran one for Laura.

Putting Laura's glass on her desk, she shoved a file aside on her own desk to make room for her own glass. Then she unrolled a blueprint and studied it. Yes, there should be room for more fans. And they could be added regardless of which office they decided on. So she was officially finished.

Every detail was in these files, and ready for Granville and Mr. Scott to make the final decision.

Though Emily knew already that it would be the second floor office—it was perfect for them. Accessible, with more space—and the numbers were better. Plus they could ask more money for the rental of this office, simply because it was on the third floor.

Best of all, the second floor office was available for their immediate use. And it had a passable conference room already. So all she'd have to do was order some furniture, and Granville and Mr. Scott could meet with the man from Pinkerton's in a proper meeting room, instead of in their current too-small office. That should impress him.

She was tidying everything back into folders and clearing off her desktop, when she heard footsteps coming down the hall. She hurried to pull on her jacket, then glanced over at Laura. "Are we expecting anyone?"

"I don't think so."

Emily was trying to straighten her lapel—which seemed to have got tucked under somehow—when the door opened. She looked up, and smiled. "Granville? I didn't expect you back until tomorrow."

"I had booked the ten a.m. stage back. Would you care to go for lunch?"

"I'd adore it. And I'm starving. Shall we bring something back for Laura?"

"Of course. Any requests, Miss Kent?" he asked.

"Anything is fine," Laura replied. "And I'll make tea when you return."

"Thank you," Emily said as she put on her summer hat. "I'll see you in an hour."

"Or so," Granville added. "I'll brief you then, Miss Kent."

Emily smiled at Laura's pleased expression. And wondered what Granville had to tell them.

As they strolled the two blocks to Stroh's Teashop, her hand in the crook of Granville's arm, chatting about nothing in particular, Emily's curiosity grew sharper. It was too hot to hurry, but it seemed to take forever until they were seated at a small table towards the back of the tea shop, and free to talk.

Their table was in a quiet spot, partly hidden from the rest of the room by a couple of large potted palms. Best of all, it sat beneath a very efficient fan. Emily was delighted by the cool breeze.

"Now that is the kind of fan I want to make sure the builders put in our renovated offices," she said to Granville as soon as the waiter had seated them and departed.

He chuckled. "I'd expected you to be grilling me about the case as soon as we sat down, not talking about fans."

"Well, I've heard you complain about the one in your office often enough. And the office is hot! As you'd know if you ever spent any time there."

She grinned at him. "Think of poor Miss Trent, stuck in that hot office all day. Besides, it is far cheaper to put good fans into an office when it is being renovated than it is to try to do it later."

Granville grinned back and held up a hand. "Peace. We can have as many fans as you can convince the architect to put in. Quiet ones, please. And I don't care how expensive they are."

"You might regret saying that."

"Not if our offices are cool." He picked up the menu, but didn't look at it. "I gather you've been looking at plans this morning?"

"Yes. In fact, I'm done. You and Scott now have three designs to look at for our new office, complete with pricing."

"You're finished? But that's terrific."

She felt just a little smug. "I know. And I know which one you'll pick. It's the obvious choice."

He started to say something and she held up a hand. "No, no. I'm not saying anything. You need to make the decision, the two of you."

"I hope we chose correctly, in that case."

"You will. Now tell me about the case. What did the coroner say, and what did you learn from Ingram's uncle?" She paused, glanced at her menu, then back at him. "And why are we here? I love the menu here, but I know you prefer a steak. Especially after spending a full day around the canneries."

He shrugged. "We're here because you like it here. And I know you were disappointed not to be included in my meeting with the coroner."

"You're trying to make it up to me? Thank you," she said. "That means a lot. But a nice lunch doesn't make up for being left out of the investigation."

"A nice lunch and a pot of tea?" he said with a grin.

She frowned at him. "You're not taking me seriously."

"I am, you know. I always take you seriously. Lunch is just to say I'm sorry for your disappointment. And to give me a chance to brief you on the investigation."

"Brief me? Oh. Then I'm sorry too." She leaned forward. "Tell me."

"After we've ordered," Granville said, picking up her menu and passing it to her. "We've only an hour before we need to be back, remember."

Emily nodded, and made quick work of ordering a crab salad sandwich, a jam pudding, and a pot of Earl Grey tea. "And the same sandwich and pudding to go, please."

He ordered two beef sandwiches and a beer.

"No pudding?" she said after the waiter had left.

He made a face at her, and she nearly choked on her tea, it was so unlike him. "So tell me," she said.

He filled her in on his meeting with the coroner the day before, and then the rest of that day and evening.

"Another body? So there are two murdered men now? Oh, that's awful," she said softly. "Does Scott know?"

"Yes, I met with him and Trent last night. It was before we discovered the second body, though, so I left a note for him with Trent when I went to the cannery this morning. And there's something else that I think you'll be interested in."

"Oh?"

"I examined the area around the lye bath this morning, with Ingram," he said, describing what they'd found, and then detailing the rest of the morning.

"May I see the maps? And the evidence you collected?" Emily asked.

He pulled out some papers. "These are rough maps that Ingram and I drew last evening on sheets pulled from our notebooks. This is one canning line." And he pointed to the first one. "With the doors opening down to the dock at this end."

Then he placed the second page beside it.

Emily looked from one to the other. The first was more finely drawn, the second had cruder strokes. "You didn't draw the second one, did you?"

"No, that was Ingram. But how did you know?"

She just gave him a secretive smile. "Go on."

He shook his head at her and turned back to the drawing. "This one shows the other canning line. The body was found here," he pointed, "and there was a bit of torn fabric caught on the leg of this canning table, here. These marks show the minuscule trail of evidence leading to the lye bath. You can see where each of the two intruders walked."

"Yes, I can," Emily said. "This is amazing. Even though it is rough, and your drawing styles are different, I can still see how it must have been last night."

"Good. I'm glad I'm not the only one it's clear to," Granville said. "And these are samples of the debris they tracked in." He carefully opened out the two small packets.

Emily peered at them. "The mud just looks like mud," she said. "And the grit is so small. Will the color tell you anything?"

"I won't know until I try," Granville said. "But it's more than I had yesterday."

He pulled out the third packet, opened it to show her the tiny bit of fabric. "I'm not sure if this might tell us anything, either."

"I know someone who can tell us," Emily said, with an inward grin. Clara would be in heaven. And Granville would hate it. Serve him right for not taking her to the coroner's, lunch or no lunch.

EMILY AND GRANVILLE returned to the office, and delivered Laura's lunch to her. She seemed pleased with Emily's selection, which was a relief. Then while Laura briefed Granville on the calls she'd taken, Emily borrowed his office to phone Clara and invite her to join them.

Clara accepted immediately, even before she had explained that it was Clara's expertise with fabric that was needed. With that added incentive, Emily expected to see her friend as quickly as she could get changed and catch the streetcar over. And she wasn't far wrong.

Clara arrived before Granville had finished telling Laura what she needed to know about the cannery case. And her fashion-conscious friend was wearing a day dress. It was pretty, but Emily had never known Clara to leave her house without changing from a day dress to something more formal.

Clara was either very bored, or she had developed even more of a taste for detecting than Emily had suspected.

"Ah, Miss Miles," Granville said as Clara entered. "Thank you for coming to our assistance. I appreciate it."

"I'm happy to help," Clara said, with a smile for Laura. Then she rolled her eyes at Emily, who had to swallow her grin. For some reason Granville was being very formal, and it sounded odd.

He seemed to realize it, too, because he shook his head a little and gestured them into his office. "Miss Kent, you're welcome to join us, if you can listen for the phone and any visitors at the same time."

"Yes, definitely I can do that," Laura said, with a pleased little smile. "And should I make that pot of tea I mentioned first?"

"Tea, Miss Miles?" Granville asked Clara.

"That would be lovely."

"Then tea it is, please," Granville said, and followed Emily and Clara into the office. He got herself and Clara settled in his and Scott's chairs at either end of the big partner's desk that dominated the office, then inquired politely as to Clara's health and her family.

Emily smothered a laugh as she wondered what Mr. Scott would think if he walked in on what seemed to have become a tea party. She was reminded again that Granville had grown up with sisters, which was probably a good trait in a husband. And it certainly made for pleasant working conditions.

Once Laura had brought in the tea tray, with a plate of tea biscuits for Clara, they focused their attention on the case. Granville brought out the folded paper, opened it and placed it on the desk in front of Clara, so they all could see the torn scrap of fabric. Clara and Laura leaned forward and peered at it, and Emily got up and came around to their side of the desk and did the same.

"It's very small," Clara said. "Where was it found?"

"It was caught on the rough edge of a piece of equipment in one of the salmon canneries in Steveston," Granville explained. "We think it may belong to a murderer."

Miss Kent gasped, but Clara just nodded, much to Emily's amusement. Her fashionable friend really had started to think like an investigator.

"May I pick it up?" Clara asked.

"Yes, of course. Just be careful not to separate the threads. There isn't much of it, so we can't afford to lose a single thread," Granville said.

Clara carefully picked up the scrap of fabric, and held it close to her eyes, squinting slightly as if to bring it into better focus. "I believe it's cotton," she said. "Heavy cotton. And a very rough weave."

"The kind of cloth a fisherman might wear?" Emily asked.

"I don't know," Clara said. "I've never seen fishermen's gear."

"You'll have to come to Steveston with us tomorrow," Granville said. "They have several shops that sell fishermen's gear."

"What a good idea," Emily said, watching Clara closely. Her friend's eyes lit up and she nodded agreement with the plan, but Emily wasn't sure if she was eager to do more detecting, or just more shopping.

"May I see that?" Laura asked, holding out her hand. Clara passed her the scrap of fabric.

Laura held it towards the window, where the sun caught it. "I think this may have once been dyed," she said. "It looks like the kind of fabric used in denim overalls, which may become bleached by wear, acid or long exposure to sunshine."

Clara wordlessly put out her hand, and Laura passed the fabric scrap back to her. Clara moved so her hand was in the direct sun, then peered at the fabric again. "You may be right," she said. Then looked at Emily. "I assume one can also buy denim overalls in Steveston?"

At Emily's nod, Clara smiled. "Then I can also look at those. For comparison." And to Laura, "Thank you."

Laura smiled, and nodded.

Clara turned to Granville. "I'd like to tease out one thread from this sample. I promise to take very good care of it—but I'll need it for comparison. And it's safer than my using the whole sample."

Emily watched Granville as he considered Clara's request. Then he smiled and nodded. "That's a good suggestion."

"Then could I have a piece of paper, please?" Clara said.

Granville pulled a sheet of paper from his desk drawer and handed it to her.

Clara folded it carefully, tore it neatly in half, then extracted a single thread and folded it into the half sheet and tucked it into her purse. "There!" she said with satisfaction, and handed the remainder of the scrap of fabric to Granville. "And what time do we leave for Steveston tomorrow?"

22

WEDNESDAY, AUGUST 15, 1900

Granville helped Emily and Clara up into the canvas-roofed wagon, then sat opposite them. The stagecoach journey to Steveston was beginning to feel very familiar. The driver had even greeted him by name this morning.

The trip was as slow and rough as he'd come to expect, as the coach swayed ponderously from side to side. The horses, two massive Percherons, seemed to haul them with little effort. It still struck him as an outmoded form of transportation to find in such an urban area at the beginning of this new century. He far preferred the more efficient tram that ran between Vancouver and New Westminster.

Emily, as usual, had taken the journey in stride, simply noting the changing streets and landscapes they passed through. Clara, however, was hilarious in her dislike for this mode of transport.

"For goodness sake, Clara," Emily had said at one point. "Have you never travelled by stage?"

"Never," Clara had replied, one hand clutching her hat, the other clutching the seat in front of her. "And I never will again."

"You mean you'll never ride on the stage after the ride home again," Emily said helpfully, one corner of her mouth twitching up as if she were fighting not to smile.

Which Clara wouldn't appreciate. At all. Granville knew his fiancée's best friend well enough by now to be sure of that.

"I will find another way," Clara vowed.

"How do you feel about small fishing boats?" Emily had asked her. "They are really the only other option, from what I understand."

Clara had given her a dark look, and tightened her lips around whatever comment she'd been about to make.

The rest of the journey passed in silence, for which Granville was properly grateful.

Once in Steveston, Clara wrinkled her nose at the smell, but was too busy taking in every detail of the small village to comment. The weather was cooler today, and there was a slight breeze off the river, which helped dissipate the odour of the canneries.

He noted that Emily didn't point Cannery Row out to her friend, but instead took the shortest route towards the small downtown shopping district. Once they reached Moncton Street, Emily was kept busy pointing out landmarks to her friend, but Clara seemed most interested in the shops.

Granville had decided to accompany them on their shopping expedition. He wanted a chance to check out the feel of the village, to see if it was any different after the second murder—and whether rumors had started to fly yet.

It would be difficult, if not impossible, to keep two murders quiet.

He could also see if anyone recognized the disk they'd found with the first body. Rubbing a thumb over the smooth plaster surface of the copy, he wondered if they'd find a second one with last night's body. The four Chinese men who'd removed the body from the lye vat hadn't commented on it, if they had.

THE INTERIOR of the chandlery on Second Street was full of anything a fisherman could want. No denim overalls, though.

Clara went straight to the clothing section. Emily saw racks of yellow rain slickers—both jackets and pants—in all sizes, and shelves of heavy wool sweaters, caps, thick rubberized gloves, sturdy work boots with thick soles and good traction. She didn't see anything that the tiny piece of fabric might have come from.

Glancing around, she could see Granville deep in conversation with the sales clerk. When she looked back, Clara had vanished.

Looking frantically around, she spotted the top of her friend's blond head above the stack of sweaters on a nearby shelf. Walking around the shelves, Emily found her friend on the other side, busily sorting through a rack full of heavy trousers and overalls. Clara had the thread in one hand, and would periodically stop and compare it to a piece of clothing.

"Did you find anything?" she asked.

"It could be any of these," Clara said. "If the fabric has been bleached out since it was purchased, the color variation here"—and she showed Emily how the fabric ranged from very white through cream to a light beige—"doesn't help us at all. But if it weren't faded, only these two"—and she pulled out two pairs of trousers that were a yellowish-cream color—"are a match."

"Can we ask the clerk who his customers for these two might be?"

"Good idea," said Clara, and trousers in hand, she marched up to the cash desk.

Emily watched in amusement as the clerk was immediately pulled away from whatever serious discussion he'd been having with Granville. Faced with Clara's vivacious prettiness, he all but fell over himself trying to answer her questions.

If he wondered what a very fashionably-dressed young woman was doing asking about a pair of workingman's trousers, he certainly didn't let on.

"Those are popular with fishermen," he explained. "Since they are woven tightly enough to keep out some of the wind, and have plenty of room for"—and he hesitated, flushing deeply—"forgive me, long undergarments."

"And do all fishermen buy them?" Clara asked.

"They are particularly popular with European fishermen—the Finns, the Greeks—as well as Canadians and Americans. A few of the Indians also wear them."

"Not the Japanese?" Granville asked.

Emily had to admire how casually he'd asked the question, as if it was no more than a passing curiosity.

"No, I don't think we've sold a single pair to a Japanese," the fellow said. "They tend to shop at McGinty's."

Clara smiled at him, and asked several questions about how the fabric wore, and the care of it, which the clerk was only too happy to answer. She ended up by buying a pair in the smallest size.

Emily wondered what in the world she planned to do with them. But when they'd left the shop and she asked, Clara smiled mysteriously and refused to answer.

On their way to McGinty's, they passed a feed store at the end of the block. Granville waited outside while Clara and Emily went in quickly to see whether they carried denim overalls. They didn't. Emily glanced from bales of hay and sacks of feed to the rack of shovels and trowels, the boxes full of seed. It seemed they had everything else, though.

McGinty's had fishing gear as well as a variety of rakes and shovels, but their main focus seemed to be clothing. Ignoring the heavy coats and sweaters and the rain gear, Clara went straight to the thick cotton garments. There were three racks of them, all stuffed full.

"We have more in the back, if you need something different," the clerk called from the front. "Just let me know."

"Thank you, we will," Emily said.

Clara had handed Emily the bag holding her purchase from the previous chandlery. She was too busy flipping through garments to even look up. She stopped every now and then to finger one thoughtfully.

Emily had seen her friend concentrate like this before, but usually it was in service of finding the perfect hat, or the perfect color of ribbon to match a gown. This was fascinating.

Clara rapidly chose two pairs of trousers and two pairs of overalls and carried them to the large window at the front of the store. "I'd just like to see these in the light."

The clerk looked bemused but nodded.

Curious, Emily followed Clara. She watched as her friend turned her back a little so the clerk couldn't see what she was doing, then drew out the thread. Carefully she laid the thread on each of the garments she carried in turn.

Handing one of the garments to Emily, Clara switched the thread back and forth between the two pairs of trousers and the two overalls, holding each at different angles, and humming softly to herself. Finally she returned to the rack, with Emily trailing behind her.

Hanging up one pair of trousers and one pair of overalls, she carried the other two pairs up to the front desk and purchased them.

Emily followed her out of the store, and confronted her on the sidewalk. "Clara, whatever are you doing?"

Clara just smiled.

Granville followed them out of the store. "Did you find what you were looking for?" he asked Clara.

"I think so," she said. "I'll need to have these laundered before I can tell you for sure, but I think these overalls might be a good match for what you found."

Granville nodded. "I spoke with the clerk," he told them both. "And many of their customers are Japanese—but they are also from every other race."

"Including white?" Emily asked.

Granville nodded. "He says so. Apparently their fishing wear has a good reputation for durability."

"Then this doesn't help us much?" Emily asked.

"No, it doesn't look like it. Though that depends on the outcome of Miss Mile's experiment."

"So what do we do now?" Emily asked.

"Now I treat you both to fresh salmon and chips for lunch," Granville said with a smile.

"That won't get us anywhere," Emily muttered softly, aware she was being uncharitable, but feeling too frustrated to be reasonable. It was a fault, she knew, but one she couldn't seem to overcome.

She looked at Granville's handsome face, with not a frown in sight, and she wondered how he stood it. He had run into far more dead ends in this case than she had. And you didn't hear him complaining.

She fervently hoped that the coroner's examination of the second body would tell them something.

Whoever was doing this had to be stopped! And they all knew it.

AFTER AN EXCELLENT LUNCH of fish and chips, Granville, Emily and Clara went to visit Rudolf Mayer, the real estate agent. From what Granville had picked up that morning, no-one in the village yet knew about the bodies in the cannery. He didn't have any more sense of racial tension in the village than he'd had the previous day.

But the realtor was a gossip. He'd be a good man to talk to.

Mayer was pleased to see them.

"Ah, Mr. Granville. And Miss Turner," he said, beaming at both of them. Though Granville noticed that the real estate agent gave Emily a wary look when he thought she wasn't looking.

The sparkle in her eyes told him she'd noticed. He did love her sense of humor.

"And this is...?" Mayer asked, turning to Clara.

Granville introduced her.

"It is indeed a pleasure, miss." Mayer said, bowing over her hand. "And what can I do for the three of you? Would you like to see any of the premises we looked at the other day again?"

"Yes, I would. Especially the chandlery and the general store, if that is possible?" Granville said.

"That shouldn't be a problem at all," he was assured.

"Good. But first, I'd like to know a little more about the business climate here. We're now two weeks past the strike. What are you hearing?"

Mayer glanced from Granville to Emily, then shook his head. "Truthfully? Very little. Except that the salmon run is a good one, and everyone from the canneries on down expect to make up most of what they lost during the strike."

"So business is good?"

"Yes."

"And there are no murmurs of discontent amongst the cannery workers? Or the fishermen?" Emily asked.

"Why do you ask?" Mayer said. "What have you heard? Are there problems?"

Evidently there were no rumors floating around, Granville thought. But Mayer was oddly worried about Emily's opinion. She must have really impressed him the other day.

"On the contrary," Emily assured him with a smile. "I've been very impressed by everything I've seen. But there is always something unseen that a prospective buyer of real estate should know about local conditions, but doesn't. I just wondered what that might be in Steveston."

Mayer did not look reassured, Granville noted. Nor did he rush to answer Emily. Who had asked an excellent question. And a surprisingly complex one.

He wondered when his fiancée had gained such wisdom about the real estate business. She hadn't learned it from their other real estate agent. Marshall was good, but not this subtle.

Clara, however, didn't look in the least surprised. She just glanced over at her friend and gave her an approving nod.

What had he missed?

"Well, yes, I suppose that is true," Mayer said at last. "And as I mentioned when last we met, Steveston does not have ready access to its markets."

"And it is dependent on fishing and agriculture," Granville added. "With most of the money coming from fishing, I believe?"

Mayer nodded. "Yes, that is true."

"So the value of businesses here depends in large part on the success of that year's catch?" Emily asked.

Mayer's lips tightened, but he nodded.

"Before you make a buying decision, we should talk to some of the cannery owners," Emily said to Granville. "Or perhaps the managers?"

"An excellent idea," Mayer said. "I can put you in touch with one or two of each, if you like?"

"Thank you," Granville said. "But I've already met Boyd from the Gulf of Georgia. He'll do for now. So, if we could start with the chandlery?"

The chandlery sold the same merchandise they'd seen at McGinty's, but it had a smaller selection of clothing. Granville and Mayer talked to the owner while Emily and Clara looked through a rack of clothing.

After much deliberation, Clara bought another pair of overalls, much to the owner's amusement. Meanwhile, Emily asked several excellent questions which confirmed that the store sold equally well to all the races, and that they ran a very profitable business.

Granville grinned as Emily left with a thoughtful look in her eye. He suspected that unless he was firmly set against it, he was going to end up owning this building too. He'd have to have a chat with his banker sometime soon.

Emily could be persuasive. And she did have an eye for a good real estate deal.

The general store, while interesting in its variety of goods, was less helpful. The few clothing items they did carry were clearly not as heavy as the fabric he and Ingram had found at the cannery on Wednesday morning.

By the time they finished, Granville had his answer. Little seemed to have changed in Steveston. Not the way it would have if rumors about the deaths at the Gulf of Georgia were spreading.

And Emily was looking pleased. She was up to something. He wondered what? And how much trouble it would get her—or him — into.

23

THURSDAY, AUGUST 16, 1900

On Thursday morning, Granville, Clara and Emily got off the tram in New Westminster. All three of them enjoyed the journey, which was both swift and smooth, at least when compared to the stagecoach journey to Steveston. Granville was particularly amused by Clara's glee, and the bantering between the two friends.

Both girls were dressed for the heat. Emily wore a pale green dress and her favorite white chip straw hat, both of which suited her and emphasized her slightly tilted green eyes. Clara was looking demurely angelic in a flattering lilac dress and a chip-straw hat with a lilac ribbon that made her eyes intensely blue. Looking at her, few would believe the stubborn will that had won out over even Emily's determination and resulted in their tram trip.

Clara had spent most of the journey enthusing about how much better the journey by tram was compared to taking the stagecoach. Emily reminded her that there was still a ferry journey downriver to Steveston ahead of them, but Clara—who apparently was prone to seasickness—ignored her. Granville chuckled to himself over the exchange.

He escorted the two women to a new tea shop Clara had heard about and been wanting to try, then strolled along Sixth Avenue to the coroner's office. Dr. Findler's clerk had left a message on Wednesday that the coroner was finished with his autopsy. Findler must have made the autopsy of the second victim a priority, to have finished so quickly. Good.

He'd considered asking Emily to join him at the coroner's today, since Constable Ingram was tied up with a robbery investigation and unable to join him. But the thought of the bloody mess they'd pulled out of the lye bath had quickly dissuaded him.

He couldn't get the image out of his own mind. He'd hate to be responsible for Emily having it stuck in hers. Having Clara along had provided the perfect excuse.

Even Emily couldn't build a convincing argument that included taking Clara to the morgue.

Dr. Findler met him at the door with an outstretched hand and a smile. Granville was relieved to see the fellow wasn't wearing the thin gloves he wore while he performed autopsies. The lab was spotless, and smelled of carbolic, not death. And there was no body on the examining table.

"I hear you're finished with our latest body?" Granville said.

Findler nodded. "And I have a bit more information this time, since you found the corpse so quickly. Poor fellow."

He walked towards a stack of large metal drawers Granville had noted on his previous visit, and hadn't wanted to ask about. It was where the low level hum was coming from.

The coroner pulled open one of the lower drawers. It gave off a blast of cold air—definitely refrigerated—and a faint reek of death. Bracing himself, Granville looked down to see what was left of the body they'd pulled from the lye bath on Tuesday night.

It had been cleaned up, and it was possible to see that the skeleton was intact. All the bones would be there. And much of the flesh remained.

Granville could feel Findler's eyes on his face. He was relieved when the coroner slid the drawer shut again.

"As you can see, I had much more to work with this time," Dr. Findler said. He walked across the room to a large metal desk with one manila folder and two brown paper bags with something in them sitting on its scrubbed top, pulled out a chair and sat down. He waved Granville to the other chair—also metal and rather uncomfortable—while he glanced through what must be his notes.

"Given that this man was also found in the lye bath at the Gulf of Georgia Cannery, it would seem likely that the deaths are related. This man is slightly taller, at just over five foot seven, than I estimated the first chap to be. He's also a lighter build, and younger. Late teens to early twenties, I'd say."

"Perhaps a boat owner and his crew?" Granville said, thinking aloud.

"Possibly. Is there a missing boat?"

"Not that we've found out about so far."

"Ah." Findler went back to his notes. "You'll be interested to hear that I found traces of bruising around what was left of the neck. And the hyoid was broken badly enough that I could feel it in the way the neck moved even before I did the autopsy."

"So he was strangled?"

"Yes."

Interesting. "Could we assume that the first man was also strangled?"

"I wish I could tell you that. But no, based on the bones, there is nothing to suggest he was strangled." The coroner looked up from his notes and smiled at Granville. "And nothing to suggest that he wasn't, either."

Granville nodded, appreciating the other man's respect for the facts. "Can you tell how long he's been dead?"

"I'm afraid not. That is a very inexact science, as you can imagine. And any signs I might have seen have been eradicated by that lye bath." He paused, closed the folder and folded his hands on top of it. "That is a very inventive murderer you're dealing with."

"Yes. I know. He's left us almost nothing to go on. But at least now we know that one, if not both, of our victims was strangled. That is progress."

"Yes, I suppose it is. I'm sorry I couldn't tell you more, though."

"I appreciate what you've given me. It can't be an easy job you have."

"No, but someone has to speak for the dead."

Granville nodded. That was how he'd come to feel about this case. Always before he'd sought the murderer to prove someone else innocent. This was the first time his real clients had been the murder victims themselves.

It was an unsettling difference.

"I can tell you that this fellow was definitely Oriental, though" the coroner said. "I had enough of his features to determine that. And I'd say he was Japanese, judging by fabric I found with what was left of his clothing."

He reached for the first paper bag, opened it, and laid some ragged bits of fabric on the desk. It looked remarkably similar to the torn-off scrap Ingram had found on the canning table. "The lye had dissolved most of his clothing, except for these bits. You can see this is a heavy cotton, probably some kind of overalls, the kind that many of the fishermen wear. Which tells us very little."

Granville pulled out the paper that held his scrap of fabric, unfolded it and showed it to the coroner. "It looks similar to this, which was found at the canner near the lye bath."

Dr. Findler bent forward and peered at the tiny bit of fabric. "It does look similar. May I?"

At Granville's nod he picked up a single thread with a pair of tweezers and placed it on a glass slide he drew out of one of the drawers in the table. He then carefully pulled a thread from one of the pieces of fabric from the paper bag, and placed it on the slide beside the first thread. Then he placed another, smaller piece of glass over the two threads, holding them flat.

Walking over to the counter, he placed the slide under a microscope and peered through the eyepiece.

"They look very similar," he said. "Definitely both cotton, and of a similar weight. But the color is slightly different. Come and see."

Granville strode over to the counter, and did as requested. He adjusted the focus slightly, and the two threads swum into view, every detail sharp. Looking closely, Granville could make out the twists of the thread, and way small filaments stood out like an aura around the thread. Both threads were the same.

Was it possible that the scrap of fabric they'd found had come from the victim's garments, and not those of the killer? "Does this mean they are from the same garment?" he asked.

"No. But it probably means both are from the same manufacturer," Dr. Findler said.

Then either the victim and the killer bought their garments from the same outlet—McGinty's, perhaps?—or several outfits carried the same brand. He would have to talk to Clara.

"Thank you," he said to Dr. Findler, who had handed back his thread. "Does the fabric tell you anything else?"

"This one does not," Dr. Findler said, returning the piece to the first paper bag.

"But this other one...," and he opened the second paper bag and drew out several pieces of fabric printed in indigo blue and white.

Dr. Findler carefully arranged them so they formed a rough square, approximately seven inches on each side. "This one tells me quite a bit."

Granville could see that it was a piece of printed cotton that had once been folded into quarters. There were ragged holes here and there where the lye had eaten into the fabric along what had been the folded edges, and the edges themselves were jagged where they'd separated. But the piece was remarkably well-preserved. "A handkerchief?"

"I think so."

Despite the holes, Granville could easily see that it was a lightweight cotton, printed in a lovely pattern of white chrysanthemums on an indigo background. The edges were carefully hemmed. Someone who loved the poor man had given him this handkerchief. A mother? A fiancée?

"He carried this in an inner pocket, carefully folded and wrapped," Dr. Findler said.

"Obviously it was important to him. Is that why the cloth is in such good shape?"

"Yes. I believe the fabric is Japanese. But you may be able to find someone who will tell you more in Steveston," Dr. Findler said.

Granville nodded. That was probably good advice. Perhaps even one of the Japanese wives, if he could find someone to translate.

He'd have to enlist Emily and Clara's help again. And Constable Ingram's.

"I'd need to borrow samples of each fragment from you," he said. "I promise they'll be well taken care of, and returned promptly."

Dr. Findler gave him a searching look, then nodded. "We need to stop this killer. I'll trust you with them. Mind that they're fragile after the lye, and will need to be handled carefully."

He opened another drawer and brought out a small envelope. Carefully placing a small piece of the first fabric inside, along with one of the quarters of the handkerchief, he handed the envelope to Granville.

"Thank you," Granville said as he tucked both into the pocket of his suit jacket. "I'll take good care of these."

"Yes, you will," the coroner replied.

Granville grinned at his tone, but nodded. "If this fellow was Japanese," he said, looking thoughtfully at the remaining segments of the blue and indigo printed cotton still spread on the table before them. "Then would you suggest that the owner of the bones was also Japanese?"

"Yes, I'd say so," Dr. Findler said. "Obviously I can't compare the bones, but the teeth share a number of similarities. And the wear pattern is similar as well—though much more developed on the first man, since he's the older—suggesting they ate a similar diet. Perhaps they even came from the same region."

Granville though of what Ingram had told him about the Japanese in Steveston mostly coming from Wakayama province, driven out by poverty. It fit.

"And this was in one of his pockets," Dr. Findler said, drawing out a metal disk and handing it to Granville. Who turned it over in his hands, studying both sides carefully.

"It didn't strike me as being identical to the first one," the coroner asked. "Though without comparing them, I couldn't be sure. Is it?"

"I don't believe so," Granville said, bringing the first one out and holding it next to the second one. He rubbed a thumb over the front face of the first disk, placed them side by side on the desk in front of the coroner. "See, the markings on this one are slightly different, don't you think?"

"Yes, I agree," the coroner said, bending forward to take a closer look.

"So the markings definitely have meaning," Granville said. And he'd have to find out what they meant.

Glancing at the coroner to make sure he'd finished his examination, Granville turned the second disk over, and considered the few scratches there. Looked at them more closely. "These markings aren't the same as on the reverse of the first one. When you looked under the microscope, did you find writing on this one, also?"

"No, I didn't. I believe the scratches on this one are random, gained through use, and not obscuring something written."

"Could you make me a copy of this one, as you did the other?"

"I have already done so," Dr. Findler said, drawing two plaster copies from the same drawer and handing them to Granville. "I believe this one is clear enough to be helpful?"

It was. The symbols on the copy stood out sharply, as they did on the original. "This one seems less worn than the other, wouldn't you say? Perhaps it is newer since the owner of it was younger?"

Dr. Findler turned the two disks over in his hand. "Yes, that seems accurate," he said. "Or at very least the first one had been carried loose in a pocket longer."

"So if our victims are both Japanese, these symbols are likely Japanese rather than Chinese?" Granville said.

"I know too little of the two languages to say for certain. But I suspect you're right." The coroner handed both disks to Granville. "I'd love to know what the disks are."

"I intend to find out," Granville said. "And I'll let you know when I do so. The killer is not going to get away with this."

"Good," said Dr. Findler. "Is there anything else I can help you with?"

"No, I don't believe so," Granville said. "Except—would it be too much trouble to make another set of copies of the coins? It would be very useful."

"Not a problem at all," Dr. Findler said. "I'd be happy to do so. If you can wait for them?"

Granville nodded.

Twenty minutes later, the new set of copies in hand, Granville was standing and shaking the man's hand. "You've been very helpful, indeed. But may I come back if I have further questions? Or if I find something that raises questions?"

"Of course," said Dr. Findler. "Come anytime. And I look forward to hearing that you've identified these poor men."

24

Emily leaned over the railing as the ferry *Transfer* cleared the harbor in New Westminster and moved out into open water. She leaned forward to see as far as possible down the open stretch of river that would take them to Steveston. The Fraser was flat and calm here, murky with the mud picked up on its long journey from the Interior.

She was hoping to see river otters, or possibly even a seal. She'd heard that they occasionally swam up-river on an incoming tide. As they got closer to the ocean, perhaps she'd even glimpse a porpoise, or the sleek black fins of a pod of killer whales, though it would be unusual to see either this close to shore.

She looked towards the hazy green of the far bank, spotting two bald eagles circling lazily over a tall pine. She'd just decided they must have a nest there, when Clara clutched her arm in excitement.

"Look there, Emily. Those dark specks there, in the river." And Clara pointed a little downriver. "Are those seals? There are quite a few of them."

As Emily's eyes followed her friends pointing finger, she spotted them too. "You're right, they are seals. They're wonderful," she said, as she watched their sleek dark heads bobbing in the waves as they dived and swum in circles around each other.

"They're playing. And I think they're showing off, too. Do you think they know we're here?"

"They seem to," Clara said, and they watched in silence for a time.

Then Granville rejoined them, and Emily turned to him eagerly. "We have time to talk now. How did it go with the coroner?"

Clara rolled her eyes, and Emily bit back a grin. She'd noticed that Clara had half-turned so she could watch the seals but still hear their conversation. Despite all her pretended disinterest.

Granville filled them in on the coroner's report. Emily suspected he'd spared them the more gruesome details, but he seemed to have told them everything that mattered.

"That poor man," she said when he'd finished, and had to stare hard at the river for a moment to keep the tears from welling up. "And someone who loves him has lost him."

"And they may never know how," Clara put in.

"We will find out," Emily said with certainty. "Granville would never leave a case like this unsolved."

He seemed about to say something, but then let it go. She considered asking, then decided it could wait until they were alone. "So there was a second disk found?" she said instead.

Granville nodded, and reached into his pocket. "Hold out your hand," he said.

She did so, and he dropped two disks into her palm, where they lay heavy and warm.

She turned first one and then the other over, then held them so they were side by side. "The symbols on the second disk are different from those on the first disk," she said.

"Yes, so I'd noticed. And the second disk is less worn, also. It's probably newer."

"It would be helpful to know what the different symbols mean. And why they are different on these two disks," she said. "Someone must be able to tell us."

"What a good thing we are headed for Steveston," Clara put in.

Emily caught Granville hiding a grin at her friend's words. It was lucky he had a strong sense of the ridiculous, since Clara seemed to be in a contrary mood today. "What are your plans?" she asked him.

"It will be some time before we dock, and by then I thought the two of you might appreciate a cup of tea. I'll go and see if Ingram can arrange for you to speak with one of the Japanese wives about the fabrics. I'm hoping he can arrange it by the time we finish lunch. If so, I'll meet with Boyd at the cannery while you two talk to her. Agreed?"

Emily nodded happily. "Yes, that makes great sense. Clara? What do you think?" she asked, turning to her friend.

"I think we should take the disks with us. We might be able to learn about more than fabrics, given the chance."

Emily was pleased when Granville handed the coins back to her with no hesitation. "That is an excellent idea," he said. "I'll still have the copies, if I need them. Just don't lose the originals."

"Of course not," Clara snapped. Then something caught her eye on the river and she turned fully to see what it was. "Oh, there's a family of otters on the bank. Look how cute they are."

Emily and Granville exchanged a smile over Clara's oblivious head.

"Between us, we'll find out who they are," she said softly. "I know we will."

<hr>

As he exited the Steveston café where he'd left Emily and Clara and walked along Chatham, Granville realized that he didn't even have to think about which direction to take. Perhaps he was finally starting to understand this place, at least a little. He barely even noticed the smell of the canneries. Turning left on Third Street, he headed for the police station—and ran into Ingram half a block before he got there.

"Granville! I didn't expect to see you today. Have you seen the coroner?"

"I have. If you have time, I'd be happy to brief you on his findings. And I have a favor to ask you, also."

"Whatever I can do," Ingram said. "The police station?"

"No, let me buy you a drink. It's too hot for coffee."

"Just a beer then. Thanks. How about the Troller? It's nearly deserted this time of day, so our meeting might go unnoticed."

"Lead the way."

As he followed Ingram into the Troller, Granville was surprised to find himself in such a dive. If the place had been on the Vancouver waterfront, Granville would have sworn he was walking into the Beaver Tavern—it was that rundown. Rough plank walls and a smoke-stained ceiling created an atmosphere completed by uneven tables with stools rather than chairs, and a sawdust floor that smelled of sour beer.

"What is this place?" Granville asked Ingram.

"Somewhere we wouldn't want to be after sundown," was the answer. "But the ale here is more than drinkable. And it's deserted at this time of day."

It was. Making it a very good choice for this meeting.

Once they were seated with brimming mugs in front of them, Ingram leaned forward. "What did the coroner have to say?"

Granville filled him in on Dr. Findler's conclusions.

When he finished, Ingram whistled softly. "So he's Japanese? And a fisherman?"

"Most likely."

"That won't be good news for the canneries."

"Not necessarily. It depends on who killed him. And more important, why? We still don't have answers to either."

"No, we don't. And Dr. Findler wasn't able to give us anything that might help?" Ingram asked.

"He gave us a couple of things. First is that he found another of the metal disks that was found on the first man." Granville handed one of the copies of the disk to Ingram. "Here's the first disk. And this one,"—as he handed it to him—"is the disk the coroner just found."

Ingram turned them over. "They're slightly different," he said, and handed them back.

Granville nodded. "And we need to know what they mean. Have you had any success in finding out whom in the Japanese community we might safely talk to about the murders?" he asked.

"Not yet, I'm afraid. It's a tricky situation," Ingram said. "But I'm getting closer."

"Good. However, I rather expected finding the right person would take some time. So I had the coroner make another set of copies," Granville put a second set of copies on the table, pushed it towards the young constable. "Those are yours."

Ingram looked up and grinned. "Mine? You want me to ask people about them?"

"Yes. It's time to start asking about them. And we'll get farther if we both do so," Granville said. "As long as we don't let on that the owners were Japanese, or that they're dead."

"Yes, I know. I'll keep the secret for you."

It wasn't for him that the secret needed keeping, but Granville let the comment pass. Ingram was still green—he'd learn.

"Though if the disks are Japanese too," Ingram said, "That won't stay secret for long."

"Doesn't need to," Granville said with a grin. He brought out the bag the coroner had also given him, and laid out the fabric scraps on top of it. "Because now we have more to go on. These were also found on the second body. One seems to be part of his clothing. The other a handkerchief or similar."

Ingram bent forward to see them.

"Do you recognize the blue and white pattern?" Granville asked.

"Only enough to know it is Japanese," Ingram said. "Why?"

"The coroner suggested that one of the Japanese wives might be able to help," Granville said. "That is the favor. Would you be able to set up a meeting?"

"I doubt they'd talk to us," Ingram said.

"Not to us," Granville told him. "To my fiancée and her friend. You met both of them the other day."

Ingram looked thoughtful. He took long enough to respond that Granville began to feel impatient. "Surely it can't be that difficult," he finally said.

"We can't afford to make things worse with the Japanese community just now," Ingram said. "But since it is your fiancée… And since they aren't talking about murder—they won't will they?"

Granville shook his head. "They will be talking about fabric. Miss Miles in particular has a passion for it."

"Oh, well in that case, I'm sure it will be fine. I will need to give them a few pointers about the culture first, of course."

"Of course," Granville said. He'd have to warn Emily. Otherwise he suspected she wouldn't take Ingram's pompous tone kindly. Which might have been amusing, except that they couldn't afford to lose the young constable's help.

"I'll let you know when I've set it up," Ingram was saying, oblivious to Granville's reaction.

"Actually, Emily and Clara are here in Steveston today. We all took the boat down from New Westminster. Is there any possibility of setting up something for this afternoon?"

"This afternoon? Well, that's—let me see what I can do. Where can I find you?"

"We'll be lunching at the White Horse." Which was the café in the building he was considering purchasing. According to Emily, the food was supposed to be good there. As was the local gossip. He didn't know how she'd found out, but he trusted that her source would have been a good one.

"Who knows what we might learn?" she'd said, leaning into him as the ferry crested a wave. How could he resist?

Ingram nodded. "I'll find you there."

"Thank you. One last question before I go. Would Monday night be a good night to pay a return visit to the cannery?"

Ingram thought for a moment, then smiled. "Yes, I think so. What time?"

"Around eight, if the cannery shuts down at six as they've been doing. We can meet here. And I must go," Granville said, glancing at the wall clock and downing the last of his beer.

He had lunch plans, and a less than capable cannery manager to see.

E mily glanced up to see Constable Ingram stepping into the White Horse just as she, Clara and Granville were finishing lunch. He joined them with a smile, and accepted a cup of coffee. "Miss Turner. Miss Miles. It's nice to see you again. How was the boat trip from New Westminster?"

"Very smooth," Clara said, with a side glance at Emily. Clara wasn't budging on her refusal ever to take the stage again, and she wasn't letting Emily forget it. "It is nice to see you again, also, Constable Ingram."

Emily watched the young constable's cheeks flush a little. He seemed a nice man, but he didn't have the core of toughness of the other policemen she'd met. Which probably came from seeing too much, and she suspected Constable Ingram hadn't been a policeman for very long. Though Granville said he had good instincts.

And he certainly seemed pleased to help.

"Were you able to arrange everything on such short notice?" she asked him.

"Yes indeed. Mrs. Sakamoto is very pleased to meet with you. She hasn't been in Steveston that long, you know, so has little

English. Your conversation may be a little awkward. But she seemed pleased for the company."

They quickly finished their tea and coffee, and left with Ingram.

Ingram ushered Emily and Clara out along Moncton Street, talking all the while. "Mr. Sakamoto has been fishing here since the 1890's," the young constable said. "He went home and brought back his wife and family last year. He had built a small house for her near the river. She's already begun a garden, though it must take her hours to water it in this heat, when she has to carry it by hand from the river."

He turned down First Street and then along Dyke Road. Emily noted the haphazard wooden buildings in the huge lots behind all the canneries. Occasionally a slight wind brought the scent of baking Indian bread or cooking rice, slipping under the pervading stench of the canneries. She tried to imagine what it must be like to live in one of those rickety buildings, and couldn't.

"One thing you'll need to remember is that the Japanese like to give gifts to their guests," Ingram was saying. "They would be most hurt if those gifts were not accepted. It would be seen as an insult."

Emily nodded, but her eyes were busily taking in a steep roofed longhouse that looked as if it belonged somewhere wilder, not crammed in between a bunkhouse and what seemed to be a cooking shed behind yet another cannery.

They kept walking

EMILY HAD BEGUN to think the canneries would never end, though there were still several more on the horizon when Ingram turned off the wooden walkway and entered one of the back lots. He headed towards a cluster of small wooden houses along a rough dirt lane. Emily and Clara had to watch their step carefully, or risk tripping.

As they approached one small house, with a gabled roof of cedar shakes and a white painted door, Emily thought she'd love to live in a little house like this. It was hard to believe that more than two people actually lived here.

"It's so sweet," Clara whispered to her.

Constable Ingram opened the gate in the white picket fence for them, and they walked into the garden. The path under their feet was soft with mulch, and wound through the garden to the front door. And what a garden it was!

Huge leafy mounds of zucchini and another squash Emily didn't know were covered with trumpet-shaped yellow blooms. The pole beans had smothered their trellis and spread to the fence, and rows of spinach and kale grew tall and proud. Bees buzzed amongst bright red zinnias and orange nasturtiums, the air was sweet with the scent of phlox, and great yellow sunflowers stood sentry around the plot.

As Emily gazed on the garden in delight, the front door opened, revealing a short, slight woman with straight dark hair pulled back into a tight bun. Her hair was so dark that it gleamed in the sun like polished ebony. She wore a kimono in dark blue with white embroidery, and a shy smile. She bowed towards them.

"Welcome," she said carefully.

Emily gave her a nod that was half a bow, and a smile in return. "Thank you for inviting us," she said clearly.

Constable Ingram stepped forward and introduced them.

"Please," said Mrs. Sakamoto with a shy smile. "Come in."

"I will leave you here," Constable Ingram said. "I wouldn't be welcome inside, not with her husband away. Can you find your way back? Or would you like me to collect you at three or so?"

"I think we can find our own way back," Emily said, after a glance at Clara, who nodded. Neither of them wanted to shorten their visit—and the chance to learn something about another way of life—just to fit in with Constable Ingram's schedule.

"Very well. The *Transfer* sails at five o'clock, don't forget," he said as he departed.

As if she would. Besides, Granville was expecting them at four-thirty. Which gave them plenty of time to visit, Emily decided.

Mrs. Sakamoto opened the door behind her and invited them into the house.

Inside the tiny house was spotless, and smelled faintly of lye soap, which Emily found ironic, given the nature of the deaths that were their real reason for visiting. There was very little furniture, just four wooden chairs and a simple table, but they were all carefully hand built and gleaming with polish.

The small windows were curtained with cheerful blue and white cloth, pulled back now to let the sun in. A small white vase full of red zinnias on the table glowed in the light. A few dust motes danced in the stream of sunshine.

Mrs. Sakamoto motioned them to chairs with a little bow, and asked if they would like tea.

"Yes, please," Emily said. "Tea would be welcome. It is so hot out."

Mrs. Sakamoto returned shortly and arranged three delicate cups and saucers and plates on the table, all with a pattern of delicate pink cherry blossoms. Ten minutes later she returned with a matching teapot and a plate of delicate cookies shaped like blossoms. She placed the cookies in front of her guests and the teapot in front of her own chair. Then she sat down with a smile and poured the tea.

Emily took a cautious sip of the pale green liquid. It was much lighter than any green tea Mama had ever served. She rather expected it to be flavorless, but to her surprise, it was delicious, with a fresh green flavor that tasted like grass looked in early spring, so vibrantly alive.

"It's very good," she said to their hostess.

Mrs. Sakamoto smiled. "I am glad," she said. "Please, try?" and passed them the plate of cookies.

Emily accepted one to be polite and took a small bite. It was even better than the tea, sweet and delicate at the same time. "This is very good."

Clara glanced at her, then took one also. When she tasted it, her eyes lit up. "These are wonderful," she said.

"You like another?"

"Oh yes, please," Clara said, as she took a second cookie. "These are too good not to have seconds."

A short discussion of how the cookies were baked, and how she'd grown such an amazing garden, followed. Emily couldn't quite believe how good the Japanese woman's English was, but it had to be tiring for her to discuss complicated topics. And she suspected it wouldn't be considered very impolite to raise the topic of murder while they were enjoying their tea.

"Now, how can I help?" Mrs. Sakamoto asked when they'd finished their tea.

"We wanted to ask you about several disks, and a piece of cloth that was found. May we show you?" Emily asked.

Mrs. Sakamoto nodded, and Clara drew the two pieces of fabric from their protective wrappings. Their hostess fingered first one, then the other fragment of cloth, her expression intent. After a moment she picked up the first piece, the small scrap of heavy, pale cotton fabric.

"My husband have coverall like this. Same..." and she made a gesture towards her hand, then rubbed the fabric slowly between her fingers.

"Feel?" Clara suggested.

Mrs. Sakamoto nodded. "Yes."

"Where does your husband buy his coveralls, Mrs. Sakamoto?" Emily asked.

"In Steveston. At McGinty's," the woman answered, stumbling slightly over the name.

Clara and Emily exchanged glances. "And the other?" Clara asked.

Mrs. Sakamoto picked up the small square of blue and white, rubbing her thumb gently over it. "This—gift. To lovely man."

To a loved one, she meant. Very much what Emily had thought herself when Granville first showed it to her.

Before she could ask another question, Mrs. Sakamoto continued. "This made by hand. See work on hem? Pattern is one used in my town."

"Where is your town?" Emily asked her.

"Mio. In Wakayama. Most men here—from there," she said with a gesture that somehow made Emily feel how very far away their hostess's homeland was.

But it meant that their victims likely had been from the same area of Japan, Emily thought. Granville would be very interested in this bit of information.

"Can you tell me any more about this fabric?" Clara asked.

"Is *hankachi*."

"Handkerchief," Emily suggested.

"Yes. Much valued." She touched the tiny hemming stitches gently. "He mourn loss."

He could no longer mourn anything, Emily thought sadly. But she couldn't tell this gentle woman that, even if Granville hadn't sworn her to secrecy.

And they had another tiny bit of information. With enough of them, they might even solve this horrid crime. Emily withdrew the two iron disks Granville had given her that morning, and passed them to her hostess. "Can you tell me anything about these?" she asked.

Gently weighing them in her palm, Mrs. Sakamoto turned them over with a careful finger. Her expression turned sad.

"These also sold in my town. Other cities, too. These Buddhist tokens. This one," and her finger prodded at the newer on. "For protection. This..." the more worn one, "for honor."

She moved her palm in a small up and down motion, as if feeling the weight of the disks for a moment more, then her eyes met Emily's. "These men, they are dead?" she asked.

Emily nodded. "Yes. I'm sorry, but they are."

Mrs. Sakamoto nodded back. "Yes. Very sad." She carefully handed the disks back to Emily.

"We are helping in the investigation," Emily said. "My fiancé will not stop until he learns the names of these lost men, and the name of their killer."

Mrs. Sakamoto nodded. "Is good."

"Is there any way to connect these disks to their owner?" Emily asked.

"No, sorry." Mrs. Sakamoto said after a moment's pause. "Too many sold to tell one."

Emily had suspected as much. She paused, considering how to ask. "We have told no-one of these disks. Would you—will you honor our secret until the killer is found?"

"Yes. Yes." Mrs. Sakamoto said immediately.

Emily thanked Mrs. Sakamoto sincerely.

As they rose to go, their hostess removed the red zinnias from their vase and wrapped them in a lovely piece of blue and white cloth. "*Hankachi*. For you," she said, presenting them to Emily.

Emily began to protest, then remembered that Constable Ingram had explained that guest gifts were part of the Japanese tradition, and their hostess would be offended if an offered gift was refused.

So she smiled instead. "These are very beautiful, as is your garden," she said, touching the bright petals softly, then the cloth. "And I will always value this."

Mrs. Sakamoto gave her a bright smile and bowed. Emily and Clara bowed in return.

"Come again," Mrs. Sakamoto said.

Emily nodded. She'd love to come back to visit. She just hoped it wouldn't be because they'd found another body.

26

Once Emily and Clara had left with Ingram, Granville paid the bill for their lunch, leaving him with the afternoon free to meet with Boyd at the Monster Cannery. He laughed a little at the name. The double meaning had become uncomfortably apt as the investigation proceeded.

The cannery manager looked startled and none too pleased to see Granville. "You're back?" he said. Then Boyd's face brightened. "You caught him!"

"No, I'm afraid not. But we now suspect that both of the dead men were Japanese. They were likely fishermen. And they knew each other."

Boyd's face paled. "We have two dead Japanese fishermen? In our cannery?" He stood up and paced to the window and back, before thumping back into his chair.

"And you have no idea who the murderer is?" Boyd gave Granville what he undoubtedly intended to be an accusing look. He actually looked rather dyspeptic.

"I'm afraid not," Granville said, stifling a smile, and ignoring for the moment the unsaid, "Then what good are you?" behind the cannery manager's expression.

"So now what happens?"

"I will be briefing Alexander Ross-Murray later this afternoon." And he rather suspected that Ross-Murray would be anxious to hear his results.

"Oh? That's all?"

"Of course not. We'll continue our investigation. There are difficulties, however. The bodies fished out of your lye bath haven't exactly given us much to go on."

"I suppose not. But you have a second one, now."

"Which is why we can say that both men were most likely Japanese."

Boyd stared at him. "And nothing more?"

"No. Which is why I came here this afternoon. To ask you for that list of fishermen who deliver to the cannery on a regular basis. And the list of those who delivered the day of each murder."

The cannery manager reached for a glass paperweight shaped like a salmon, ran a thumb over its glossy scales. "Dirks has them," he said. Not looking up.

"You didn't ask him for them?"

"Of course I did," Boyd said. Hands busy with the paperweight. "But he just keeps forgetting."

"Forgetting," Granville repeated.

Boyd reddened, shrugged. Put down the paperweight. "It's clear to both of us that he never intends to produce it."

"And why would that be?"

"I don't know."

Was afraid to know, more likely, Granville thought.

The cannery manager met Granville's eyes. His own looked defeated. "It's—a game Dirks plays. It doesn't mean anything. And I —I pick my battles."

Granville wondered if Boyd really believed that. "So you don't think he's involved?"

"In the murder? Dirks? No. Impossible."

Right. "Regardless, at this point in our investigation, it is critical that there be no rumors about the finding of the bodies."

Boyd flushed slightly and fiddled with a pencil on his desk.

"Have you heard something?"

Boyd didn't look up.

Granville knew what that meant. "Who did you talk to?"

"Me? I didn't..." began Boyd indignantly, then met Granville's eyes. "Just Dirks," he said. Then, defensively, "He needed to know."

Right. Of course he did. "When?"

"Yesterday afternoon." Boyd's voice was weak.

"Could you ask him to join us here, please?"

While Boyd was off on his errand, Granville scribbled a quick note to Scott, and sealed it. He'd have someone give it to Trent later. He needed to meet with both of them, and the sooner the better.

He'd just tucked the note into his pocket when Boyd returned with Dirks.

"Dirks," Granville said.

"Granville."

"Why don't you both have a seat?" Granville said.

Boyd tried to give him an angry look, then quickly looked away.

Dirks just looked from one to the other with a smirk that he didn't even try to hide.

Granville smiled. "I have some questions," he said.

"You..." Boyd began, then thought better of it. "He has questions for you," he barked at Dirks. Who slouched even further in his chair.

"I gather Boyd told you about our second murder," Granville said. "Have you heard any gossip about it?"

Dirks shook his head. But he didn't lose the smirk.

"Has anyone mentioned a couple of missing men?"

Another head shake.

"Did you tell anyone?" Granville threw the words at him. He wondered again whether Dirks had deliberately left the cannery unlocked the other evening. And what the fellow was really up to. Was this their murderer?

"I just asked my line supervisors some questions," Dirks said. He shrugged and Boyd scowled at him.

"Well, we need to know if someone's missing," Dirks said as if Boyd had asked a question. "You told me he needed help, Boss. How'm I supposed to help if I can't ask questions?"

The smirk was back. Granville wanted to knock it off his face. But violence wouldn't serve now.

"I'm meeting with Alexander Ross-Murray tomorrow," Granville said. "He'll have to be briefed on the progress of my investigation so far. And the kind of help I've been receiving here."

The smirk vanished. And Boyd looked ill.

"So, did your line supervisors have any answers for you?" Granville asked.

"Nah. They didn't know a thing," Dirks said.

"And I trust you swore them to secrecy?"

"Well, I told them to be careful."

"What?"

"Who they talked to, y'see. And what they asked. When they asked around."

"Asked around," Granville repeated. He turned to Boyd. "You can assume the whole cannery knows by now."

Boyd's eyes widened, and he pursed his lips. "But I—I never— he..." He shut up, and glared at Dirks. "You weren't supposed to say anything."

"Then how d'you think this'll get solved? He isn't going to do it. He doesn't know the first thing about canneries."

"That's enough," Boyd barked. "Get back to your job. And I don't want to hear about you talking to anyone else. Or I might decide you don't know anything about the cannery business either."

Dirks smirked at Boyd—leaving Granville to wonder what the foreman had on his manager. Then he sauntered out of the room, closing the door softly behind him.

"He's a fool," Boyd said, raising his hands helplessly. "I certainly didn't tell him to do all that."

Not directly, perhaps. But Granville had a pretty good idea what the fellow had said. And it was neither complimentary nor helpful to the investigation.

"Well, you'd best make sure that the rumors are contained as quickly as possible," he said. "And that it doesn't get out that the victims are Japanese. Or this cannery will be shut down and you'll both be out of work."

Boyd's mouth flapped like a fish, but Granville didn't wait to hear what he might have to say. He strode back into the outer office. "Trent?" he said to the clerk.

"Outside," was the answer.

Which seemed odd, until he found Trent sitting on a weathered wooden railing, sipping a soda and staring at the river.

"Granville!" the lad said when he noticed him headed his way. "I was hoping I'd see you."

"And why is that?" Granville asked, handing Trent the note he'd written earlier. "Get that to Scott, would you?

"Sure thing," Trent said. "And because the place is full of rumors today. Everyone knows about the two deaths."

"They know where the bodies were found?"

"Not that I've heard. And nobody seems to know who they are, either."

"Well that's something, at least. Thanks—and keep your ears open. I need to know what's being said. But get that to Scott now, and I'll see you both later."

Trent grinned broadly. "We're meeting again? Good."

He gulped down the last of his soda, and hopped off the railing. "I'm on it."

GRANVILLE CONSULTED HIS POCKET WATCH—PLENTY of time to talk with the bookkeeper before Emily and her friend were due back. He turned back into the Monster Cannery and made his way down the hall to the bookkeeper's dark little office. Leon Grazzini looked up from his stacks of paper when the door creaked open.

"Mr. Granville," he said with a smile. "What can I do for you?"

"Just Granville is fine," he said as he edged his way into the cramped room.

Grazzini inclined his head. "Call me Leon. Now please, sit."

And he waved Granville to a chair, then turned his wheelchair to face him. "Don't know how long there'll be air in here. Not with you as well as me," Leon said, keeping a straight face as he gestured around the small room. "So, what can I do for you? Best tell me before we both die from lack of oxygen."

It was an unfortunate choice of words, Granville thought. Unless he was playing with him. "I just have a few questions for you, if you would."

"Of course. How can I help?"

"You said you've been working here since the cannery opened?" Granville said.

"That's right."

"Then you'll know a lot about how it operates."

"Not really. I only know it on paper, on the reports that come through that door," he said. "This chair isn't welcome on the canning floor."

"I know a few bankers who are convinced that the numbers always tell the real story," Granville said. "And that everything else is a distraction."

Leon shrugged, gave him a sideways glance. "Well, bankers. They would say that."

Which was true enough. "Yet if they're right, it means you should be the one person here that really knows what is going on."

"This why you've come to see me again?" Leon said, with a surprisingly deep laugh. "You'll be disappointed, I think."

"Well, I do have some questions about the reports," Granville said slowly, as if thinking it through.

"Yes?" Leon leaned forward in his chair, his expression open.

"How do the reports for the owners get put together every month?"

"Well, Mr. Boyd does that. I just put pages of figures together for him. Like I always have. Like I used to do for Mr. Owen, you know."

"So you're using Owen's system? Boyd just follows it?"

"Well, yes, I guess so," Leon said with a shrug. "It works, doesn't it? Why change it?"

Interesting. "So where do you get the figures you give to Boyd?"

"From Dirks. He keeps track of how much fish is bought, what's paid out for it, and when."

"And you get those figures from him every month?"

"Ev'ry month. Like clockwork."

"And give them to Boyd for his reports."

"Yup. Just like always."

So why was Boyd not getting the figures Granville had asked for? Or was the cannery manager more devious than he appeared? "Do you ever have trouble getting the reports from Dirks?" Granville asked.

"Nah. Well, sometimes he's a few hours late…"

A few hours? That was all? "And can you tell if the records he gives you have been changed?"

Leon shrugged. "It's all in pencil, and it's a holy mess when I get it."

"And does Owens ever complain?"

"Mr. Owens? No. He stops by now and again. Thanks me for the job I'm doing."

Owens did? The cannery owner had struck Granville as shrewd enough to notice if there were problems. Especially if he had set up the system for the monthly reports in the first place. "You've been doing this work a long time," he said to the bookkeeper. "Everything look right to you?"

Leon gave him a long look, shrugged. "The numbers work, same as always. Beyond that? They got nothing to worry about. These wheels of mine don't exactly work too well down on the docks, now do they? I can't very well go count fish. Or stacks of cans."

His look, combined with his words, told Granville that fellow did know something was wrong. Or suspected it, at least. But whatever it was clearly didn't show up in the numbers. Owens would have been looking for anything off.

"Anything in particular you can tell me?" Granville asked. "And Leon? We're looking for a killer."

Leon's face was pale in the dim light of his office. "I've heard that. And no, I have nothing that would help you. All I hear is rumors. And the occasional commotion in the hallway."

And he gestured towards the closed door behind them.

"Oh?" Granville said.

"Hmmm." Leon's chin sunk to his chest for a moment, as if his head had grown too heavy for him to hold up. Then he raised his face, met Granville's eyes. "It's no secret that Dirks and Boyd don't get along. Or who is the strong one of the two. And the numbers?" He paused.

"Go on," Granville said.

"The numbers are good," the bookkeeper said.

"But?"

"But they show too little change from year to year."

"How do you mean?"

Leon shrugged. Reached into a drawer in his desk and, after some shuffling of paper, brought out a single sheet, and handed it to Granville.

Who examined the neatly written columns of numbers. It seemed a very straightforward accounting of total sales and total costs over a five year span. The numbers were big, but there was a substantial profit every year. What was he missing? He looked inquiringly at Leon.

"Ask a bookkeeper," Leon said, correctly interpreting the look. "He'll tell you. Profits don't stay so close to the same year to year. Some go up. Sometimes a lot, sometimes not. Other numbers go down. Same thing. Overall it might look much the same. But it shouldn't be, if you look at the detail."

He glanced over his shoulder as if expecting to see someone. "Here at the Monster? Even the detailed numbers don't change enough."

"You're saying someone is copying the previous year's numbers to hide what is happening this year?" Granville said.

"I'm saying the numbers show too little change from year to year. Listen to what I say. Talk to a bookkeeper. Show him that."

Granville nodded. He'd do that. And he knew just the man. Mac McAndrews was probably due for a new challenge, anyway. "Thank you. I will," he said, and took his leave.

27

It was nearly four-thirty and Granville was checking his watch when Emily and Clara returned to the cafe, slightly out of breath. The visit had taken longer than Emily had anticipated.

"I'm sorry we took so long," she told Granville before he could say anything. Bracing herself for the complaints about her lack of timeliness she was used to from her family. "We're ready to go. And I have news."

He grinned. "You're right on time. Let's get ourselves to the dock, then the two of you can fill me in."

Tucking her hand in his arm, Emily beamed at him. She kept forgetting he was different. And she loved him for it. "How did your afternoon go?"

"Not well," he said. "Though I think I finally might be making progress."

But in the chaos of loading and departure, Emily didn't get to ask the questions his provocative statement raised. It wasn't until they were standing on the rear deck watching the canneries of Steveston slip away behind them that they had a moment of quiet.

"How can there be so many canneries?" Clara asked in awe,

wrinkling her nose at the smell they hadn't quite left behind. "I count at least seven. Surely they must run out of fish."

"There's a lot of money to be made in canning," Granville said. "There are twelve canneries now, with several more under construction. And the sockeye salmon runs are phenomenal. There's no shortage of fish. From what I understand, even thirteen canneries running flat out will not be enough to handle the volume of fish expected in next year's run."

"So many?" Clara just shook her head, her eyes fixed on the receding cannery town.

"But tell me," Emily said, unable to restrain her curiosity any longer. "What have you learned? You talked to the cannery manager, didn't you?"

"I did. And he's talked to the wrong person about our investigation. It isn't much of a secret anymore."

Emily considered that for a moment. So he was saying "the jig is up" as the detective stories liked to put it? Then why was he not more upset? She would have been furious.

Granville laughed. "Your expression, Emily."

Clara spun away from the view to stare at the two of them. "What? What?"

"Emily knows that I'm not nearly angry enough at this betrayal," Granville said to Clara. "And she's trying to work out why."

Emily nearly laughed herself at Clara's expression as her friend looked from Granville to Emily and back.

"He really loves you, Emily," Clara said at last in a low tone.

Emily nodded. He understood her too. She still couldn't quite believe it. "I know. But I still can't work out why he's so calm about it."

She paused, considered Granville's expression once more. "Except that this has confirmed something for you, hasn't it? Whoever leaked the secret, you're now sure you can't trust him. And that he's tied into this murder somehow. That's it, isn't it? You have a lead?"

He grinned at her. "That's it. A tenuous one at the moment,

because I can't yet see how it will all tie together—not without knowing who our victims are. But I have a lead."

Emily smiled back at him. "Then perhaps this will help. Clara and I spoke with Mrs. Sakamoto, and she was very helpful. She recognized the disks as Buddhist tokens, as we'd suspected. They are Japanese, and common in her part of Japan. She says the symbol on the disk with the worn edges is for honor, and the symbol on the newer one for protection."

Clara had moved a little away, to give them privacy, but at Emily's words, she turned back to them.

"And the cotton scrap is typical of overalls or trousers the Japanese fishermen would wear," Clara said. "We have the names of several stores where they might shop. Including McGinty's. And even more important…"

Here she stopped and glanced at Emily. "You tell it."

Emily shook her head. "Go ahead."

Clara beamed at her. "Most of the fishermen living here came from the same province in Japan. And even the same city. Mio."

"They're that closely linked?" Granville asked.

Emily and Clara both nodded.

"Mio is in Waka—Wakayama province," Emily said carefully. "And she said that the blue and white cloth is definitely from a handkerchief, which would have been made for him by a mother or a sweetheart."

She stopped, and swallowed back the lump that thought unexpectedly brought to her throat. "She—she guessed he was dead. But she promised to keep it secret. And she has offered to answer any other questions we might have."

"That is excellent work, both of you," Granville said. "And if the Japanese community is that inter-related, it should help us find out who the dead men are."

"Yes, but who do you suspect might be a killer?" Clara said.

Emily watched as Granville's eyes swept the deck around them. No-one was close enough to hear. Nor were the other passengers paying them much attention. Most had gone inside, the river journey a routine part of their lives.

He turned back. "The cannery foreman, Dirks, is clearly up to something," Granville said to them, including both Emily and Clara in his words. "He has little respect for his boss, and I've suspected for some time that he is stealing from the cannery. At best."

"He's the one that leaked information about the investigation," Emily guessed.

"He is indeed."

"And you think he's involved in the murders?" Emily asked.

"Yes. I'm not sure how deeply. But Scott and I need to be paying a great deal of attention to him and what he's up to. I also have something else that might prove to be a lead. Or it might be nothing."

He drew the folded page of figures the bookkeeper had given him out of his jacket pocket and passed it to Emily. Who turned her back so the wind couldn't catch it and unfolded it carefully.

"What is this?" she asked.

"The cannery bookkeeper gave it to me, and suggested I show it to a bookkeeper."

"Mr. McAndrews?" Emily asked.

"That's what I was thinking."

Her eyes scanned the page. "He thinks this is evidence of fraud, then? The bookkeeper, I mean."

His fiancée didn't miss much. "Or at least an indication of it, from the little he was willing to tell me. His argument is that the profits should increase more, from one year to the next."

"That makes sense," Emily said. "Though this seems to be just a summary of costs and sales for each of the last five years? I don't see how he can tell how much profit should increase, much less spot a fraud from only the figures he's written here."

"That was my reaction, too," Granville said. "I'm looking forward to hearing what McAndrews has to say, though."

Emily nodded. She glanced over at Clara, who had turned back to the view—clearly not interested in a page of figures—and handed the page back to Granville. "If the bookkeeper gave you this information willingly, then he is likely not involved in whatever is going on at the cannery?"

"Or he is much trickier than most of the fellows I deal with," Granville said with a grin.

"I wonder which it will prove to be," Emily said thoughtfully, as she turned a little to watch the scenery flow past.

2 8

Granville sat behind his desk, toying with a pen-wipe. It was just past eight, and the building was nearly deserted. Emily and Miss Kent had gone home long ago, but he'd wanted time to think through the cannery case.

He'd already mailed the list of figures Leon had given him to McAndrews, with a note explaining the circumstances, and asking for his thoughts on it. The accountant should have it tomorrow.

Now he was waiting for Scott. And hoping that his partner would get here before he had to leave for his meeting with Ross-Murray. Which he was not looking forward to.

He looked up at the sound of footsteps in the hall, echoing in the mostly empty building. He knew those heavy steps. Striding to the doorway, he looked into the outer office just as a key scratched in the lock and the door to the hallway was flung inwards.

"You made good time," Granville said as Scott strode in. "You sailed here?"

His friend was wearing rough tweed trousers with a wilted shirt of heavy cotton, and the reek of the canneries overlaid by fresh sea air. His eyes were tired and his hands bore the fresh marks of heavy rope work. He didn't look like he'd slept.

Scott nodded. "A bit of wind came up about three so we left as soon as the canning line shut down."

Trent crowded in behind Scott. He didn't look much better than Scott did.

"Am I glad to see you two," Granville said.

"Well, that's good," Scott said with a grin. "Missed us, did you?"

"Not at all," Granville said with a straight face. "But I think I might have the beginning of a lead on this case. I need to know what you two have heard at the cannery."

"Mind if I sit, first?" Scott said, suiting action to words.

That earned him a grin. "If you must," Granville said. "Trent, pull up a chair."

He pulled the whiskey bottle from his bottom drawer, poured drinks for the three of them. " So, how bad are the rumors from the cannery now?"

"Everyone is talking about the two murders," Trent said. "And they know most of the details."

He groaned. "I was afraid of that. Dirks is a fool."

"No argument there," Scott said.

"So what exactly do people know?" Granville asked.

"They know there's two bodies been found, and some of them have figured out they was in the lye vat," Scott said. "People also know the victims haven't been identified yet."

"I had a few people tell me that the Cannery Association's hired someone to look into it," Trent said.

"Worse, some of those I spoke with know it's our firm's been hired. And why," Scott added. "They haven't figured out who I am, though. Not yet, anyhow."

It had grown worse since he talked to Dirks, then. Granville cursed the fellow roundly. He'd learned a few choice phrases in the Yukon that were uniquely appropriate for this moment.

Scott grinned at him. Trent looked impressed.

"Well, there goes any possibility of keeping a lid on this situation," Granville said. "Anyone mention a missing man? Or men?"

"Nothing I heard," Scott said.

"Me neither," Trent said.

"What about theories?"

"Lots of em," Trent said.

Scott nodded. "Especially conspiracy theories. Mostly they don't trust the cannery owners, think they're up to something."

"Not surprising, after that strike," Trent put in. "I had four people tell me how awful it was when they brought in the militia."

"The sad thing is, no-one seems to know anything," Scott said. "Which is kinda good, when you think about it. At least they're not planning a riot."

"I'm glad to hear it," Granville said. "Though it's faint consolation. When I heard that Dirks had been stupid—or cunning—enough to tell his line supervisors, I'd hoped that at least the resultant gossip would give us a lead."

"Guess not," Trent said. "And I think me or Scott would have heard." He gulped some whiskey, choked, and fell into a coughing fit.

"Slowly. This is a decent brand. You're supposed to savor it," Granville said dryly.

"I'm wondering if there's any point in our staying working at the cannery," Scott said. "Since the deaths are out in the open now, we could just ask people questions."

"I'd considered that," Granville said. "I'm planning to go back and ask a few questions myself, now that I can do so openly. It would be good to have you with me."

And to have the two of them out of the plant, and away from Dirks. Who might or might not be a murderer. But who was definitely dangerous.

"Me too?" Trent asked.

"Of course," Granville said. Trent beamed.

"But you said you had a possible lead?" Scott said. "Who?"

"Dirks. He's up to something. At best he's stealing from the cannery. At worst? This latest move of his has me suspecting that the murders are connected to whatever it is he's up to. What do you think?"

Scott nodded slowly. "Could be. He has too much power at the cannery, that's for sure."

"And everyone's afraid of him," Trent added. "Him and his bullies."

"Bullies?" Granville repeated.

Trent and Scott both nodded. "A few of the line supervisors," Trent said. "If Dirks is around, they're never far away. They're his muscle."

"How many?" Granville asked.

"Two for sure. Maybe a third," Scott said. "Enforcers."

Granville knew exactly what he meant. They'd run into the type on the creeks of the Klondike. Big, strong men, with little conscience, who took orders from someone else. "Killers?"

"I wouldn't doubt it," Scott said.

"What about Dirks himself?"

"He looks like a coward to me."

Granville agreed—that was his own read on the man. "Hence the enforcers."

"Yeah."

"He'll bear watching," Granville said. "What do you know about these enforcers of his?"

"Two are line supervisors, like me," Scott said. "But they don't talk much. The third keeps his distance from the rest of us."

"Want me to see what I can overhear?" Trent asked.

"I'd like both of you to find out what you can about them. But quietly. If we're right, these men are dangerous. And you know how fast rumors can spread in a village like Steveston."

He looked from Scott to Trent as he said it. Scott didn't need the warning, but Trent was young enough, and impetuous enough, to get himself into trouble before he realized it. "Agreed?"

Both nodded. Granville gave Trent a hard look, and the boy shrugged a little, gave him a half grin, then dropped his eyes. Good.

"We're still lacking a motive in this case," Granville said. "If Dirks is our killer, I can't fathom why he'd have killed these particular men. Or had them killed. Those rumors you heard.

Was there any hint that our dead men might have been Japanese?"

Both Scott and Trent shook their heads.

"What about missing boats?" At their baffled looks, he smiled. "I'm sorry, I forgot I hadn't told you what the coroner found. Not to mention Emily and Clara."

And he proceeded to fill them in. "So if both of them are from the same town, they might well have been fishing together. And if they had a small boat..."

"Where is it?" Trent said, leaning forward, his face intent.

"Exactly," Granville said.

"I'm wondering if there's any possibility that they were father and son?" Scott said. "If they came from the same village, carried similar disks."

"It's a good question," Granville said. "Though I gather a good part of the Steveston fishing fleet came from the same town, or at least the same province."

"If they were father and son, on a two man boat, no-one might have missed them yet," Scott said.

"That's a strong possibility," Granville agreed. "But if they are father and son, they'd be memorable. Someone out there knows them."

"And we've the disks and the handkerchief to go on now," Trent said. "We didn't have anything before."

"I plan to be on the first stage to Steveston tomorrow," Granville said. "And I could use some help."

"Sure. But we'll need to go into the cannery and quit first," Scott said. "Then we can meet you."

"Why not telephone Boyd and resign that way?" Granville asked.

"Because Boyd doesn't get in until after nine, and by then we'll be on our way," Scott said. "And we've a ride back arranged with the boat that brought us."

"Yeah, at four a.m.," Trent said, scowling.

At least the lad was predictable. "It won't kill you," Granville said, hiding his grin.

"It'll give us a chance to hear any rumors that've brewing overnight," Scott said. "Maybe learn a bit about Dirks's men. And I want a chance to tell my fellow workers who I am, and why I was there. They'll find out anyway, and this way they might still be willing to talk to me."

"As long as Dirks's men don't decide either of you is a threat."

Scott grimaced. "Because they're on home ground. And we're not."

"Exactly."

"Maybe we'll wait a bit before we ask questions," Scott said. "Right, Trent?"

"Sure," Trent said. Not very convincingly.

Ignoring him, Scott glanced at Granville. "We can meet you at the dock behind the cannery around eleven tomorrow morning?"

"That works for me," Granville said. He had a few things he needed to do on his own anyway.

Trent muttered something, but shook his head at Scott's look.

Scott grinned and cuffed him lightly. "Don't go gettin' ideas."

Trent scowled. "I wouldn't."

Which worried Granville. They were getting too close to a killer to be taking chances now.

GRANVILLE STRODE into the bar at the Vancouver Club. It was after nine, and the lights were low. Small clumps of men sat around tables, leaning forward in quiet conversation, or slumped back in their chairs, whiskey in hand. Ross-Murray had suggested the location, and Granville was happy to meet on neutral ground, since his news wasn't good.

Ross-Murray, impeccably groomed as ever, came forward to greet him, hand outstretched.

"You have news?" Ross-Murray asked as they shook.

"Yes, but it isn't good news, I'm afraid," Granville said. "You'll have heard that there's been another death?"

"Yes, Owens called me on Tuesday," Ross-Murray said. "It certainly wasn't what I had expected to hear. But please, have a seat."

And he waved Granville towards a small table in an empty corner of the bar. Granville noted that there were already two crystal tumblers filled with a golden liquid, an ice bucket and a small silver pitcher sitting on a silver tray. Ross-Murray had already ensured privacy for their conversation.

"Care for a scotch?" Ross-Murray offered.

"Two fingers."

Ross-Murray poured a generous two fingers, and the same for himself. He picked up the small silver water pitcher. "Water?"

At Granville's nod, Ross-Murray poured a small amount into each glass. "Tell me, how is your search for the killer coming?" he asked as he put the pitcher down and slid the drink towards Granville.

"None too quickly, I'm afraid," Granville said. He raised the glass to his host in a silent toast, drank. Took a moment to savor the rich taste. It was excellent whiskey, and went down very smoothly indeed.

"We have established that both victims were most likely Japanese, and possibly from the same village," Granville said. "As of yet, we have no idea who they are. Nor do we know who killed them, or why. Though we do know that the second body was brought into the cannery by way of the fishing dock."

"That's something, I suppose," Ross-Murray said "Though I had expected more details at this point."

"I'm sure." Granville paused. "But I'm sorry to tell you that news of the two deaths is out, though people have few details. And they also know our firm has been hired by the Canneries Association."

Ross-Murray frowned. "And just how did that happen?"

"The manager of the Gulf of Georgia Cannery brought his

foreman into it. And the fellow decided to question his line super-visors. The story spread from there."

"I see. How unfortunate. And it will likely have consequences for all of us."

Granville nodded.

"It shows poor judgment on the foreman's part. I will need to talk to Owens about it. But what do you intend to do about it?"

"My plans haven't changed," Granville said. "I intend to identify the victims, and find their killers."

"Indeed. And how do you plan to do that?"

"By following the few details we now have to wherever they might lead us."

"Just keep in mind that we cannot afford to have another strike. Or worse," Ross-Murray said. "You need to solve this."

"We will find the killer. Or killers," Granville said. "And bring them to justice."

"We are counting on your doing so." Ross-Murray said. "Quickly."

"Of course," Granville said firmly. There was no point prolonging this conversation. "Thank you for the whiskey."

Draining his glass, he left with a nod.

29

FRIDAY, AUGUST 17, 1900

It was nearly noon on the following day when Granville walked into The Troller in Steveston. He scanned the room. Constable Ingram was seated at a small table, scowling at two rowdy drunks arguing with the bartender. He seemed ready to launch himself into the middle of the situation, but was holding back. So far.

The young constable had chosen a back table, and seated himself against the wall, facing the door. Granville approved—he didn't like people sneaking up on him either. And no-one was close enough to overhear their conversation. Ingram was learning.

At the sight of Granville, Ingram turned away from the argumentative drunks. He checked his pocket-watch, then smiled broadly. He raised a hand in greeting, then motioned towards a second mug of ale sitting on the table across from him.

Nodding his thanks, Granville seated himself and took a deep drink of India Pale Ale. Ingram had even got the right brand, he noted.

"Thanks. I needed that," he said. "Dealing with liars is thirsty work."

"You're welcome. And let me guess. You've been talking to Dirks?"

"No. Boyd."

"Boyd? I wouldn't have pegged him for a liar. As far as I know, he's been straight with us."

"He's been lying to himself. Which is worse, because it means we can't trust a word the fellow says."

Ingram frowned thoughtfully and took a swig of his own beer. "He doesn't want to admit that Dirks is really running the place, and not him?" he ventured after a moment. "Is that it?"

Granville nodded, impressed. "Yes, that's it. How did you know?"

Ingram shrugged. "I hear things."

"So it's an open secret here in Steveston?"

"No, not an open one. Mostly it's what isn't said. But I listen."

Granville had begun to appreciate that about the young constable. He wondered if Ingram's colleagues did.

"So why does he do it?" Ingram asked. "Boyd, I mean."

Granville stifled a grin at the naive question. He might have the right instincts, but Ingram still needed seasoning. "The longer Boyd can pretend he's still in charge, the safer he is."

"Safer? Dirks threatened him?"

"Not directly, I don't think," Granville said. "But Boyd is beginning to recognize that Dirks is getting deeper into whatever he's up to, and with it could become a physical threat to him. And he's denying it for all he's worth."

"Physical? You mean you think he'd kill Boyd?"

"I don't know how dangerous Dirks is right now. But I suspect that either he himself or one of his coterie of bully-boys is our murderer."

Ingram stared at Granville, then downed a good portion of his beer, plunking the half-empty mug back down on the table. "Dirks? A killer? You sure? Did Boyd say that?"

Granville smiled as Ingram's questions tripped over each other, so urgently was he asking them. "Not yet. But apparently Dirks has the lists of who had sold fish to the docks on the days the murders occurred. And Boyd said that it's now clear to both of them that Dirks will never release them."

Ingram just stared at him, mouth half-open.

"So I'm hoping you had better luck collecting some of that information," Granville said.

"Oh," Ingram said. "Yes. I mean, I got some of it. I don't know who was selling fish to the Monster Cannery, but the harbor master has records of which boats were in port that day."

"It's a start," Granville said. "But we'll need to find out which of those boats might have tied up at the Monster Cannery on the days of the murders. It'll take us a while to ask those questions—and we're running out of time. We really need those sales records."

Ingram was nodding. "I'll see what I can find out. But if Dirks has them already..."

"There may not be much we can do," Granville finished for him. "Did you find out about any missing fishermen? Or anything that might identify our victims?"

"I'm afraid not. But my uncle's been at sea since before the second body was found. He's back in port now. And unlike some of the others, I know he'll tell me if he's heard anything."

Granville smiled. "Good. We'll need to visit the docks again. And we also need to know what Dirks is up to. Can you think of anyone who might talk to us?"

"To me? No," Ingram said. "And I'm afraid word is out about you, also."

"Yes, so I've heard," Granville said with a wry smile. "What about the men Dirks has collected around himself? Boyd described three of them to me. All are white males. Big men, heavily built, dark haired. One is half-a-foot taller than the others, and heavily muscled. Recognize any of them?"

Ingram noted the descriptions down, then shook his head. "No. But I can ask around."

"Quietly. These men are dangerous."

"I'll be careful."

"See that you are." Granville said, raising his mug to the young constable. "And we'll meet here around five-thirty or so?"

"Sure thing," Ingram said. He glanced back at his notes, then up at Granville. "You know, Dirks is one who enjoys making people suffer. Some of his victims might be willing to talk to you."

"Where would I find them?" Granville said.

Granville found Scott and Trent leaning against a rail fence beside the Monster Cannery, watching a fishing boat unload six or seven feet below them. With such a long dry spell, the river was low, so the dock was riding low as well.

He could see seaweed and barnacles crusted along the outer walls of the cannery that showed how much higher the water had been earlier in the year.

The fishing boat they were watching looked to be a typical Coast Salish skiff, single-masted and made of cedar. And remarkably sea-worthy. She was heavily laden enough to ride low in the water. Two Indian fishermen were using wooden spears and something that looked like a long-handled garden spade to fling salmon from the boat up to the dock.

On the dock, a pair of Japanese workers in heavy cotton overalls were shoveling the fish into large wooden bins on wheels, while another of their colleagues moved the filled bins to the bottom of a ramp and attached a complicated rope and pulley system. Above them, several more men stood inside the double doors, and were hauling the full bins up and wheeling them into the cannery itself.

The day was bright, but there was a slight wind out of the west, and the muddy water of the Fraser was showing a light chop. Half a dozen white gulls dipped and swung overhead, watching for scraps to fall overboard. It was a noisy scene, between the hoarse cries of the birds, the rhythmic grinding of the chains that secured the dock and the yelling of the fishermen to each other and to the men unloading their fish.

The salt smell of the wind was enough to defeat the odor of the cannery, but it blew the heavy, fecund scent of the marsh straight in their faces. Smiling to himself at the irony, Granville let his eyes wander.

What could this scene tell him about their murders?

Gaining access to the docks from up here would not be difficult. The only barriers were the low wooden railings, and a five foot high chain link fence with a locked gate that protected the entrance to the dock itself. It wouldn't be hard to scale that.

He considered the six foot difference between the wharf and the big double doors of the cannery. The ramp they used to move the wheeled bins up from the dock and into the building made it a laughable obstacle.

There was another fishing boat tied up at the far end of the dock, presumably waiting its turn. This one, while also single-masted, was similar to the flat-bottomed Columbia boat that Ingram's uncle sailed, but much bigger. He could just make out the identifier painted on the side, *H1789*. Her crew of four looked to be Japanese, though it was hard to be certain at this distance.

As Granville watched the chaotic scene, a sense of order began to unfold. It was an elaborate ritual, with each man having a part to play—all of them focused on bringing freshly caught salmon to market.

His eyes narrowed on the men standing on the dock itself, heavy shovels flashing in the sun as they cleared fish onto the wheeled carts. Japanese. A team of two.

Just like the men who'd been killed. And working right there, on the docks.

Right next to the double doors through which his evidence suggested the victims had been carried into the cannery.

Could it be that simple?

The cannery records said not—no employee had gone missing during the days in question. But given Boyd's hints earlier, he suspected that Dirks had far too much control over the cannery records. It was highly unlikely that those records were accurate. Especially not on this matter.

So if two of the Japanese dockworkers had gone missing, who would know?

He turned to ask Scott, just as a passing ferry blew his whistle, the blast drowning out any possibility of speech. Granville winced at the volume, and gave up. It was too noisy to talk here.

And probably not the best place for a conversation anyway, in full view of anyone who chose to look out.

Not that he'd mind if Dirks saw the three of them here. Fear of discovery could push the foreman into doing something rash—and he'd have him. "See anything interesting?" he yelled in Scott's general direction, and grinned at the face his partner made.

"I'm never eating salmon again," Scott yelled back with a scowl.

"Now that would be a true loss," Granville said.

He'd grown fond of the taste of salmon. Living here on the west coast, he had even decided that sockeye salmon fresh from the ocean edged out the flavor of fresh-caught Scottish trout, which he'd formerly thought incomparable.

Though he had to confess that a few weeks spent in Steveston had made the thought of eating salmon slightly less appealing. But it was a temporary effect. He hoped.

Trent grinned at the both of them, his too long hair blowing into his eyes. Scraping it away with an impatient hand, the lad pointed towards the waiting fishing boat.

"They came in fifteen minutes ago," he said, pitching his voice just loud enough to be heard over the clamor. "And they're Japanese. They'll probably eat on land before heading back out to fish tonight. Maybe we can find a way to talk to them."

It was a good thought, though not necessarily an easy one to implement, Granville thought. How many of these fishermen would speak enough English to be helpful? And be willing to talk to them?

He suspected it would prove fruitless, but still. "Where would they go for a meal?" he asked looking from Trent to Scott.

Scott shook his head, but Trent laughed. "From what I've heard, if they speak any English at all, they'll be at The Anchor," he said.

Which was where Ingram had told Granville he might find Dirks's victims. It was worth a try. "Good. Let's go," he said, matching action to words and turning back towards downtown.

"Whoa! Not yet," Trent said as he raced to catch up with Granville's longer stride. "No-one will get there for at least an hour. We have time to get ourselves something to eat. I'm starving. And the food at the Anchor is enough to poison even a sailor."

"Lunch it is, then," Granville said.

J ust over an hour later, Granville, Scott and Trent had taken over a back table at the Anchor, and were pretending to be deep in conversation while they watched the bar's patrons come and go. It was a big place, with the familiar sawdust floor and smell of stale beer, and obviously popular, judging by the hard use the wooden tables and plank benches had seen. At the moment it was fairly bright, with the sun streaming in through small windows high up on the back wall. At night it was probably dim, smoky and loud, judging by the meager overhead lighting and the size of those windows. Just the way he liked it, Granville thought

It was still early enough that business was slow, which made spotting the crew of the *H1789* an easy task. Within half an hour, all four of the Japanese fishermen they'd seen earlier arrived, and after a rapid interchange with the bartender, they headed for a table two over from where Granville, Scott and Trent sat. At least one of them must speak some English, then.

Less than ten minutes later a fat man in a greasy apron came out of the kitchen in the back and slapped heaping plates of fish and chips in front of the *H1789's* crew. Granville could smell the grease from where he sat, and was grateful Trent had suggested they eat before they came here. Though if he'd been about to head out to sea in an unheated boat, he'd probably be glad of greasy fish and chips, too.

He gave the four fishermen a few minutes to take the edge off their hunger, then nodded to Scott. The two of them stopped by the bar, then sauntered over. The crew of the *H1789*, who were definitely Japanese, looked up warily as he and Scott stopped, towering over their table. They exchanged glances as Granville set a beer in front of two of them, Scott repeating the motion with the other two.

One of the four, the spokesman, met Granville's eyes. "What you want?" he said.

"To talk," Granville said, pulling out an empty chair. "May we?"

The spokesman gave a sharp nod, and Granville and Scott sat down.

"We're looking into the deaths of two of your countrymen," Granville said. "Men who may have vanished near the Monster Cannery. Perhaps they even worked or fished for the cannery. We were hoping you might have heard something, or be able to tell us who we could talk to."

The spokesman watched him for a moment, and Granville had the impression that he himself was being weighed as much as his words.

"Who you work for?"

"The canneries hired us. But I am personally committed to finding out what happened. And to ensuring that the dead men are properly buried, and under their own names."

There was another heavy silence, then the spokesman turned to the other three and spoke rapidly in Japanese. A heated interchange followed.

Granville found it fascinating—he understood none of the words, but he could almost follow the conversation through their intensity and how they reacted to each other. At last the spokesman turned back to him and gave him a funny half-bow.

"Someone find you. With answer," he said.

Accepting that this was all the answer they would get—for now—Granville returned the bow. "Thank-you," he said as he stood. "And safe fishing."

"Well, that was different," Scott said as they walked back to their table. "So who's going to be looking for us?"

"I have no idea," Granville said. "As long as someone is, we might be closer to naming our victims than we've been since this case started."

Two hours later, the three of them were still at the Anchor. The cannery line had just let out, and the place was busy, noisy and crowded. Scott and Trent were still at the back table they'd been occupying for the last few hours, hoping some of their fellow workers would join them. There was no sign of whomever the crew of the *H1789* was sending to talk to them.

Acting on Ingram's earlier advice about possible informants, Granville had moved to one of the stools along the bar. Might as well make it easy for anyone who might want to talk to him. The barstools on either side of him were still empty.

They knew who he was, alright. Now to see if anyone wanted to talk.

It took another three-quarters of an hour before a short, grimy man who wouldn't see fifty again sat down on his far side. He wasn't Japanese. Granville assumed this must be one of Dirks's victims, and not someone the crew of the *H1789* had referred to them.

"Buy you a beer?" Granville said.

His new neighbor started. Turning slightly, he stared at Granville for a bit out of bloodshot gray eyes, then nodded. "Yeah, thanks."

Granville signaled the bartender, then waited. He'd nearly finished his beer when the fellow leaned closer.

"I hear you're investigating the murders at the Monster," he said in low tones.

"That's right," Granville said. And waited again.

"I might have some information." A pause. "What's it worth to ya?"

"Goodwill," Granville said.

A snort. "I want money," the fellow said, and drained his mug.

"I can buy you another beer," Granville said, and, catching the bartender's eye, held up two fingers.

"That's it? I thought you were some fancy investigator."

"I'm looking for a killer." He glanced over at the wiry, worn-looking man beside him. "And I'd guess you are looking for justice."

The fellow's mouth snapped shut and he glared at Granville. "Can't eat justice."

"Perhaps not, but I understand salmon's pretty cheap this time of year."

His companion made a disgusted face. Funny how the more plentiful something was, the less it tended to be valued. Apparently it worked for sockeye salmon equally as well as it did for gemstones.

"Still, having your pride ground down day after day?" Granville continued. "That's more costly."

His new friend slugged back the top third-of his beer, wiped the foam off his lips with a grimy sleeve. "You got that right." He looked Granville over carefully. "You know Dirks?"

"I've met the man. Didn't care for him."

"No, me neither." And another third of the beer disappeared. "He won't like it, he hears I was talking to you."

"I won't tell him," Granville said, suddenly amused. "But if you like, we can go for dinner, someplace with fewer folks likely to talk."

The fellow hesitated. "You buying?"

"Of course."

"And my name stays out of it."

"My word on it."

"Okay. Make it the Bolthole. In half an hour." He drained his mug. "I'm Carson. And I'll leave first. You wait a bit."

He slid off the stool, and marched out. Granville watched him go. A short, thin man, with no meat on his bones, but perfectly steady on his feet despite the two pints he'd just downed in quick succession.

The Bolthole was nearly empty. A seedy, depressing place, it reeked of old grease and stale smoke. Granville spotted his source—or so he hoped—at a table on the far side of the small room, out of view of the front windows. Which were probably too dirty to see through, anyway.

As he approached the table, Carson nodded at the cook—visible through a grease-spattered window in the fry kitchen beyond—and held up two fingers. Granville noted that there was already a pitcher of ale and two mugs on the table.

This one was going to cost him.

"I ordered you a special," the small man told Granville as he sat down. "You'll like it. Place doesn't look like much, but the food'll surprise you. 'S why it'll be jammed to the rafters, later."

"Why is it so empty now, if the food is good?" Granville asked, as much out of curiosity as to establish rapport.

"Folks're busy drinking now. They don't get around to eating until they've drunk off the day. Takes a while," he said. And downed most of his mug of ale.

Right. "So what can you tell me about Dirks?" Granville asked.

Carson's hand stopped in mid-air, and the fellow stared at him for a moment. Then instead of putting the mug down, Carson's arm rapidly moved back upwards, and he slugged down the rest of his drink.

"Don't surprise a fella like that," he said with a scowl after he'd banged the empty mug on the table. "It's not good for the digestion. And pour me another, would ya?"

With a grin, Granville obeyed. He was starting to like this fellow. "Well?"

Half of the fresh glass vanished. Then Carson put the mug down, wiped his mouth on his sleeve and sat back with a sigh. "Dirks is bad news. Someone needs to stop him."

"So I've been hearing. What I haven't heard is exactly what he's into," Granville said. "What can you tell me about him?"

Thin lips twisted in a wry grin and Carson let out a harsh sound that was probably supposed to be a laugh. "Not very subtle, are ya? Well, neither is Dirks, so maybe that's okay. He's heavy-handed with the workers. He runs the place like he owns it. Plus he's stealing, is what he's doing. Petty stuff, mostly. But he's also shorting the salmon loads, and pocketing the difference."

Interesting. "He fiddles the books so it doesn't show, then?"

"Yeah. Boyd should'a caught it long ago, but he's never paid enough attention. I doubt he's any too bright, either."

Granville had to fake a cough to hide his sudden spurt of laughter. Who was this Carson? He hadn't always worked at a cannery, that was for sure. "Anything else?"

Carson shrugged. "Dirks "loses" a lot of equipment, but that's small stuff. And he's overpaying his own private little army."

"The line supervisors?"

"Yeah. Not all of 'em, though."

Which is what Granville had suspected. "How can you know all this? I know Dirks is arrogant, but surely he can't be so obvious everyone can see it."

The flash of white teeth that was Carson's sudden grin took

Granville by surprise—both by its humor, and because he hadn't expected this sign of good dental care. "I'm one of them, then, aren't I?"

Granville had the feeling he'd been had. And that he'd seriously misjudged Carson. "One of what?"

"Dirks's line supervisors. Just like your pal Scott."

If it was true, no wonder Carson had a clear sense of what was going on. "Dirks wouldn't have hired you. You're too quick to be one of his men."

Granville didn't have any doubt about that either.

"He didn't," Carson said. "Man before him did. Dirks inherited me, and once I had his measure, I was careful not to give him any reason to get rid of me. It's a good job for these parts. Or at least it was before he got here. Now he's ruining things for everyone."

"Which is why you're speaking up," Granville said, suddenly understanding what was going on. "But why now, after all this time? Why not say something sooner?"

"To whom? Boyd?"

"Owens?"

"You think he'd listen to the likes of me?"

"I thought he'd worked his way up in the canneries."

"He did. Sometimes they're the worst kind. The ones who've made it, I mean. Short memories."

Granville knew what he meant. He'd met men like that, though he wouldn't have taken Owens for one of them.

He wondered if there was history between Owens and Carson. Which was probably irrelevant—he suspected Carson was trying to distract him. "And two recent murders have nothing to do with why you're talking to me now?"

"Well, you're only here for me to talk to because of the murders, so of course they'll have something to do with it," was the ingenuous response.

Carson was definitely trying to distract him.

Before Granville could follow up, two heavy earthenware plates were slapped in front of them, the contents still sizzling loudly from the grill. He drew in an appreciative breath. Sausage hash with mashed turnips and potatoes, spiked with bacon and peppers if he didn't miss his guess. And from the smell, Carson hadn't been exaggerating about the quality of the food.

"Dig in," the thin man said, and did so.

With a mental shrug, Granville did so. Clearly he wasn't going to get another word out of his dinner companion until the fellow's plate was empty.

Which didn't take long.

As soon as Carson's fork went down, Granville put down his own fork and leaned forward. "About the murders. It's obvious you know something. And I won't give up until I know what it is."

Carson opened his mouth, and Granville held up a cautioning hand. "And by now, I can tell when you're lying."

Carson grinned, his teeth much too white in that tired face. He poured himself another mug of ale and sat back, very much at his ease. "I believe you can. And I've decided I kinda like you, so I'll talk. Eat, though. This food's too good to waste."

He was right about that. "You tell me what you know, I'll spring for another plate for you."

Carson's grin widened. "Words that are music to my heart. Fine. Just keep the ale flowing and I'll tell you what you want to know. But it'll take a little time. Eat."

Granville picked up his fork, and prepared to spend some time sorting fact from fiction. But the fellow surprised him. Again.

"I've been watching Dirks since he started," Carson said. "Carefully, once I realized what he was. He's a thief, sure, and he has no morals at all that I've seen. But I don't think he's a killer."

Granville put down his knife and fork "One of his men, then?"

Carson stared at the fork until Granville picked it up again.

"Could be, I suppose. But none of them have much gumption. Idiots, all, as you so wisely noted. And Dirks—he's not nearly as bright as he thinks he is. I don't think he could have pulled it all off on his own. Eat."

About to ask another question, Granville just nodded, and ate a slice of sausage. It was superb.

"The murders are too perfect. There's too little evidence, from what I've heard, to even point to someone, much less prove murder," Carson said.

Granville just nodded.

"I think Dirks might have disposed of the bodies. Or had his men do it. It would be easy for them. And if anyone saw anything—and I'm not saying they did, mind—they'd never speak up against him. But I've seen nothing—ever—that would make me think Dirks a murderer. Boy's a coward at heart, and that's the truth. No, he's covering for someone."

"Who? And why?" Granville asked.

"Well now, that's for you to discover, I'm thinking," Carson said, finishing the last of his ale. "I've done what I can for you. And I thank you for dinner."

And with that the wiry little man was up and vanishing out the door before Granville had a chance to protest.

When Granville got back to the Anchor, it was considerably busier than it had been earlier. Scott and Trent were still at their table in the back, sitting alone, fresh pints in front of them. Granville collected a pint at the bar, then joined them.

"Well?" he asked. "Anyone show up about the *H1789*?"

"Nope," Scott said. "Not a sign of 'em. We talked to a few people from the cannery, but they mostly wanted to find out if we really were investigators, and what we'd learned."

"A couple knew something," Trent said unexpectedly, leaning forward. "They were dancin' around saying it, too. But they never came right out with it. It was like they were too scared to talk. Right?" he said to Scott, his tone challenging.

"Right," Scott said with a grin and a wink at Granville.

Who wasn't sure he wanted to know what was going on

between the two of them. They'd have to sort it out. They always did.

"You think any of them would talk to us? Later?" he asked instead.

Scott shook his head. "I think they're too scared," he said, and Trent nodded.

"Of Dirks?"

"Yeah," his partner said. "Man controls a lot of jobs there. No-one can afford to be fired at this point in the season. Too much money lost to the strike."

It made sense, Granville thought. Unfortunately.

And it fit in with what Carson had said. If Dirks—or his men—had been responsible for disposing of the bodies, and if they'd been seen… Rumors would have spread. But very quietly.

Except they'd heard none of them. And Carson didn't think Dirks was capable of murder.

Or so he said.

Around them people started to finish their beers and depart. The tables all around them cleared out within minutes. Scott glanced around, then leaned closer, lowering his voice. "Was that Carson I saw you talking to earlier?" he asked.

Granville nodded.

"Your informant?"

"Yes." Lowering his own voice, Granville filled them in on what he'd heard from Carson.

Scott listened without saying a single word. At one point Trent started to interrupt, but Scott gave him a look and the boy subsided. Only when Granville had finished did Scott speak.

"Sounds like Dirks," he said.

"Which? The theft? Or the statement that he isn't a murderer?" Granville said.

"No, I can see him as a murderer," Scott said. "But the man's a coward. He'd kill to protect himself. Or his secrets. But only if it didn't come back on him."

"So what do you think Dirks is hiding?"

"Murder. I think he either did it himself, or he's protecting someone."

Granville nodded. That made sense. The question was who? And why would Dirks protect him?

Dirks's actions could simply be driven by a need to hide his own crimes, whatever they were. Whether he was their killer or not, it might well be in his best interests to make it impossible for them to identify the real murderer. He might even be trying to incite another strike.

Which would make Granville's job truly impossible.

"But Carson's a tricky one himself," Scott added. "I wouldn't be so quick to discount Dirks just on his say so."

"Oh? You haven't mentioned Carson before. What do you know of him?"

"He knows the business, and he knows the cannery. And he's smarter than he looks," Scott said, squinting a little as if he was seeing Carson as he spoke. "But he's sneaky. He's never where you expect him to be."

"So he avoids working?" Granville asked.

"No, he's a hard worker. But he asks too many questions. And I'd see him watching people—like he's collecting secrets."

That fit the man he'd met, Granville thought. He'd met men like that before—ones who seemed to have an endless need to know what was going on around them, even though they had no good use for the information.

Which might explain why Carson had chosen to turn informant. It gave the fellow access to Granville and the investigation, didn't it?

Trent had been glaring at Scott. Now he turned to Granville. "Can I talk now?"

"Go ahead," Granville said, hiding his chuckle.

"I like Carson. Any time he had me running errands, he was straight with me. Not like the others. And he tipped well."

At Scott's laugh Trent grimaced. "You can laugh, but it matters. Dirks's other supervisors—including you, by the way—treated me like a servant. Just the errand boy."

"I was blending in," Scott said, holding up his hands.

"And they treated the workers worse," Trent said, ignoring him. "Like one was the same as the next, and none of them mattered. Carson was different. He pays attention, and if someone's struggling on the line, he does something about it."

"And Dirks didn't notice?" Granville asked, fascinated by this glimpse into the inner workings of the cannery.

"No, I think he did notice him. He just kinda pretended he didn't. I saw Dirks not notice Carson a few times, if you know what I mean."

Granville did know. And he was impressed. Both that the lad had noticed, and that he'd recognized what he was seeing.

"But Dirks seemed reluctant to challenge him, too," Trent was saying. "Like Carson has something on him."

He probably did, Granville thought with an inward grin. There was a story there. Someday he'd find out what it was. "What d'you think, Scott?"

"The lad's right. Carson—he's irritating, like a mosquito buzzing around. But only when he gets too close. Mostly I didn't really notice him. He did a good job of being invisible. Maybe on purpose."

Scott paused, absently smoothed his beard. "Probably why I don't trust him, at that. But I did see Dirks ignore him a couple times. Like the man really was invisible to him."

"And invisible men can see a lot of what's going on," Granville said thoughtfully. "So if we assume Carson is telling us the truth about Dirks—then what would it mean for our investigation?"

"Trouble," Scott said. "Not just that we don't know who our victims are. If it isn't Dirks? It could mean that the killer is someone we haven't even considered. We'd have to start all over."

"But Dirks knows," Granville said softly. "Even if Carson is right, and Dirks isn't the killer. All we have to do is get Dirks to talk."

"Yeah, good luck with that," Scott said.

"I think we need to talk to Ingram. All of us," Granville said, glancing at his pocket watch, then draining his mug. "He'll be waiting for us at the Troller. Let's go."

By mid-morning, the office was already far too warm, despite the faint breeze from the harbor that came in through the open windows. The air itself felt sticky, Emily thought as she rolled up several sets of rejected blueprints. She was glad to be seeing the last of them.

She glanced over at Laura, who was typing briskly from some notes Granville had left her the previous day. The heat didn't seem to bother her, and Emily wondered how she did it. Especially with her fingers flying so quickly. Maybe that was why Laura was concentrating so hard—it helped her ignore the heat.

Well, at least their new space would have good fans, Emily thought. She had made sure of it. And it wouldn't be long now. Granville and Scott Investigations would be moving to their new offices on the second floor by the end of September. The work of renovating the space was scheduled to begin on Monday.

All except for the renovations to the second floor conference room, which were already completed, or nearly so. Elegant—but very functional—ceiling fans had been installed three days ago. The painters and paperers had finished there only yesterday. Today the furnishings were being delivered.

And tomorrow Granville and Scott would hold their meeting there with the man from Pinkerton's. Pinkerton's! She smiled to herself at the thought.

Then glanced up at the sound of the outer door opening.

"Mr. McAndrews. How nice to see you," she said. "Were we expecting you?" She couldn't resist a glance at Laura, who was blushing slightly, and refusing to look up.

Emily held back a grin. She'd thought there was something between the two of them. Now she was sure of it.

Mr. McAndrews looked a little flustered, too. "Well, I wasn't sure if Granville was in. Did he tell you I might be coming by?"

"No, he didn't mention anything to me," Emily said. "Did you know?" she asked Miss Kent. Who shook her head. And still wasn't looking at Mr. McAndrews.

"He's out of town on a case," Emily said. "We aren't expecting him back to the office today. Is there something I could tell him?"

"Well. I suppose so." He paused, looked from Emily to Laura. "Is he in Steveston today? At the cannery?"

"Yes," Emily said. "How did you know?"

"He asked for my opinion on something that came up there," McAndrews said slowly.

Emily had the impression he was searching for a diplomatic way to avoid telling them anything. In case they didn't already know. Men. Far too fond of keeping secrets from women, the lot of them.

Though that wasn't usually a problem Granville had.

"You must have received a note from Mr. Granville's with the figures from the cannery," she said. "I know he had some concerns about it. Is that it?"

To his credit, McAndrews looked pleased. "It is indeed. And I've spent some time trying to make sense of them, let me assure you."

"They are that complicated?" Laura asked.

McAndrews shook his head. "That's the problem. What's recorded here is very straight-forward. It's really only a high-level summary of income and expenses over a five year period."

Laura frowned a little. "Then what is the problem?"

Emily waited with interest for his reply.

"It looks wrong," McAndrews said. "The numbers are too similar from year to year. But without the detailed figures that these reports are based on, I can't verify that. And there are any number of explanations as at why the figures could be so close."

He pulled a well-thumbed file out of his battered briefcase.

"I keep feeling I'm missing something obvious, though. Maybe I'm looking for something too complicated. And your abilities to spot inconsistencies had a great deal to do with our success in that last case," he said, and his glance included both of them, though Emily noted his eyes went first to Laura. "I'd appreciate it if you would take a look, and see if anything leaps out at you. If you've the time, that is?"

"Of course we do," Emily said. "Perhaps we can meet in Mr. Granville's office. Laura, you can hear the telephone from there, can't you?"

"Of course," Laura echoed, gather up her note pad. "After you, Mr. McAndrews. And would you like some tea?"

"Oh no, after you," McAndrews said. "And no, there is no need for tea."

"Perhaps later," Emily said diplomatically, looking from one awkward face to the other. "Now, what is it Mr. Granville asked you to look into?"

McAndrews pulled out a note in what Emily recognized as Granville's hand and placed it on the edge of the desk. Emily and Laura moved closer so they could both read it.

"His informant—the bookkeeper, I believe," McAndrews said. "He says that the profit for the cannery hasn't changed much from year to year, despite improvements in the process. And these figures," he pulled out another sheet of paper, lined with columns of figures in a different, very neat hand. "They seem to verify that."

"May I?" Emily asked. At his nod, she picked it up and scanned the figures again. She saw nothing more than she had when

Granville had shown them to her on the ferry. Emily passed the page to Laura, and waited.

When Laura handed it back to McAndrews a minute later, Emily said, "And what is your opinion, Mr. McAndrews?"

"These figures do indeed seem to bear out the fellow's statement. And on the face of it, he's right—it's rare for even the most efficient operation to stay so close to the same income from year to year."

Emily nodded. "And you wanted our thoughts? On what, exactly?"

"I'm not sure. The numbers are different, but not different enough. As I said, my training is to look into every detail—which I don't have—and I'm afraid I'm missing something. Something obvious."

Emily glanced at the page again, shook her head. "Nothing I can see. Laura?"

Laura leaned over and picked up the page again. "It seems to me that these figures have been inflated by a small percentage each year. And that the increases consistently increase by the same amount. Is that possible?"

McAndrews stared at her for a moment, then pulled a note pad, pencil and slide rule from his briefcase. The watched in silence as he calculated and scribbled figures. Finally he looked up. "Yes. You're right. Every figure increases by 1.35 percent every year. Which makes no logical sense. But how could you see that?"

Laura smiled. "I don't know. I just do."

He stared from his figures to Laura and back again. Without saying a word.

Finally Emily said, "But what does it mean?"

"It means someone, somewhere, worked out what these figures should be. And then worked backwards to create the detailed records that add up to these figures," he said.

Laura was nodding.

"Fraud," Emily said.

"Yes," McAndrews agreed.

"Where does this list go?" Laura asked. "Is it a report that goes to management? Or an internal document?"

"It must be internal," Emily said. "It would be too obvious otherwise, wouldn't it?"

"Yes, it would," McAndrews said. "Though there would be a profit and loss statement done at some point, but it may not be as simplified as this one. This is either an original master document created by one of those committing the fraud ..."

"In which case the bookkeeper must be implicated," Laura said.

"Though in that case why would he give it to Granville?" Emily said. "He'd just make himself look guilty."

"Or if someone—likely the bookkeeper—was suspicious enough to take figures from the reports that do go to management and used those figures they showed to create this document..." McAndrews said.

"That would have been a lot of work," Laura commented.

"And it would be the last thing the thieves would expect," Emily said slowly. "Because we all knew from looking at the result that something was wrong, even though it took Laura's eye for patterns to recognize exactly what that was."

"Exactly," McAndrews said. "The numbers on their own are worrying enough. But once the pattern is recognized, it's clear that this can be nothing but fraud. It is too precise to be anything else."

"Not something any thief would leave lying around where a bookkeeper could find it," Laura said.

"Especially not one who is in a wheelchair, with limited access to anything beyond the office area," Emily said. "Which is apparently true for this bookkeeper."

"So where does this leave you, Mr. McAndrews?" Laura asked.

"Leaving a note for Granville, explaining my findings and your contributions. If he's expected back late, can you leave it somewhere he won't miss it?" he asked them both.

"Of course," Laura said. "I leave a stack of documents for both him and Mr. Scott every evening. It will be a simple thing to leave your note on top."

"Good. Tell him that I'll be happy to discuss it with him. But that either of you two," and Emily noted that his glance lingered a moment longer on Laura, "can probably answer most of his questions."

34

Granville pushed open the doors of The Troller, blinking as his eyes adjusted to the dimness after the still bright day outside. Long and narrow, with small windows, the place was a true hole in the wall, a fact he hadn't realized the other morning. And it was nearly empty.

A quick glance around found Ingram sitting at a large table in the back. And he wasn't alone. Motioning to Scott and Trent to follow, Granville strode to the table. "Ingram," he said with a nod. And waited.

"John Granville, Joe Sakamoto," Ingram said.

Granville knew the name. This short, wiry man must be the husband of the woman Emily and Clara had talked to the previous day. Was he also the man sent by the crew of the *H1789*?

Sakamoto bowed. Granville returned the gesture, then introduced Scott and Trent.

Once they were all seated, Ingram sat forward. "Mr. Sakamoto sought me out, asked if I could set up a private meeting with you. Somewhere you wouldn't be observed. I suggested he join us here."

It wasn't quite a question, but Granville answered it anyway. "Good thinking," he said, and Ingram gave him a relieved grin.

It was in moments like these that Granville suddenly recognized just how much he'd gained through the hardships and struggles that were the Klondike Gold Rush. Less than a decade separated him from Ingram, but the lad seemed so young, so untried. He met Scott's eyes over Ingram's head, and they shared a quick flash of amusement. A year or so in the Klondike would toughen the lad up.

With an inward grin at his own whimsies, Granville turned to their guest, more than curious to hear what he had to say. "Mr. Sakamoto?"

"Mr. Granville," the fellow said. "I believe your—fiancée—came to see my wife yesterday." He stumbled only a little over the word.

"That is correct."

Sakamoto nodded. "My wife liked her. Very much."

"I'm glad to hear it. I know my fiancée felt the same about your wife."

"Ah, good." He inclined his head in an almost-bow. "So, when the crew of the *H1789* came to speak with me..." He paused.

So this was their representative. "Yes?"

"I was most happy to agree. There are things you need to know. I believe you investigate two murders of my countrymen?"

"Yes. But we have very little information to help us find out who killed them, or even who they were."

"Perhaps I may help. You have things that belong to them?"

Of course. Emily had shown the cloth and the disks to this man's wife. Granville, nodded, taking a guess at what he'd want most to see. Reaching into his pocket, he placed the pair of disks on the table.

Sakamoto reached for them, then hesitated, and looked to Granville for permission. "May I?"

"Yes. Absolutely."

The wiry Japanese man picked up the disks, held them cradled in his palm for a long moment. Then he turned them over with one scarred finger, and traced the patterns on the other side. He looked sad.

"You knew them?" Granville asked.

"*Hai*. Yes."

Silence fell, broken only by scattered yells coming from the street outside the window.

"I understand your wife could only say the disks likely came from your home town," Granville said, choosing his words carefully. The man was grieving. And they could not afford to offend their only lead.

"Yes. But I knew them well. This one?" Rubbing a thumb over the more worn of the two disks. "I saw often. These marks?"

Turning the disk over, Sakamoto ran a forefinger over the faint scratches. "Hari told us often how this saved him. Wind come up, he need to drop anchor fast. Rope ran over this, saved his hand." And he ran the same finger over the palm of his own hand in demonstration. "Disk should have fallen, but did not."

It made sense. Granville could recall moments like that one around campfires in the Klondike, men passing around objects that had become sacred to them, telling the story of how this knife had saved them from a grizzly, or that compass had got them home in a blizzard.

"And their names?" he asked quietly.

"Hari Akizuki and his son Ben. Ben only seventeen," Sakamoto said after a moment. "And young still—his father protects him. But good men. Very sad."

"I'm sorry," Granville said. "They were fishermen?"

"Yes. They sail the *H3340*. No-one has seen the boat for a week. Maybe more."

So not dockworkers after all. Fishermen. At least they'd been right about that, Granville thought.

"Where were Akizuki and his son last seen?" Ingram asked, leaning forward. He sat back when Granville shot him a look.

Sakamoto didn't notice the interaction, seemingly watching something only he could see. "They sail from here same day strike end. Most left Steveston then. No-one wish to miss the salmon, not after long strike."

"And no-one has seen the boat since?"

"No."

"Could someone else be sailing their boat now? Under a different name?"

Sakamoto looked troubled. "Perhaps. I have not heard, if so."

"Did Akizuki and his son bring their catch back here to sell?" Granville asked. "Or to the cannery float?"

"To the cannery float, I think. I will ask."

"Which cannery did they fish for?" Granville asked.

"They own licenses. Mostly they bring fish to the Gulf of Georgia, though. I work there too. Mending nets, building boats." Sakamoto held out hands covered with the thick scars from handling net ropes and wood-working tools.

The Monster Cannery again. "Were they involved in the strike?" Granville asked. "Or in your Benevolent Association?"

"Yes, but same as many others. Not as leaders."

Another dead end. "Who would want these two men dead?" Granville asked. "Had they enemies?"

"No. Everyone likes them. And Hari? He makes us laugh."

There seemed nothing to say to that.

"You have the names. You will find killer?" Sakamoto said after a long moment of silence.

"Yes. You have my word I will find him. Or them," he said. "And bring them to justice for what they have done."

"Good," Sakamoto said with a firm nod, and rose. He bowed towards Granville, then towards the table in general. "I will learn what I can. You will let me know what you find?"

Granville inclined his head in return. "Yes, of course. We'll relay the information through Ingram here," Granville said, noting out of the corner of his eye that Ingram sat taller with his words.

GRANVILLE, Scott, Trent and Ingram watched in silence as Sakamoto departed.

Then Granville turned to Ingram. "So now we know who our victims are. But we still don't know why they were killed. Were you able to talk to your uncle today?"

Ingram nodded. "Yes. And he'd heard rumors that one of the Japanese fish boats was missing, but no more than that."

"Boyd told me a few days ago that there are sometimes feuds over the fishing grounds. That true?" Granville asked Ingram.

Ingram nodded. "My uncle talks about it."

"Are the feuds serious enough to murder someone over?"

"Not that I've ever heard. Doesn't mean they haven't been. Or couldn't be. My uncle might be able to tell you more."

And just how open would any of the fishermen be on such a subject? Granville wondered.

"More often, it's the wind and the tides that betray the fishermen and sink their boats," Ingram added.

Which didn't help them in this case. "Would a fisherman kill in order to steal a boat?" Granville asked.

Ingram looked appalled, but nodded slowly. "It's possible. Or even for their fishing licenses. If the thieves were desperate enough."

So where was that boat? "Would your uncle have known Akizuki?"

"He might have. Or at least of him. They lived here, in Steveston, after all. But my uncle—I mean, we don't really mix with the Japanese."

What wasn't he saying?

"Why not?" Granville waited, watching Ingram's expression closely, until the young constable flushed a little and looked down.

"We're too different, I guess," Ingram said at last. "They don't understand our customs and we don't understand theirs."

Just as Granville was wondering how that affected his ability to police this community, Ingram surprised him.

"But I've been seeing that we're more alike than different, since I started wearing this uniform," Ingram said. "We're both nations that live very close to the sea, and have long depended on fishing. We're both a long way from home, and trying to live with a third culture very different from ours."

Ingram meant the English—since British Columbia was still far more English than it was Canadian, at least in Granville's experience. It was an astute observation. His respect for Ingram rose.

"Funny, Japan and England are both islands," Scott commented, a small frown of concentration between his brows. "And Finland..."

"Might as well be one," Ingram said with a broad smile. "We're cut off enough."

"So sea travels come natural," Scott said. "And us Americans— well, we're right next door. And we have a history of going west. But what are the Chinese doing here? Their country is huge."

"And definitely not an island," Granville said with a grin. "But the Chinese have a long history of exploration, and undertaking very long sea voyages. Remember the thousand-year-old Buddhist tokens from the Weston case?"

"And then the Chinese came to work on building the railroads," Trent put in. "And to escape a famine, Bertie says."

Trent had learned more from the Taylor's Chinese houseboy than Granville had realized. He felt a surge of pride in their apprentice.

"The Japanese did the same," he said, recalling Emily's words. "There was no work, and they were starving, so they came here, where the salmon runs were plentiful."

"Just as the Finns did," Ingram said with a nod. "Times were bad, and word came back that fishing here was good."

As it still was. Despite the strike, there were enough fish for everyone to make a decent living. So why were their victims dead?

"If our fishermen killed for their boat, where is it?" Granville asked, following that thought.

"You think that wasn't the reason they were killed?" Trent said.

Scott leaned forward. "If it was Dirks killed them—for whatever reason—he doesn't need a boat. Likely whoever wanted them dead doesn't either. And since we found the bodies in the lye vat? Prob'ly they were killed near the cannery. Maybe someone just sank the boat there, too."

"We can check," Granville said. "But it doesn't sound right. Akizuki was killed a week before his son. If the boat was sunk when Akizuki was killed, then where was the boy?"

"He must have been held somewhere else," Scott said.

"There are abandoned sheds and things along the river that could have been used, if the boy was bound and gagged, so he couldn't be heard. Or escape," Ingram said.

"Or maybe I was right before, and Akizuki's body was brought in from the fishing grounds to be disposed of here," Scott said. "His son could have been left alone on the boat."

"And didn't go for help for an entire week?" Granville said.

"Maybe the boat was crippled," Scott said.

"It still doesn't make sense that they'd kill one and leave the other free," Granville said. "Ben must have been held captive. But why? What did they want from him?"

"Not the boat," Scott said. "Once Akizuki was dead, they probably already had that."

"Exactly," Granville said. "But if whoever killed these two didn't want their boat, then what did they want?"

"What if there was some kind of accident, and Akizuki drowned?" Ingram said. "Then Ben could have been alone on the boat, and unable to manage on his own."

"Doesn't explain why both corpses ended up in the lye vat," Granville said.

"Well, it kinda does, if someone didn't want it known that Akizuki was dead," Scott said. "If the body washed up somewhere, and whoever found it wanted to pretend he was still alive..."

It was possible. If unlikely. "They'd have to have some reason for wanting Akizuki to be alive."

"They might've thought to blackmail Ben," Ingram said. "They had his father, and unless he gave them what they wanted, they'd kill him."

"They didn't need to pretend Akizuki was alive. With his father gone, they could just threaten to kill Ben himself if he didn't tell them whatever it was," Granville said. "And I find it hard to believe that two Japanese fishermen could be that big a threat to our killer."

"They're dead, aren't they?" Scott said.

"Yes. But your theory has too many assumptions in it. With the facts we have, it doesn't make any sense," Granville said, fighting back his frustration.

He'd been operating under the assumption that once he knew who the victims were, it would become obvious who had killed them. And why.

Instead, it seemed that knowing who their Japanese fishermen were only made the case more complicated.

"So we need to figure out who the killer is," Trent said. "Then we might know why he wanted them dead."

Trent had a point, Granville thought. He turned to Ingram. "We've learned a few things since you and I last spoke," he said, and filled him in on what they'd learned since that morning.

"So if Dirks isn't our killer—a possibility we can't afford to ignore—then someone else is behind this. The question we need to answer is—could Dirks be taking orders from someone?"

Ingram frowned, looking rather absurd with his thick brows clumped together in the center of his forehead. "I guess. But it's clearly not Boyd."

Scott let out a crack of laughter. "Definitely not."

"Owens?" Ingram suggested.

Granville shook his head. "Owens would only gain in a situation like that if the cannery was in financial trouble. I checked. It's sound. In fact, it's in such good financial shape that they haven't noticed the thefts."

He paused, thought about what he'd just said.

"Then maybe it's one of the owners of another cannery?" Scott suggested. "Hoping to put the Monster out of business before next year's big salmon run."

"That doesn't work," Granville said absently. "From everything

I've been told, there'll be more than enough fish for everyone next year. No—this would have to be an inside job."

"But there's no-one left," Trent said. "I mean, if it isn't Boyd, or Dirks, then who's left?"

"Carson?" Scott suggested.

"You just don't like him," Trent said.

"True."

"Nope, it has to be Dirks," Trent said, rapping his fork on his plate for emphasis until a glance from Granville had him putting it down quickly.

"If Owens hasn't noticed the thefts, why hasn't he?" Granville said slowly, still thinking about his earlier statement. "The fellow gets regular reports."

"I thought Dirks was doctorin' the reports," Scott said.

"I'm sure he is," Granville said slowly. "But they also must have someone doing the accounts."

"The bookkeeper?" Scott asked.

It was possible. "Dirks certainly can't be changing everything himself. Maybe the bookkeeper is in on it. Somehow." Leon Grazzini was smart enough, even if he was stuck in that chair of his.

"Leon?" Trent said. "That funny old man? He never gets out of his cave."

"You think he might be involved?" Scott asked.

"I liked the fellow, but we can't afford to ignore anyone. As the cannery's bookkeeper, Leon could easily be part of this, whatever it is. At the very least, he could be a useful go-between for someone," Granville said. "Even if he's not involved, he might know something useful."

"So why don't we just go talk to Leon now?" Trent said.

"He isn't going anywhere. And if he is involved, he'll likely be a minor player. First we need to see if we can find any evidence that Akizuki's boat was sunk," Granville said, pushing his plate back and standing up. "Ingram, is your uncle's boat still at the dock?"

Ingram checked his pocket watch, and frowned a little. "They were to sail soon," he said. "They won't want to miss the tide. But if we're quick, we might just catch them."

"Then let's go," Granville said.

35

Joe Ingram's boat was still tied up, though it was clear she was about to get underway. Joe himself stood on the wharf, yelling instructions to one of his men. He looked surprised to see Ingram, then his gaze lighted on Granville.

"So, you have more questions for me, have you?" he called.

"Just two," Granville said. "Then we'll leave you to get underway."

"All right. Go ahead."

"If you wanted to hide a small Japanese-built fishing boat somewhere near here, where would you do so?"

"You are talking about the Akizuki's' boat. The *H3340*," Joe Ingram said shrewdly. "I heard talk no-one had seen her for a few days. Near here?"

He looked down-river, then up. And pointed to several decrepit sheds dotted along the shoreline. "Any of these would do. The hard thing would be getting the boat ashore."

Granville turned to Ingram. "Can you search them, Constable?"

Ingram nodded. "Yes. As soon as we're done here."

"Good." Granville turned back to Joe Ingram. "And if you

wanted to sink the *H3340*? So that she was never found? Where would you do so?"

"Scuttle her?" A look of sadness crossed his face and was gone. "So it is Akizuki and his son who are dead, is it? That is bad."

He considered the river, narrowed eyes following the banks, the currents. "The tide is strong here. You dump something in the right place, the tide pulls it out to the deeper parts. If they put a big enough hole in her side, dump her at the right place? You won't see the *H3340* again."

His gaze shifted to Granville, his grey eyes penetrating. "You think that is why no-one has seen the *H3340*?"

"It's a possibility we're looking into, no more. And I'll ask you to keep our discussions quiet for now."

"Oh, aye. I'll do so," Joe Ingram said. "For Hari's—Akizuki's— sake."

"You knew him?"

"Not well, but I liked him. Everyone did. He will be missed."

Granville nodded.

"Rumor is you found the second body in the cannery a few days ago. That right?"

There was no harm in telling him. Thanks to Dirks, word was out anyway. "Yes," Granville said. "We found him Monday night."

"It was Ben?"

"Yes. I'm afraid so."

"And Hari?"

"They found him a week ago Monday."

Joe Ingram just nodded, his face set. "You want to find out if the *H3340* was scuttled here?" he asked unexpectedly.

Granville looked up, surprised. "I thought you said we'd never find her."

"Depends on how smart Hari's killers were. And killing him was stupid, if they hoped to get away with whatever they've done. Hari —he has friends."

"Then yes, I definitely want to know if she was scuttled here."

"Good. Then come aboard. But I can only take three of you," Joe Ingram said. "We're nearly ready to cast off."

"I'll stay," Trent said unexpectedly. "I'll go back to the bar at the Sockeye Hotel. Listen to the talk. If that's OK?"

"Be careful," Granville said. "There's a killer out there."

Trent grinned at him. "I'll be fine. Go. Find that boat."

FIVE MEN on the *G2977* was a tight fit, but the boat felt solid under Granville's feet as it rocked across the light chop brought up by the breeze. While his uncle and the other crew member rowed, Ingram was competently pulling on some ropes and adjusting others. Clearly he knew his way around a boat.

Granville wondered where they were heading as he watched the waves of their passage flowing behind them. They weren't going far, as it turned out.

On Uncle Joe's word, they dropped anchor just a few hundred yards beyond the Monster Cannery. Granville found it odd to see the familiar building from this perspective—looming up from the docks, the doors at the end gaping darkly in a solid wall of metal. Their boat, by contrast felt even smaller, and flimsier.

He looked up and down the river. The canneries dominated the view. Twelve of them, one after another—their docks jutting into the water and corrugated metal walls glinting in the evening light. On shore, in the gaps between the canneries, he could see a pale red glow that marked the location of the bordello lanterns, reflecting off the cannery roofs.

The water was dark here, and rippled by the wind. The air smelled heavy, with algae and oil and mud. He could hear shouts and off-key singing drifting over the water from the bars that lined Bayview, raucous even here. There were few boats in the river now.

"This is where it gets deep," Ingram explained. "The tide will turn soon, and the currents are strong enough here to drag nearly anything out to sea."

Granville looked down into the opaque, greenish-brown depths. "There's still a lot of mud in the river here. You aren't expecting to see any trace of the *H3340's* wreckage here, surely?"

"No. But you needed to see what Cannery Row looks like to a fisherman. And I want to try something."

Turning to his nephew, Uncle Joe said something Granville couldn't hear. Ingram unearthed a grappling hook on a long line from a nearby locker, and gave it a couple of practice swings. He nodded to his uncle.

"Raise anchor," Joe called out. "Sails."

Granville could hear the anchor chain start to turn a creaking groan. Ingram waited, grappling hook held ready. The sails billowed out, and the boat turned towards shore.

At a signal from his uncle, Ingram swung the hook back, and let it go. It flew several yards back of the boat, and sank without a trace.

Other than the rope that now trailed behind the boat and the occasional ripple of surface, Granville could see nothing but flat, muddy water. Even the lowering sun didn't reflect back.

"You dragging the bottom?" Scott asked with great interest as he watched Ingram anchoring the other end of the rope the grappling hook was on. "I thought it was too rocky here for that to work."

"It is," Uncle Joe said. "Unless there's something big enough down there to catch onto it."

"Like a wrecked boat?" Granville hazarded.

Uncle Joe grinned at him. "Just like that. It's why Billy here used a shorter line than usual."

He thumped his nephew on the back, and Granville was amused to note that the young constable seemed unable to decide whether to look pleased or mortified, settling on an uncomfortable expression somewhere between the two.

"Think we'll find anything?" Scott asked.

"It's a long shot," Ingram said.

There was a loud grating from beneath their feet, and the boat slowed abruptly, nearly knocking Granville and Scott off their feet.

"But clearly one worth taking," Scott said with a straight face, as he steadied Granville with a hand under his elbow.

"Drop anchor," Uncle Joe yelled. "And reel that hook in."

They didn't need to be told twice. While two crew members released the anchor, Granville, Scott, Ingram and the other crewman rushed to haul in the grappling hook, and whatever it had snagged.

"It's heavy," Ingram said with a groan after they'd been hauling for what seemed like forever but was likely under a minute.

"Probably stuck on something," Uncle Joe said with no sign of sympathy. "Keep hauling. Before the tide takes it from you."

After several more minutes that had all of them cursing with straining muscles and rope-burned palms, there was a loud crack. Then a groaning sound, partly muffled by the water.

Suddenly a dark mass covered in river weed popped to the surface. It moved rapidly towards their boat.

"Ease off," yelled Uncle Joe. "She'll put a hole in the boat. Pull to starb'rd. Now!"

He'd been faster to identify the long, curved boards than Granville had. As the heavy, water-logged boards slid safely along-side the *G2977*, and they started to pull them aboard, he could clearly recognize what had once been part of a boat's hull.

Joe moved closer. Pulling a knife from his boot, he scraped away a clump of weeds. Exposing black letters, dark against the white-painted boards.

"The *H3340*," he said heavily. "Hari's boat."

They'd found it. Or rather, what was left of it.

"But why scuttle a perfectly good boat?" Scott asked. "Doesn't make sense."

"It makes sense to someone," Granville said. And if they could figure out why, they'd be one step closer to whoever was behind all this.

36

SATURDAY, AUGUST 18, 1900

"You know, I've been thinking about Dirks," Granville said, setting down his knife and fork and focusing on Scott's face.

Around them the din of the other diners kept their words confidential. Breakfast at Mary's Diner was a tradition for those in the know—and a good one. It had seemed the perfect way to prepare for their meeting with the fellow from Pinkerton's. Especially today, when it would be hard to pull his mind from the case they were so close to solving.

Today, even the chance to affiliate with the powerful international detective agency was low on Granville's list of priorities. But the meeting had been set weeks ago, and could have a major impact on his future, on their firm's future. No matter how it went.

But he couldn't stop thinking about the battered remnants of the *H3340* they'd dragged out of the river the previous day. Somehow those, even more that the pitted bones of the murdered men, spoke to him of life and hope lost.

Emily's stories from Mrs. Sakamoto had made him appreciate that these men had left their lives behind, risked everything for the chance of a better life in a new, raw country—much as he had when he'd headed for the Klondike Gold Rush. To see the shattered pieces of the boat that was to make their dream possible, the boat they'd saved everything to build, just brought that home to him. And he kept thinking about their killer.

"About Dirks?" Scott said, scooping up a forkful of eggs scrambled with cheese and some kind of sausage. "That's enough to give a man indigestion."

Granville smiled a little bitterly at the sally. His sense of humor was suffering on this one. "Perhaps. But the more I think about what was left of the Akizuki's boat yesterday, the more I think we're missing something."

Scott narrowed his eyes at him. "Like what?"

"Suppose Carson is right about Dirks not being our murderer? How would that change our investigation?"

"What d'you mean?"

"Think about it. Even if Dirks had a motive for killing the two fishermen—one we haven't uncovered yet—I can't see what he could gain by having their boat destroyed," Granville said. "And he strikes me as too greedy to destroy something he could repaint and sell."

"Yeah, that's Dirks, all right."

"If it had been one of the dockworkers who'd been killed, I could understand they might have seen or heard something that Dirks would find threatening. But why kill two fishermen?"

"From the little we learned about them, the two victims rarely came into the cannery to unload," Scott said. "We need to find out why they did that day. Maybe they had a reason. One that would threaten Dirks."

"We also need to find out where they went when they were here," Granville said. "It sounds like Hari Akizuki was well-liked, and talked to everyone. Maybe he put some pieces of information together."

Scott nodded. "I can talk to a few people, see where Hari went that day. Who he talked to."

"Which might help us figure out why they were murdered,"

Granville said. "But the more I think about Dirks? The more I think our informant is right. Dirks is too boastful to have got away with these murders. He just isn't bright enough to be doing everything that we're being told he's doing."

"Murderin' those two men and dumping the bodies in his own cannery wasn't smart," Scott said.

"True. Not if it was Dirks's idea, anyway. Given that we immediately focus on him when the bodies are found. But if Dirks isn't the man behind all this…"

"Then he makes the perfect patsy," Scott said, putting down his own fork and leaning forward.

It took a lot to take Scott's focus off of his food, Granville thought. His theory must be making sense. Which was good to know. He'd been worried that it was too much of a stretch.

"But for who?" his partner was saying.

"Exactly. What if someone else is benefitting from whatever's been going on in that cannery? Someone who is the brains behind all of this. Someone who is making the real money here. And who doesn't hesitate to kill to protect that money."

"Someone else at the cannery?" Scott asked.

"Perhaps, though that seems unlikely," Granville said. "The only ones with more authority than Dirks are Boyd…"

"Who's even stupider than Dirks," Scott put in.

"And Owens himself," Granville finished with a grin.

"Owens? But I thought you said…"

"I did a little more thinking on that one last night. I don't think we can ignore Owens," Granville said. "Not at this stage."

"But why would the man steal from himself?"

"And from his partners, don't forget. Owens might not be getting what he feels is a fair share in that partnership. He worked his way up from nothing, remember. Such men often don't get the best of any deals they make with the monied classes. Depending on how his partnership is set up."

Scott nodded, scowling.

Which had Granville wondering what kind of experiences his

partner was recalling. There was a story there—one that bore looking into. Later.

"We need to look into exactly what the setup is for that cannery," Granville said. "Who the partners are, how much money they each contributed. And where the profits go. Especially given what the bookkeeper told me yesterday."

"If it's true," Scott growled. "Sounded like mumbo jumbo to me."

He grinned. "Accounting mumbo jumbo. I asked McAndrews to take a look, and I'm hoping to hear from him today.

"Huh. You really think Owens could be behind these murders?"

"I think we still don't know why these men were murdered," Granville said. "So far, all we have is speculation. We haven't uncovered a single reason. And there must be one, however twisted. These murders don't strike me as random violence."

"Not like Jack the Ripper or someone like that," Scott said, nodding. "Where it's all about blood and gore."

"Exactly. If we hadn't found the second corpse so quickly, all we'd have been left with would be two sets of bones. No blood, no flesh. Just bones."

"Maybe that's why they were dumped at the cannery," Scott said.

Granville frowned. "I'm not following. Why?"

"Well, if you were the opposite of a Jack the Ripper, if you didn't want any mess at all—the lye bath is perfect. Where else would you find something that would get rid of everything but the bones, and so quickly?"

Scott was onto something, he could feel it. "Go on," Granville said, picking up his coffee cup.

His partner leaned forward.

"This wasn't about killing," Scott said, his voice low and fast. "The killer got no excitement from it. The two victims—he wanted them gone, completely gone, their bodies, their boat, everything."

"There was no passion in it," Granville said thoughtfully, putting the cup down. "They got in his way."

"That's it. And so he got rid of them. Quickly and cleanly."

"Methodically," Granville added. "Which still doesn't tell us why they had to die. But it tells us a great deal about whomever is behind this. And it makes me sure that these were hired killings."

"How're you so sure?"

"Think about it. This wasn't about the killing itself. There was no blood lust. And the killer was very careful to leave no evidence behind when he disposed of the bodies.

"Almost no evidence," Scott said.

That earned him a grin. "Who acts like that?" Granville finished.

"Hired killers, cause it's just another job. Yeah, I see what you mean. Except I've never heard of a hired killer being so careful about the traces they left." Scott drank some coffee, wiped his mouth. "And specially not if it was Dirks or one of his henchmen who was hired."

"And that's what tells us the most about the man behind it, the one who hired the killer and his helper," Granville said. "He planned this very carefully, must have given very specific instructions to the men he hired. Knowing they weren't the methodical types.

He drained his coffee, placing the cup carefully back in the saucer. Looked up, met Scott's fascinated gaze. "This was very deliberate. He meant there to be no links between the two Japanese fishermen and the bones found in the cannery. A mystery no-one would ever solve."

"When they never returned to port, everyone would have assumed they'd been lost at sea," Scott said.

"Yes. Leaving no-one wondering what secret they'd died for. Dead and gone, mourned, but with nothing to revenge."

"Nasty," said Scott after a moment.

Granville nodded.

"He has to be someone at the Monster Cannery," Scott said. "Someone who knows everything that goes on."

"Why?" Granville asked. "Dirks is an insider, which gives our man access to everything Dirks knows."

"You really think he's working with Dirks?"

"I think Dirks is working for him," Granville said. "He has to be."

"Because Dirks controls most of the cannery operations?" Scott said. "Yeah, this wouldn't work without someone like Dirks."

"Exactly. And whoever this is, he's a thinker, a planner. And probably an expert manipulator. The kind who likes to stay in the background, while their plans are carried out by others."

"Like a spider. Trapping 'em in his web," Scott said. "But how could two Japanese fishermen be dangerous to someone like that?"

"That's what we'll have to figure out, if we intend to find this spider," Granville said, liking the analogy. "And I do."

EMILY LOOKED up to see Granville coming in, followed by Scott, and hurried to the door to meet them. They were both sharply dressed for their upcoming meeting with the fellow from Pinkerton's, and she thought they looked very handsome. They probably wouldn't appreciate being told so, though.

"I was hoping you'd be here before the meeting," she said, her words coming out in a rush despite her best intentions to speak slowly and calmly.

It was knowing that the man from Pinkerton's—Pinkerton's!—would be here in little more than an hour that made everything feel so urgent. And it didn't help that she hadn't slept much last night for thinking about the case, and those numbers. "I wasn't sure how late it would be when you got back from Steveston."

"Late," Scott said with a scowl.

Emily could tell he didn't meant it. "I know you'll need to discuss strategy for your meeting, but Laura and I need to talk to you for ten minutes first, if you can make the time? Mr. McAndrews came in yesterday, and it's about the numbers."

Out of the corner of her eye, she could see Laura's look of surprise. She hadn't even wanted to raise her concerns with Laura, in case there hadn't been time to discuss them with Granville before the meeting.

And maybe she was worrying for nothing. She might be wrong. Or Granville might not plan to discuss his current case with the Pinkerton's agent at all. But...

"You can have all the time you need. We met for breakfast, and have talked things through already," Granville said, glancing at Scott, who gave him a brief nod in return.

"Good," Emily said, trying not to sound as relieved as she felt. "We can go into your office. We'll still hear the door in case the Pinkerton's agent..."

"Mr. Foster," Laura put in.

"Mr. Foster, arrives early," Emily finished.

Granville was nodding agreement when the opening of the door had them all turning to look. Emily could feel her panic rising. No-one had expected the Pinkerton's agent to arrive an hour early.

But it was only Trent.

"Oh, good," Emily said. "Trent, your timing is perfect. Can you sit at Laura's desk for a bit in case Mr. Foster from Pinkerton's arrives early? We'll just be in Granville's office for a few minutes."

Trent looked like he wanted to argue, but after glancing from her to Granville, he quickly agreed. Emily was impressed. Trent's ability to read a situation by interpreting expressions and body language was improving fast. Which was a very good thing, given a few of the blunders he'd made in the past.

On that thought, she turned and made her way into Granville and Scott's shared office, pausing only to note that the stack of urgent items, with McAndrews' note on top, was sitting on Granville's half of the big partner's desk. Picking it up, she handed it to Granville as he came in.

"Read this first," she said. "Scott too. Then we can talk."

Waving off Granville's unspoken offer of his more comfortable desk chair, Emily pulled one of the lighter guest chairs up to the longer end of the desk and sat. Laura did the same. While Granville read, Emily watched his face, and ignored the questioning looks that Laura was giving her. She'd obviously picked up on Emily's tension, and wanted to know what was going on.

Granville read the note quickly, then spent a little time looking back and forth between the note and the sheet with the five year income figures on it.

"So McAndrews says what is going on at the Monster Cannery is definitely fraud, and on a pretty grand scale," Granville said at last, as he passed the pages to Scott. "Whoever is behind this seems to have figured out how much profit they needed to show every year, then changed the detailed reports accordingly to hide their take."

Scott ran a forefinger along the edge of his beard. "Sounds complicated." He glanced through the two documents. "And you were right that they'd need to be keeping two sets of books."

"From what Leon told me, I suspect they just copy the previous year and make a few strategic changes," Granville said. "Simple. It's ingenious, in its own way."

Emily had a hard time holding her tongue, but it was important that they reached this point before she said anything. She didn't want to influence their thinking too early, not when she might be wrong. Laura too was sitting forward in her chair, as if to join in, but she seemed to be taking her cue from Emily.

As Scott put down the pages, Granville turned to Emily with a smile. "And?" he said. "What are we missing?"

"Possibly nothing," she said. "It was Laura who pointed out the formula being used to set each year's profit numbers. Which not only mean that it has to be fraud, but that there is probably a great deal of money involved."

"Agreed. So what is worrying you so much?" Granville asked.

Trent wasn't the only one that could read expressions. And Granville was starting to read her very well indeed. Emily smiled at him. "What if we're wrong?"

Then as Granville reached out for the sheet of figures again, she held up a hand. "Oh, not about the figures, or what we think they mean. But those came from the bookkeeper, didn't they? Are they written in his handwriting, do you know?"

"I can't be positive, but there were other documents in his office written in the same hand, so I think it a safe assumption," Granville said.

"But you haven't seen the books that back this up?" she said.

"No."

He could see where she was going with this, Emily thought. They all could, judging by their expressions. "So what if the bookkeeper has simply invented this?"

"Why would he?" Scott asked.

"To hide something else," Emily said.

"According to Mr. McAndrews, that formula alone is enough to suggest a major fraud," Laura said. "And the formula was just hidden enough that we had to work a bit to find it. Which is very clever indeed, if these figures aren't real."

"Because the deceit wasn't immediately obvious," Granville said slowly. "Making it seem as if we weren't mean to find it. Which gives it much more credibility, and lessens the chances that we'll look for a different answer once we have found this one."

"And I think you said the bookkeeper suggested you have another bookkeeper look at it. Didn't he?" Emily said, feeling excited. The more they talked about it, the more it seemed she'd been right.

"Yes," Granville said. "Making sure we wouldn't miss the hidden formula."

"And even then, we might have, except that McAndrews felt he was missing something, and Laura spotted it," Emily said.

"If this is a fraud," Laura said, waving at the sheet of figures Granville held. "It was done by a very, very clever man. He didn't make it too easy, but it's obvious once you see the formula."

"A nice piece of misdirection," Granville said.

"But if that's so, then what's he really up to?" Scott asked.

"Whatever is in the other direction from where this information would have you look," Emily said promptly.

"If this is about profits," Laura said. "Maybe you need to look at losses."

"That makes sense," Emily said.

"You mean we're back to thefts?" Scott said.

"But possibly on a more systemic basis than we've thought Dirks was capable of," Granville said.

Looking from her to Laura, he explained, "We now know who our victims are, and we found their boat. And Dirks might not be the one behind the murders, though he's undoubtedly involved." And he filled them in on everything they'd learned in Steveston the day before.

"Wait a minute. What?" Emily said. "You thought yourself that Dirks was the killer. Or maybe had hired the killer."

"Yes. I did."

"And now you know that it was two Japanese fishermen who were killed. From Mio, just as Mrs. Sakamoto thought. And that they probably weren't killed for money, or anything they owned, since the boat was scuttled. Right?"

"Right."

"But you don't yet know of any reason someone would want to kill them?"

"No. But it's possible someone is trying to make it look like Dirks is responsible for all of it. I do think Dirks is involved, but I doubt that he's the brains behind it all. Especially if we're talking about a major fraud. I also don't think Dirks ordered the killings."

"I don't understand. Why ever not? Isn't he the obvious bad guy in all of this?"

"Yes. Too obvious, perhaps. But it's the disposal of the bodies, and of the boat that give it away. They were carefully planned. Too carefully for Dirks. Or any of his men."

Emily blinked. It was quite a change since the last time they'd talked.

"Scott and I have been talking about a spider," Granville said. And he quickly explained their earlier discussion. "If our theory is right, then perhaps Leon—the bookkeeper—really is our spider. He's clever enough for it."

"He'd have to be, to pull this off from a wheelchair," Scott said, a hint of admiration in his voice.

"Or..." said Emily slowly.

All three turned to look at her. "Or?" Granville said.

"Or this document is real, and points to what McAndrews calls a massive fraud," Emily said. "One that your bookkeeper was clever enough to spot. Which would put him in danger for talking to you."

She looked from Scott to Granville. Held his gaze with her own. "Either way, your spider—whoever he is—must be real, too. And has a great deal to lose." She swallowed hard. "Be careful."

37

An hour later, Granville and Scott walked shoulder to shoulder into their new conference room. The fellow from Pinkerton's rose from his seat on the far side of the polished mahogany table and held out a hand. "William Foster."

"John Granville," he said, and shook the outstretched hand.

"Sam Scott."

Granville glanced around the room. Emily had done wonders in getting it decorated and furnished so quickly. It looked pretty good. Simple and businesslike, but expensive. Even a touch elegant. This was much better than the current setup in his and Scott's joint office, which, aside from being too small, was looking a little tired from all the people that had been meeting there.

He was particularly pleased to note the ceiling fan whirling silently overhead. Not a clank to be heard, and the draft of cool air was most welcome. Especially to their visitor. Foster was wearing a well-cut navy suit that looked a little too heavy for today's heat, though his white shirt was crisply immaculate. Summer in Seattle was said to be cooler than here.

On Granville's return from the Skeena, and based on the strength of their growing business, he had invested in several custom-tailored summer-weight suits, and been heartily glad of them. July had been stifling, and August showed little signs of cooling off.

He glanced at Scott, whose navy suit was also custom-tailored—a necessity on his large frame—and made him look very much a partner. Which he was.

At least for today Scott had left off the thick cotton shirts he seemed to have adopted in Steveston, Granville thought with an inward grin. They'd have had a harder time convincing Pinkerton's that they'd be a valuable affiliate had Scott been dressed as he was the previous day.

"I'm very pleased we're finally meeting, and thank you for coming up from Seattle," Granville said as they all sat down

"Happy to do it," Foster said. "We're becoming players in this province, but badly under-represented here in Vancouver, and your firm is building quite a reputation for itself."

"Thank you," Granville said. "We are starting to make decent progress."

Foster nodded. "And you're growing, as well, he said. "Your firm has four employees now, I understand. In addition to the two of you."

Four? And he'd worried three was growing too fast. Emily hadn't gone and hired someone, had she? Who had the fellow been talking to?

"There are three, actually. Our clerk, our assistant, and our... photographer," Granville said. He couldn't quite think how else to describe Emily, though he saw Scott stifling a grin at the description he'd chosen.

He wondered what words Emily might have used. He'd have to ask her how she'd like to be described.

"Ah, I had understood you had an accountant as well," Foster said. "My mistake."

"No, you're correct," Scott said. "We have an accountant who does our books, and has assisted us on several cases. But he's a contractor, rather than an employee."

"I see. And how has that arrangement served you?" Foster asked.

"Very well indeed," Granville said. "But why do you ask?"

"We've— Pinkerton's, that is—have had some difficulties with contract employees in the past. Issues of confidentiality and the like," Foster said. "On the whole we find it works best to simply hire them."

Granville and Scott exchanged glances. "That's useful to know," Granville said. "It's early days yet, but we've been considering making the arrangement permanent. As soon as our income justifies it."

Foster nodded. "A wise caution," he said. "I've seen too many firms put under by growing too quickly. Though I understand you're in little danger of that, since your firm is in great demand these days."

Granville wondered if Foster had talked to any of the cannery owners lately. He knew Pinkerton's had been hired by the Cannery Association in the strike, and clearly they had checked him and Scott out thoroughly before setting up this meeting.

Foster had probably talked to Ross-Murray personally. He wondered what the fellow had heard.

He didn't wonder for long.

"I've been following your cases," Foster said. "Most impressive. And I gather you've been working for the Cannery Owners Association on solving two murders recently."

"We have," Granville said.

"And how has that been going for you?" the fellow asked with a slight smile.

Granville considered him for a moment. He noticed that Scott was sitting back, watching Foster's responses carefully. They'd compare notes later.

He considered giving Foster a diplomatic answer, but decided on honesty. They were considering a partnership of sorts, after all. He wanted to know what these potential partners were made of. Aside from their reputation.

And if they couldn't deal honestly now, their association was doomed anyway.

"About as well as you probably expect," Granville said. "Since we're dealing with two particularly nasty murders. I gather you've worked with the Association on several jobs."

Foster's expression gave nothing away. "Yes, most recently on last month's strike," he said. "We did some background for them on that issue. An interesting situation."

Granville suspected that was something of an understatement. And Foster was watching him carefully too.

"You would have met most of the cannery owners, at one time or another, I assume?" Granville asked him.

Foster gave him a sideways glance. A nod.

"And what's your take on Owens?"

"Owens at the Gulf of Georgia Cannery?" Foster said. "That who you're dealing with?"

"He's one of them, yes," Granville said.

"That's an easy one. I liked him," Foster said. "He knows his business, and he strikes me as one of the more honest of the owners. What you see is close to what you get with him."

Granville was a little surprised, both by the fellow's openness, and by his opinion of Owens. He was inclined to trust both, though. "And Boyd?"

Foster rolled his eyes. Granville had to smile. That was exactly how he felt about the cannery manager.

"I wondered if Owens would pawn Boyd off on you. Having fun?" Foster said.

"Not really," Granville said. "But I'm curious as to why you'd put it like that? Pawned off?"

Foster grinned. "You haven't heard?"

"No."

"Boyd is Owen's wife's cousin."

That explained a great deal. And Foster's words confirmed that Granville didn't need to take Boyd seriously. Not that there'd been much danger of that.

However, the fact that Foster had chosen to disclose that specific fact implied that Pinkerton's really were interested—very interested—in working with him and Scott. Further, he judged that Foster did nothing without careful consideration.

So this conversation with either part of an elaborate test, or confirmation that he and Scott had already passed Pinkerton's test. Either way, the meeting was off to a good start.

And two could play at that game.

Granville had planned to use this meeting to get more information from Foster on the situation at the Monster Cannery in any case. And to see if he had any knowledge of their elusive spider. Since the document the bookkeeper had given them meant that the spider must actually exist—outside his and Scott's imaginations— whether he proved to be Leon Grazzini himself or some shadowy figure they hadn't yet identified.

And this spider was a cold-blooded killer.

Now Foster had given him the go-ahead, as they said in the Klondike. "You ever meet with a fellow called Dirks?" Granville asked.

"The foreman at the Gulf of Georgia? No, I never met the man," Foster said. "However I did hear a fair bit about him."

"Oh? From whom?"

"Various people," he said with the sideways glance that Granville had already decided was characteristic of the man. "You have to understand that our investigations were confidential."

Checking to see how he'd answer, obviously.

"Then perhaps I can tell you a bit about what I've learned about the fellow," Granville said, choosing what he disclosed carefully. "Dirks seems to be as crooked as they come, and I suspect he's stealing from the Gulf of Georgia Cannery. Which is ironic, since he's the one really running things there. But he's too obvious a suspect. Despite some leading clues, he may not be the one responsible for the murders."

"But if it isn't him, Dirks probably knows who it is," Scott added. "Not that he'll tell us anything."

"Interesting," Foster said slowly, then smiled as Scott shot him a hard look from where he lounged on the other side of the table.

"Isn't it?" Granville agreed. "And if Dirks is not our murderer, there must be something bigger behind this. And someone else whom we haven't identified yet. Otherwise these two murders make no sense."

"Not enough motive," Scott put in.

Foster looked from one to the other. And nodded. "You're digging deeper," he said.

The fellow sounded a little surprised, Granville thought.

"Of course," he said. Why wouldn't we? he thought but didn't say. "You know anything that might relate here?"

"Not at this moment," Foster said. "We'd heard something about Dirks, of course. But nothing that would drive the murders you're investigating. What have you found so far?"

"You'll keep the information confidential?"

Foster smiled. "Of course. I consider any discussions about our clients or former clients, including this entire conversation, confidential. And that confidentiality would of course extend to our affiliates. Am I right?"

"You are indeed," Granville said, returning the smile. "Very well, then. The two victims were Japanese fishermen. A father and his son. We've found no motive for their death as yet. But we did find what is left of their boat, wrecked in deeper waters off the Gulf of Georgia Cannery."

Foster looked surprised. "Their boat was wrecked?"

Granville nodded. "It tends to remove the profit motive for the murders—those boats have value. Might be someone sending a message."

"A pretty strong message, if that's the case," Foster said thoughtfully. "It was the Japanese who first went back to work in August, thus essentially breaking the strike. Then the cannery owners protected them, called in the militia. There must still be hard feelings about that?"

"If there are, they're well-hidden," Granville said. "Everything

I've uncovered suggests that the fishermen—of all nationalities—
are focused on bringing in as many salmon as possible. Most of the
bad blood has been put aside, at least while the sockeye are
running."

"I hear the same thing at the cannery," Scott said. "Everyone's
working too hard to act on any grudges they might be holding. But
finding what's left of the boat in the waters outside the cannery?
That ties the murders to the cannery. Even more tightly than
finding the bodies in the lye bath did."

Foster sat forward, his eyes on Granville's face. Paused for a
moment, then nodded slightly. "You might want to look into where
the money is going, then. The canneries are big business, on an
international scale. From what you've said—and from everything
I've heard—Dirks is indulging what is essentially petty theft.
Though on a slightly larger scale. Your murders could mean
someone has a lot to lose."

"I agree. You're suggesting we follow the money trail, and find
out where the money is being made," Granville said. And find a
spider?

It was exactly what they'd been talking about earlier.

"Yes," Foster agreed. "It's the kind of case Pinkerton's likes to
take on. And very much in the way you seem to be doing. I'm
impressed with your approach. And I think our two firms can do
business together."

So it had been a test. On both sides.

Granville considered both the man's expression and his words.
He too was inclined to like Foster's style.

He glanced over at Scott. His partner closed one eye in the
wink. Good enough.

"Then let's talk terms," Granville said.

Granville and Scott walked out into a wall of heat, unnerving after the relative coolness of the conference room. Without speaking, their feet turned down towards the water. It was still hot, but there was a hint of a breeze coming off the ocean. It tasted of salt, and mountain air. Granville still found it amazing how clean the air was here, compared to the sooty smog so common in London.

"So we're following the money?" Scott said, his feet slapping against the board sidewalks in an impatient pattern. "It sounds simple enough. But what does it mean here? Are the bookkeepers' numbers real or aren't they? Emily made a good argument either way. And the only place we've see the money going is Dirks."

"He's the obvious target—which is partly what makes the existence of the spider plausible," Granville said. Thinking as he spoke of some of the examples of his brother's wheeling and dealing he'd seen back in London. "Sometimes the obvious choice is exactly that. Too obvious. And we're meant to overlook a spider."

"You ready to ignore Dirks?"

"No. I think he's part of it. But likely a much smaller part than we'd been led to believe. We need to be sure we're focused on that spider. And not looking too hard in the wrong place."

"So where does that leave us?" Scott asked.

"Exactly where you were suggesting earlier. Finding out why our two Japanese fishermen were killed," Granville said. "Since it wasn't for their boat. And they had no money."

"They must've been a threat to someone. It doesn't seem to be Dirks—but are you sure that isn't yet another trick?"

"Not according to Carson," Granville said. "And you'll note that Foster didn't contradict any of our information."

"So that's why you asked him that question."

"Exactly. As you said earlier, we need to think bigger. If we start with the assumption that Dirks is either not involved in the murders at all…"

"Or he's working for somebody else," Scott broke in. "Our spider?"

Granville nodded. "But then who is the spider? And what scheme are they protecting?"

"Has to be something big. The fraud the bookkeeper warned you about?"

"Perhaps," Granville said. "Though we still have no actual proof of that. Just Leon's word. And some numbers he put together."

"And he might be our spider. Or not," Scott said. "Whoever he is, the guy is good. The spider, I mean."

Granville was still thinking about the kind of money it would take to incite someone to murder. Twice.

It wasn't all that different from an earlier case, now that he considered it. That one had been about the amount of money someone stood to inherit. This was about the amount of money someone could make by stealing from one of the most profitable industries in the region.

But how? And who?

The answers lay in Steveston.

"We need to get back out there," Granville said. "First thing Monday."

"Agreed. We could pack up now, go back to the warehouse tonight," Scott said.

Granville's feet moved automatically towards the ocean, as his eyes took in the stately stone buildings they were passing. This was the heart of Vancouver's financial district. Not all of the answers lay in Steveston.

"No. First, we're going to see a banker," Granville said.

Scott stopped walking and stared at him. "A banker? What, now?"

"We're dressed for it, aren't we?" Granville said with a grin. "You're even wearing a proper shirt."

Scott fingered the fine cotton of his shirt, ran a finger around the neck. Grinned at him. "This? It's too tight for the heat. I prefer my fisherman's shirt."

"I've noticed," Granville said dryly. "But since you're presently suitably attired—we might as well talk to someone. We'll need to rethink how we handle our finances in any case. What with the expansion, and our new partnership with Pinkerton's."

At Scott's look of disbelief, Granville let out a crack of laughter, slapped his partner on the back. "Follow the money, remember?" he said. "And who better than a banker to know about where money is going?"

WILLIAM WARDLE'S office felt familiar to Granville—which was odd, given that he'd only been here once before. The plump banker hustled forward to shake hands. He was dressed in a dark business suit that concealed his girth. And a beaming smile. He looked entirely the prosperous banker, well-clothed, well-fed, and smoothly pleasant.

"Mr. Granville! A pleasure to see you again, sir," he said, casting an inquiring look at Scott, who stood looming above them both.

"My partner, Sam Scott," Granville said.

A sideways glance told him Scott looked very business-like—

except for his size, and the lack of a tie. He wondered what the very proper banker would make of Scott if he'd met him in the rough corduroy pants and worn-in deerskin jacket he'd favored in the Yukon.

Wardle probably wouldn't care—there was more subtlety to this man than he'd first seen. And Scott's presence implied that both partners made decisions about their growing firm. A fact that Wardle wouldn't have missed.

"It's a pleasure, indeed," Wardle was saying, shaking Scott's hand. "I've been hearing good things about your firm. I've even been hearing that you're meeting with the Pinkerton's Agency. And that things are looking good on that front, also. Very good indeed."

Now how had he learned that? Granville wondered. They'd kept that information very quiet. But it meant they'd come to the right place for information on the business deals in town. "Your sources must be good ones."

Wardle beamed at him. "They are indeed." He gestured them towards a grouping of well-upholstered leather chairs. "Please, make yourselves comfortable? Coffee?"

"No, nothing for me," Granville said, and Scott shook his head.

Once they were seated, Wardle leaned forwards. "Might I hope that you have come to discuss your banking needs as your firm expands?" he asked. "Or is this in regard to the coin you shared with me the other day? I'm afraid I've had little success in tracing its origin, though my contacts have been most helpful. I hope to have something for you shortly."

"Thank you," Granville said. "On both fronts. Though we aren't here to discuss either matter. Not today."

Knowing that Wardle would hear the subtle promise that they would return to discuss their banking business with him another day.

According to Emily's father, subtleties were Wardle's bread and butter. Turner had been quite voluble on the topic. Apparently Wardle was a man who made it his purpose to know everything there was to know about the financial underpinnings of this town —and those they traded with.

Which meant he was very well-connected, but it also meant he paid attention to every rumor, every hint. And knew how to fit them back into the overall picture.

Wardle's glance acknowledged that promise, moving from him to Scott, then back again. "Then how may I help you both?"

"We need some information," Granville said, leaning forward. "About the canneries."

"Oh, I'm afraid I'm no expert on canneries," Wardle said, leaning back. "I confess, I've never even been inside one. The smell, you know. The noise."

He waved a hand, as if clearing the air.

"It is the financing of the canneries that we're most interested in," Granville said. "How much money is made there, and who profits. At the Gulf of Georgia Cannery, particularly."

"I see." Wardle steepled his hands together, his face oddly smooth. "They don't bank with me, you know."

"I suspected as much," Granville said. "All the better."

Wardle gave him an inquiring look.

Granville smiled. "Since they aren't clients, you have no duty to protect their interests. And I've asked around. You are considered the man most likely to know what deals are going on in the business community. And where the money is going."

"Well, thank you," Wardle said. "I'll tell you what I can. But I'll need to have some idea what you're looking for before I can be much help to you."

Granville considered the man, nodded. "Very well. But we'll need to be sure anything we tell you is kept in confidence."

"I'm used to keeping business dealings confidential," the banker told him. Then added, with a hint of reluctance in his tone, "Of course, the highest level of confidentiality is usually reserved for my clients..."

It was masterfully played. And all three of them knew it.

Wardle had just convinced Granville that this was the man he wanted as their banker.

After a quick exchange of glances with Scott, Granville held out a hand. "I'm looking forward to our ongoing business relationship."

"As am I," Wardle said solemnly.

"We were brought in to solve the murders of two fishermen, and intend to do so," Granville said. "These are men who seem to have had no enemies. Our killer is someone who hides in the background, someone with something to protect, something big. And enough at stake to risk killing those two. Finding out what's at stake should lead us to the killer."

Quickly Granville explained he'd been hearing rumors about the prosperity of the Monster Cannery. "In particular, I'm hearing that the same profit is being reported year after year. With the insinuation that those numbers do not reflect reality. I'm wondering what your sources might have told you?"

As they talked, Wardle's eyes lit up. "I need to do some digging. There is a money motive behind all of this, you can bet on it. And money always leaves a trail. Somewhere," he said, scribbling a few notes.

"Come back on Monday. Early. I should have something for you."

SO WHAT DO you think of our new banker?" Granville asked Scott as they strode along Hastings Street, maneuvering through the shoppers and delivery men that thronged the plank sidewalk.

"I liked him," Scott said. "Didn't much expect to. Man's looks are deceiving."

"They are that. But I think he'll make a useful addition to our team."

"So it's a team now, is it?" Scott said. "How big is this business you're planning going to be, anyway?"

"Big enough to help us solve our cases effectively," Granville said.

"We're not getting very far solving this one."

"We will. We're getting closer. We've identified the victims, and the way they died tells us a great deal. And we know the spider exists, if not who he is. With any luck, Wardle will have something for us by Monday that will prove helpful."

39

SUNDAY, AUGUST 19, 1900

Sunday morning Granville stepped down from the stagecoach to find a quieter Steveston than he'd yet seen. All of the canneries stood silent and the hot, still air smelled of mud and river water and sea air. Not fish. He could hear several church bells, calling the various congregations to service. It was hard to believe this was the same frantically busy village where he'd spent most of the last two weeks.

He turned down Bayview—which was mostly deserted today—since it too early for the both the saloons and the bordellos—towards the Monster Cannery, lengthening his stride. He had a watchman to interview.

The side door leading to the offices was ajar when Granville arrived. Nick Jones was expecting him. Or at least, he hoped that was why the building had been left open. Otherwise, the cannery had even more problems than he'd realized.

Soft-footed, he made his way to the reception area, where Howell had taken his breaks. He assumed Jones did the same, but there was no sign of the fellow. He must be on his rounds.

Granville looked around him. Sun streamed in through the windows and dust motes swirled randomly in the air, creating an atmosphere very different than the last time he'd seen it. The night the second body was found.

He listened, but heard nothing but the occasional creaking of the dock below him. No footsteps. Wherever Jones was, it would take him a few minutes to get back here. He glanced through the windows. Saw no-one.

Perfect.

Granville made his way quietly down the hall to the bookkeeper's office. Turned the handle. But the door was locked.

He listened again. Still nothing.

He walked soft-footed along the hall to Boyd's office. The handle turned easily under his hand, and he swung the door inwards. Blinked against the sun streaming in through the big windows, far too bright after the darkness of the hall.

Stepping inside, he closed the door behind him. Turned towards Boyd's desk, which he saw at a glance had been cleared off. There was no paperwork anywhere in sight.

Boyd must have an efficient secretary—the fellow just wasn't this organized. But there would be information he could use, somewhere. He scanned the office.

His gaze stopped at the far corner, which the sun barely reached. There was a dark, human-sized shape sprawled half against the wall.

For a long moment he thought he'd found another body, and froze. Then he heard a gentle snore.

Right.

If this was Jones, he wasn't much of a watchman.

And if this was Jones' regular routine, anyone could have dumped Hari Akizuki's body into that lye bath on Sunday morning. By the time Howell came on shift, the lye would probably have cleared enough so that the night watchman wouldn't have noticed anything.

Unless he'd stood directly over the vat and looked in. And there had been no reason for him to do so.

He had a feeling Owens wouldn't much appreciate the report

he'd be writing at the end of this case. And Boyd and Dirks would have some explaining to do.

To confirm his suspicions, Granville made his way into the main cannery area. As he'd suspected, the double doors at the end were wide open. Creating an easy passage for a murderer.

WALKING arm in arm with Granville along English Bay, Emily savored the freshness of the faint breeze that had sprung up across the water as the sun began to set. After the long, hot summer, there was finally a hint of coolness in the air.

And at last she had the chance to hear how their hunt for the spider was going.

When Granville had arrived this evening, she'd been forced to sit through an interminable dinner with her parents, where she had to be on her best behavior and couldn't talk about anything meaningful. She'd sat in uncomfortable silence to keep from asking questions that would have horrified her parents.

And now, finally, she had him to herself. It felt so good, just walking beside him, that she could almost contain her curiosity, just to prolong the moment. Almost.

Granville had been fuming about something all through dinner —she could tell. But he'd done a good job of hiding it. She didn't think her family had even noticed. But she had.

"What's wrong?" she asked. Stopping him with a firm hand on his arm.

"What do you mean?"

She just looked at him.

He grinned. "My brothers always told me, never take a wife who knows how to read you," he said. "But what do they know? I'm going to prove them wrong."

He raised her hand to his lips. "And in answer to your question, it's this case. We're moving too slowly. I'm worried there will be another murder before we can stop him."

"The spider, you mean?" she asked, feeling her cheeks flush at his gesture.

"Yes."

"You still think he exists?"

"I'm now convinced of it. But we're getting no closer. And my hands are tied until Monday."

"But you were in Steveston this morning, were you not?"

"Yes. I went to talk to the fellow who guards the Monster Cannery on a Sunday. Found him sound asleep in Boyd's office."

"Oh no. And I gather it isn't an unusual situation?"

He grimaced. "Not at all. Oh, he tried to deny it, but the truth came out pretty fast. It's what Dirks should have expected for trying to save money by hiring a fisherman. The fellow'd been out fishing for the last six days. He was exhausted, couldn't stay awake."

"So he didn't even try?" Emily was shocked.

"Actually, he did. He rationalized that on a Sunday morning everyone would be at church. By napping then, he could be alert the rest of the day."

"He thinks criminals go to church?" Emily said. "Really?"

"I think he's too tired to think straight," Granville said.

Emily thought about that. "The first body must have been dumped during the morning, then. Someone knew what the Sunday watchman was doing."

"Yes, I think so. But it widens our suspect pool, rather than narrows it. It's the stupidity of it all that frustrates me."

"Yes, I can imagine." They began to stroll again "But tell me—what has happened since yesterday morning? And how did it go with Pinkerton's?"

"Whoa, slowly. Where do you want me to start?" Granville said.

His sideways glance was enough to tell her he was joking.

"Tease," she said. "Tell me about the Pinkerton's meeting, but quickly. I want to hear about the rest of the investigation, too."

He grinned at that, covering her hand on his arm with his own for a moment.

"It went very well," he said. "We've essentially agreed to an affiliation, and to the basic terms of the agreement. William Pinkerton himself will come out to formalize it, most likely next month, unless an urgent case comes up first."

Emily let out a small squeal of excitement, then clapped her gloved hand over her mouth. "I'm sorry. But it's so exciting, I feel like pinching myself. Pinkerton's. And you'll—we'll be working with them."

He laughed. "I feel a bit like that myself. It's an incredible opportunity. And I have you to thank for putting the original idea in my head."

"Well, it seemed too obvious," Emily said. "But now that it's actually happened, for some reason it doesn't seem obvious at all. Why is that?"

"I have no idea," Granville said. "But I'm forever grateful that you look at life that way."

"Oh. Well," Emily said, refusing to blush again. "Anyone could have come up with the idea."

"The way I see it, you didn't come up with the idea, so much as you saw a possibility. One that I hadn't seen. And you believed it could happen."

"Well, yes. Because it could," Emily said. It was logical, wasn't it? "And it did!"

"Yes, it did," Granville said, smiling at her.

Emily smiled back. "But tell me more about the case," she said, suddenly embarrassed. "Have you learned anything more about the spider?"

"Not yet. And that's the problem. I'd thought that once we found out who the victims were, it would be much clearer who the killer is."

"But it isn't," Emily finished. She stopped walking, stared at him. "Or perhaps it is."

"What's that?" Granville said, stopping also and turning to face her.

"Well, before you knew who the victims were, you were

focusing on Dirks. Now you know who they are, he doesn't fit anymore as the villain of the piece."

"That's true," he said. "He doesn't. We still have no evidence, though."

"You haven't been back to Steveston since you started thinking about the spider," Emily pointed out.

He started to say something and she held up a hand. "Except this morning. Which doesn't count, because the cannery is closed." She gave him a sideways glance and a conspiratorial smile.

He smiled back, and they walked on.

"But really, think about it," she said. "You can't find this spider from here. You have to be in Steveston. And until yesterday, you didn't even know you were looking for him—because everything was pointing you towards Dirks. Right?"

"Right," he said, with a grin.

She was glad she was amusing him. Especially when she knew she was onto something, and that he knew it too.

"Now that you're focused on the spider instead of Dirks, you'll solve it," she said with a decided nod. "You'll have the killer behind bars in no time. And then I need your help with this office move." She batted her eyes at him.

He burst out laughing.

As she'd intended him to. Emily felt pleased with herself as they walked on, admiring the first hints of a brilliant orange and pink sunset blooming out over the ocean.

Right up until the moment he glanced over at her and asked if she'd talked to her mother yet.

"To Mama? Why yes, I speak with her all the time," Emily said with an impish smile.

She knew quite well that he'd meant about moving their wedding date up by a year and a half. But she'd hoped to avoid the topic, at least until this case was over. Everything he'd said about the spider worried her.

Though perhaps the thought of having that particular conversation with Mama worried her more. Which wasn't a thought she wanted to face. Not yet.

He laughed again, as she'd hoped. And squeezed her hand. And asked the question she hadn't expected.

"Have you changed your mind about marrying me?" he said quietly.

She stopped dead. "Granville! No!"

Of that she was sure.

"Then that is all that matters," he said, his eyes on her face, his expression serious. "When we marry doesn't matter. As long as you are comfortable with the timing of it."

Emily felt a huge sense of relief. And promptly wondered why.

She hadn't been worried about being married so soon—had she? Surely it was just the pressure of her mother's notion of a proper wedding that was worrying her.

Her sudden silence didn't seem to worry Granville. He brought her hand to his cheek, held it there for a moment. "As long as you know that I will be happy to marry you on any date and in any location you decide on, with or without your mother's assistance," he said, a laugh in his voice but an intent look in his eyes.

Then his eyes danced. "Even if you decided to elope with me. Think of it. We could marry without any bother at all, and take a long honeymoon until all the fuss died down."

It was a surprisingly appealing notion. "A long honeymoon," she teased him. "You'd take me to the Klondike?"

"Anywhere you like," he said, kissing her hand, then tucking it into the crook of his arm. They strolled on.

40

MONDAY, AUGUST 20, 1900

The following morning found Granville and Scott in Wardle's tidy office early, well before the bank opened. Sitting facing the banker across his massive desk, Granville hoped Wardle had learned something useful.

Wardle beamed at them. "I found it," he said, quietly enough that Granville had to lean forward to hear him. "It took some time, and some very careful questions, but I found it."

"What? Where?" Scott asked.

Apparently he'd had no problem hearing the banker.

"The Gulf of Georgia Cannery is the biggest of the lot, with two canning lines running full speed at all times, while other canneries only run one line," Wardle said. "A couple of the others may run two lines occasionally. But the Monster is the one that's fully staffed for two lines at all times."

Granville nodded. He'd heard all this from Dirks. "So?"

"So with nearly double the production, and similar distribution outlets and costs to the other canneries, the Monster should be making nearly double the profits of the others."

"And I assume they aren't?"

"They are not," Wardle said, sitting back. He crossed his hands and rested them on his tweed waistcoat. "I've been able to verify that they are running from fifteen to nearly twenty percent behind where my calculations say they should be."

"Could be a problem on the canning lines," Scott said.

"Once, perhaps. But not only are there indications that this will be the case when this year's profits are counted, it was the same story last year and the year before that, as well. As far as I've been able to gather," Wardle said.

Which made it near certain, Granville thought. And it fit with the figures the bookkeeper had given them. "So we were right? There is something going on here."

"Yes, I believe so. I've uncovered a few rumors, but no confirmation as yet, of under-the-table sales of canned fish—especially the half-pound cans—that could account for the amounts missing from the Monster Cannery."

Granville remembered Dirks's explanation of the canning process. "The half-pound cans are hand-done, and more expensive than the one pound cans. And I was told they make less of them."

"Interesting. Yes, they sell at a premium," Wardle agreed. "So Dirk's statement suggests fraud—consistent, very well-organized fraud. And on a large scale, judging by these numbers."

He'd have to have another look at those half-pound cans, Granville thought. They hadn't looked any different from the others.

But then he hadn't been looking for differences in the product. He'd been looking for a killer. Still was.

Wardle looked from Scott to Granville. "From what you've said, I gather your initial suspect couldn't have managed it?"

"Dirks?" Granville said. He and Scott exchanged glances. "No, he couldn't have. Not on this scale."

"He's not smart enough," Scott added.

Granville nodded. "Either Dirks's thieving is in addition to what you've found. Or he's part of it, but in someone else's pay."

"I haven't found anything to suggest who that someone might be, unfortunately. I've found nothing even hinting that anyone connected with the Monster Cannery is making more money than they should be. Neither Boyd nor Owens seem to be living above their incomes," Wardle said. "For what it's worth."

Interesting. Whoever was behind this was more than careful. And they knew what they were doing.

But who? Granville couldn't think of anyone who would fit. "Then why haven't the cannery owners noticed? Owens has partners, it isn't just him," he said. "If you could see this pattern, surely they would, also?"

"It's possible they're relying too much on the detailed reports they receive," Wardle said. "They'd see some variations in production, up or down, from month to month, and from product line to product line. Not exactly predictable patterns, but reasonable ones. I've noticed that some owners of enterprises tend to do focus on those figures. Me, I'm a banker. I don't look at the reports, I just look at the money, and what it is doing."

The reports again. Granville had a few more questions for the bookkeeper.

"Thank you," he said to Wardle. "You'll be hearing from us."

"Good luck," Wardle said as he ushered them out.

They'd need it, Granville thought, as he and Scott headed for the stagecoach depot. They had a spider to catch.

A poisonous one.

* * *

As he and Scott stepped down from the stagecoach in Steveston—the rattling of which he'd ceased to even notice—Granville thought how oddly appealing little village was, despite its roughness. He'd noticed in the past that objectivity was quickly lost as a place became familiar. As an investigator, it was something he needed to be wary of.

They'd left both Trent and Emily behind today. Over the vociferous protests of both. He'd have to make it up to Emily, he thought, remembering her disappointed face. Probably to Trent, too.

But this last play needed fewer players. The spider was too wary to risk alerting him to the trouble headed his way.

Looking down Cannery Row at the rough board housing for the workers that covered the back lots, Granville realized he'd also become inured to the stench. Then the wind changed slightly, blowing off the river now. And he got hit full face with the smell.

It smelled like something rotten. It made him feel sick to his stomach.

Just like the thought of the spider did.

"You know, after we talk to Boyd, I'd like to have another chat with Leon," Granville said suddenly. "He gave us what seems to be a pretty clear picture of the fraud going on here—which Wardle's information has just confirmed. But that in itself doesn't clear him. Emily is right. Leon's help could still be a clever bit of misdirection. If he were our spider."

"Leon wouldn't have the strength to kill anyone, though," Scott said.

"No, but he might have hired someone," Granville said, thinking about the man he'd talked to. With his quirky sense of humor, the bookkeeper had the intelligence to plan it all—though he really hadn't thought Leon had the personality to be behind something like this.

"You think it's him?" Scott asked.

"I think it's possible. And we have to check. We can't afford to ignore anyone."

It was why they were here, after all—to unearth that rotten core. And eliminate it.

S cott by his side, Granville headed straight for Boyd's office. Spider hunting.

He didn't wait for the fellow's secretary to announce him, waving off her protestations with an impatient hand and a smile that had her beaming back. The cannery manager looked up as Granville closed the door behind himself. Boyd paled, just a little. Fear?

"Morning," Granville said. "Glad you're in. Boyd, my partner, Sam Scott. Sam, the manager here. William Boyd."

Scott nodded acknowledgement.

Boyd's eyes were fixed on Granville's face. "What is it?" he demanded, the harsh tone ringing false. "Why are you bursting in like this? You find him?"

"The murderer? No." Granville pulled out a chair facing Boyd's desk, made himself at ease. "But you owe me some answers."

Scott took the second chair, his eyes fixed on Boyd. He'd let Granville ask the questions here—his job was to watch Boyd's every move.

It was a ploy they'd used before, very successfully. It tended to make even the strongest nervous. Boyd didn't stand a chance.

"I didn't do it," Boyd said hurriedly.

"Didn't do what?" Granville asked.

Now the cannery manager looked flustered. His eyes flicked from Granville to Scott and back. "Um, what answers?"

"You didn't do what?" Granville said.

Boyd grimaced. "Kill anyone."

"No?" Granville said. "But you know who did." It was a flat statement.

Boyd shook his head. "No. No, I don't know anything. That's why we hired you."

"Way I hear it, you had nothing to do with the decision to hire us. Did you?"

"Well, no. Not directly, anyway," Boyd said weakly.

"Enough lies. We need the truth now."

"But... "

"You know something," Granville said. "Or you're afraid you do. And if you don't want to find yourself arrested for murder today, I suggest you start telling me what that something is"

"Oh, but..." Boyd met Granville's gaze, and his protests died off.

He pulled the edge of his blotter towards himself, then looked at it as if wondering what it was for. His fingers plucked at the edge of it, then wound themselves together in his lap. "I... I...."

Boyd looked like a beached flounder, all staring eyes and flapping mouth. Granville felt like rolling his eyes. The fellow was pathetic. "Just tell me," he said. "It will be easier."

"I... I really don't know anything," Boyd said. He glanced at Scott's granite face. "But Dirks might. He—he's the one who knows what goes on, there on the cannery floor. He knows the workers, too."

"What has he told you?" Granville asked.

"Nothing. Nothing, I swear."

"But?"

"But he's made some veiled threats," Boyd said in a rush. "Stuff he can easily deny. He's made it clear he expects me to keep out of his business."

"And what exactly is his business?"

"Well..." Boyd looked away, had the grace to look ashamed. "He —has a lot of independence in how he operates here. I mean, I rely on him to keep the cannery running..."

"He's stealing from the operation, isn't he?" Granville said. "Is that it?"

"Well, I don't know," Boyd said. Glanced at Granville's face, then Scott's. Paled. "I really don't. He—doesn't tell me much. And everything I see looks fine."

"But you suspect. And it wouldn't be too hard for him to cook up something plausible, would it? Not with the way you run the plant."

"No. I mean, yes. I mean—he's the one who knows what's going on. I only know what he tells me."

Right. "And Owens is fine with that arrangement?"

"Well, no. Of course not. I mean, he doesn't know about it. I mean..."

"Never mind. I know what you mean," Granville said, tired of this pathetic little man. "Tell me what you have seen. Something made you suspicious of Dirks."

"Um..." Boyd began.

"Didn't it?" Granville said, giving him a straight look. Beside him, Scott hadn't moved.

Boyd quailed. "Yes, you're right. He's changed."

"How has he changed?"

"He's—never been exactly open, but now he's become secretive. If I walk into his office, he covers whatever he's working on. He doesn't like me showing up on the floor. And I keep seeing him talking to the same three or four men."

"How long has this been going on?"

"A year or so. Maybe two."

Two years? That was ridiculous. "What is Dirks up to?"

Boyd opened his mouth.

"I know you don't know, but I want your best guess," Granville said before the other man could speak.

The fellow nodded. He looked beaten. "He's probably stealing a bit here and there from the cannery," Boyd said softly. "Or maybe pilfering equipment, tools."

And maybe both, Granville thought. And worse, if he was working for the spider. There was no point asking Boyd anything further. The cannery manager had clearly shut his eyes to all of it. "I'll need access to your books."

"You have it. I already said you could."

"Yes, but I want to take your books with me, review them at my offices," Granville said.

"But why?" Boyd asked.

"I don't know who to trust here. Or how the figures might change overnight."

"But—well—oh, very well. Ask Leon when you're done here," Boyd said, looking hunted.

"Thank you. Now, back to Dirks. You know who his men are?" Granville asked.

Boyd nodded. "Some of them are line supervisors. Not all of them, though."

"Do you know which ones are involved?"

"Not for sure."

"Describe the ones you know about."

"They're all big men, heavy shouldered. All are white. All brown-haired. One fellow I've seen with them is taller than the other two by half a foot, and more heavily muscled."

That last could be one of the killers, Granville thought. The strong one they'd seen traces of around the lye bath. "We'll need to talk to them."

"But Dirks..." Boyd began weakly, then glanced at Granville. Stopped. "Fine."

"Names?"

Boyd shook his head. "I have no idea."

Right. The sad thing was, the fellow probably was telling the truth. Granville suspected that the cannery manager didn't know any of the men who worked for him. With the exception of Dirks.

He glanced at Scott, raised an eyebrow. Scott gave him a slight nod. Good. Scott recognized the descriptions.

Granville turned his attention back to Boyd. The cannery manager had struck him from the first as unusually divorced from the day to day running of the plant. And what the fellow had just told him about Dirks explained some of that distance he'd seen. Foster's revelation about Boyd's connection to Owens' wife probably explained the rest. But how had things got to that point?

It seemed Dirks held all the answers. And the foreman wasn't going to break easily. He basically ran this plant, and Boyd knew it.

Dirks held too many cards.

"How did Dirks get such a hold over you?" Granville asked bluntly.

Boyd seemed to have expected the question. All the fight had gone out of him, and he didn't even attempt to deny it.

"It started small, little things where he'd not turn in a report, or he'd skirt some rule or other," the cannery manager said. "But he kept the cannery running smoothly. I let him get away with it. We both know I can't run this place without him. Then it was something bigger. Finally he just stopped doing the daily reports."

"You lost control of the operation," Granville said.

Boyd nodded. "Without even realizing it. At first. By the time I saw what was going on, the damage was done. I couldn't afford to have him leave. Or tell Owens."

From the look in his eyes, Boyd couldn't decide which was worse. Granville suspected not even Owen's wife could save Boyd once the cannery owners realized how bad things were here.

"And yet you're telling us," he said. "Why?"

"It's gone too far. You're a smart man. And your partner is— well... You were going to find out, anyway." Boyd swallowed hard, seemed to force the next words out. "And I'm afraid Dirks might not just know who the killer is. I'm afraid he might be the one behind the killings."

The cannery manager really had closed his eyes to what was

going on around him, Granville thought. Including the character of his own people.

Unless he'd seen something Granville had missed. Which was unlikely.

But possible.

Granville glanced at Scott.

"Dirks is slimy," Scott said. "But he's no natural killer."

His partner was right. And Boyd was pointing fingers again. So how much did Boyd really know?

Granville turned back to the cannery manager. "You have bigger problems here than Dirks."

The cannery manager gaped at him. "What do you mean?"

"My sources tell me that your profits aren't what they should be, not when you're running two lines. You're missing money. A lot of money," Granville said, watching Boyd closely. "What can you tell me about that?"

It was a risk to saying anything to someone who could still be a suspect. But it was one he was willing to take. It was time to shake loose the truth.

Boyd's eyes widened. He went white. "A lot? Missing?" It was a whisper. "But how? Who?"

"You tell me," Granville said. Boyd's surprise, and the fear that quickly followed it, were real, he'd be prepared to swear on it.

But exactly what was the fellow afraid of? Being exposed for a thief? Or simply as an incompetent manager?

"I don't know," Boyd said. "I don't. I swear it."

"Right. I'm sure Owens will love to hear that from you. And your explanation of how it is that you knew nothing about it."

"But—I don't understand."

He probably didn't. "Someone is stealing from this cannery, right under your nose."

"Dirks…"

"Both of us know that Dirks isn't operating on that level. Don't we?"

Boyd shrank back in his chair. "I—guess. But if it isn't Dirks, how is it happening? And who is behind it?"

"Let's ask Dirks that, shall we? I'd be most interested in hearing his answer."

Boyd didn't look like he agreed, but he rang for his secretary anyway.

<hr>

GRANVILLE WAS AMUSED to note that less than five minutes after the secretary left to inform him that he was wanted, Dirks stormed into Boyd's office. The fellow halted two feet from Boyd's desk. Stared at Granville and Scott, now standing either side of the cannery manager's chair.

"I was told Owens wanted to see me," Dirks said to his manager. "So where is he?"

Boyd just stared at him.

Dirks scowled back. "And what's he doing here?" Waving an arm towards Scott.

Time to step in. "I'm afraid this meeting was my idea," Granville said in his most polished tones, fairly certain the accent alone would irritate Dirks further. "I have a few questions for you."

The tone appeared to work. Dirks flushed an unlovely shade of puce, and glared at him.

"What's the matter? Your investigation not going well? Can't find the man who killed your Japs?" Dirks laughed harshly. "Want some help with that?"

"Actually, yes, we do," Granville said.

"Thought you might like to tell us who really killed those men," Scott said, stepping forward so he towered a good foot above Dirks.

Dirks glanced up, then away. "How would I know?"

"Yes, that's the question I had," Granville said. "But after Boyd here told us about the way you actually run the place,"—Boyd made a protesting gesture, then subsided at a look from Granville—"and with all the missing money, well…"

"Wait a minute. Missing money? What missing money?" Dirks said.

"And it all points back to you," Granville said, ignoring him. "Why did you kill them? And in your cannery, of all places."

"They weren't killed here," Dirks protested. Then realized what he'd said. "And it wasn't me. I didn't kill them."

"Sorry. Had them killed, then," Granville said.

Dirks's pitted skin showed white along the jaw. "It wasn't me."

"No?" Granville considered him for a minute, letting the tension build.

Dirks tried not to squirm under the look, but couldn't manage it.

"Who was it then?" Granville finally said.

"I don't know."

"Now you're denying all knowledge of it? Not very believable, I'm afraid."

"Won't wash, pal," Scott put in. "You're in for it now."

Dirks glanced wildly around, then straightened, raised his chin. Glared at Scott and Granville. "No one will believe you two. You've failed to find the killer, and you're desperate to pin it on someone. So you try to blame me. They'll all see through you. Fools!"

"You look guilty, Dirks," Boyd said, apparently caught up in the moment. "And it's well known you're stealing from the cannery."

Dirks turned to Boyd. "And you. You're pathetic, and everyone knows it. If there's been any stealing, you're the one they'll look to. You're supposed to be the damn manager, after all."

"Blaming others won't help you now, Dirks," Granville said, watching the fellow closely. "We found the boat, you know."

Dirks stopped, swallowed hard. "What boat?" he asked, but the confidence had gone from his voice.

Granville was quick to follow up. "The *H3340*," he said, watching Dirks expression closely. "The Akizuki's' boat. It was quite a risk, scuttling it right outside. Too bad it didn't pay off for you."

Dirks shook his head. "I told him it wouldn't work," he said, almost to himself. "Current's too unpredictable there. But no, he had to know better. Him and his damn tide charts."

Tide charts? On a river?

"You confessing, Dirks?" Granville asked. "Because it will go better for you with the courts if you tell us everything now."

"Courts? What're the courts to do with me? I haven't done anything wrong."

Granville bit back a laugh at the expression on Boyd's face when Dirks said that. Dirks seemed to realize he'd gone too far, but it was too late."

"You haven't done anything wrong?" Boyd said. "After our last conversation, you can stand there and say that? You—haven't—done—anything—wrong?" His voice grew louder with each word.

Granville hadn't thought the portly little fellow had it in him. His face went red and he seemed to swell up. It appeared to take Dirks by surprise too. He took a step backwards, putting a hand up, as if to fend off the enraged manager.

"Unless you tell us everything," Boyd said, his gaze fixed on Dirks. "I am going straight to Owens. I'll tell him everything, and request an investigation into everything about the way this cannery is run. Then we'll see who's done what wrong."

Dirks glared back. "I have nothing to say."

"You sure about that? Man sounds serious," Scott put in. "If I were you, I'd tell him what he wants to know."

"I'm sure," Dirks said.

"You have nothing to say?" Granville asked. "I'll be recommending you be charged with murder, you know."

"I..." Dirks began, then clamped his lips tight. "I have nothing to say."

"There's also a lot of money missing," Granville said. "Thousands of dollars in sales."

Dirks looked stunned, then angry—at the figure? Granville wondered—but just tightened his lips. Said nothing.

Granville watched him. "That much money won't be overlooked, you know. And two murders?" He shook his head.

"You'll be hanged for the murders alone," Scott said.

Dirks dropped his gaze to the floor. His whole body seemed to stiffen. But still he said nothing.

Granville wondered what hold their spider had on Dirks.

Whatever it was, it was effective. He glanced over at Boyd, who dismissed the seething Dirks. There was nothing more to be said. For now.

But what was that about tide charts?

Granville was still thinking about those tide charts when he and Scott strode down the hall to the bookkeeper's office. Leon Grazzini looked up as they entered, beamed at them both. "Granville. So you came back," he said.

"Good morning, Leon," he said, opening the door wider. "I'd like you to meet my partner, Sam Scott. Scott, Leon Grazzini."

"Mr. Scott," the bookkeeper said, inclining his head. "Call me Leon. I'd get up, but as you can see,"—and he patted the side of his wheelchair.

Scott stepped past Granville, reached down and shook hands. "Pleased to meet you. And it's Scott."

"We've learned a few things, so we have a few more questions," Granville said.

""Fine by me. Please, sit," Leon said, waving Granville to the captain's chair as Scott leaned back against the now-closed door.

The bookkeeper turned his wheelchair to face them. "How can I help?"

"You mentioned last time we talked that the detailed numbers were changing too little from year to year," Granville said. "How much money could be hidden that way?"

Leon smiled. "A very interesting question. It would depend, of course. But theoretically, you could maybe hide ten, fifteen, even as much as twenty percent. In a good year."

"How would that work?" Scott asked.

"Someone would need to be keeping a second set of books. One set is used to send information to management, the other is the real account of what's happening."

"But aren't you the one keeping the books?" Scott growled. "Shouldn't we be lookin' at you, then?"

The question—and Scott's approach—didn't seem to bother Leon at all.

"Yes, I'm responsible for keeping the books," he said. "But as you can see, I can't easily get around the canning floor. So I can't verify the numbers I'm given," and he waved at his chair. "If there were a second set of books being kept, then you would need to look at the man who's sending those numbers to me."

"Dirks?" Granville said.

"Dirks indeed," was Leon's answer.

It struck Granville as interesting that no matter who he spoke to, everything came back to Dirks. And that Leon's wheeled chair was serving as his alibi. Very conveniently, too.

Much as he was inclined to like the fellow, he couldn't ignore him as a suspect.

"I didn't know Dirks had the training to keep books," he said.

Leon shrugged. "He might not. But someone else close to him might."

"And—theoretically—could you put a name to that someone?" Granville asked.

"I am sorry, but no. I don't see enough of anyone on the canning floor to know who might have that skill," Leon said.

Granville wondered just how true that was. "I see," he said.

"You mind if we have a look at these books of yours?" Scott asked.

"If you have the manager's approval, go right ahead."

"We have it," Granville said. "But we'll need time to examine them. How long can you manage without your books?"

"You want to borrow them?" Leon said. "Then a few days, I suppose. But you'll need to sign each one out. And Mr. Boyd will have to countersign."

The books must really be on the level, then. At least the set Leon was prepared to lend them was. But perhaps McAndrews could find something useful in them, anyway.

"I'll arrange it, then," Granville said. And make sure McAndrews took a long hard look at those books. "Thank you for your time."

And he and Scott left the room quickly, dragging the door closed behind them.

"Phew. Feels good to be out of there," Scott said once they were out in the cooler air of the hall. He dragged an arm across his sweating brow. "How can he stand working in a place that close?"

"Never mind him," Granville said as they left the cannery and turned towards Cannery Row. "What do you know about tide charts?"

"Tide charts?" Scott said. "You've just spent fifteen minutes asking questions about bookkeeping, and getting no closer to a killer. Now you're worrying about tide charts?"

"It was something Dirks said. About tide charts and someone not listening," Granville said. "Did you hear him?"

"I figured he was just trying to blame all this on someone else," Scott said. "And doin' a poor job of it. Why?"

"We need to find Ingram," Granville said, turning up Third Street and quickening his pace. "Maybe he can tell us."

With a resigned sigh, Scott followed him.

"Tide charts?" Ingram said when they tracked him down near the police station. "Why are you asking about them?"

"Dirks said something about someone—and from the context I'm assuming he was referring to the man behind all this—not listening to him about the tide charts," Granville said. "I want to know if the tide charts would play a part in us finding the Akizuki's' boat. Or not finding it."

"Nice of you to explain it," Scott muttered.

Granville ignored him, watching Ingram, who had a small furrow between his brows.

"Well, I'm no expert, you understand," Ingram was saying. "We'd need a fisherman to be sure. But we're so close to the river's mouth, we get incoming and outgoing tides. And a strong outgoing tide can have a huge influence, even this far upriver. It might have been enough to carry the *H3340* out to sea, where it would never have been found."

"But the boat got caught up on something?" Granville asked.

"From what I heard my uncle say, I think so," Ingram said. "The river bottom just offshore is uneven. I think large logs and such get caught up, especially in that area. If they scuttled the *H3340* on anything but a strong outgoing tide, even in pieces, she wasn't going anywhere."

"How common is that knowledge about the tides?" Granville asked, his voice urgent. "Here in Steveston, I mean."

"Well, any fisherman would know it. And probably most of them working at the canneries would know too, since they see the rise and fall of the river every day," Ingram said. "Sometimes the tide is stronger than others, though."

"So Owens should know," Granville said, half to himself. "And Dirks obviously did. What about Boyd?"

"From what I heard, he hasn't bothered to learn much," Scott put in.

That didn't surprise him. "Dirks was working with someone who either didn't know, or thought he understood it better than Dirks did," Granville said slowly. "Either way, we're looking at someone who wouldn't listen to Dirks."

"Arrogant," Scott commented.

"Indeed. And whoever it is has enough knowledge of the canning industry to sell nearly a fifth of their products elsewhere."

"He's got contacts, then. Somewhere," Scott said. "The spider, I mean."

"Exactly. Now all we have to do is find him," Granville said. "I'm off to talk to Gates. Ingram, is he in today?"

"Chief Gates?" Ingram looked surprised. "I think so."

"Good. Then you're with me."

Ingram looked even more surprised, then pleased. Granville hid his smile as he turned to his partner. "Scott, you're headed back to the Monster Cannery?"

Scott nodded.

"Think you can get a look at the labels on the various cans? Without being too obvious?"

"Without getting caught, you mean?" Scott said.

"Exactly. And preferably without letting Dirks know you're back again. He's likely feeling cornered now."

"Yeah, like the rat he is," Scott said. "No problem. I learned a few things, working there," he added with a grin. "It's the half-pound tins Wardle mentioned that you're interested in, right? You thinking they're selling some of them under another brand?"

"I think it would be interesting to find out," Granville said. "Meet me at the Buck n' Ear at noon?"

"That the one at the Sockeye Hotel?"

"It is."

"Good. I like the food. Make it one, then. And try to be on time," Scott said with a grin as he turned towards the water.

Granville watched him for a moment, then headed for the police station, Ingram in tow.

———

GRANVILLE AND INGRAM strolled into the crowded front office of the police station. "I'm looking for your Chief. Is he in?" Granville said.

"Yes, he's here," an overweight constable said with a sour look.

Clearly the Acting Chief was still having difficulties here, Granville noted, feeling sorry for the man.

Ingram looked uncomfortable. "I'll go and see if he's free," he said, stepping forward.

"Thank you. And if he is, are you free to join us?"

Ingram nodded and shot him a grateful look before hustling away. Moments later he was back, and beckoning Granville to follow him.

Gates smiled a welcome as they came in, coming forward to shake hands before waving them both to the chairs opposite his desk. Granville thought the fellow looked more worn than the last time he'd seen him, and wondered what he'd been dealing with.

"What can I help you with today?" Gates asked after they were all seated. "Not another body, I hope?"

"No, thankfully, we have only the two victims still," Granville said. "And we may be getting closer to finding the killer."

"Oh?" Gates said, as Ingram sat forward a little in his chair, attention riveted on Granville. "That is good news. But you don't look particularly cheerful about it. What's wrong?"

"Finding the man who killed the Akizukis may be fairly easy. I suspect it might be one of Dirks's henchmen. But it's the man behind the killer that we really want. And proving him responsible will be hard. That's where we need your help."

Gates considered Granville for a moment before giving a slight nod. "Anything," he said.

And the fellow meant it. Granville was surprised and pleased at the Acting Chief's reaction—Gates was the kind to deliver on his promises, whatever the personal cost.

"You may regret those words," he said with a slow smile. "I suspect we'll end up setting a trap to catch the fellow. And that we'll need all your resources to make it work."

"We have two grisly murders here," Gates said. "And from what you're saying, I gather it's part of a larger plot?"

"It seems so."

Gates leaned forward. "Those are the criminals we need to catch," he said intensely. "Even more than the ones who get drunk and stab their buddy in an argument. Because they're the ones who don't stop. Until we stop them."

Granville thought of a spider, quietly working in a dark corner, spinning a bigger and bigger web. And nodded.

Glancing at Ingram, he was amused—and rather pleased—to see traces of hero worship on the lad's face as he looked at Gates. There might be hope for the Acting Chief after all.

"You've been a policeman here for quite some time?" Granville asked Gates.

"Yes. Nearly a decade," the Acting Chief replied. "The whole area has been my beat, at one time or another. But especially the village itself."

"And the canneries? You must have seen most of them built here over those ten years."

"Most. A few were here already."

"You must know a few things about the canneries and the men who run them, then?"

Gates shrugged. "I don't know that I'd say I know much. But you do hear things over the years—and the canneries are a major industry in this village. You might say I have a feeling for them."

"What can you tell me about the Monster Cannery? How profitable is it?"

Gates shrugged. "It's one of the biggest, and one of the most profitable, from everything I hear. A lot of money passes through that place."

Which matched what Wardle had told Scott and himself. "From your experience, is anyone making more money than they should be?"

"Aside from Dirks, you mean?" Gates said with a sideways glance at Ingram.

The young constable had been keeping his chief up to date, then. Good. "Dirks is the obvious suspect in all this, isn't he?" Granville said. "Yes, aside from him."

"Too obvious, is he?" Gates said. "Very well. The cannery manager, Boyd, is considered weak. And Owens and the other owners are outside most people's experience. No, the rumors tend to focus on Dirks, because he's the one most people notice."

Exactly, Granville thought. Which was what their spider counted on, spinning his webs there in the dark.

It was time to shine some light into his darkness.

43

At one Granville and Ingram met Scott outside the Sockeye Hotel on Fourth Street. Granville hadn't intended to bring Ingram—the lad wasn't exactly seasoned—but Gates had specifically requested they include his constable in whatever actions they took going forward. He couldn't very well refuse the fellow.

Even when his gut told him they were getting too close to a killer.

Scott bustled them all inside, distracting Granville from his thoughts. Choosing a table for four in the quietest corner, they ordered quickly, then got down to business.

"Well?" Granville said to Scott. "Any luck?"

Scott picked up the fresh mug of ale the waiter had just slapped in front of him. "I'll say! To good information," he said, and emptied half the mug.

"Hear, hear," Ingram cried, and took a deep swig.

"And not getting caught," Scott added.

"What did you do?" Granville asked.

"Poked around a bit. Nothing too dangerous," Scott said with a wide smile.

Of course not. And that heady feeling of relief after danger had passed had nothing to do with why Scott's beer was vanishing so quickly, either.

"So what did you learn?" Granville asked, raising his own mug.

"Well, I scouted around some, checked out the canned salmon. Especially the half-pounders. First off, the labels on the cans are all the same. So that's no help. But then I went looking for the finished cases. Found something odd," Scott said, downing the rest of his beer and signaling for another.

"Oh? And what's that?" Granville said. Bracing himself.

"Well, they crate the cans, label them for shipping, probably just like any cannery," Scott began.

Granville glanced at Ingram, who was nodding.

"The finished crates are stacked in a back room, rows of 'em. All waiting for the next sailing ship to dock," Scott said. "The ships converge on Steveston, load up their holds full of canned salmon for the trip around the Horn to England."

"It's quite a sight," Ingram said. "Last season, there were eleven sailing ships anchored just past Steveston Island, waiting for the tide to turn so they could sail in and load up."

"And?" Granville asked.

"And I poked around some in that back room. Everything looks fine at first, but there didn't seem to be as many crates of half-pound cans as there should be, given what I'd seen going into cans on the canning floor."

"So you investigated further," Granville said. "No wonder you were glad not to be caught."

Scott grinned at him.

"You are keeping in mind that they've already killed two people to protect their secret?"

"Hey, I was careful," Scott protested.

"You should at least have had someone along to watch the door for you. But since you made it out again—what did you find?" Granville asked.

"Stack after stack of half-pound cans. Hidden way in the back, and kinda off to one side of everything else," Scott said. "And from what I could tell, the labels on those crates used a different numbering system than the other ones in the storeroom. It'd be easy to keep them separate when they were loaded."

"So that part of the shipment might end up being delivered somewhere other than where it was supposed to be going?" Granville said thoughtfully. "And sold through a different delivery chain."

"But how would they pull that off?" Ingram asked.

"Different shipping labels, invoices. That'd allow the profits to go to a different company entirely," Scott said. "That's probably what the second numbering system is about."

"Which would explain the missing revenue that Wardle uncovered," Granville said. "But it would definitely require that there be two sets of books kept."

"You think Leon—their bookkeeper" Scott said for Ingram's benefit, "—is in on this?"

"I still don't know," Granville said slowly, thinking over their recent conversation. "He was pretty persuasive. And that chair of his does limit his movements. But we can't ignore him, either. Someone is keeping that second set of books. I can't see Dirks keeping all of this straight by himself."

Scott chuckled. "Me neither. But the bookkeeper will keep. Because that's not all I found."

"What else?" asked Ingram, leaning forward, eyes gleaming.

"I also found out that Hari Akizuki was really angry that day," Scott said. "The guys I talked to say Hari was a genial sort, just like we heard. But he hated injustice, and it would get him hotter than anything."

"So our first victim had a passion for justice? And a temper?" Granville asked. "That doesn't seem to fit the man Ingram's uncle talked about."

"No, it fits," Ingram said slowly. "Hari Akizuki was well-known here. And I knew this about him, you know? But his temper showed so seldom, I never thought about it."

"Well, something had got him hot that day," Scott said. "He and his son had been fishing just outside the mouth of the Fraser. He'd landed at the cannery barge, tied up, was going to unload there. Was just waiting his turn, so he sent his son aboard to collect their mail."

"Their mail?" Granville asked.

"Cannery ships brought it out on a regular basis, as a service to the fishermen," Scott explained.

It was a strategic move on the part of the canneries, Granville thought—yet another thing to bond the fishermen tightly to a specific cannery. "And something Akizuki read in his mail upset him?"

"That's what the other men who were there think. He didn't talk to anyone about it, if so. But he didn't seem himself, according to them. Wasn't making his usual jokes, didn't stop to chat. Just muttered to himself and to his boy, then called over that he was going to take his catch into town, and cast off. That's the last anyone saw of him."

"When was this?" Granville asked.

"The Friday, two days before his body was dumped at the cannery."

"And did he sell his fish here?"

"Dunno," Scott said. "Aren't those the records Dirks is refusing to release?"

"They are indeed," Granville said. Time for another little chat with Boyd. And this time, the cannery manager was going to have to step up and do his job. For once.

He looked from Scott to Ingram. "And what was in the mail that upset Akizuki so?"

"No-one knows for sure. But that day, they all got their statements on what they'd been paid for their catch the previous week," Scott said.

"They did?" Granville found that every bit as interesting as Scott seemed to. "And just what information does that statement give them?"

His partner grinned. "I figured you'd want to know that. So I tracked down a fisherman I know, and borrowed one of his state-ments." Pulling a much folded piece of paper out of his shirt pocket and passed it to Granville.

Who unfolded the slightly slimy page carefully. And examined it equally carefully.

"This is just the dates, the total paid, and the number of fish that total is based on," Granville said after a moment, passing the page to Ingram. "Hardly seems enough for two murders. I had hoped for more."

"Yeah, so did I," Scott said.

"Most of the fishermen hereabout keep at least a rough track of the size of each cargo they sell," Ingram said thoughtfully. "They'd know as soon as they checked if the totals match up. If they didn't, I can see Hari being pretty steamed.

"It wouldn't be the amount being paid that angered him?" Granville asked.

"Nope. After the strike, everybody had settled at nineteen cents per fish for sockeye—Japanese, Indian, Chinese and whites alike," Ingram said.

"Then if Akizuki was mad, it must have been about the number of fish he'd been credited for," Scott said. "Someone was shorting the loads?"

"Sounds like it," Ingram said.

"Who has the access and the authority to do that?" Granville asked. "Besides Dirks," he added when Ingram opened his mouth as though to speak.

"Oh. Um. It could have been an error on the cannery barge. Or the loading dock," Ingram said slowly. "You know, the places where they unload the fish."

"But Akizuki left the cannery barge," Granville said. "Without asking questions?"

"Yup. That's what I heard," Scott said.

"What are the odds Akizuki went back to speak with the fellows on the loading dock?" Granville said quietly to Scott. Who nodded.

"I'd say they were pretty good," Ingram broke in.

The lad had very sharp hearing—and no manners to speak of, Granville thought with a wry grin.

"But why not ask questions on the barge?" he asked them both. "Why cut short his fishing and sail all the way back to town?"

"Maybe he knows—knew—someone on the loading docks," Scott said. "Someone he could trust, someone it was safe to ask a question like that."

"Or someone he thought he could trust," Ingram said. "He is dead, after all."

Granville shot Ingram a look, and the young constable took a step back.

"Well, he is."

"A little respect wouldn't come amiss," Granville said. "Akizuki was a good man, from everything we've heard."

Ingram looked away.

"Or perhaps Akizuki wanted to talk to someone else entirely," Granville said. "And it got him and his son killed."

He turned to Scott. "Can you find out who he talked to?"

"I think so. If I keep asking questions of the right people," Scott said.

"And where he went after he left the docks?"

"I'm having little luck with that, so far."

"As in he may not have left?"

"As in everyone I've spoken to either has no idea, or clams up and insists they have no idea," Scott said.

"You don't believe them?"

"No."

"I see." Granville turned to Ingram. "Well, what if we suppose he did talk to the fellows on the dock. And they didn't have the answers Akizuki was looking for? Where might he go then?"

"Oh, um... I don't know," the young constable stuttered out, suddenly interested in the arrangement of cutlery on the table. Poor though it was.

Figured, Granville thought, turning to Scott and quirking a brow.

"I asked about that," Scott said, deadpan. "Seems all the numbers from the docks went to Dirks. With a copy to the book-keeper."

Leon again.

Granville thought about the wry little man in his dark office and wondered again how much he knew. And how accurate the set of books he'd promised to loan them would prove to be. The book-keeper was either innocent of any part in whatever was happening here, or very clever at deception. He wondered which it was.

It was obviously past time to find out.

"What was that you said earlier, about how the canned salmon was stacked, ready to be shipped out of here?" he asked Scott.

"Yeah?"

"Someone's already put those deals in place. Deals to ship the stolen cans out, and deal to buy them at the other end. And whoever it is has arrangements with someone at the cannery itself —most likely Dirks, based on what we've learned so far—to get those cases tagged and set aside."

"The spider," Scott said.

"Agreed. But what kind of threat would a fisherman like Hari Akizuki pose to him?" Granville said. "If someone—likely Dirks—was shorting the fishermen's pay by under-reporting their catch, it wouldn't have anything to do with the stolen cans. So why would the spider care?"

"Because it must be how they keep the reports clean," Ingram broke in excitedly. "You said earlier that Owens hasn't noticed the theft. So the reports he gets must be legitimate. And if they under-report the number of salmon caught…"

"They can under-report the number of salmon canned," Scott said.

"And hide a good portion of the overall catch," Granville finished. "Good thinking, Ingram. You might be right."

The young constable beamed.

"Though the estimates we've been given suggest that as much as a fifth of the catch may be being stolen. That's a lot of fish to under-report. Surely some of the other fishermen would have noticed."

"Not if it's only a fish or two here or there for any individual fisherman. Spread out over a four month season," Scott said. "Well, three months this year."

"Most don't actually count the fish themselves," Ingram put in. "Hari, though? He would have, from what I've heard."

"So it is feasible," Granville said. "And perhaps Akizuki was angry enough—and well-respected enough here—to be a threat to the whole operation. Which means that Hari Akizuki and his son were murdered because they spotted a piece of the fraud."

"That's why their bodies were thrown in the lye bath. So no-one who saw how upset Hari was could make the connection," Scott said. "And now that we've made it—that's why no-one will talk about where he went that day. They're all afraid."

"With good reason," Granville said. "Saying anything might put them in danger, too."

"So how do we find the spider?" Scott asked. "Whoever it is might not even work at the cannery."

"He probably doesn't work there," Granville said as he stood up. "But he'll have his sources. I can guarantee he'll hear pretty quickly if there's anything going on at the cannery. Let's go."

"Where are we going?" Ingram asked, trailing along behind them.

"The cannery," Granville said. "And we'll need your help. Can you give us a couple of hours, then meet us in front of the cannery?"

"So meet you at three-thirty? Sure, I can do that," Ingram said. "But what are we going to do?"

"It's time for this investigation to go public."

"We going to stir things up some?" Scott asked.

"We are indeed," Granville said. "We have a spider to trap."

4 4

The cannery floor was as noisy and frantic—and smelled as rank—as ever. But unlike the first time he'd been here, the all-out assault on his senses didn't faze Granville. He registered it all in a quick glance, then tuned it out to focus on his targets.

The floor supervisors reporting to Dirks. Especially the very tall ones.

It was time to talk to the men who'd hauled the body into the lye bath. One of them had been very tall, and very strong. He was the one Granville was looking for now.

And he was easy to spot.

The fellow stood at the far side of the cannery line, clustered together with several other of the supervisors. And he stood half a head above all of them. Dark-haired, dark-eyed, with broad cheekbones and a hard mouth, he looked like someone Granville wanted to avoid meeting in a dark alley.

Granville nudged Scott, inclined his head in the direction of the cluster. "Who's the tall one?"

"Jeb Brazinski. Smarter than he looks, but Dirks hired him mostly as muscle. Sending him in to sort out an argument is usually enough to scare anyone back to work."

"Makes sense." Granville noted the rough cotton coveralls that Brazinski was wearing. They looked like they might match the threads they'd found near the lye bath. "Let's see if he wants to chat."

Brazinski looked up as they approached. His face showed no apprehension. Instead, he smiled broadly at Scott. "Scott!" he said, loud enough to be heard easily over the clanking of the canning machine.

Scott smiled back. "We've a few questions for you, Braz. If you will?"

"Yah, sure. Dirks know?"

"He does now," Scott said.

"Okay, then. You want to talk here?"

"Too noisy," Scott said. "Follow me."

And Brazinski followed Scott back to an empty office Boyd had made available to them. Granville brought up the rear, just in case someone decided to object. Or Brazinski decided to run. Which he showed no signs of doing.

So far, he was the least suspicious suspect that Granville had ever run across.

"So. What'd you want to know?" Brazinski asked when he was seated across the small meeting table from Scott and Granville.

Granville sat back, happy to let Scott take the lead. He wanted to observe their suspect. Who wasn't behaving anything like a suspect.

Had they been wrong in their interpretation of the traces he and Ingram had found at the lye bath?

"You know by now that I'm a private investigator?" Scott was saying.

Brazinski smiled broadly. "I didn't believe it. For real?"

"Yeah, 'fraid so."

"Well good on you. You any closer to finding who did those killings?"

"Not really. That's why we," gesturing towards Granville,

"wanted to talk to you. You mind answering a few questions about that?"

"Nope. I'm happy to."

"Well, good then," Scott said, then glanced at Granville.

Neither of them had expected this level of cooperation, and Granville could see it had thrown Scott a bit. In addition, he suspected Scott rather like the seemingly genial fellow, which would make questioning him even more difficult for him.

"Thank you, we're grateful," Granville said. "Can you tell us if you were working the days of the two murders?"

Brazinski looked blank, so Granville gave him the dates.

"Ah. Sure. I've been working every day except Sunday all month. Gotta get the catch in, you know," he said to Scott.

Who nodded.

"And do you remember seeing anything unusual either of those days?" Granville said.

Brazinski thought about it. "Nope. Nothing comes to mind."

"Tell us what kind of work you do for Dirks?"

"We keep an eye on the cannery line, keep it moving," Brazinski said. "Like Scott here did. Break up any arguments, if they come up. Like that."

"It gets physical, then?"

"Yeah, sometimes. Not often. I've never had to break any bones, or nothing."

"Do you remember if you were asked to do anything unusual on those nights?"

Their suspect laughed. "Like dump a body into the lye bath?" he said. "I think I'd remember that. No. I wasn't. And no-one else was, either."

"Any idea how that body got there?" Scott said. "Cannery was running pretty long hours on both those days. It'd be hard to dump a body without being seen."

Brazinski leaned forwards. "It had to be after hours," he said. "He'd have been seen, otherwise. Had to be someone strong, to fling a body in there. Someone who knew the layout here, and how to avoid gettin' lye on themselves. The stuff burns, y'know."

"In fact, someone very like yourself," Granville said.

"Yeah. Exactly," Brazinski said. "Wait a minute. You lookin' at me for this? 'Cause I wouldn't do something like this. And none of the others would, either."

"Well, someone did. And there aren't too many people who fit the description you just gave us," Granville said.

Brazinski just looked at him. Then at Scott. And held out his hands, as if expecting to be handcuffed.

"You confessing?" Scott asked him.

"Seems you've made up your minds it's me," Brazinski said. "Not much else I can say, is there?"

Interesting. He'd made no attempt to run, yet the man was big enough to take on both himself and Scott. He might not win, but it would be close. Granville wondered why he'd given up like this.

"You could give us another name," Scott said. "If you didn't do it, who would have?"

"I wish I knew," Brazinski said. "But I don't. I didn't see anything then. Haven't heard anything since."

"Seems like you want to be arrested," Scott said."

"No. I don't."

"Then maybe you should think a little harder about who might have done it," Scott said. "There were two of 'em. Both strong. At least one was tall."

"Both missing around nine, nine-thirty. On both nights those nights," Granville said. "Where were you, then?"

"Bunch of us went out for drinking."

"Where?"

"The Troller."

"Who went along?" Scott asked.

Brazinski frowned. "Everyone, I think. All the supervisors, I mean. Except you, 'cause you weren't even hired the first night, and wouldn't join in the second one."

Scott ignored the sally. "And did everyone stay together?"

"Sure. Well, after midnight I'm not sure, 'cause I don't remember much. But up till then, yeah."

"You notice anyone missing around nine, nine-thirty?" Granville said.

"Nope. I didn't. I…" Brazinski's voice tailed off.

"Well?" Granville said.

"Well, I don't know what happened to Carson. He's kinda short, so I doubt he's who you're looking for. But seems to me he vanished for a bit, the first night, anyway. I'm not so sure about the second. Probably around that time."

"Carson?" Scott glanced at Granville, then back at Brazinski. "You sure?"

"Yeah, I think so. No, I am. Carson wasn't there. He might have just had a beer somewhere else, though. He does like his beer."

"Anyone else missing, even for a bit?" Granville asked. "Anyone other than Carson?"

Brazinski shook his head. "Not that I noticed. The others might have seen, though."

"Which is why we'll be talking to them next," Granville said. "If you make any attempt today to talk to them about our discussions here, it'll be seen as an admission of guilt. Which we'll act upon accordingly. Agreed?"

"Yeah, sure." Brazinski said. "I got nothing to hide."

That remained to be seen, Granville thought. Brazinski was still their best suspect, on size alone.

Two hours later, Granville and Scott had talked to all four of Dirks's supervisors, including Carson. One of them remembered the same thing Brazinski had. One didn't wasn't sure, but thought everyone had been there all night on both nights.

Carson thought he remembered Brazinski and one of the others as both being missing at the key times.

"So who's lying?" Scott said to Granville as the door closed behind the last of their interviewees. "Carson? Or Brazinski and his pal?"

"Probably all of them, to one degree or another," Granville said. "We have more questions to ask. And if Brazinski is telling the truth about who was missing on at least one of those two nights, then Carson may well be involved. In which case, he had an accomplice. Let's see if such a fellow exists."

Just before four p.m., Granville, Scott and Ingram strode into the main room of the cannery. Both canning lines were running at full speed. Half-pound cans clattered as they were loaded into crate after crate.

Granville wondered how many of them would show up on Owen's next statement. His gaze swept the room. No sign of Dirks.

Granville nodded to Ingram. Who straightened his shoulders, took a step forward.

"Where is Dirks?" Ingram demanded loudly, his voice barely rising above the noise. "I need these lines shut down. Now."

He got a few confused looks.

Several of the men they'd just interviewed were looking their way. Brazinski gestured and took a step forward. Another fellow held him back. Whatever they were saying was lost against the ordered mayhem of two canning lines running full out.

There was no sign of Dirks. Where was he?

Just as he was about to ask Scott to look for the foreman, Carson stepped forward. "Need some help?" he asked Ingram. But his eyes were on Granville.

It surprised Granville a little that Carson would be willing to be seen helping them. But this was the police, after all. Not a private investigator. Perhaps that mattered here.

Ingram was nodding. "I need these lines shut down. Now. Where's Dirks at?"

"He was here a minute ago," Carson said. "I can look for him for you, if you like. But he won't shut it down. We'd lose too much time."

"That's up to Dirks," Ingram said. "Get him for me."

Ingram was holding up surprisingly well, Granville thought. Especially in keeping his composure when faced with a man twice his age. And Carson was making it easy for the young constable, though he cast a speaking look at Granville as he set off to find Dirks.

Granville, Scott and Ingram stood where they were, watching Dirks's men and the unceasing activity of the cannery.

Fifteen very long minutes later, Carson was back. There was no sign of Dirks, but an annoyed looking Boyd was following at Carson's heels.

"I couldn't find him," Carson said.

"What's all this?" Boyd said loudly, as he puffed up to them.

"I need to talk to Dirks," Ingram said. "Now. Where is he?"

"I don't know," Boyd said. "He should be here." He glanced around. Then walked to Dirks's office and peered inside. Shook his head.

"Did you check the back rooms?" Scott asked Carson.

Who nodded. "No sign of him."

Scott looked up towards the cannery loft overhead. Carson's eyes followed.

"I'll check there," he said. "Never thought of that. Can't think why he'd be there, though."

Gesturing to one of the Chinese men sealing cans, Carson motioned towards the loft and said something.

The fellow trotted off, climbed the ladder and poked his head into the cannery loft. If he was talking to someone, none of them could hear it. After a moment, the fellow's body and legs disappeared as he wiggled his way up into the loft.

He re-emerged a few minutes later, shaking his head at Carson before he got more than halfway down the ladder.

"So where is he?" Boyd said.

A commotion from the loading docks had all five of them hurrying down the cannery floor towards the double doors at the end.

Looking out, they could see a fishing boat tied up for unloading, a bin half-full of fish, and another full bin which was stopped part-way up the trolley. Along the edge of the dock, shovels in hand, stood the four workers who should have been unloading the catch. They were yelling loudly, waving their arms and pointing at something large floating in the water.

Whatever it was bumped gently against one of the pilings with every small wave. Then a partially submerged log collided with the object, causing it to roll a little. Granville could see an eye, and half of a nose.

They'd found Dirks.

***

WITHIN THE NEXT FIVE MINUTES, Ingram had called for assistance, then gone down to the wharf to arrange the recovery of the body. Carson had gone back to his work. Scott and Granville were left standing with Boyd, looking out over the wharf.

"We need to question everyone here," Granville said to Boyd. He had to shout to be heard. "Find out who saw Dirks last. And where."

"Shut down the canning line, you mean?" Boyd said. "No. You can't."

What was wrong with Boyd? "Your foreman was just killed. We need to find the man who did it," Granville said.

"But—he did it himself," Boyd sputtered. "Must have. It just proves he's the murderer. The man you've been looking for, the one behind all this."

Granville and Scott exchanged glances.

"Don't you see? Boyd said. "He was guilty. You were questioning his men. He knew you were getting too close, that he had no chance. So he chose to end it."

By drowning? "We can't know that until the coroner examines the body," Granville said.

"Well you can't shut down the lines," Boyd said. "They wouldn't have seen anything anyway."

Which was quite likely, given how fast the lines moved. The workers' focus was on the task at hand. "We'll have a look at Dirks's body first, then," Granville said.

"Until the shift ends. And then we'll talk to the line supervisors again," Scott said. Pitching his voice so it carried. "They were probably the last to see him anyway."

"Humph," Boyd said. But he left them to it.

"You think Boyd's right, that Dirks killed himself to escape being exposed?" Scott said quietly.

They had walked back along the canning lines and gone into Dirks's office when Boyd left. Here they could talk without shouting. Granville took a quick look around them, to ensure they couldn't be overheard, then turned back to Scott.

"I think we'll find that Dirks has a nasty crack on his head, which could possibly have been caused by hitting his head against one of those pilings down there," he said. "But which the coroner will discover was from a blow delivered at an angle that could only have been delivered by an opponent."

"Another murder then, you think?"

"Yes."

Scott nodded. "Thought so. Now that we're rid of Boyd, where do you really want to start?"

"Is there any possibility someone saw you go into the shipping storeroom the other day?"

"It's possible, I guess," Scott said. "Why?"

"Because maybe someone saw you go in, and knew how long you were in there," Granville said. "So he knew he was at risk. When we started questioning the line supervisors, he knew we were getting close. He was afraid Dirks would turn on him."

"The spider? He's here?"

"I believe so."

"So he killed Dirks, what? To shut him up? As a scapegoat?"

"Probably both. But also as a diversion, I suspect. Let's go."

"The shipping storeroom?" Scott said. "You think he's there?"

Granville nodded. "Either he's there now or he'll follow us there."

"This way," Scott said, turning down a narrow passageway running behind Dirk's office. "But I can't see him going there."

"He'll be covering his tracks," Granville said. "Making sure Dirks gets blamed if you found everything earlier."

"You mean he's not going to run?"

"The spider? No. He'd rather outsmart us all."

Scott grunted at that. "He'll be armed, though."

"Oh, yeah. He's the poisonous kind. And Scott?" Granville said. "Don't get too close to him. Just in case."

"I can take him," Scott said. "No matter how big he is."

At first glance, the shipping storeroom seemed deserted. As Scott eased the heavy fir plank door open, Granville could see that the back portion of the room contained a solid wall of wooden cases, stacked more than ten feet high. The ceiling was a good six feet higher. But there were lights shining dimly overhead.

Someone was in there.

Scott pointed to his left, quietly crossed the empty floor and began to work his way down a narrow aisle between the outer wall and the first row of cases. Granville followed behind, the gun he seldom carried—but had strapped in place today—held ready.

The air felt thick. Hot, dusty and hard to breathe. Through the wooden thick walls, they could hear the muffled clamor of the canning lines. The room full of people they'd just left seemed far away.

Scott vanished around a corner, Granville close behind him. Another corner. Then another.

They seemed to be moving along a narrow corridor with shipping cases on one side and the back wall of the room on the other. Granville wondered what it was for. And how many men were in the spider's pay, to accomplish this.

They moved in silence, Granville stopping when Scott did. Both choosing every step carefully. Listening hard.

As the spider undoubtedly listened for them.

Though hopefully he was arrogant enough to expect his 'diversion' to have kept them occupied while he covered his tracks.

And Dirks, who'd schemed so hard to be important here, was reduced to a diversion. Poor fellow, Granville thought. Unpleasant though he'd been, no-one deserved to die like that.

Scott stopped again. Waited for Granville to come up behind him. Pointed forward, indicating a bigger space ahead with a couple of gestures.

Granville checked his partner also held his gun at the ready. Nodded.

Scott held up two fingers. Dropped one. Then the other.

The two of them surged into the smallish opening in the midst of the stacks of cases. Guns out.

"Don't move," Granville said. "Not even a finger."

Carson looked up at them from three feet away, pen in hand.

Carson?

On one level Granville wasn't really surprised. The fellow had been a possibility since their conversation with Brazinski. On another he was shocked that he'd misjudged him so badly.

"But I was just finishing these," Carson said, gesturing towards the boxes. "With Dirks gone…"

"Not another word," Granville said. "Drop the pen."

"But really, I was only…"

"You heard him," Scott said. Quiet. Deadly. "Shut. Up. And turn around."

With exaggeratedly careful motions, Carson placed the pen on the protruding edge of a nearby case, and began to turn.

Granville didn't like the smirk he gave as he did so.

But even so, he wasn't ready for how quickly Carson moved. Small as the fellow was, he was all wiry muscles.

And he was fast, moving like he was on springs.

Carson had a hand in his pocket and had launched himself at Granville before either Granville or Scott could move.

That was when the small space they were standing in worked against them. They couldn't risk a shot.

Both Granville and Scott surged forward. Banged into each other.

Scott knocked Granville back. Out of danger.

Before Granville could recover, Carson's arm was driving towards Scott's heart. A needle glinting in his fist.

Where had that come from?

Granville used the solid stacks of canned fish behind him to push off of, diving headfirst into the spider's midsection. Driving the smaller man down and away from Scott.

But he was too late.

Carson's needle caught Scott's arm, stabbing down before Granville's momentum tore it free and drove both of them to the ground.

One quick blow to the jaw and Carson was done.

Granville drew in a harsh breath and got to his feet. Turned to Scott.

"How bad is it?

THEY RUSHED Scott to the Japanese Fisherman's Hospital, only a few blocks away.

"He barely nicked my arm," Scott protested from the back of the grocer's delivery wagon, where he half lay, with Granville supporting him. The wagon had been the closest transportation available when they'd carried Scott out of the cannery.

"Yes, but with what?" Granville said, his glance on Scott's arm, already red and swollen. It looked worse every minute, despite the tourniquet—his necktie—that Granville had put on within minutes of the attack.

He'd also considered cutting into the wound, like he would for a snakebite, but the needle looked as if it might have scraped along the surface rather than punctured deeply. He was afraid a cut would simply suck the poison deeper into Scott's arm.

But what kind of poison had Carson been using?

Granville would've taken great pleasure in shaking that information out of out of him, but the fellow had been in handcuffs and still unconscious when they left.

Ingram would take care of getting Carson incarcerated—with some help from Brazinski. And the young constable had promised to send information on the poison to Granville at the hospital the minute Carson was conscious.

Which might be too late for Scott.

"Don't talk. It'll spread the poison faster," he said to his partner.

"I'm fine," Scott protested. "It barely hurts at all."

Looking at the arm, Granville didn't believe him. But Scott's color was still good. And he was coherent. Not the symptoms Granville would have expected from a fast-acting poison.

And Carson would have used a fast-acting poison, to give himself an advantage.

Perhaps the villain had only managed to nick Scott's arm.

And the hospital wasn't far now. They might be in time. He just hoped the Japanese doctor would be good with unidentified poisons.

"Just hang on," he said, bracing Scott against the jolts of the wagon. "We're almost there."

Scott said nothing, just scowled at him.

"Faster," he said to the driver. Who turned to glare at him, before urging his horses to a faster pace over the rough roads.

TUESDAY, AUGUST 21, 1900

"But how is Scott doing now?" Emily asked, tucking her hand into the crook of Granville's arm as they walked along English Bay. She was so glad they finally had the time and privacy to talk. She'd been on tenterhooks of anxiety, waiting to hear how their search for the spider had turned out.

Then the news about Scott had come, in a hurried phone call from the hospital, while Granville waited for news. And she'd been nearly frantic, realizing in that one moment just how badly it could all have gone.

"He'll be fine," Granville said. "He was just lucky the doctor at the Japanese Hospital had the right solution to wash the poison from his arm. And kept doing so. Despite everything he could do, Scott's arm swelled up pretty badly, so the doctor there kept him overnight."

"But Scott's okay?"

"He was stable by this noon today, so I hired a coach to take us back to Vancouver. And got him to St. Paul's Hospital. They've cleaned his arm again, and they're keeping him in for observation. Despite his protests."

Emily smiled at that. "And what do they say about his arm?"

"They say it'll be fine. It's blistered a little. And it will be sore for a while. But Scott was right. Carson's needle barely scraped his arm."

The news was a relief, especially after waiting all day to hear. It was late afternoon, and they had nearly an hour before they were expected at her parents for dinner. The heat wave had finally broken, and a cool breeze danced off the ocean. Emily could feel it lifting the tendrils of hair around her forehead.

"And what of your spider?" she asked. "Carson, is it?"

"All he'll have is a sore head. At least until they hang him."

"And there's not much doubt of that, is there?"

"Not when half the cannery saw him talking to Dirks, a few minutes before the fellow washed up against the pier. Turns out I was wrong about how Carson killed Dirks, though," Granville said. "Nothing so mundane as a blow to the head would do for him."

"Poison again?"

"And a nearly undetectable one at that," Granville said. "Carson was a sailor, before he was injured and couldn't handle the life any longer. He had friends in every port—or so he tells it. And he collected deadly knowledge. His poison of choice derived from a plant native to Indonesia."

"So who killed the Akizukis?"

"Carson. Once he'd been arrested, a few people came forward to tell us that Carson was one of the fellows Akizuki had gone to talk to. They hadn't made the connection before."

"So if people had known about the murders earlier, would Carson have been caught earlier?" she asked.

Dreading the answer, but needing to know. And suspecting that he needed to talk about it.

"Could we have saved Ben Akizuki if we hadn't been so concerned about the news of a murdered Japanese man igniting a riot or another strike?" Granville said. "That question—along with Scott's injury—kept me awake last night. But from everything I've learned today, I believe the answer is no."

He walked in silence for a moment. It had to be hard for

Granville—with all he'd learned about the victims—thinking about the pointless deaths that Carson had caused. Emily shuddered a little. Carson really was the spider they'd named him.

"Carson was—or rather is—deceptive," Granville said finally. "No-one suspected him. Even if the news about the murders had been shared much earlier, I doubt anyone would have made the connection. It was Carson's arrest that put the pieces together for them."

Emily watched his expressive face. She'd come to know him well over the last few months—and while he knew what he'd said was true, some part of him would always wonder if they could have saved Ben if he'd acted differently.

Just as some part of her would always wonder if there was something more she could have done.

"Was that why Carson told you he thought Dirks was innocent of the murders?" she said. "He wasn't trying to clear an innocent man. He was trying to manipulate you?"

She looked out over the calm ocean to the mountains hazy with distance, taking solace from the stillness. "He was your informant, right?"

"Yes on both counts. As the mastermind behind the scheme, Carson had set everything up so that there was very little evidence, but what there was pointed straight to Dirks. By becoming an informant, he got closer to the investigation..."

"So he could know what you were up to. And also he could feel smarter than you, because he was fooling you."

"Exactly. And setting himself up as being on our side. And because he had nothing to back up his story, and there was so much surface evidence pointing straight at Dirks, he actually intended to pin an even bigger target on Dirks..."

"Except that he triggered your own doubts about Dirks being just too convenient a fall guy, instead," Emily said. "Which he certainly hadn't intended to do."

"No, that he hadn't," Granville said with a grin. "He was a little stunned to see us in the storeroom. He hadn't expected us to catch on so quickly. Unfortunately, it didn't slow him down any."

Picturing that moment, Emily could feel her stomach tying itself in knots. Granville might make light of it now, but they'd been up against a cold and cunning adversary.

Carson might be small, but he'd proven himself to be deadly. They could so easily have been killed, both of them.

"You're sure Scott will be fine?" she asked urgently.

"I'm sure. The doctors assured me he'll have no after-effects at all."

"Good," she said.

"We also got Carson's accomplice," Granville said.

Emily recognized an attempt to distract her, but she wanted to know all of it. "Go on."

"One of the fishermen," Granville said. "Tall fellow, strong, but slow-witted. Carson told him some tale, convinced him to help with the bodies. Let him in after hours, they dumped the bodies in the lye bath together. And it was done."

"How did Carson hide them?"

"Turns out he'd been there so long, he knew the cannery better than anyone. He'd made it his business to do so. And I just talked to the coroner."

"Oh?"

"He had another look at Ben Akizuki's body. Once he knew what to look for, he found what was left of a deep puncture mark on Ben. And the same poison in his tissue as they found on Scott's arm."

"But I thought they'd both died from a broken neck?"

"They did. Carson isn't the biggest fellow around, nor the strongest. So he used the poison to incapacitate his victims. Then broke their necks. Just in case."

Ugh. "So why did Ben die a week later than his father?" Emily asked, dreading the answer.

"Akizuki confronted Dirks in the hallway. Dirks brushed him off, leaving Akizuki muttering to himself. Carson overheard them.

He told Akizuki to meet him at the cannery after they closed, and he'd help him find what he needed."

"Akizuki didn't bring Ben?" Emily asked.

"No. Told him to stay with the boat."

She tried to picture it and shivered, knowing what the outcome would be. "And Carson just killed him? Mr. Akizuki, I mean."

Granville nodded. "He says it was an accident."

"But you don't believe him." Emily could read it in his face.

"No. Especially when Carson chose to hide the body. Then the blackguard went out and told Akizuki's son that Akizuki wanted Ben to take their boat and leave town. To find a quiet cove, and hide for seven days. Then Ben was to come back, because Akizuki and Carson would have everything safely sorted out."

"All so there wouldn't be two bodies found at once," Emily said. "It makes a horrible kind of sense. And Ben believed him?"

Granville nodded, his face solemn. "Apparently. When we spoke with Sakamoto, he said Akizuki had protected his son, that Ben could be naive."

"And Carson used it to kill him." Emily found it unbearably sad. "All to protect his illegal income."

She frowned. "I suppose that's why he destroyed the boat, too?"

"Yes. An empty boat creates questions. Carson didn't want those. Or anything that might identify his victims."

"Why did he kill Dirks?"

"Carson won't say. I suspect Dirks knew too much," Granville said. "And perhaps he hoped we'd take the easy way out—blame everything on Dirks and close the case."

"You? Not likely," Emily said with a sideways glance. Which he met with a quick grin. "But did the coroner find the same poison in Dirks?"

"He did indeed. A very fast acting one, I gather."

"But what I don't understand is why Carson would choose to make money this way?" Emily said. "It seems an odd choice for a former sailor."

"Carson had worked on a few of the sailing ships that make the canning run. He's smart, he'd picked up a bit about the canning industry. And he had the connections to get large quantities of stolen tinned salmon loaded and delivered without being caught. He used them."

"And why the Monster Cannery? Did he already know Dirks?"

"No. Owens," Granville said. "They'd had a run-in somewhere along the line, and Carson never forgot. He believes in revenge served cold."

Emily winced. "And all this for a few cans of salmon?"

"More than a few cans, but yes. It was all about the money. And Carson had big plans. Next year is a fourth-year run for the sockeye, a big year. The Monster has been gearing up to run three cannery lines full time."

"And he had plans to steal even more of the profit?" Emily asked.

"Yes, he did. And even bigger plans to take that money and retire to a life of leisure in Indonesia. Build a home there."

"Indonesia? Really?"

"Apparently he liked the lifestyle there."

Including a readily available poison? Emily shuddered.

"And speaking of homes," Granville said.

Emily knew what was coming. Hoped he wouldn't say it.

He did.

"The closing date on our house is getting close. Have you thought any more about when you'd like our wedding date to be?" he asked.

"Not yet," Emily said. She stretched up, threw her arms around his neck and held him close.

Not caring who saw them. She'd come too close to losing him this time. "But soon. I promise."

Especially with the notion of eloping with him dancing in her head.

I lived in Steveston for a number of years. The last of the big canneries closed a year or so after I moved there, and I remember clearly the overwhelming stink of it when the wind was in the wrong direction. Steveston was, and is, still a fishing village at heart, though there is no trace now of the rougher edge that was Cannery Row in its heyday.

In the early mornings before work I'd walk along the riverfront, past the huge metal cannery buildings, slowly rusting away—and gone now to upscale condominiums—to the old town and the dock, where every weekend I'd buy fresh fish or prawns in season, sold right off the boat. The harbor is still home to the fishing fleet, row after row of trollers, gillnetters and trawlers, gleaming with fresh paint in the spring, battered and weathered by late fall.

The old Gulf of Georgia Cannery, the Monster, is now a heritage site and museum, as is the Britannia Heritage Shipyard. Both are a fascinating place to spend time, breathing in the air of the past.

The Gulf of Georgia Cannery Museum has a full canning line set up, with tours that take visitors through every step of the canning process. I've always loved history, so when I first moved to Steveston, taking that tour was one of the first things I did. The museum changes and updates their exhibits regularly, but on that beautiful May morning, the canning line was set up as it would have been in 1900, before the cutting of the salmon was mechanized. As the tour guide took us down the line, he pointed to a large iron tub about three-quarters of the way down the line. "That's the lye vat," he told us. "Full of lye, and very caustic. They'd put the finished cans go in there to get the gunk off of them. You wouldn't want to fall in there." A pause. "But it would be a great way to dispose of a body."

He got a laugh. And little light went on in my brain.

"Hmmm," I thought. It took me more years than I'd expected, but the first spark for this book came from that tour guide's throwaway line. Unfortunately I don't remember his name, but I'd like to thank him, and the all staff and volunteers at both the Gulf of Georgia Museum and Britannia Heritage Shipyard site over the years.

I've taken a few liberties with history—as far as I know, there was no actual fraud at the Gulf of Georgia Cannery—not on this scale, anyway. So I've created fictional people to run the cannery—but the roles they carried out were real. So was the fishing strike of 1900. The cannery owners really did set the militia on the strikers.

And Steveston and Cannery Row in 1900 are as accurate as my research can make them. I always want to know what it felt like to live in a particular time and place—to work on a cannery line, in all that smell and noise—and I try to share that feeling with my readers. I hope I've succeeded, at least a little, and that you enjoy spending time on Steveston's Cannery Row as much as I did while researching and writing this book.

Particular thanks go to Linda Roggeveen for her exceptional copy edit. Any errors or omissions are, of course, mine.

In addition to the museums, I'd like to thank the staff at the Steveston Museum, the Vancouver Public Library Special Collections, the Vancouver Archives and the Richmond Historical Society.

A number of historical works and on-line sites have been invaluable to me in researching this book; many of them are listed on my website at www.sharonrowse.com.

THE HIDDEN CITY MURDERS
A John Granville & Emily Turner Mystery

1

SATURDAY, AUGUST 25, 1900

Emily Turner sat with her aunt at a round tea table dressed with immaculate white linen tablecloths, one of ten tables that had been set up in the shade of the oaks on Caroline Harris's side lawn. From that vantage point, the ladies present could hear the waves crashing against the rocky cliff to the beach twenty feet below, or look out over open ocean as far as Salt Spring Island.

It was a warm summer day, with just the tiniest hint of a breeze off the ocean. Floating on top of the crisp scent of fresh cut grass, Emily could smell the vanilla and sugar of scones baking. She drew in an appreciative breath, wishing Granville could be here to share this with.

Or perhaps her friend Clara—Granville would be decidedly out of place at a ladies tea. Not that he'd care. He'd simply charm them all, she thought with an inward grin, drawing in another deep breath.

She drew in another deep breath, frowning a little over the unmistakeable scent of fresh, ripe blackberries. Had the Harris's cook broken with tradition so far as to serve a *blackberry* cream tea? It was probably too late in the season for the more usual fresh strawberries served with Devon cream on their scones, after all. Though strawberry preserves would have been the usual substitute.

Mrs. Harris's cream teas were a summer institution in Victoria society, and Emily never been to one before. But Aunt Louisa had insisted that Emily join the party.

"You'll be married before too long, given what your mother tells me, and there's no-one better than Mrs. Harris to show you what entertaining should look like," her aunt had said. "Though I understand you're avoiding any discussion of your actual wedding day," Aunt Louisa had added with a sideways look that made Emily wonder exactly what Mama had told her.

She didn't plan on doing a great deal of entertaining once she and Granville wed. She was far more interested in helping him with his detective business. But there was no point explaining that to her aunt.

It would simply result in yet another argument with Mama. And arguments with Mama were an exercise in frustration, and to be avoided at all costs.

No, it was pure curiosity that brought her here. She'd heard about the Harris teas for so long—and the discussion usually ended up with a *sotto voce* comment about the Harris's Chinese houseboy, and what a treasure he was.

Apparently Mr. Ying could whip up a cream tea to rival anything served in England. Someone else would chime in with the tale of the latest attempt to bribe or steal him away from the Harrises—but Mrs. Harris had apparently won the man's permanent loyalty, though no one was quite sure how she'd managed it.

Society's matrons—something Emily planned never to become —relied on their Chinese houseboys for every facet of running a household, which often included the cooking. And the English-style cream tea was the ultimate test of a cook's skills.

There were several extremely good tea shops in Vancouver that served cream teas, as well as those in Victoria, and Emily had developed a taste for them because her friend Clara loved them.

She wished again that Clara were with her today—her friend would have loved everything about this lavish entertainment. But Clara's eldest sister Cecily was getting married next week, and as a bridesmaid, Clara was far too caught up in Cecily's wedding preparations to leave Vancouver, even for a weekend visit. Today wouldn't be the same without Clara's decided opinions on what made the best scones, though.

To Emily's mind, Victoria's grand Empress Hotel served the best cream tea she'd ever tasted. The tea was perfectly steeped, the finger sandwiches delectable, the scones the perfect blend of butter and sugar and vanilla, with sweetened thick cream and strawberry-rich jam—she smiled at the memory. She'd never tasted a cream tea done better, and certainly not at a private home.

Clara, of course, didn't agree. She insisted that the Hotel Vancouver did a better cream tea, though she'd never been able to convince Emily of that.

Emily couldn't wait to taste Mrs. Harris's famed offerings and see how they compared to the two hotels. And to tell Clara about it.

Just as the last of the ladies took their seats, several maids began to bring out trays holding steaming china teapots, with matching cream and sugar sets. Emily smiled to see the black gowns, frilled head caps and white aprons they all wore. The old-style costumes gave the event a formal feel, though she noted that the girls wearing the caps and aprons were all quite young. Probably they had been hired just for this occasion.

Once everyone had tea, the maids began to bring out plates of plates of warm scones, with pots of Devon cream and little pots of sauce. The table Aunt Louisa had chosen was furthest away from the house, so they were among the last to be served, giving Emily time to watch everything and appreciate the coordination it must take to put on an event like this.

Just as a plate of scones was placed on their table, there was a scream from the back of the house, the shrill sound rising and falling.

It was a young woman's voice.

Ignoring her aunt's protest, Emily leapt to her feet and dashed around the corner of the house, following the sound towards the kitchen. As she grew closer, the scent of blackberries and vanilla grew stronger, underlaid now with hint of an odd coppery tang. Could that be blood?

Someone was hurt.

Heart in her throat, Emily ran faster, wishing she wasn't wearing these fancy boots—they were much harder to run in than her ordinary pair. It was a good thing her aunt's maid hadn't laced Emily's stays as tightly as her aunt had suggested, or she'd not have been able to run at all.

The screaming was coming from inside. What on earth was happening here? She hurried into the large airy kitchen that took up most of the back of the house.

All was confusion, with pots and trays everywhere, flour scattered across the floor, and a pot boiling over on the stove, filling the air with the scorched scent of burnt sugar. Three of the maids milled around in a state of panic, their voices rising sharply towards the hysteria of the whoever was still screaming. There was no sign of Mr. Ying.

Ignoring the chaos around her, Emily focused on the source of the sound. She followed her ears across the width of the kitchen, to where a hysterical young maid stood in front of a large standing cupboard.

Emily's heart pounded in her chest as she hurried across the room. She was shocked but not surprised to see the prone form of another young woman—who was also wearing a frilled head cap and full apron.

She didn't see much blood, but the scent of it lingered in the air, and the girl's stillness was worrying. Perhaps she'd simply passed out from the shock of her injury?

Breathing too quickly, Emily knelt beside the girl and picked up her wrist, feeling for a pulse. For a moment, she thought she had it, then realized she was feeling her own pulse pounding in her fingertips. She drew in a long, slow breath, willing her heart rate to slow. The screaming behind her didn't help any.

"Please be quiet," she said sharply to the hysterical young maid. "I need to see if she's alive.

All the while, Emily's eyes were scanning the victim, looking for signs of blood, and trying to see how badly she might be injured. The poor girl was lying half on her side, as if she'd collapsed while turning away from someone or something.

Emily kept one hand on her pulse, while with the other she pressed down gently on the girl's shoulder, moving her slightly so that she she was lying mostly on her back. Then Emily bit back a cry of horror.

There was a bone-handled knife protruding from the girl's chest, near her heart. It was hard to see the knife against the white of her apron, though a few drops of blood spread crimson against the starched cotton.

Emily kept feeling for the girl's pulse, though she suspected it was hopeless. Granville had told her that if death is immediate, a wound often bled very little, especially in a stabbing where the knife was left in the wound.

Like this one. Emily's heart was heavy with the knowledge as she turned her head towards the other three maids.

"Did anyone see what happened?"

"No," said the taller of the three on a sob. "She—Betsy—was here. Like this. After we came back from taking the scones out."

"She was alone when you found her?" Emily asked.

The three maids all nodded.

"But she... shouldn't have been. Ying was here," the tallest maid said.

Emily glanced around. There was no sign of the Harris's house-boy. "But Mr. Ying wasn't here when you found her?"

"No."

"Then one of you needs to call for the police now," Emily said, instinctively using her mother's tone of command. "And the doctor. The other two, take your friend outside and calm her down."

Emily was instantly obeyed, a fact that surprised her. It was probably a good thing she didn't want servants, or it might go to her head—an idiotic thought to be having under the circumstances, she chided herself.

But then she was sitting in a suddenly empty kitchen holding a dead girl's hand, in the middle of one of Mrs. Harris's famous teas. It was hard to think of anything that would be appropriate for this.

Enjoyed this preview?
THE HIDDEN CITY MURDERS
is available for order through retailers everywhere